HIGH STREET

Also by Anna Jacobs

Salem Street

High Street

Anna Jacobs

CORONET BOOKS
Hodder and Stoughton

Copyright © 1994 Anna Jacobs

First Published in paperback in 1995
by Hodder and Stoughton
A division of Hodder Headline

A Coronet Paperback

First published in Great Britain in 1994
bye Hodder & Stoughton

A CIP record for this title is available from the British Library

ISBN 0 340 62290 3

Typeset by Avon Dataset Ltd, Bidford-on-Avon

Printed and bound in the United Kingdom by
Mackays of Chatham plc, Chatham, Kent

Hodder and Stoughton
A division of Hodder Headline
338 Euston Road
London NW1 3BH

To my amazingly energetic mother-in-law, Connie Jacobs, and to the memory of my lovely father-in-law, David Jacobs, whose wry sense of humour was a talent in itself.

Anna Jacobs is always delighted to hear from readers and can be contacted at:

PO Box 628
Mandurah
Western Australia 6210

If you'd like a reply, please enclose a self-addressed envelope, stamped (from inside Australia) or with an international reply coupon (from outside Australia). Anna Jacobs can also be contacted by e-mail on jacobses@iinet.net.au

Contents

Chapter

One

MAY 1845

After a hard day's work at the mill, the occupants of the Rows had come home through the light spring rain to relax for an hour or two before seeking their beds. In the very last house of Salem Street, Number Eight, two people were quarrelling, as they had quarrelled all their lives – except when family loyalty or self-interest caused them to unite against the harsh world around them.

"They're all coming to live with us when we move, and that's flat!" declared Annie, her pale complexion slightly flushed and her eyes glinting green in the candlelight.

Tom jabbed the poker at the fire and then thumped another piece of coal into the red heart of the flames. Spring it might be, but the evenings were still chilly. "You've run mad, our Annie, mad! It's Dad's job to provide for his second family, not ours. We've enough on our plates with the business. We'll never make a success of it all if we have that lot hangin' round our necks, eatin' us out of house and home!"

Getting on in the world was one of the few things about which the two of them were usually in agreement.

"They're our brothers and sisters, Tom." Annie's voice was clear and pleasant, her accent no longer that of the Rows. She had escaped from Salem Street when she was twelve to go into service with the local doctor and his wife, and had only returned when she was seventeen because a rape had left her pregnant.

Rejected by her sweetheart, Matt Peters, for the same reason, Annie had later shocked everyone by marrying Charlie Ashworth, commonly known as Barmy Charlie. He was older than her own father, as well as slow of speech and thought after an accident in the mill. But Charlie was not too slow to make a good living from second-hand junk, and not too stupid to save the money he earned. Unable to father a child of his own, he had welcomed Annie's bastard son, William.

Annie had grown quite fond of her husband, in a motherly way. She had looked after his physical needs, invested his hoard of money and helped him to expand his junk-collecting business. At the same time, she had built up a thriving business of her own, refashioning second-hand clothes or making cheap new ones to sell at the weekly market. And as the years passed, she had continued to save their money and to invest it wisely.

When Charlie had died the previous year, Annie had brought her brother Tom into the junk trade as a full-time partner. With two sharp-witted people at the helm, the business had gone from strength to strength.

But it was not the business that concerned them now. "They're our brothers and sisters," she repeated. "We can't let them want."

"They're only *half*-brothers and sisters! An' they're dear Emily's brats, too, which puts me right off them."

Annie spoke quietly, but there was steel underneath the soft tones. "Emily's dead, Tom, and two of her children with her. Now, Dad needs our help. He can't manage on his own, with four children to look after."

"Let Rebecca help him, then. She's the same age as you were when our mam died. You managed."

"Rebecca couldn't cope. Mam had taught me how to do things. Emily couldn't look after the house herself, let alone teach Rebecca how to do it. Those children are as ignorant as the toss-pots in Claters End."

"All the more reason for not takin' them to live with us." His voice became coaxing. "Look, Annie, we can slip them the odd shilling or two to help out. We can see that they don't want."

"No. They're coming to live with us."

Tom slapped his hand on the table, and the thump made his nephew William, sitting quietly in the back room, glance apprehensively at Kathy, who lived with them and helped with the sewing and the housework. Kathy shook her head. Best to stay out of it when Annie and Tom were quarrelling. They might not look alike, for Annie had inherited their mother's red hair while Tom had their father's tight brown curls, but they were alike in so many ways that clashes were inevitable.

"Besides," Tom went on scornfully, "Dad'll soon find another woman to look after him. It didn't take him long after our mam died, and it'll take him even less time to forget Emily!"

"I don't intend to give him the chance to find another woman this time. If he lives with us, he won't *need* anyone else."

Tom gave a snort of laughter. "You should know him better than that. He can't do without it! He'll soon find someone to comfort him, trust old randy-pants for that!" Not that he blamed his father, really. A man's body had its needs, and Tom only hoped he could enjoy that sort of thing for as many years as John Gibson obviously had, judging by the number of children he had fathered. Mind, the same urge could drive a man to do foolish things, like his father marrying that silly bitch, Emily. Tom was not going to be caught like that. He looked at Annie speculatively and tried another tack. "It'd not be fair on your William to have the other kids living with us."

Annie snorted and shook her head. "I think it'd be good for William. And you needn't try to get at me that way, Tom Gibson, because it won't work. You're the one who showed me that I was spoiling him, and taught him to stand up for himself. You were right then, but you're not right now. William will love having company. He already follows our Mark around like a lost puppy dog whenever he can." Her lips thinned, "And as I've no intention of ever marrying again, I shan't be giving William any brothers or sisters, shall I?"

They were silent for a moment, both busy with their own thoughts. Tom was glad on the whole that Annie had kept all men at a distance since Charlie died. It meant she was less likely to marry and bring someone else into the business. Sometimes, however, as a man, he could not help thinking that it was a waste for a woman as lovely as his sister to stay so determinedly single.

Annie's thoughts were still on her plans. She went over and linked her arm in his, her voice becoming coaxing. "What's come over you, Tom Gibson? You were quite pleased about my idea last night. If Dad had been at home, we'd have told him then. What's made you change your mind today?"

Tom put his hands on her shoulders and held her at arm's length. Blue eyes stared into green, and neither would give way. He was not much taller than she was, but powerfully built, with a hard, muscular body. From his crinkly brown hair to his squarely planted feet, he seemed to exude strength and vitality. Lucy Gibson's children were of a different breed to those of poor Emily.

"Look, Annie, I've had time to think about it since then. It makes no sense to lumber ourselves with Dad and four young children, just when we'll need all our wits and every penny .'e can scrape together to expand the business."

"Sally left me all her money—"

"Ill-gotten gains!" he mocked, for their neighbour Sally had started life as a whore and ended it as a kept woman, and he knew how much Annie valued respectability.

She flushed at his words. "I don't care. She may not have been respectable, but she was a good friend to me after Mam died. And she left me a tidy sum, as well as the two cottages. Poor Sally!"

Tom opened his mouth to continue the argument, but Annie gave him no chance to speak. "Anyway, I explained it all to you last night. Dad'll go on working at Hallam's Mill. He'll bring in enough money to clothe and feed them all. And Mark's a clever lad. He's twelve now, old enough to be a real help to you in the business. I know Luke's a bit slow, but he'll improve, now that he hasn't got Emily nagging at him all the time. How she could treat her own son like that, I'll never understand! It's no wonder poor Luke's so nervous. She never stopped picking on him. And Rebecca's nearly ten. She'll be a big help in the new house, and she can learn to sew and help me in the salon as well."

"Aye, you said all that last night. An' Joan's five, a snotty-nosed, whining brat who looks just like her sister, May."

They were silent again, as they both thought of their stepsister May, child of Emily's first marriage, who had left home a few years ago and was now living with their full sister Lizzie somewhere in Manchester. An unsavoury pair of girls, they were. Tom hoped he would never set eyes on them again. They made his flesh creep. Unnatural, they were. Man-haters, the pair of them.

"Aye, it'll be a pleasure to have little Joan snivelling round the house, won't it?" he jeered, pressing his advantage.

The old Annie would have lost her temper and flung something at him. The new one, seasoned by death and illness, shook her head and said very quietly, with tears in her eyes,

"I'm set on it, Tom. I won't see them want while we can help. Either you accept that – and them – or you go your own way." Her expression was too old for someone who was only twenty-five.

Tom's eyes were the first to drop. Funny, he found himself thinking, not anxious to capitulate but seeing no way round it, funny how lovely a woman Annie was when she'd been such a scrawny stick of a child. How he used to tease her about her red hair – a rich auburn now – and her green cat's eyes! Those eyes were large and luminous, in a finely drawn face. If she'd encouraged them, the fellows would have been queuing up to court her, regardless of whether she had money or not. But she didn't encourage any familiarities. After the rape, she had been glad to marry an old man like Charlie Ashworth, glad that he could give her no more than his name. Tom stared at her for a minute longer, but she gave no sign of yielding. "Damn you, our Annie!" he said feelingly.

"What does that mean?" Her voice was cold.

"It means you've got your own way, like you always do, but damn you, Annie, for makin' me do it! An' it'd just better work out all right, that's all!" He turned and flung the front door open. "I need a drink. You can go an' tell him yourself." He slammed out of the house before she could answer, out to Claters End and his friend, his very good friend, Rosie.

A few days later, Annie walked briskly along Bilsden High Street, enjoying the early morning sunshine. Her full black skirts swished about her ankles and the black ribbons on her bonnet fluttered cheerfully in the breeze. So eager was she to get to her destination that she did not notice the gentleman sitting waiting in his carriage who raised his hat politely to her.

"By Jove!" he murmured to himself. "Annie Ashworth's turning into a real stunner!" Frederick Hallam, largest mill owner in the town, was a noted connoisseur of female beauty. "Quite the lady of fashion too," he added thoughtfully. "Well, well! Who'd ever have thought someone from Salem Street would turn out like that?" His eyes lingered on the slim figure until it turned the corner.

Annie would not have classed herself as a lady, or even aspired to be one. She was a businesswoman and proud of it. Today, however, business was forgotten and she could not hide the excitement that was bubbling up inside her. Frederick Hallam was not the only man to turn and stare at her. Her eyes were sparkling and her lips were half-parted in a smile of anticipation. Even the weather seemed to reflect her joyful mood and was making a glorious halo of the auburn curls that had escaped from under the bonnet brim, for the sun was shining brightly after yesterday's showers, giving a promise of warmth to come after the long hard winter that had tried them all sorely and taken the lives of so many of the weaker inhabitants of Bilsden.

Annie turned right into Market Street, followed the road as it curved upwards away from the town centre, then turned left into North Road. And there at the first corner she turned left again and stopped for a moment to draw a deep breath of satisfaction and survey her future home, Netherleigh Cottage. No terraced rows of narrow houses here in Moor Close, but neat detached villas with carefully tended patches of garden, and one or two slightly larger houses with iron railings – how different it all was from Salem Street! And how beautiful the trees were, with their froth of young leaves! There were no trees in Salem Street, only a sour patch of earth under the high wall of Hallam's Mill that cut off the light and cast permanent shadows on the little terrace of eight houses.

At Netherleigh Cottage Annie stopped again and sighed happily, running her fingertips along the top of the low stone wall. She owned this house and was here to receive the keys from her former tenant, Michael Benworth, overseer at Hallam's Mill. As soon as she could, tomorrow if possible, she would be moving in. After a while, she realised that she had been standing by the gate for several minutes, lost in thought, and glanced round guiltily to see if anyone had noticed. But the street was quiet and the only people in sight were those walking past the end of the little cul-de-sac.

"Netherleigh Cottage." Annie murmured the name aloud as she pushed open the gate. The house was an anachronism so near the busy centre of a Lancashire mill town, for it had been a farmhouse in its day. Even its name was a misnomer, for it was much larger than a cottage. It had somehow managed to escape demolition when the farm land was sold to a cotton spinner, and had even retained half an acre of land hidden at the rear behind a high stone wall. It stood part way up the lower slope of Ridge Hill, just above Hallam Park and a little higher than the town centre. She looked upwards at the crest of the hill behind it which you could see between the houses. Unlike her cottage, the houses up there on the Ridge were huge, commanding a sweeping view of the grey slate roofs of their poorer neighbours and of the brooding mills with their tall chimneys.

Frederick Hallam, just turning into his own drive on the Ridge, would not have thanked you for a rural vista. His father had built Ridge House to be a part of Bilsden, and like his father, Frederick enjoyed looking down on the town that his family had helped to create, relishing the unlovely signs of wealth in the making. "There's progress for you!" he would declare. "Forty years back, when I was just a little lad, there were only a few cottages and some scrubby farms, and now look at it all! Those Rows are like a bloody great beehive, teeming with life. That's real progress, that is!"

Frederick's wife, recently dead in the influenza epidemic, had hated Bilsden, hated her husband too, for his blatant womanising and sarcastic tongue. And as the years passed, he had not troubled to hide his scorn for her timid ways, though she had never dared to show her resentment of that. Now, Frederick admitted, though only to himself, he was enjoying life without Christine's drooping presence. How many times had that miserable face driven him out of the house to seek pleasanter companionship?

Near the park, its spire just showing from Moor Close, stood the grimy little parish church of St Mark's. It had been lavishly endowed in a bygone age by the Darringtons who were still, technically speaking, lords of the manor of Bilsden. The present Lord Darrington, however, chose to live elsewhere and kept only a skeleton staff at the Hall to look after his elderly aunt who refused to be moved from her childhood home. It was rumoured that she abused her nephew roundly whenever she saw him for deserting his land and duties. Frederick Hallam had tried once or twice to buy the Hall, which was a great barn of a place with the best views on the whole Ridge, but even George Darrington balked at this. Jonas Pennybody, the family lawyer, had been instructed to inform Mr Hallam that it was useless to persist. One did not sell one's birthright.

Annie had nothing to do with St Mark's Church. She worshipped her Maker at the Todmorden Road Methodist Chapel on the other side of the town. The latter was an ugly red-brick box of a building only thirteen years old, standing at the western end of the Rows. In it, the largest group of Nonconformists in the town met to worship; there, too, they held their Sunday school and their evening classes in reading and writing. Annie herself had learned to read and write in that humble chapel, becoming one of the few girls to progress to the advanced class and be taught by the minister, Saul Hinchcliffe.

At the eastern end of the Rows stood the Catholic Church, a small shoddy place, also in grimy red brick. It had been built to encourage the Irish to settle in the town at a time when labour was scarce. To the parson of St Mark's, it was living proof of the dangerous radicalism of the times that papists were allowed to build churches and conduct their Romish rites on English soil. And as for this shocking idea the Chartists had, of giving every man a vote, just let them try it! He and every right-thinking English gentleman knew where that sort of thing led. Look at France! What good had the Revolution done the common man there? None! They'd had to bring back a king again, hadn't they? And things were still not settled there, either. Europe was in a mess, that was evident, and it was free-thinking which had wrought the havoc. Men of the poorer sort should know their place and stay in it.

Theophilus Kenderby did not hesitate to trumpet his views from the pulpit, but his words fell upon stony ground, and attendance at his services was perfunctory and mainly female. Most of the manufacturing classes of Bilsden were self-made men who had *not* been content with their station in life.

Frederick Hallam said outright that the old parson was still living in a bygone age and would not recognise progress if it hit him smack in the eye. Frederick only attended the church at Easter and Christmas for appearance's sake, though his daughter was very devout and attended St Mark's regularly. He considered church-going a waste of time, but it gave the womenfolk something to do, so he had subscribed to the odd charity in Christine's name and allowed his coachman to drive her and Beatrice to and from the weekly meetings of the Ladies' Society for the Relief of the Deserving Poor.

While Frederick Hallam was staring out over the town in which he owned at least a quarter of the property, Annie was walking along the path to the front door of Netherleigh Cottage. She noted with satisfaction that the garden was neat and tidy and that the windowpanes were twinkling in the sunlight. It was a pretty house, square and symmetrical, built of stone, with large dormer windows punctuating the grey expanse of slate roof. Benworth had been a good tenant. Even when his children had grown up and left home and his wife had died, he had stayed on with his one remaining unmarried daughter because of his love for the place. Annie thought this wastefully extravagant when he could have been putting his money to better use.

Well, she thought smugly as she knocked on the door, he'll have to get out now that my years of frugality are starting to pay off. I had enough money saved to snap up Netherleigh Cottage before anyone else knew it was for sale. It stands to reason that half an acre of land so near the town centre will be worth a lot of money one day. And I have the two other cottages as well, thanks to Charlie's savings. They're smaller places and not nearly so well-situated, but they're mine. There I go, forgetting again! I've got four cottages now, including the ones Sally left me.

The front door of the house opened and Michael Benworth came out to stand on the step as he greeted her. He was two years younger than her father, the same age as the century – forty-five – but he looked fifteen years younger than her father, she thought, returning his stare coolly. My dad's worn-out, after all those years in the mill. And being married to Emily didn't help much, either. She looked again at Benworth, whose hair was only lightly flecked with grey, and whose body was still lean and muscular. Before he knew that she owned the house, he had made an attempt to court Annie, but she didn't need or want a husband; she could look after herself.

"Good morning, Mrs Ashworth. You're very punctual. It's a lovely day, isn't it?"

"Good morning, Mr Benworth. Is the house ready for my inspection?" She couldn't bear to waste any time on chit-chat now that she was here. She wanted the house to herself for an hour or two to gloat over. That was why she had told Tom not

11

to join her till later in the morning.

Benworth's gaze was admiring, but he followed her lead. "Yes, everything's ready. My daughter's just finishing the last bit of clearing up in the kitchen. Won't you come in and look things over?"

Annie stepped over the threshold and paused for a moment to admire the square hallway. Fancy this much space, just for an entry! It was as big as most rooms in the Rows. Her eyes missed nothing and she was pleased to note how spotless it all was. You could feel a clean house, somehow.

Without waiting to be asked, she opened the door to the front room that her family must now learn to call the parlour. Houses in Salem Street had two rooms on the ground floor, front and back, and two tiny bedrooms upstairs. This house had several rooms on each floor. In this house, she would have her own bedroom and the parlour would be nicely furnished and kept for best. Her standards would come as a shock to her half-brothers and sisters after their mother's slovenly ways, but they were young enough to adapt. It was only her father she was worried about – how would he fit in? She wasn't going to let him start telling her what to do, father or not! She had been her own mistress for years and she liked it that way.

Annie followed Michael Benworth round the ground floor and then upstairs, still musing about the future. "Yes," she said as they came back downstairs, "you've left everything nice, very nice indeed."

"It's Mary who must take the credit for that. She's a good housewife. I don't think you've ever met my eldest daughter, have you?" He opened the door at the back of the hallway and ushered Annie through to the kitchen. "Ah, there you are, my dear."

Annie was expecting a girl, but it was a woman of about her own age who turned to greet them. Mary Benworth was tall, almost as tall as her father, towering over Annie, and she

had his wavy brown hair and bright blue eyes. She didn't seem
in the least put out to be discovered with her sleeves rolled up,
a dirty apron over her dress and her hands immersed in soapy
water. Annie liked her better for that.

"How do you do, Mrs Ashworth. I'm afraid I can't offer to
shake hands with you, because mine are wet. I've nearly
finished in here, and then that'll be it."

"I was just saying how nice everything looks."

"I like to keep things clean."

"I hope that you've found somewhere suitable to live."

"We've found a house in Church Lane. It's a nice little
house, but Father will miss his garden."

"I'm sorry about that. We know nothing about gardening.
We shall have to learn."

Benworth moved over to look out of the window. "It's a
good garden and always repays a bit of work. The soil's rich
and the fruit trees bear well."

She could hear the love in his voice. "Fruit trees! I hadn't
realised . . ." She smiled apologetically. "I don't know one plant
from another. None of us do!"

"I'd be happy to help you and your brother until you know
enough to look after the garden yourselves."

Mary swung round. "Now, Father, let it go!"

"I couldn't impose on you!" said Annie.

Benworth ignored his daughter's frown and said eagerly,
"It'd be no imposition. Our new house," he grimaced and
looked longingly out of the window again, "has no garden at
all and I shall not know what to do with myself at weekends.
And we shall miss our fresh vegetables, shan't we, Mary?"

Mary shrugged, but said nothing.

Annie stared out of the window again. "Would you mind
showing me round the garden, Mr Benworth? If you have the
time, that is. I wouldn't know what to look for."

He looked appealingly at his daughter who shrugged again.

"I can walk back to Church Lane if you like, Father, and you can follow when you've finished here. Goodbye, Mrs Ashworth. I hope you'll be happy at Netherleigh Cottage."

Annie let Michael Benworth show her all round the garden, though much of what he said was meaningless to her. She had not really taken into consideration the fact that land could be productive, and could give them food, since she had never had a house with a garden before. By the time the tour was finished, she had made up her mind to seize this opportunity. "I wonder if we mightn't come to some arrangement, Mr Benworth, to our mutual advantage?"

"Mrs Ashworth?"

She gestured to the garden. "Tom and I know nothing about gardening. And we won't have a lot of time to spare to learn about it. If you would like to keep on with the gardening, we could share the produce and . . ." she had another idea, "my brother Luke could help you and learn how to do things." When Benworth did not say anything, she added hastily, "I hope this suggestion doesn't offend you. I shall perfectly understand if . . ."

To her embarrassment, he pulled out a large checked handkerchief and blew his nose, imperfectly disguising his emotions. "I don't know what to say, Mrs Ashworth. Wouldn't it annoy you to have me pottering about? A garden needs a lot of care, you know. I'd have to be here every weekend and sometimes during the week."

She laughed. "There'll be so many people around here, Mr Benworth, that I don't think another will make much difference. I was thinking more of your time and trouble."

He was in control of himself again. "To be frank with you, Mrs Ashworth, it would not be a trouble but a pleasure. And the produce would be very welcome. There's nothing like home-grown vegetables." He sighed. "Mary insists that we must start saving, try to buy a house of our own, however small, for the day when I'm too old to work. She's right, I suppose, but I've never been much of a saving man. I've enjoyed my life, you see, enjoyed every minute. But she insists . . . and Mary can be a very determined person. I think she would approve of a businesslike arrangement about the garden. She's even talking of looking for employment herself though there's no need for that." He broke off. "I'm sorry! I'm inclined to run on a bit, given the slightest encouragement. You should have stopped me."

"I was interested," Annie said frankly. "Besides, I feel – well, rather guilty at turning you out. You've been here for years."

"It's your house, my dear Mrs Ashworth. And your need is greater than ours. You father has told me that he and the children will be coming to live with you. I think your father is as lucky in his daughter as I am in mine."

She bowed her head in acknowledgment of his compliment, liking the way he spoke well of his daughter, liking him better than she ever had before. "Then it's agreed, Mr Benworth?"

"It is indeed, Mrs Ashworth!"

She did not approve of the warmth in his glance and added firmly, "This is purely a business arrangement, Mr Benworth. I'm not interested in anything beyond my business interests and my family."

"That, Mrs Ashworth, is a waste," he replied, "but I take your point. I shall not presume. And at least I shall still have my garden."

"Then I'll not detain you any longer today. You must have a lot of things to sort out in your new house."

When he had gone, she wandered back into the house and exhaled with sheer pleasure. "Mine!" she said aloud. "All mine!"

Two

NETHERLEIGH COTTAGE (1)

Annie walked slowly round the kitchen. It was far larger than any kitchen she had ever had, because it had been a farm kitchen, with space to feed the family and farm hands as well as to cook in. The pantry was enormous. How could they possibly fill all those shelves? Leading off from the back of the kitchen was a small entry which led to the scullery and another large room that had once been the dairy. Well, she wouldn't need a dairy, that was for sure, but the room was so big that it could surely be put to good use with so many of them to house. Behind that was a proper washhouse with a copper boiler. Wonderful! That would make things so much easier with a large family.

As she walked round them, Annie noticed the old-fashioned pump in the corner of the scullery. She ran her hand over the worn handle, then worked it up and down until water gushed out. Who knew where that water had come from? They would continue to boil everything they drank until the new Bilsden Municipal Water Company came into operation, and then they would apply to be connected to that. Dr Lewis himself was promoting that venture in conjunction with Frederick Hallam and some other dignitaries.

Annie smiled wryly. Such philanthropy! It wasn't civic pride or concern for their fellow citizens that was driving most of the shareholders; it was concern for their own health. The richer people were just as afraid of dying as the poorer sort. Many families had lost someone in the recent epidemics and suddenly the things that Dr Lewis had been saying for years about sanitation and a clean water supply were being listened to.

Eyes narrowed, Annie studied the pump. Her son had nearly died in the scarlet fever epidemic and she had read about other types of epidemics. Typhoid was an ever-present spectre. She did not intend to risk anything as far as William was concerned.

Then a smile crept over her face. If she was going to put in proper water supplies to the house, why not do the thing in style? There was room in the dairy for more than just a bedroom for her father. She had heard Dr Lewis talk about modern sanitation and had long had a secret hankering for one of the new bathrooms she had seen pictured in the ladies' magazines which Pauline Hinchcliffe lent her. With a house full of people, they would need to improve the facilities here or they would be for ever queuing up to use the outside privy, or to heat water and use the wash basin and tin bath in the scullery. What had been thought proper a hundred years ago when the farm was first built seemed very primitive nowadays – though still an improvement upon sharing two privies with a street full of people, not to mention sharing with three other streets a water tap which sometimes froze in the depths of winter and which was switched off at nights. And having your own laundry room was a huge improvement on going to the Municipal Washhouse, though that had been Kathy's job for years now.

She strolled back into the kitchen, and her smile broadened as she looked at the wide hearth with its iron bar for hanging pots and its kettle crane and pothooks. She had seen pictures of the new types of kitchen range which heated water as well as providing two cooking ovens and a hob. She intended to have one of those installed as well, eventually. Why not now? Tom would find a way to have things done as cheaply as possible – he could always be relied on for that.

"I'll do it!" She wasn't even aware that she had spoken aloud. She looked at the lamp-holder on the wall and pursed her lips thoughtfully – and why not gas lighting as well? The Bilsden Gas Company had been in operation for several years. People were used to the new gas lamps in the town centre now, and indoor gas lighting was common in the more go-ahead business premises, but very few people wanted to install it in their own homes. She was going to install gas inside her High Street premises. Why not here as well?

She walked out of the kitchen, still with a smile on her face, loving the sound of her footsteps echoing on the bare polished boards of the hall and the feeling of space everywhere.

Standing in the parlour, she pictured how it would look one day and again the laughter bubbled up. Why, she hadn't even got any furniture to put in it, apart from a few of the pieces Sally had left her, let alone carpets, ornaments and draped curtains. The room would have to stay half-empty for quite a while. Good sanitation and cooking facilities were far more important than parlours, especially with nine of them in the house. Nine! How would she cope with that? For all her brave words to Tom, she had to admit to herself that she felt a few qualms about it.

The back room on the ground floor would make a good bedroom for Tom. Who needed a separate morning room when there was a big kitchen to sit in? The dining room would have to stay as empty as the parlour, but one day . . .

In a sudden burst of delight, she pirouetted round the hall, then she chuckled at herself and climbed the stairs. She moved up them slowly, taking the time to admire the turned banisters and run her fingers along the highly polished hand rail. They'd need a carpet on these stairs, or the varnish on the wooden treads would get scuffed. But that'd have to wait, too.

She shook her head, for she was surprising herself today. Fancy someone from Salem Street even being able to contemplate such orgies of spending. She would have to be careful with her money, though. Above all, she must make sure she had enough left to set up the elegant dressmaking salon upon which she had set her heart. With that she couldn't skimp. It had to be so elegant that it astounded the ladies of the town. It had to make them itch to go inside and buy something. Bilsden's only dressmaker, Miss Pinkley, was, at the most charitable estimation, no more than competent as a seamstress. Her stitchery could not be faulted, but her sense of design was appalling. Annie knew that she could do better, far better.

"I'm going to make a lot of money!" she said aloud, then doubt shook her for a moment and she clasped her hands at her chest. Was she fooling herself? Did she really think she could take some of the trade away from the Manchester and London salons which the town's ladies visited from time to time? Were the gowns she created going to be special enough? Then she shook her head and pushed away the doubts. No good came of that sort of thinking. You had to set your mind firmly on success and then work towards it. And as for those creeping doubts, well, if Pauline Hinchcliffe believed in her, then she must have the capacity to succeed, for Pauline was a very shrewd businesswoman.

Upstairs were four bedrooms, one large and three small. The large one was at the front, with two dormer windows, and had been intended for the farmer and his wife, no doubt. "I shall have this one." It might be selfish, but she had a longing for a private place of her own after all the years of sharing with Kathy. There was a good fireplace in it and she would put a table and chair under one of the windows so that she could do her accounts up here or work on her designs. She had been practising drawing again and she intended to take watercolour lessons as soon as she could find a teacher. It was no good *telling* a customer about a dress, you had to *show* her! And things looked so much better in colour.

Annie wandered into the smaller bedrooms. Her little sisters could have this one; William, Mark and Luke could share the second largest; and Kathy should have the third one, the tiniest of them all, to herself. Thank heavens for the old dairy. Without that, she'd not have been able to give her father his own room.

There was a knock on the front door and a voice called, "Annie? Are you there?"

Time to stop day-dreaming. "I'm just coming, Tom."

"Had enough gloating?" he asked, as she let him in. He grinned at her with his usual impudence.

She beamed back at him, forgetting their recent differences. "Oh, Tom! It's going to be so marvellous living here! I'd forgotten how much space there was."

He let her lead him round the house, more impressed than he would have admitted by the thought of living in it. "We could do with a bit more furniture. What'll we put in those big rooms at the front?"

"The parlour and the dining room, you mean."

"Sorry, my lady! Won't you step into the parlour, pray?"

"Shut up, you idiot! There'll only be Sally's things in them to start off with, as well you know – unless you can find us some odd bits and pieces when you're out collecting junk for the yard. I shall need all my money for my salon. Well, most of it."

"Salon!" he teased. "Oh, my, we shall be posh!"

She was impervious to his mockery. Nothing could upset her today.

"You'll get used to it, my lad. Now, wait till you hear what I've decided . . ."

21

There was an imperious tattoo at the front door. They looked at each other, startled.

"Who can that be?" she asked, still feeling more like a visitor herself than the owner of the house.

"You'll never know if you don't go and open the door – or do you want me to do it for you?"

"No. Oh, no! I'll go."

The knocker sounded again as she walked across to the door. She took a deep breath and opened it.

"Ah, Annie. I thought I might find you here." It was Pauline Hinchcliffe, the Methodist minister's wife, once Annie's employer and now her friend. It still amazed Annie sometimes that a member of the landed gentry should befriend someone from the Rows, but when you were rich, you could afford to be eccentric. When you had to make your own way in the world, like Annie, you had to stay utterly respectable.

Behind Pauline, Annie could see the carriage with its glossy brown horses pawing at the ground. In Salem Street the carriage had had to wait around the corner and the driver had had to endure the taunts of grubby urchins. Here, it could stand outside the house in peace. Even that detail made her feel good.

"Well," said Pauline, "aren't you going to invite me in?"

Annie smiled a little shamefacedly. "I'm sorry, Pauline. I've only just taken the house over and I'm still in a bit of a daze. Won't you come in? You're my very first visitor. I wish I could offer you some refreshments, but as you can see, we haven't brought anything over here yet."

Pauline stepped into the hall in her usual confident way. "I've just had a cup of tea with Mrs Purbright, so I'm not in need of refreshments, but I'd love to see your new home. Hello, Mr Gibson. How are you?"

Tom came over to shake hands. He had grown used to the minister's rich wife and her way of ordering people around, but he still found her a bit overpowering at times. "I'm fine, thank you, Mrs Hinchcliffe."

"Good. Don't let me detain you. I shan't be offended if you want to get on with something."

Rightly taking this to mean that his presence was not wanted, he winked at Annie and excused himself. "I'll go and start loading the furniture on the cart then, shall I, love? I'll be back in a couple of hours. There's no time like the present."

"Move in today?" Annie couldn't seem to think clearly.

"Today, love. I, for one, have had more than enough of Salem Street. I don't care if we have to sleep on the bare floorboards tonight. I want to move in here just as much as you do, and if you think you can stop William from coming here today, you're wrong!"

"He was excited this morning, wasn't he? Yes, well – right, then. We'll move in today." Annie glanced apologetically at Pauline. "I don't know whether I'm on my head or my heels."

"That doesn't matter. You have a right to be excited. I'm pleased for you. Now, show me your house!" It was a royal command.

Pauline followed Annie round, making approving comments. "Yes," she summed up when they'd finished, "you did well to buy this place. It's a very sound structure. Now, I want you to give me an hour or two of your time."

"But Tom will be back with the—"

"Never mind Tom! He knows what to do and that girl of yours can help him. What's she called? Kathy. It's important that you come with me today, or I wouldn't take you away from your house-moving, I promise you."

There was no gainsaying Pauline Hinchcliffe when she was in this sort of mood. "Where are we going, then?" asked Annie as the carriage drove off.

"Home. To Collett Hall. I have something to show you." Pauline refused to say any more and spent the rest of the journey questioning Annie about her plans for the new dressmaking salon.

When they arrived at Collett Hall, a lonely, windswept mansion out on the moors, it was nearly half an hour later. Pauline led the way in, ignoring her guest's slight hesitation. Annie had worked as a maid at this house when she had been dismissed by the doctor's wife for being pregnant, after the rape. She had spent several very unhappy weeks here, hating the bleak setting and the wind that whistled round the house when the weather was bad, hating most of all the loneliness, for the other servants had made it plain that they considered her a charity case and one, moreover, whose morals were suspect. Now she was here for the first time as a guest and it further increased the feeling of disorientation that she had been experiencing all day. Moving from the Rows was going to change a lot of things in her life. If things went as she planned, no one would ever again class her as "poor".

Mrs Marsh, the housekeeper, greeted them deferentially, showing no sign of surprise at the sight of Annie.

"Mrs Ashworth and I will be going straight up to the attics," declared Pauline, "and when we've finished up there, you may serve us a light luncheon in the morning room. Did you have the lamps taken up? And the aprons?"

"Yes, ma'am, and the lamps were lit as soon as we heard the carriage."

"Good. Is the master around?"

"He's in the library, ma'am, writing his sermon for Sunday."

"Ask him if he will join us for luncheon in, say, an hour and a half. This way, Annie."

Feeling somewhat irritated by this high-handed treatment, Annie followed Pauline up the stairs. As if she needed showing the way to the attics where she used to sleep! How well she remembered these stairs! Three flights, each narrower than the one before, and the last carpeted only with cheap drugget to dull the sound of the servants' footsteps.

Pauline strode past the servants' bedrooms and up a further half-flight of stairs that led to the first of the lumber rooms high under the roof. They had been going to clean these out, Annie remembered, when she had left to marry Charlie over seven years ago. Poor Charlie!

"There!" said Pauline, flinging open the door triumphantly.

A musty smell wafted out to greet them and Annie gazed in bewilderment at the heaps of furniture, old trunks and piles of dusty rubbish. She looked questioningly at Pauline. What was this all about?

"I thought of it yesterday," said Pauline with smug satisfaction, "when Stephen came up here exploring and grazed his knee. That child can be very wilful at times."

Just like his mother, thought Annie, managing not to smile. Pauline did not have a strong sense of humour.

"It's for you, Annie! The furniture, I mean. For your new house."

Annie stiffened.

"Don't you dare get that stubborn expression on your face, Annie Ashworth! You can *see* that it's doing no good here. We shall never use these things again. But I knew that you didn't have much furniture, so I decided you should have this."

"I can't —" Annie began, but was cut off short.

"Oh, yes, you can! You're in no position to look a gift-horse in the mouth. Besides, I shall be glad to get rid of all this stuff. I've been meaning to clear it out for years."

Annie looked round again, greatly tempted just to say yes, her common sense warring with her pride, for she had sworn to do things on her own, to maintain her independence and to be beholden to no one from now on.

Pauline sighed in exasperation, then spoke again in a coaxing tone. It was not often that she bothered to coax anyone. "I thought we were friends."

"We are. But—"

"No buts. I'm not offering you money, just junk, things of no possible use to us. And what's more," she smiled, "most of them are either worn or broken."

"Pauline, I . . ." Annie hesitated. Mrs Hinchcliffe was an eccentric woman who had chosen and wooed a husband of a lower class than herself, and a Nonconformist at that, so that she could retain absolute control of her family estates. She had befriended Annie many years ago, but it still seemed strange to address her by her first name, even though Annie had by now grown fond of her.

"If you don't take them, I'll have them carted into town and dumped in the street outside your front door."

"You would, too." Annie shook her head. "I don't know what to say, Pauline."

"Say thank you and if it really upsets you to take them, don't charge me for my next dress."

Annie's face cleared. A dress wouldn't be nearly the same value as this furniture, but still, it would be something. She nodded. "Very well. I'll do that. You know we agreed that you need some more stylish garments."

Pauline smiled in relief. "Good. Now, I asked Mrs Marsh to leave some large aprons up here. Yes, there they are. Put one on and we'll start hunting for things that'll be useful." She raised her voice. "Minnie!"

"Yes, ma'am." The reply from outside was so prompt that the maid must have been waiting nearby in the servants' quarters.

"Tell the men to come up now."

It was well over an hour before the two women came down for luncheon, both hot, flushed and very pleased with themselves. Annie was now the owner of several squares of carpet, all worn in places and all in great need of a thorough beating. She had also acquired a bewildering selection of furniture, most in need of repair, some just scuffed and old-fashioned, but all of a very high quality.

She could not now remember exactly what she had got, because Pauline had also given her some things for her dressmaking salon. She suspected that Pauline had worked quickly on purpose to give her no chance to protest. There were several pairs of curtains, that she did remember, all of them faded and frayed, but so big that they could easily be cut down to fit the much smaller windows of Netherleigh Cottage and perhaps, if she were lucky, of the salon. There was even a large mirror in an ornate gilded frame, which, Pauline said disparagingly, had belonged to her grandmother and was rather vulgar. It would be perfect for the salon, though.

Head swimming, Annie went to use the recently installed water closet and then wash her hands in what had once been a guest room, and was now a bathroom. She had been surprised when Pauline told her that a bathroom was to be installed. Her friend did not often make changes to Collett Hall. There had been no water closets in the house when Annie had worked here. How she had hated carrying the ewers of hot water all the way up to these rooms! "That's progress for you," she declared to the empty bathroom. "They can keep their steam-engines. I'd rather have piped water and inside privies, thank you." Then another idea struck her and she stood stock-still in the middle of the room. "Oh," she said exultantly, "I'll do it! I'll do that, too!"

She realised that she was wasting time and rather nervously she went downstairs to have luncheon with Pauline and her husband, the first meal she had ever eaten as a guest at Collett Hall. She came through this ordeal quite well, she considered, but she caught a fleeting look of resentment on the parlourmaid's face as she saw whom she was serving.

Saul Hinchcliffe, who had known her since she was a small child, greeted Annie kindly. He had put on weight steadily since his marriage and his face looked pink and well-fed against his receding hairline. He was rather preoccupied during the meal and Pauline dismissed him as soon as it was over. "He's never very sociable on a Tuesday," she said, as she led the way up to the nursery to show off her sons. "Sometimes, when he's writing his sermons, he won't even stop to eat until he's finished. Ah, there you are, you two! Come and greet Mrs Ashworth properly."

Stephen Hinchcliffe, aged six, came over at once and bowed to Annie. "How do you do, ma'am," he said politely.

"I'm very well, thank you, Stephen."

"Wesley!" Pauline said sharply.

A chubby little boy of three had to be brought over forcibly by his governess, protesting loudly at having to leave his wooden blocks.

Pauline reached down and took his hand. "Say how-do-you-do to Mrs Ashworth, and then you shall return to your toys," she commanded.

He gulped his tears away. Even at that age, he knew better than to disobey a direct order from his mother. "How d'oo do," he lisped, staring briefly up at Annie, then gazing back at his half-built castle.

Annie shook the chubby hand that he was waving at her and then laughed at the speed with which he returned to his toys. She exchanged smiles with the older boy who was still standing politely beside his mother.

"He's only a baby, ma'am. He doesn't mean to be rude," Stephen offered in apology.

How like his mother this one was! The same pale skin, straight mousy hair and alert expression. "I know. I have a son of my own. I remember what he was like when he was three."

"How old is your son now, ma'am?"

"He's seven, nearly eight. His name is William."

"The gardener's boy's called William too, but everyone

calls him Will. I'm not allowed to play with him. If you had brought your William with you, I could have played with him, couldn't I? I've seen him in chapel, I think. He has hair the same colour as yours but a little darker, hasn't he?"

"Yes, he has. Perhaps you'll be able to play with him another time."

Pauline squeezed her son's shoulder briefly. "Go back to your toys now, Stephen. We'll go out for a ride together later."

He nodded happily and ran back to the toy soldiers which were lined up on the table in neat rows.

"They're fine boys," said Annie as they walked out to the carriage. "But isn't it rather lonely for them here?" She wondered if she should have said that, but she remembered how lonely she had been at Collett Hall herself.

Pauline looked at her in surprise. "I suppose it is. But there's no one suitable for him to play with, and this is my family home, after all."

"Then let him play with someone unsuitable! It won't hurt, at his age, if he gets to know the gardener's boy. Children need the company of other children. I made the same mistake myself with William for a time."

Pauline stared down her nose. "Hmm. I'll think about it. Now, you'd better get back to your new house. You'll no doubt pass the big cart carrying your things. There won't be time to send a second load today, but I'll send the rest across first thing tomorrow."

The carriage deposited Annie at a Netherleigh Cottage filled with chaos. Her possessions were piled all over the hall and Kathy was working furiously in the kitchen to put a stew on the fire, as well as trying to help with the unpacking.

"Thank 'eavens you're back, Annie! I didn't know where to start. Rebecca! If you've put them cups away, you can go an' look for the plates. An' try not to get straw all over the floor this time."

Annie's half-sister peeped shyly out of the pantry. "Hello, Annie."

"Mrs Carson couldn't come in today to look after your dad's lot, so I've got the girls with me an' the boys are with Tom. We didn't know where you was." Kathy stared at her accusingly. "An' there's a big black cat keeps tryin' to creep into the kitchen. The children *will* leave the door open! Sammy'll go mad if it's still around when Tom brings him over tonight. You know how that dog hates cats!"

"Oh, dear! I'm sorry I had to leave you, Kathy, but Mrs Hinchcliffe took me over to Collett Hall. She just wouldn't take no for an answer."

Kathy raised her eyes to the ceiling. "Aye, I know what she's like, that one. Didn't you tell her we were movin' in today?"

"That's why she came. She has an attic full of old furniture. She knew we'd be short of things here, so she's given me some pieces – lots of pieces, actually."

She broke off as Kathy darted past her, flapping her apron. "There's that dratted cat again! Shoo! Go on! Get away!"

At the same time there was a knock on the front door. "I'll go," said Annie, feeling that she had come home to a madhouse.

Mary Benworth was standing on the steps. "I'm sorry to trouble you, but I think Sooty must have tried to come back to his old home." She saw that Annie was looking blank. "Our cat," she added. "A big black one."

"Oh, yes. He keeps trying to get into the kitchen. Won't you come in for a moment?"

"I'm sorry to intrude at a time like this, but I thought he might be making a nuisance of himself." She laughed. "He thinks he owns the place. I meant to wait until you were settled and call on you properly then. I wanted to thank you about the garden. Dad was more depressed at losing that than at leaving the house."

"I think the arrangement is more to our benefit than to yours," Annie said frankly. "I feel we're taking advantage of Mr Benworth."

As she started to lead the way towards the kitchen, there was another knock on the front door. "Oh, no! Who can that be?" It was the cart with the first load of furniture from Collett Hall. One of Pauline's gardeners was standing near the door, grinning broadly, while the driver was putting feeding bags on his horses.

"Can I help?" asked Mary impulsively, seeing the frantic way Annie rolled her eyes and floundered for words. "I've nothing much to do, because we moved most of our stuff the day before yesterday, but you seem very – er – busy." She smiled warmly at little Joan who was peeping round the kitchen door, but the child drew back into the kitchen and the safety of Rebecca's presence. Seeing Annie hesitating, Mary took her bonnet off and rolled up her sleeves. "What shall I do?"

Annie accepted her offer gratefully. "It's a load of furniture which Mrs Hinchcliffe has just given to me. I haven't thought where to put it yet. I can't even remember what there is. If you could send anything that's for bedrooms upstairs – it doesn't matter where they put it – and tell them to pile the rest in the parlour or the dining room . . . Oh, and if there's anything for the kitchen, just send it through."

Kathy poked her head into the hall. "Rebecca chased the cat outside. It's sitting up in the tree now. Oh, sorry, love! I didn't know you had someone with you." She goggled at the two men who were trying to get a huge, overstuffed sofa through the door.

"I was trying to tell you, Kathy," Annie explained, "that Mrs Hinchcliffe's given us a pile of her old furniture and the first cartload is here already. Oh, and this is Miss Benworth who used to live here. It's her cat. She'll take it away with her later, but for the moment she's kindly offered to help us. I *must* go and change into one of my old dresses before I do anything. I can see a bundle of my clothes over there." She vanished upstairs clutching the bundle and looking flustered.

"I'm Kathy. I work for Annie," Kathy volunteered, with her usual shyness, but that vanished as the two men began to complain loudly that they couldn't get the sofa through, and she and Mary Benworth were forced to set to work to move the piles of things littering the hallway.

By four o'clock the men had unloaded all the furniture and carpets from the cart and Mary Benworth had gone home, taking the cat with her tied up in an apron and yowling loudly at the indignity of that. Tom and the boys had brought several loads of things over from Number Eight. Now that they had the furniture from Mrs Hinchcliffe, Annie was able to send one or two of her old pieces back to Alice, her other employee, who was to stay on in their old house in Salem Street.

The last load of their own stuff arrived around six o'clock driven by a weary-looking Tom with the boys walking behind. "How have things gone?" asked Annie, going out to meet them.

Tom rolled his eyes heavenwards. "What a rotten day! Our William hasn't stopped talking and asking questions since you left this morning. And Alice was trying to get her stuff into Number Eight before we'd even moved ours out. Hey, you boys, start unloading that lot, eh?"

"What about Mark and Luke? How have they been?" she asked in a low voice. She knew Tom was still not convinced that her father and his children should come and live with them.

He shrugged. "Mark's all right. He's got his head screwed on, that one has. But Luke creeps round after him like a shadow and jumps if anyone else speaks to him."

Annie nodded. She had noticed how protective Mark was towards the younger boy, but she had also noticed how well Luke tackled any task that Mark set him, even though the younger boy didn't often take the initiative to do something himself. She linked her arm in Tom's and walked with him into the house. "I think you've done wonderfully," she was beginning, when William burst into the kitchen dragging Sammy behind him on a piece of rope. "That dog's filthy! Just take him straight out into the garden again, William, and make sure the side gates are closed so he can't run away!" She watched through the kitchen window as the old dog started to sniff his way round the garden, running to and fro behind William as fast as his stiff legs would carry him.

A little later, when the other two boys joined William in the back garden, Sammy started limping from one to the other in an ecstasy of excitement. It was a good thing, Annie thought, pouring a cup of tea, that Mary had taken her cat back to his new home before Sammy arrived.

The three boys tired of watching the dog and came back into the kitchen, William leading the way confidently, the other two following hesitantly as if unsure of their welcome.

"Mother?"

"Yes, William, what is it? Can't you see that I'm busy? Here's your cup of tea, Tom. Kathy, give the boys a piece of bread and jam each, will you?" She did not need to ask if they were hungry. In the past few days, she had found that her half-brothers and sisters were perpetually hungry.

William brandished his jam butty at her. "Mother, why can't Mark and Luke move in tonight with us?"

"Because nothing's ready, William. Don't be silly!"

"But Mother, we want to be together the first night. It won't be the same if I'm on my own." Once he had an idea fixed in his mind, it was hard to divert William from it. "Please, Mother!"

Mark tugged at his young nephew's arm. "Don't pester her, William. I told you we wouldn't be able to. Our Annie's tired."

Luke said nothing, but he watched everything with his large pale eyes, mouth slightly agape in concentration and head turning from one speaker to another.

Tom gulped down the rest of his tea and looked across at Annie, a grin dawning. "Why not?"

"Why not? Because there's nothing ready for them, that's why not! I haven't even *begun* to sort out Dad's house yet, let alone bring their stuff over here."

"They won't mind if they have to sleep on the floor. Will you, boys?"

"No!"

"And we can sort their things out here, surely?"

"They'll have to eat here with us anyway," put in Kathy. "There's nothin' ready at their place."

Annie began to waver, but she was not yet ready to cede the point to Tom. "If they stay, the girls'll want to stay too. And what about Dad? The old dairy's not ready for him to move into yet. We can't leave him on his own at Number Three."

Tom grinned. "He can come in with me for a bit. He's not fussy, Dad isn't. An' I don't mind sharin' my room. Besides, I think we've all had enough of Salem Street. Let 'em come if they want. Why not?"

"Oh, Mam, do let them!" begged William.

Mark held his breath, dying to move into this palace, but not wanting to upset his sister.

"What did you call me?" demanded Annie.

William scuffed one foot on the floor. "Mother, then. Please, Mother! Mother, Mother, Mother, *darling* Mother! Please let them come."

"Well . . ."

William saw that she was wavering and rushed across the room to fling his arms round her. "Do say yes, Mother. Please! I can't bear it if you don't."

"All right, all right! Yes."

Mark let out his breath in a whoosh and beamed at them,

and even Luke's wary expression relaxed into a smile.

"Come on, then, lads," said Tom. "Let's harness up that poor old donkey again. We'll have to go an' get some of your things an' tell Dad when he comes home from the mill."

Three bodies tried to push through the back door at once to get to the shed where Blackie was now housed. With much laughter and squealing, the boys tore across the back garden and Tom, with a wink at Kathy, drained his cup of tea and followed them. He was not ready to admit such a thing to Annie, but he had enjoyed the boys' company that day. And she was right about one thing. Young Mark was a bright lad. Very bright. Maybe it wouldn't be so bad, after all, having them here.

Rebecca made her way hesitantly over to her half-sister and Joan trotted after her, clutching her skirt. "Can we really stay here tonight, our Annie?"

"I said so, didn't I?"

Although Annie's voice had been sharp, the little girl heaved such a blissful sigh that Annie and Kathy both burst out laughing.

"Kathy, I think we'll have to send Rebecca over to the baker's for a meat pie. One of those big ones. And a couple of cakes or tarts or something." Annie suddenly felt reckless, light-hearted. They would celebrate in style tonight. "And get a jug of ale, too. Dad likes an occasional glass and so does Tom. No, Rebecca will never carry that much. Could you go with them? I'll keep an eye on that stew and set the table."

But when they had gone, she stole a few minutes to tiptoe into the parlour and sit on the big dusty sofa with the wobbly leg and imagine how it would look when they got it all done up properly. And she felt young and carefree again, full of hope, just like she had when she was sixteen and walking out with Matt Peters.

Three

BRIGHTON: ANNABELLE LEWIS

While Annie and her new extended family were moving into Netherleigh Cottage, Annabelle Lewis, the estranged wife of Bilsden's only doctor, was arranging her cosy terraced house in Brighton to her exact liking. She intended to call on all her old acquaintances and make new friends in the town. She had never been as happy as she had been in Brighton, and had been scheming and planning to come back here for years. Jeremy's stupidity in moving to Bilsden was one of the many things she despised about him.

Annabelle travelled down to London by train at the height of the Bilsden epidemic, seething with fury at her husband for the first part of the journey, snapping at Cora and even at the porters who transferred her luggage from one train to another. How dared Jeremy treat her like that, throwing her out of his home and life as if she were just a servant who had not given satisfaction? Shouting at her, with all the household listening, too! And how dared he deprive her of her share, her *rightful* share, of his family silver? She was his wife, wasn't she? She had put up with him for all those years, hadn't she? He had just better keep his promise and send on the rest of her boxes, that was all!

She smiled, a tight nasty smile. She had taken every single item she could from that house in Bilsden, every rag that was rightfully hers. Jeremy had said nothing about sheets and table linen, so she had made sure that she got a major share of those, not to mention extra blankets and pillows and a myriad of other small items. He was such a fool, so easy to cheat. He didn't even insist on his poorer patients paying him for his services.

The anger died down somewhat and she began to wonder what to tell people in Brighton about her move. Separated wives were not always welcomed into their social circles by other ladies. She sat staring out of the train window for nearly an hour, brows furrowed as she worried away at that question and considered the implications of the various alternatives.

She had originally intended to say that she had been forced to come back to Brighton for the sake of her health, that her doctor husband had absolutely insisted she leave Bilsden for fear its smoky atmosphere would ruin her lungs completely. But in order to maintain that fiction, he would have to come to visit her in Brighton or she would have to visit him occasionally in Bilsden. And at the very least, she ought to have Marianne come down to visit her every year. No one would believe the tale of poor health and her husband's insistence on her living in Brighton if she never even tried to see her own daughter, tiresome as the chit was.

After a while, another tight smile curved Annabelle's lips briefly. Who would know where she was going if she went away for little holidays from time to time? She could always say she was going to Bilsden to be with her dear daughter, or was meeting Marianne in London, but in fact she could go anywhere as long as no one from Brighton saw her. Why, she could even go on one of those new excursions to France which a gentleman called Mr Cook was advertising? Had she not always longed to visit Paris, to see for herself the capital of fashion? She might not be able to afford to buy her clothes there, but she could come back with ideas, couldn't she? Just as she used to do when she visited London.

A scowl replaced the smile for a moment. She would have preferred to stay in Bilsden for another year or two to save some more money from the housekeeping and then to bargain with Jeremy about a decent allowance. Now, with him furious and only allowing her a miserly sum, she would have to be extremely careful how she lived in Brighton. Her whole life seemed to have been plagued by a lack of money. How wonderful it must be to be rich, really rich! She glanced sideways at Cora. Perhaps she had been rash in bringing a lady's maid with her? It might be considered an extravagance now. She would have to see how things worked out. But Cora was good with her needle – not as good as that slut, Annie Gibson, had been, but good – so perhaps Cora could earn her keep that way. It was *so* important to keep up a good appearance.

In London, Annabelle stayed in a discreet little hotel where the charges were very modest and allowed Cora to sleep on a truckle bed in her room because that saved money. She did not linger in the capital, but pressed on the very next day to Brighton by train. Such a difference the railways made to travelling nowadays!

She sighed with pleasure as she told the driver of the cab she took from the railway station to detour along the sea front before taking her to her neat little house. Should she stop at dear Barbara's and tell her what had happened? No. Not yet. She rather thought she would tell no one about the true state of affairs, not even her best friend.

She stared sideways at her maid, the only person who knew what had really happened between her and her husband. "I do

39

not wish people in Brighton to know that I have left my husband, Cora."

"No, ma'am."

"In fact, if you breathe one word to anyone, I shall dismiss you instantly."

Cora jerked back in her seat in surprise, then took a deep breath and sat up straighter. In for a penny, in for a pound. If she did not make some sort of a stand now, Mrs Lewis would make her life a misery. Like her mistress, Cora had been wondering whether she had done the right thing in coming down to Brighton, but jobs were scarce, especially for those who could not get a reference from a former mistress. "You have no need to threaten me, ma'am," she said, pleased that her voice sounded calm and confident. "I enjoy working for you and I quite understand the situation. I shall do and say nothing to spoil your social life. After all, our interests both lie in the same direction, don't they? Well, they do as long as I'm working for you, anyway."

Annabelle sucked in her breath in shock at this veiled threat and stared at Cora as if she had never seen her before, then slowly she leaned her head back and allowed herself to smile. "I had not realised that you were such a sharp little piece, Cora." She let that sink in, then nodded. "However, it may suit both our purposes if you stay with me. And if I have your absolute loyalty, I shall have no reason to dismiss you, shall I?"

Cora forced herself to breathe evenly and not to let out a loud puff of relief. "None at all, ma'am. If I might say so, it's a pleasure to turn out a mistress who does justice to my skills. I could never work for an ugly woman – or a fat one." She relaxed a little as she saw Annabelle's smile widen. Oh yes, milady, she thought to herself, you love a bit of flattery, don't you? Well, you're not the only one as likes Brighton, and if it costs me a few extra compliments to stay here, it'll be well worth it.

The small elegant house was shut up and smelled cold and musty, but Annabelle hardly noticed that as she walked inside. To her surprise, she felt like weeping for joy. She had come home. She had escaped from that dreadful place – and from him – for ever.

She gave the cab driver a tip, the size of which made him mutter audibly about skinflints, then she turned to Cora. "I think we can carry these valises upstairs between us, don't you? Then we shall have to consider our needs. Food for tonight, of course – you'll have to go out to a cookshop – but more important, the question of other servants. You do realise, Cora, that I am not as affluent as I would wish. We shall have to be very careful with our expenses."

Cora inclined her head. "Yes, ma'am." You'll enjoy being parsimonious, that new cheeky Cora inside her thought. You get a real pleasure out of penny-pinching at the expense of your servants, you do. Well, just you try cheating me of my rights.

For the first time, as she helped carry the luggage upstairs, Cora realised that she was both taller and stronger than her mistress. Why she thought, if I play my cards right, I'll have the silly bitch eating out of my hand from now on.

In Bilsden, the last of the influenza epidemic died down and other parents mourned their children, but the doctor's daughter, Marianne, suffered only a mild dose. As Ellie Peters cosseted her young mistress into a full recovery, Jeremy worried over how he was going to tell his daughter about her mother's defection.

The first day she joined him downstairs for dinner, however, Marianne broached the subject herself. "I heard you and Mother quarrelling," she said, fiddling with her spoon handle.

"Oh. I'm sorry about that."

She gave him a long level look. "Father, I'm sixteen. Nearly grown up. And – I've known for years that you and Mother didn't get on very well."

He did not know what to say to that.

"Mother isn't – wasn't – an easy person to love, was she? I mean, she hardly ever talked to me and she didn't take me out or – or anything that the other girls' mothers do."

He could see the tears in her eyes, so he leaned forward to lay his hand over hers. "I'm more sorry than I can say about that, my darling."

She blinked her eyes rapidly to dispel the tears. She was determined to appear grown-up and in control of herself tonight. "It's not your fault. I should be used to it by now, shouldn't I? And *you* talk to me and spend time with me, and I have Ellie, so I haven't been too unhappy. It's just – well, I thought we ought to speak about things, now that Mother's gone for good."

"You're right." He gave her a rueful smile. "I've been trying to think what to say to you, and worrying about it all. The truth will be by far the easiest thing, but please keep it between the two of us."

Marianne nodded. "Why exactly did you tell her to leave? I was a bit dizzy and I can't remember it clearly."

He drew a deep breath. "When you were ill, we didn't know whether it was anything serious or not, but your mother decided to leave anyway. I think that was the final straw for me. I told her that if she went, she was not to come back to Bilsden again, that you would be better off without a mother who abandoned you when you were ill. I'm still not sure whether I was right or not, but anyway, it's done now." And I'm glad she's gone, he thought to himself.

"So she left." Marianne squared her shoulders. "And she didn't even come in to see me before she left, to – to say goodbye, did she?"

"No."

Marianne bowed her head for a moment, struggling to hold

back the tears. "She's taken all her clothes, even the old ones she had stored in the attic. I went to look in her room. The sheets and blankets are gone as well, and the new feather mattress. She's gone to the house in Brighton, hasn't she?"

"Yes. She bought it with some money her mother left her. I expect she had some money left from her inheritance to live on or she wouldn't have gone. Though I shall be making her a small allowance."

"She's bound to have something tucked away. Mother would never tolerate poverty, would she?" The words sounded very grown-up, but the tears were still threatening, so Marianne clenched her hands until the nails bit into her palms.

The soup lay cold and untasted in their dishes. On Jeremy's side plate there was a pile of breadcrumbs.

Suddenly, Marianne could hold the tears back no longer. As her face crumpled, she pushed her chair back and cast herself into her father's arms, weeping hysterically. Susan, waiting outside the door to clear the table and bring up the next course, tiptoed back down to the kitchen.

"Miss Marianne's crying her heart out up in the dining room. I should keep the next course warm, if I were you, Mrs Cosden." She glanced at Ellie. "What do you think's wrong? I thought she was better now."

"I expect he's telling her about her mother leaving," said Ellie calmly. "He should have waited till after the meal, really, but she's been asking me about it and she's seen how everything's gone from her mother's room, so perhaps she was the one who asked him."

"The mistress's bedroom's picked as clean as a chicken bone," said Mabel with relish. "Everything she could fit into them boxes she took with her."

"And left that poor little lamb behind!" said Mrs Cosden. "To think of a mother abandoning her own child like that!"

"Cora's done all right for herself out of it all," said Mabel.

"We're well rid of her, sneaky bitch that she was."

"Watch your language!" Mrs Cosden glanced meaningfully at Susan, the young general maid.

Mabel sniffed and tossed her head, but said no more.

Ellie cleared her throat. "Dr Lewis has discussed matters with me. He wishes me to act as both houskeeper and companion to Miss Marianne for the time being. I hope you won't be offended by that, Mrs Cosden. I know you've been here longer than I have. If you want to take over as housekeeper . . ."

Mrs Cosden sighed. "No, I'm not offended. To tell you the truth, I don't want the extra work, love. I'm not as young as I was. You'll leave me to manage the kitchen as I see fit, though?"

Ellie gave the rich chuckle which was so much her own. "I wouldn't dare do anything else, Mrs Cosden."

Mrs Cosden's face relaxed into a smile. "Then I daresay we can rub along together."

"Well!" Mabel folded her arms and glowered at them both. "I think that's a bit rich, Ellie Peters. Talk about worming your way in! What do *you* know about managing a house? *I* know more than you do – and I've been here for longer than you have, too. It's me as should have been made housekeeper and I've a good mind to tell the doctor that."

Ellie sighed. She had expected Mabel to kick up a fuss, and she knew that the other woman would not be easy to manage. She looked at Susan and the new young general maid, Ruth, who were listening to every word, open-mouthed. They wouldn't give her any trouble. "I hope I don't need to tell everyone that nothing must be said about Mrs Lewis leaving permanently, for Miss Marianne's sake. Dr Lewis intends to tell people that Mrs Lewis has had to move to Brighton because of her health."

"No one'll believe that!" jeered Mabel.

"No, of course they won't, but the gentry will pretend to

believe it. They always prefer to keep up appearances and they like Dr Lewis. He's going to ask a cousin of his to find someone to come and live here, so that Miss Marianne will have a lady to act as chaperone and companion, but that won't affect the rest of us. Whoever comes will have no responsibility for the house. He says I'm to manage everything."

Mabel was still glaring at her, but she said nothing more.

As Ellie left the kitchen to go and sit in her room, Mrs Cosden exchanged glances with Mabel. "It's an ill wind . . ." she said, tapping her nose.

"You don't think she and Dr Lewis . . ."

"No, of course not! *He* wouldn't do anything like that under his own roof, he's too much of a gentleman, and anyway, he's got someone over in Manchester, a right hussy from the way his clothes reek of cheap perfume sometimes."

"Well, someone of Ellie Peters's age doesn't normally get to be housekeeper," Mabel said, lips pressed into a tight unfriendly line.

Mrs Cosden put a hand on Mabel's arm and gave it a comforting squeeze. "I expect it's because she's looked after Miss Marianne so well. And she's certainly done that; she's been more a mother to that girl than the mistress has."

"I bet you're a bit upset about the housekeeper's job, though, underneath it all," Mabel probed.

Mrs Cosden sighed and rubbed her hip which started aching whenever she was on her feet a lot. "No, I'm not, actually. Once I might have been, but not now. It's you who've had your nose put out of the joint, Mabel, my girl. Still, you'll have to admit that we shall all be a lot happier without Mrs Lewis breathing down our necks. So in that way, we'll all be better off. Let's look on the bright side, eh?"

"As long as Ellie doesn't try to imitate *her* cheapskate ways."

"I don't think she will. I think it's Miss Marianne that Ellie cares about, really, and always has done. Ellie Peters is the sort who should have had children of her own by now, not be mothering a girl of Miss Marianne's age."

"Well, it's not likely that she'll ever marry and have children of her own, is it?" sneered Mabel. "If she's not here, she's off visiting her family, or that Annie Ashworth. And she never has walked out with anyone either. It's funny that. It's not for want of fellows asking her, but she just tells them no. I've never been able to understand her, never."

That's because you can't see one inch beyond your own nose, thought Mrs Cosden. She measures everyone against the doctor, Ellie Peters does, so it's no wonder she finds them lacking, for he's a good-looking chap, still, and the kindest gentleman I ever worked for. But she's never tried to do anything about how she feels about him, I will give her that. She knows what's right and what's wrong, and she does her job properly. So how she feels about him is her own business. He certainly doesn't think of her in that way.

Four

NETHERLEIGH COTTAGE (2)

John Gibson came across from Salem Street to Netherleigh Cottage before the furniture on the moving day. He was still dirty from the mill, with bits of cotton fluff clinging to his threadbare clothes like flakes of snow. Annie's heart ached to see how tired her father looked, and how thin and grey his hair was becoming.

" 'Allo, lass. This move's a bit sudden, isn't it?" He hovered on the front doorstep, making no effort to come in. "I thought we weren't comin' here for a few days yet."

"Well, the children were so keen to sleep together tonight that Tom and I couldn't say no. Aren't you going to come in, Dad? This is your home too now."

John looked down at himself dubiously. "I'm in all me muck."

"That doesn't matter. Wait till you see the mess inside!"

He allowed himself to be led into the hallway and paused to stare round. "By, you've getten yersen a palace 'ere, love! I couldn't believe I were at t'right place when I stopped outside."

"It is a nice house," she agreed, then took his arm. "Why

47

don't you come and sit down in the kitchen for a few minutes, Dad? I was just going to make myself a pot of tea. We can have a cup together, then I'll light one of the lamps and show you round. You can't see much with a candle."

"Aye, lass. That'd be lovely. I'm allus dry as dust of an evenin'. That cotton gets in y'r throat. Let me light the lamp for you while you brew up. Now that's a job I'm good at, lamps. You 'ave to keep 'em clean. That's the secret. Keep t'wicks trimmed and t'chimneys clean, then they'll burn proper an' give you a good light."

"Thanks. They're all in a bit of a mess, I'm afraid. We haven't had time to do them properly for days. It'll be better when we get the gaslights installed."

"Gaslights! Inside the 'ouse!" He stood there gaping at her.

"Yes, Dad. And a kitchen range and a proper bathroom, too. I'd rather spend my money on conveniences than fancy furniture."

"Nay, then. Just think of that!"

She busied herself with the tea and he with the lamps. There was only the ticking of the clock and the crackling of the fire to keep them company. It was nice to have a few minutes of peace after the frenetic bustle of the day.

"I'll 'ave a bit of a wash after I've done this, if you don't mind, love. I allus used to 'ave a wash at night for your mother. Proper fussy, Lucy were. An' you're t'same. Em'ly weren't fussy. Poor creature, I miss 'er, though! You get used to a person, faults an' all."

"Yes, you do. I miss Charlie still. He'd have liked to live here. We were always talking about moving out of Salem Street one day. He was so looking forward to having a garden of his own." She took a deep breath, blinked the tears from her eyes and deliberately changed the subject. "Thanks, Dad. That's a big help. Now, why don't you sit down by the fire and drink your tea? Take the rocking chair. It was Charlie's. It's very comfortable."

He sat down with a sigh, willing to rest a little, now that he'd made some contribution. He rocked to and fro slowly, testing the chair. "Aye. You're right. It is comfortable. It's got a nice balance to it."

"I thought you'd like it. That'll be your chair from now on, then."

He nodded, drank his tea, then accepted a second cup. "Good tea, that. You can't beat a drink of tea after a hard day's work." He sat toasting himself and watching her, happier than he'd been for weeks. How pretty she looked and how lucky he was to have such a daughter! She was just like her mother; she brought out the best in people. Look how Tom had changed since he'd gone to live with her!

Annie bustled to and fro, laying nine places round the scrubbed wooden table, stirring the stew, putting some more water in the blackened kettle and swinging it deftly over the flames on its well-balanced chimney crane.

"Lass . . ."

"Yes, Dad?"

"I don't know how to thank you. For what y're doin'. I'm right grateful, that I am."

"That's all right, Dad. We'll all be able to help one another, I think." She could feel the tears rising in her eyes again at his humble tone and added quickly, to lessen the emotion in the air, "Besides – you wait till I start nagging you all. I like to have things done my way. You might not be so grateful then!"

John smiled his slow wide smile. "Nay, I reckon we shall all need a fair bit o' naggin'. Emily weren't much cop, poor old lass, an' them childer 'aven't been taught their manners – nor owt much else, neither. You nag away, love." He handed her the cup, then held his hands out towards the fire, sighing in pleasure at its warmth. "It still gets cold of an evening," he said, "an' you feel the cold more as you grow older." After a moment or two, however, he pulled himself together. "Now, lass, if you've got a bowl of water, I'll give meself a bit of a sluice down."

She picked up a tin bowl and poured in some hot water from the kettle. "Get one of the lamps and bring it through into the scullery so that you can see to wash yourself. There's a proper drain from there into the garden which'll make things easier for Kathy." She topped the kettle up automatically with cold water from the bucket they kept nearby and swung it back over the flames.

He looked round and cleared his throat. "Eh, I still can't believe you'd the money to buy a great big place like this, love."

"I've got Charlie to thank for that. He had a lot of money saved up when I married him. It may sound awful, but it was one of the reasons why I said yes. I didn't tell you at the time, but he got Number Eight rent free and five shillings a week from Mr Hallam as well, because of the accident. That's why we were able to keep on saving, even when other people were on short time."

"Nay, fancy that! Still, old Mr Hallam did allus favour Charlie. Him an' Charlie's father was lads together, you see. You never said owt to me about all that, though."

She didn't tell him that she had kept quiet because of Emily. "No, I thought it best not to. I still had to live in Salem Street, didn't I? Folks would have been jealous, an' they might have turned spiteful. I just bought the two houses over in Peter Street with Charlie's money and got Tom to collect the rents for us. Then Charlie and I worked together to save some more money. When this house came up for sale, Mr Pennybody told me about it and I snapped it up."

He shook his head. The idea of having money to spare after a week's living was so foreign to him after his years of marriage to Emily that he did not pursue it. "I'll hand my wages over to you, love, from now on, like I used to do with your mother. I shouldn't want you to be out of pocket over the childer. If there's a bit to spare for my baccy, that's all I s'll need."

"Are you sure about that, Dad?"

"Oh, aye, I'm sure. You'll make the money go further than I ever could, an' I don't need much for myself. You can allus let me have clothes from the stall when I need 'em."

She would make sure he had some really good clothes, she thought, looking at how threadbare his things were.

Afterwards she linked her arm in his and showed him all over the house. He was duly impressed by the size of it, but what caught his interest most was the furniture Mrs Hinchcliffe had sent.

He stroked the arm of a chair with the gentle fingertips of a lover. "That's good stuff, that is. You've only got to look at it. You can see the shine on it! And this is a lovely little table! Look! It only needs a bit of glue and a few screws to make it as good as new. I'll mend it for you at the weekend, if you like."

"I'd forgotten that you could do that sort of thing, Dad, fixing furniture, I mean."

"Oh, I used to be a bit handy like, given the chance."

"Well, that'll be marvellous! Tom's no good at repairing things and most of these pieces need something doing to them."

He straightened his shoulders. "You just leave it to me, lass." Then his face fell and his shoulders sagged once again. "Nay, I were forgettin' – I 'aven't got any tools. We 'ad to sell 'em a few years back, when I were ill that time. The childer were hungry."

And of course Emily never saved a penny for a rainy day, Annie thought. But she did not voice the thought. Her dad was loyal to those he loved, whatever their faults. Then she remembered something. "Dad, I've still got Charlie's tools.

Tom doesn't use them, but I didn't like to give them away. I thought William might want to have them one day. You could use those."

He was happy again, a man with a contribution to make. "Right then, love! You just find them an' leave the rest to me! I'm right good at fixin' things, if I do say so myself."

She had not thought that he would be a useful person to have around the house. Hadn't thought either that he'd need to be able to help, for his pride's sake. She gave him a hug which made his face light up.

"Well, you 'aven't done that for a good few years, lass," he said, but it was an expression of pleasure, not a criticism.

"Well, I'm doing it now."

When she showed him the dairy and explained how she planned to alter it, to give him a room of his own looking out on to the garden, he dashed his hand across his eyes and said thickly, "Eh, lass, lass!" and she too was nearly in tears again. She was glad that Kathy and the girls got back just then.

"Hello, Mr Gibson. How are you?" Kathy placed a huge pie on the table. "I got the big size, Annie. Thought we'd need it. Had to put a shilling deposit on the dishes, but we'll get it back next time."

Rebecca placed two apple pies in the pantry, then she turned and threw herself at her father. "Dad, Dad, come an' see our room! It's that big an' clean! It's right lovely." Little Joan padded over behind her to clutch at his sleeve.

He winked at Annie. "You show me, then, our Becky."

She put her hands on her hips. "You know I don't like being called Becky."

"Sorry, love." He grinned as he lit another lamp and allowed his two youngest daughters to pull him out of the kitchen. Rebecca's voice trailed back down the stairs, talking excitedly about the wonders of the new house and what they'd been doing all day.

Kathy smiled at Annie. "Everythin' all right, love?"

"Yes. Everything's fine. I was just chatting to Dad."

"He's a nice man, your dad is. He's nice with the children an' he allus says thank you. Some don't. It'll be a pleasure to look after him properly, a real pleasure."

When Tom and the boys got back, the house was immediately filled with noise and bustle. William dragged Luke off to help him feed the donkey and bed him down in the old garden shed. Mark and Tom humped the rest of the bundles inside and piled them in the hallway, then dragged the empty cart round the back before joining the two younger boys to fill the kitchen with demands to be fed. Immediately, at once! They were all famished.

They made no attempt to unpack until after they'd eaten, but crammed themselves around the wooden kitchen table, elbow to elbow, and wolfed down their food.

Every morsel of the stew, the meat pie and the whole quartern loaf vanished from the table. Kathy brought the apple pies out from their solitary splendour on the stone cool-shelf in the near-empty pantry and they were greeted by loud cries of appreciation, and then silence as they were demolished. William was so wildly excited by the companionship that he could hardly eat for talking, little Joan fell asleep over the remains of her apple pie and Luke smiled shyly at Annie from Mark's side. Even Sammy looked at ease, lying in front of the fire, his belly round with the plate of scraps he'd consumed and his paws twitching as he chased dream rabbits.

After the meal, Annie and Kathy went upstairs to sort out beds for the children. Annie was horrified to see that the bedding they'd brought consisted mainly of sacks with one ragged old blanket each, but there was nothing she could do about that just then. She hadn't many spare blankets herself. The boys carried up two thin, lumpy straw-filled mattresses and spread one on the floor in each room.

"We 'aven't got proper beds," said Mark gruffly.

Annie could sense his embarrassment. "Well, we'll have to get you some, then," she said matter-of-factly. "It doesn't matter for tonight."

When William came up, he insisted on pulling his good feather mattress off his bed, so that he could lie on the floor with his young uncles. Annie was glad to let him, because his bubbling high spirits at this novel experience masked Mark's embarrassment.

"Hurry up, then!" she ordered. "I want you boys washed, in bed and asleep within ten minutes, because we've a busy day ahead of us tomorrow."

Luke watched wide-eyed as she kissed William and, after a moment's hesitation, Annie went over to kiss him and Mark. And it was Luke whose arms went briefly round her neck as he returned her embrace.

She went into the girls' room. Here, Kathy had already made up the bed. Joan was fast asleep on one side and Rebecca was smiling drowsily up at Annie from the other.

"Our Annie?"

"Yes."

"It's like a palace 'ere. I keep thinkin' it'll 'ave vanished when I wake up in t'mornin', an' we'll all be back in Salem Street."

"Well, it won't! We've left Salem Street for good. So you go to sleep now." She bent over and kissed Rebecca, who gave her a smacking wet child's kiss back.

"I allus kiss our dad every night. Mam doesn't – I mean, she didn't like kissin', so he allus kisses us twice, to make up for it. Now I've got you to kiss as well, but I shall still kiss 'im twice, 'cos he's a lovely dad." She yawned. "G'night, Annie."

On the landing Kathy was waiting. "I got Tom to take my

bed frame down for your dad. I thought it'd shame 'im to 'ave to lie on the floor when Tom 'as a proper bed. Don't say anythin'!"

"Kathy, you shouldn't have!"

"It doesn't matter to me. I can sleep anywhere. 'Specially tonight. I'm dead on me feet. But a man's got 'is pride."

How strange, Annie thought, that Kathy should consider her father's pride so naturally, when she had not. "Thank you. And thank you for all you've done today, Kathy. I don't know how we'd have managed without you."

"I've enjoyed meself today," said Kathy happily. "It's nice havin' a few kids around the place, isn't it? I wouldn't like to be Alice, on 'er own in Number Eight."

"I don't think she minds. And someone has to keep the second-hand business going over there. We can still make money from it." Annie stretched and yawned. "Ooh, I'm exhausted. I ache all over!"

"Why don't you go up to bed? I can soon tidy the kitchen."

"No. You're as tired as I am. Come on! It'll be quicker with two of us."

They skirted the piles of bundles in the hallway. "Tomorrow!" said Annie firmly. "Don't look at them! They're invisible till tomorrow."

Kathy giggled. "I can't see owt."

In the kitchen, the kettle had been filled and was boiling on the fire. The table was already cleared and the dishes stacked in the scullery. John was holding his unlit pipe and his tobacco pouch. Annie wrinkled her nose. The smell reminded her of her childhood.

He looked across at her anxiously. "It's all right, isn't it, love? Me smokin' in 'ere, I mean. Tom said you wouldn't mind, but I waited to ask. He's gone off to bed. Said he'd got t'make an early start in t'morning. I don't need as much sleep as you young 'uns."

How awful that he should hesitate to smoke inside his own home! "Of course it's all right in here, Dad, though not in the parlour or dining room, if you don't mind." She sniffed again. "It reminds me of when I was a child, and Mam was alive. And thanks for clearing the table."

He nodded, poked a spill in the fire and began to light the pipe. When it was burning nicely, he blew out a cloud of smoke and gave her that gentle smile that was so typical of the man he'd become. She looked at the neatly stacked dishes and remembered how her father had always helped her mother around the house. Tom was wrong about the rest of the family being a burden, and she'd tell him so in no uncertain terms if he ever dared to mention it again.

When Annie at last got up to her own bedroom she found that Kathy had made up her bed and she sighed with relief. What a day! What a wonderful, terrible day! She went and stood by the curtainless window for a moment, looking out at the lights of the nearby houses and savouring the peace and privacy of having her own room. But she was too weary to linger there for long with a clean soft bed waiting for her.

She did not wake up until after seven the next morning. Her father had already left for the mill. Kathy said she had got John his breakfast and put him up some lunch and a bottle of cold tea. Tom had left even earlier, setting off on his rounds before it was properly light. This was the day he collected produce from the small outlying farms to sell at the market the next day, and move or no move, he couldn't miss that. The children were still fast asleep.

"You should have woken me, Kathy!" Annie said reproachfully.

"You were tired."

"So were you!"

"Aye, but this is my job. I'm the 'ousekeeper now. You said so. And you're the modiste. Besides, I like lookin' after people." Kathy poured her a cup of tea and speared a piece of bread on a toasting fork. "You can make your own toast, though."

One by one the children woke and crept downstairs, drawn by the smell of hot buttered toast. Kathy made them wash their hands and faces in the scullery, and sent them back up to get dressed and put their shoes on. They clattered about in their clumsy, ill-fitting shoes and Annie exchanged glances with Kathy.

"Sound like a bunch of cart horses, don't they?" said Kathy. "They'll have to have some slippers for round the house. If you get me some black felt an' some leather scraps, Annie, I'll sew 'em of an evenin'."

A loudly protesting William was dispatched to school, but Mark and Luke stayed home to help their half-sister. It wouldn't hurt them to miss Granny Marker's classes for a few days. Annie wasn't sure that it was even worth them going back to the small dame school. She hadn't much faith in the old lady who had little to offer her pupils beyond some simple tuition in reading and basic arithmetic, with sewing for the girls.

After they had all eaten, four faces turned expectantly towards Annie. "What do you want us to do, our Annie?" asked Mark, who always acted as spokesman. "Me an' Luke's strong enough to move stuff around for you an' our Rebecca's allus a good help, Dad says. An' she'll keep an eye on Joanie."

Luke and Rebecca nodded agreement.

Annie smiled at them. "Thanks. I can do with some help. I hardly know where to start, there's so much to do. And there's another cartload of stuff to come from Collett Hall today. Don't ask me what! We were in such a hurry in that attic yesterday that I can't remember half the things we chose! And there are the things in the hall still to clear away, too. And the stuff for the shop will have to be stored in the old dairy until we can move in."

"Why did Mrs Hinchcliffe give you all that stuff?" asked Mark. "It's good stuff, Dad says. Don't she want it?"

"She has a house full of newer furniture, a huge house, much bigger than this one. These things were just lying around in an attic no use to anyone, so she gave them to me – to us. She knew we needed them. She's been a good friend to me."

"You've got a lot of posh friends, our Annie," said Rebecca.

"Oh, just one or two," said Annie lightly.

"I've never talked to posh people before."

There was no answering that, so Annie set them to work. She got the boys to string ropes between the trees in the garden and then they hauled the pile of dusty carpet squares outside. Annie set all four children to beating the dirt out of them with the carpet beater, the broom and some big sticks. It would be sensible to get the carpets laid before another pile of furniture arrived.

When they were all occupied she walked slowly indoors, thinking and planning. They would still have to buy some things for the house, in spite of all Pauline's gifts. "Bedding," she said aloud.

"What?" Kathy paused over the washing-up.

"We need some more bedding. I'm not having those children sleeping under sacks in my house. We're not living in the slums now. We've moved out of the Rows."

Kathy nodded. "It's lovely, isn't it? Living in a house that's all on its own, I mean, instead of in a terrace where you can hear what the folk next door are doing."

Annie nodded. "It's wonderful." She gazed out of the window for a moment, enjoying the sight of a green garden instead of the dirty brick of the mill wall which had been only three strides away from her front door in Salem Street. Then she came back to the topic of equipping her new family for life in a more respectable neighbourhood here on the lower slopes of Ridge Hill. "The children need new clothes as well.

Their things are little more than rags." And, she thought angrily to herself, neither her stepmother nor the woman her father had paid to look after them all since his wife's death had kept the family clean. The four children smelled sour. It was the sort of smell poor people always had, the sort of smell she had fought against during those long years in the Rows.

"I'll go and sort their things out." She marched upstairs and came back to the kitchen a short time later with a bundle of dirty clothes under her arm. "We'll have to have a washday as soon as we can, I think, Kathy. Just look at these! In fact, send them out to be washed. Does Mrs Timmins still take things in?"

"She does, but there's no need to send them to her. I can see to them. We've got a proper laundry with a copper boiler here, don't forget."

"Just this once there is a need to send them out. We've got too many other things to do in the house."

"All right." Kathy looked at the pile of ragged things and shook her head. "You'd think a woman would at least look after 'er family properly, wouldn't you? Your dad's nearly allus been in work. They were never really without money, even if there were some weeks on short time. What did Emily do with his wages?"

"Drank it or wasted it."

"Shame on her! With a nice husband like him! We'll need some proper beds too, won't we, Annie? It fair makes my blood boil to see them old straw mattresses an' sacks. Poor little devils! It reminds me of my family – only they were even worse. You rescued me as well, Annie, an' I'll never forget that."

"You've more than earned your way, love." Strange. Kathy almost never spoke of her family.

"They've nearly all gone now," said Kathy.

"Who have?"

"The people who used to live in Salem Street. There's only Widow Clegg left. How old do you think she is?"

"Who can tell? She never seems to change."

"She was the one who birthed me."

"Me, too." Annie didn't add that Widow Clegg had also been there when her mother died bearing the little brother who had never even drawn breath. Or that Widow Clegg had delivered Annie's own son, William, with the help of Dr Lewis. He was a nice man, the doctor, and he was better off without that wife of his. Annabelle Lewis was a shrew and a domestic tyrant and it had been no pleasure to work for her. Ellie said they were all a lot happier at Park House nowadays. Except for Mabel.

Annie smiled as the memories rolled back. In her days in service she had wanted to learn to cook, not be a lady's maid. Strange how things turned out. If Mabel had not broken her arm and Annabelle Lewis had not taken Annie with her to Brighton instead, things might be very different. Mrs Lewis had taught her so much about fashion and how a lady should dress, had taken her to London and Brighton, and expanded her horizons in many ways. Without that, Annie would not know enough to open a modiste's salon. Well, she was grateful in some ways, but you could never like Annabelle Lewis.

Besides, anyone who deserted a sick child deserved the worst that life could offer in Annie's opinion. Why, Ellie Peters said that even before that, Mrs Lewis had never kissed or cuddled her daughter that any of the servants had seen, not even when Marianne was young. A cold, vicious woman, Annabelle Lewis. If there were any justice in the world, she would suffer for her sins.

Kathy went back to her cleaning and cooking, but her casual words had started Annie thinking. Strange that of the people who had lived in Salem Street when Annie was young, the only one left was Widow Clegg at Number Four, who had seemed ancient to her then and still seemed no different. Charlie was dead and so was Sally from Number Six. The Peters family from Number Seven had moved on to better things a while back. Though they didn't seem to be any happier for it.

Ellie Peters said that her mother had become so obsessive about cleanliness that she was almost impossible to live with. Ellie didn't know how her dad stood it. Still, he was out at work all day during the week and at chapel on Sundays, so that must help. He loved his job as doctor's assistant and everyone knew how good he was at it. Widow Clegg said that Sam Peters had a deft touch with sick and injured people, especially those from the Rows, and from her that was high praise.

Annie sighed. She wished she could see Ellie Peters more often. They had been friends ever since the Peters family moved into Salem Street when Annie was ten. They were still as close as sisters, in spite of the way Matt Peters had treated Annie after she had been raped. Annie blinked away a tear. She would *not* let herself waste her time thinking about that dreadful period of her life. She had vowed to put it completely behind her and she had done just that – most of the time, anyway. But oh, how deeply she had loved Matt when she was sixteen, how much she had looked forward to marrying him. Would she ever be so happy again? Well, she had managed without Matt. She had married Charlie instead and Charlie had been a wonderful father to William.

Perhaps Ellie would be able to drop in more often now that she was housekeeper to Dr Lewis. Housekeepers had more freedom than their staff. Ellie rarely went home and she never visited her brother Matt, who had lodgings in the better end of town, not so far away from Moor Close. That thought made Annie shiver. She hoped they would not run into each other. Matt had not married, or even tried to walk out with anyone since he had rejected Annie and her bastard child. He always passed her in the street as if she wasn't there and that hurt, even now.

The O'Connors were still good friends of hers, but they too had left Salem Street and they now lived outside the town on a little farm bought for them by their eldest son, Danny, who had done very well for himself working on the railways. Annie did not want to think about Danny O'Connor, for he had disturbed her peace more than any man since Matt. She tossed her head angrily at the mere thought of him. Danny was altogether too disturbing a person. He had dared to say he wanted to start courting her and had intimated that he was only waiting for a decent time to pass after Charlie's death. Well, just let him try it! A little chill ran down her spine at the mere idea. There was something about Danny O'Connor that frightened her. No, not frightened, but definitely disturbed her. He was so very large and vibrant with life. He had only to walk into a room for all eyes to turn to him, and women smiled and nudged one another as he walked past in the street.

Anyway, courting her was probably just a whim on Danny's part. Annie certainly wasn't going to encourage him. He moved around the country a lot, working on the railways, and rarely spent much time at home in Bilsden. It would be dreadful to have a husband who worked away and who faced danger every day. Bridie, his mother, had been beside herself with worry the previous month when the new viaduct had collapsed at Ashton-under-Lyne, and it had taken them ages to reassure her that Danny wasn't working anywhere near Ashton. Fifteen men had been killed there, and for the first time, Bridie seemed to have realised how dangerous working on the railways could be. Now she was begging him to settle down.

Well, what Danny O'Connor did with himself was nothing to do with Annie, and she didn't know why she was still thinking about him. She wanted nothing to do with any man, ever again. She could make her own way in life. She was a businesswoman. Now, that was quite enough daydreaming. There was work to be done, her whole future to plan!

Five

FAMILY LIFE

John Gibson's children would not have agreed with Kathy's description of them as "poor little devils". They were shrieking with delight and sheer exuberance out in the garden as they beat the carpets and tried to dodge the clouds of dust that their efforts raised. They had come to live in a big fancy house with their rich sister and they were full of good food. What more could you ask of life? And as for beating carpets, why, that was great fun! Even Mark lost his worried expression and forgot his responsibilities towards his siblings in the pleasure of whacking the carpets, teasing his sisters and chasing Sammy out of the way. The old dog seemed to have got a new lease of life and was running round the garden and getting under everyone's feet as if he had never heard of stiff joints.

At nine o'clock, Alice, who was Annie's second in command in her clothing business, turned up to get her orders for the day. "How's it goin', Annie, love?"

"We're starting to make sense of things. How about you? Are you enjoying the peace without us at Number Eight?"

"Peace? It's too quiet by half. I'll have to get an apprentice or someone to live with me, or I'll go mad. If that's all right by you, that is?"

"Wait until you've seen the High Street shop before you decide on anything. There's a big set of attics there, which you might prefer living in to Number Eight."

Alice laughed. "Tryin' to get us all out of the Rows? Anyone'd think you didn't like it there."

Annie spoke quietly, but the expression on her face gave strong emphasis to her words. "I hated it there."

"Well, I don't hate it." Alice's voice was flat and uncompromising. She jerked her head to indicate Netherleigh Cottage. "It's this place I wouldn't like to live in. Too big. And too cut off from the neighbours. I like to know that if I'm in trouble, I can yell or bang on the wall, an' someone'll hear me."

Annie stared. "You never said anything about this before. All the time I was planning the move, talking about you living above the shop in High Street, you never said a word!"

"I didn't want to spoil things for you."

"But, Alice, I need someone to live there, to keep an eye on things for me."

"You'll soon find someone else, someone who'll like living all alone there." She hesitated, then burst out, "Look, you're not the only one who likes to think things out, Annie. I've done a fair bit of thinking lately. What with Sally dyin' an' all. And what I've decided is that I like it where I am. I really like livin' in Salem Street, after those years in Claters End. An' now that I've got my own house, well, I reckon I'm in clover." She tried to take the sting from her words. "I'll still be workin' for you. It won't affect the business, love."

But it will, thought Annie. It'll affect everything. You'll still be living in Salem Street, which means I'll have to visit you there sometimes to cut things out and check through the old clothes that've been altered. She didn't say anything, though. Alice had a right to live where it suited her. Instead, she changed the subject and asked Alice to take Mark and the handcart and go and buy a whole roll of unbleached cotton seconds from Dawton's Mill. "That'll give us a start on new sheets for everyone. And afterwards, would you go and price blankets for me in Hardy's – no, they'll be too expensive. Try the . . ."

"Why not wait till tomorrow and get some from the market? There's a fellow started coming over every month from Dewsbury with blankets, an' tomorrow's his day. He says he'd come every week if we had a branch line here. Says we're behind the times in Bilsden not havin' a railway. The cheek of the fellow! He has a stall at the other side of the market from us, but you allus know when he's there. Shout! You can hear him all over. If you need to buy a lot of beddin', you'll get it cheaper from him. Set your Tom on to bargain with 'im. He'll enjoy that, will Tom, an' he'll get things cheaper than you or I could."

Annie frowned. "I wanted to get the beds sorted out today."

"Those kids won't mind waitin' a bit longer. They've been sleepin' under sacks all their lives. A day or two more won't hurt 'em. You can't change everything in a day, love." Alice patted Annie's hand.

"Yes, I suppose you're right. It just seems so awful for them to have only sacks for cover, and to have to sleep on the floor. I wanted everything to be nice here."

"It is nice, but nothin's ever perfect." Alice stood up and walked round the kitchen, then peered through the door at the hallway.

"Come and have a look around." Annie could see that Alice was nearly dying of curiosity.

They strolled across the hallway and Alice reached out to stroke the wood of the banisters. "It's a rare fine 'ouse, though."

"Yes, it is, isn't it?" Annie looked round her and smiled.

"You're right, Alice. I have been trying to do too much at once." She gave the other woman a hug. "What would I do without you on hand to keep my feet on the ground?"

"You'd probably fly to the moon."

They both burst out laughing. When the laughter had died down, Annie took her friend and employee's arm and led her through the rooms, then they went back to the kitchen and returned to the business at hand. "Right, then. After you've got the sheeting, I want you to go through our stocks and sort out some clothes for the children. They've got nothing but rags to wear. I'm ashamed for them to be seen like that. Our very best stuff, mind. Leave the other work and get someone in to help you with the sewing. I want those children looking decent for chapel on Sunday."

"All right, love. I'll get Hilda James to come in. She needs the money an' she's the best sewer we've got."

"I thought she didn't want people to know she took in sewing." Hilda James was a lady, a widow who had come down in the world, thanks to her late husband's reckless investments.

Alice winked. "She's decided that it's perfectly respectable if she calls herself a dressmaker. An' it isn't as bad as goin' hungry. She's eager to do more for us. She'll never be any good on the cuttin', but she's got a neat hand an' she never gets the work dirty."

"Fine. Get her to come in. And give her as much work as you can from now on. She might be all right for the salon, once we're ready to take on staff there."

Luke stared pleadingly at his half-sister as she gave Alice and Mark her final instructions, but she refused to take the hint and let him go with them. When Mark was not around, Luke seemed to shrink into himself and Annie intended that he should start learning to stand on his own feet from now on. Besides, she needed his help.

When Alice and Mark had left, she turned to the others. "Right, Luke and Rebecca, come and help me get that red carpet into the parlour before the cart arrives with the rest of the furniture." They both turned obediently to help her, but Luke had a droop to his shoulders and an apprehensive look on his face as if afraid of doing something wrong. Annie noticed that her youngest sister was still clinging to Rebecca. "Joan, go and help Kathy in the kitchen! You're too little to carry carpets."

Rebecca gave her sister a push. "Go on, Joanie! Do as our Annie says. Dad said we were to 'elp." Joan trailed off, sniffling miserably. She clung to Rebecca as Luke clung to Mark. Rebecca turned apologetically to Annie. "She still misses our Edward. They used to play together. She'll be all right when she gets used to it 'ere. She's not a bad kid, really."

The two children helped Annie to haul the clean carpet into the house. Its pattern showed up nicely now that most of the dust had been beaten out of it. When they spread it out on the parlour floor, they found that by positioning it carefully, they could hide the worst of the worn patches under the sofa.

"That's lovely. You did a good job on that." Annie saw them exchange relieved glances, and she hid a smile.

When she swung round to get the other carpet, Luke flinched visibly. Did he think she was going to hit him? Surely not? Why were they so nervous of her? She did not realise how very different to them she seemed, with her clear speech, her elegant clothes and most of all, her air of authority and confidence.

"Come on then, you two! We'll get another carpet hung over the line, then you can beat it for me. That'll be a good help. I don't know how I'd manage without you today and that's a fact." Luke's sigh of relief was quite audible to his elder half-sister.

In the middle of the morning, the cart arrived from Collett

Hall, driven by the same two men. As she directed their labours, Annie realised very quickly that Pauline had added some more things to the load, but there was nothing she could do about it. She would not dare send anything back. Her friendship with Pauline was not quite as equal as that. And then, as Pauline had said, none of the stuff was new and much of it was damaged. If Annie did not take it, it probably would be thrown away or given to a junk dealer like Tom, so to refuse it would be sheer waste. But somehow, the gifts still rankled. Annie had wanted to be independent from now on, to do things herself. She vowed that this would be the last time she would ever take or need charity – even from her friends. She didn't know why she minded so much, she just did.

Being Annie, she buried her annoyance in a flurry of orders that kept everyone hopping around for the rest of the day.

When Tom got back from his rounds, the donkey-cart was even more heavily laden than usual. Without being told, Mark and Luke went straight out to help him unload, with William trailing behind them. Kathy followed to take her pick of the foodstuffs before the rest were stored in the old dairy room ready for market. The newly enlarged family would take a lot of feeding.

While that was going on, Annie set Rebecca to unpicking the seams of some clothes she wanted to alter.

"Don't you ever sit still, our Annie?" Rebecca asked.

Annie was puzzled by that question. "Why do you ask?"

"Well, our mam, she used to just sit there. Thinkin' things over, she said she was. It were when she were drinkin', though."

Annie ignored the reference to Emily's fondness for gin. Her stepmother was dead now, so that did not matter any more. "No, I don't sit still much. I suppose I do my thinking as I work. It's a waste of time, just sitting. I like to get things done."

The child stroked the material on the table. "It's nice, this is. I shall like havin' new clothes." She stared down at the skimpy ragged garment she was wearing, then looked sideways at Annie. Even her sister's working clothes seemed splendid to her. "But I don't know how to sew."

"When we get settled I'll teach you to sew properly. If you're good enough you can come to me in the salon as an apprentice and then, when you grow up, you'll have a trade of your own."

"Our mam said I were to go into t'mill," Rebecca volunteered. "Shan't I 'ave to do that now?"

"No. Did you want to?"

"I don't know. It's 'ard work, an' they get hurt sometimes when there's an accident, an' the fluff fair makes you choke. But they 'ave a bit of fun as well. An' it'd be nice to 'ave some money of me own. Dad says Mr Hallam's a good master an' pays fair wages. But our dad still didn't want me to go into t'mill. He shouted at Mam when she said she'd get me set on as soon as she could."

"Well, things have changed now. None of you are going into the mill. We'll do better for you than that," Annie promised. That was one thing she agreed wholeheartedly with her father about. She had never stopped being grateful that she had not had to go into the mill herself. Ellie Peters had worked there for a while and the noise and ever-present fluff had made her sick. Annie had taken over the housekeeping when her mother died, instead of going out to work, and was proud of how well she had coped. When her father had remarried, she had gone straight into service with Dr and Mrs Lewis. Even Emily, much as she disliked her stepchildren, had not tried to get Annie set on in the mill.

Later, when he had other mouths to feed, John Gibson had not been able to afford to be choosy about where his girls worked, and Annie's sister Lizzie had worked in the mill for a few years, before she went off with Emily's daughter May to live in Manchester. The two of them had not been heard of for a while, but Annie didn't miss them. Lizzie had been the bane of her young life and had grown up into a sullen young woman. She realised that Rebecca was speaking and banished those memories.

Rebecca stroked the faded brocade of a pile of Pauline's old curtains with her thin little hand. "This is pretty, too, isn't it? An' your clothes are lovely. Even that dress, your old one. But I like your fancy things best. I like the way they swish when you walk."

Annie leaned towards her and whispered, "I'll tell you a secret. I like the way they swish, too. It's the taffeta petticoats that make that sound."

Rebecca giggled. She was such a thin, serious child that her rare bubbling laughter always came as a surprise.

A little later, as she continued to unpick, she said thoughtfully, "Kathy says she'll teach me 'ow to cook prop'ly as well. Mam only did stews or fry-ups. An' we didn't have no apple pies." She licked her lips at the memory. "Annie . . ."

"Yes?"

"Annie, I hated our mam. That's wicked, isn't it, to hate your own mother? It says so in t'Bible. Mr Hinchcliffe read it to us one Sunday. Annie – will I go to hell for that?"

"Honour thy father and mother," said Annie automatically. "It's one of the Ten Commandments. And no, you won't go to hell for the way you felt about your mother." Or if you do, I shall as well, she added mentally.

Rebecca's voice was so low that Annie could hardly hear her as she said, "I couldn't help hatin' 'er. She used to hit us, 'specially when she'd had a few gins an' she hit Luke most of all. She was allus goin' on at him. But Luke hit 'er back once just before she got ill, an' then she didn't hit 'im no more. She didn't hit Mark, neither. He used to go wild at her sometimes, Mark did, when she hurt our Luke. You haven't hit anybody, our Annie. Don't you hit people?"

That partly explained the children's nervousness, Annie

realised. She must take care how she answered. "I don't need to hit people. We're all working together for the family now, aren't we?"

Rebecca considered this idea gravely for a moment or two, her head on one side like a bird about to peck at a seed. "It's nice, that is, all workin' together. For the family. You didn't seem like family before, not really."

"Well, I hope I seem like family now."

"I'm gettin' used to you. An' I'm glad you don't hit people."

Annie didn't know what to say to that, but Rebecca didn't need any encouragement to carry on talking.

"Our dad doesn't hit people, neither. I like our dad. I used to like our Peggy, too. I was best friends with her. We allus did things together. I miss her now she's dead. I don't miss Edward, though. He were a little sod an' I allus had to look after him and he allus cried. Fair got on your nerves, it did! But it were bad when he died, though. He got all red an' his skin started to peel." She shuddered at the memory.

In a few bald, dispassionate phrases, Rebecca had painted a graphic picture of the unhappiness of the children's previous life that made Annie want to weep. She did not want to encourage her young half-sister to talk about hating her mother, but in fact, Annie too had hated Emily, who had virtually turned her out of her own home at the tender age of twelve. "Well, I hope you and I will become good friends, Rebecca. After all, we're sisters, aren't we? But it's better not to say 'sod' or swear at all, because polite little girls don't talk like that. Now that we don't live in the Rows, we have to be more polite, you know."

"All right," Rebecca agreed happily. "I don't mind. It's nice bein' rich. If rich people don't swear, I won't neither. Are we havin' apple pie again for dinner?"

By Sunday everyone in the family was respectably clad, so that Annie did not feel ashamed for them to be seen in public.

John accepted a loan of one of Tom's better shirts and, with Annie on his arm, led his children to the morning service at the chapel with pride shining in his face. The only flaw in John's day was that Tom refused to attend.

When this threatened to lead to a quarrel, Annie stepped in.

"Tom's old enough to make his own decisions about things like that, Dad."

"But, lass—"

"He's old enough to decide for himself, Dad." She saw John start to open his mouth. "And if there's anything else said about it, I'll not go either." She linked her arm in her father's again. "Come on! We don't want to be late."

The arm was stiff and unyielding at first, but she held on to it, and after a few moments, John started chatting happily about something else. Annie reminded him so much of his first wife that he could not hold out against her.

Tom was out when they got back and Annie guessed that he was off visiting his friend Rosie, but she said nothing. Maybe her father didn't know about Rosie. No, he was bound to know. Tom had been friendly with Rosie for years. Gossip said Rosie would like to marry him, but Annie knew that he never would. He was too keen to get on in the world, and a woman like Rosie would not fit into his new life.

In the afternoon, John went through Charlie's tools and found what he needed to repair the little table. Kathy found him an old pan to boil the glue tin in and Mark and Luke hung around trying to help, with William crowding their heels. From the happy expression on John Gibson's face, he didn't mind if the job took twice as long, and he explained everything he did to the three lads in his soft voice as he worked.

Rebecca and Joanie went off with Kathy to the kitchen, eager to learn about the mysteries of making fruit pies, so Annie took the opportunity to go up to her bedroom and sort out her own clothes. It was wonderful to have a place of her own and not have to share with Kathy, not to mention a proper cupboard in which to hang her clothes and a room that was not piled high with bundles of second-hand garments waiting to be altered. They might only be living on the lower slopes of Ridge Hill, but it seemed like a huge step up in the world from Salem Street and the Rows.

A little later in the afternoon, Michael Benworth came round. "Would it be convenient if I started to dig over the vegetable patch now, Mrs Ashworth?"

"Certainly. Can Luke help you? I want him to learn how to look after the garden."

"Of course. Send the lad out. Afternoon, John. How are you settling in?"

"Fine, thank you, Mr Benworth."

Annie took Luke out into the garden herself. She found Charlie's spade and thrust it into his trembling hands.

"This was Charlie's. It's yours now. We'll all have our jobs to do here and one of yours will be to help in the garden."

His mouth slightly open, Luke examined the spade as if he had never seen such a thing before, then he followed her to the bottom of the garden with it clutched awkwardly to his chest.

"Mr Benworth, here's my brother Luke. He doesn't know anything about gardening, but he's very strong for his age. He was a great help to me yesterday."

"Hello, lad. So you're going to be the gardener, eh? I envy you. This is a fine big garden."

Luke's large, pale eyes were fixed on Michael Benworth's face, but still he said nothing. Annie could see that his fingers were trembling on the spade handle and she noticed Michael Benworth's eyes flicker to the boy's hands.

"Come on, then, lad. We have to turn this garden bed over. Soil needs to breathe, just like you and me. This is how we do it. See – you get your foot on the spade, like this, and you push it into the soil. Good. Good. That's the idea." He watched

Luke for a moment or two, then turned to Annie. "He'll be all right, Mrs Ashworth. He's got the makings of a good worker, I can see that. Now, if you'll excuse us men, we'll get on with this digging." He winked at her and went over to join Luke.

When Annie took them out a cup of tea an hour later, she could see that Luke had relaxed and was enjoying himself. He and Michael Benworth were bent over some plants in a corner and the boy looked up as Annie approached, giving her one of his rare smiles. He even volunteered a remark.

"Look!" His grubby fingers lifted some threads of pale foliage tenderly. "The weeds were chokin' 'em."

Annie raised an eyebrow at Mr Benworth and he nodded in answer to her unspoken question. "I think you've got a budding gardener here, Mrs Ashworth. Taken to it like a duck to water, he has."

A proud smile flickered briefly on Luke's solemn face.

By evening, John had finished mending the table, and it was ceremonially installed in the hallway, where the parquet floor was now embellished with a small rug Kathy had found among the things from Collett Hall. On top of the table, Annie placed a pretty vase that had also turned up among the things. They could fill it with fresh flowers later on. She would ask Michael Benworth to show Luke how to grow some. In the meantime, that shining table seemed to epitomise their new life and Annie's aspirations for the future, and for the next few days she could not help smiling at it every time she passed through the hallway.

The following week passed in a blur of activity and hard work. There was so much to be done in the house, not to mention the task of clothing her brothers and sisters decently, that Annie scarcely knew what to tackle first. She had to leave most of the second-hand business to Alice and found to her relief that Alice could manage quite well on her own, especially as she'd now arranged for Hilda James to live and work with her in Salem Street. They were an odd couple, and Annie knew that Miss James, an ardent churchgoer, would have hysterics if she knew about Alice's less than respectable past, but they worked well together, and she knew that the second-hand business was in good hands.

Nothing more was said about school for Mark and Luke, although William kept going to the Grammar School. Starting on the Monday, Tom took both his half-brothers down to the yard with him every day, because he too was busy and needed help. Old Mr Thomas had been yet another victim of the influenza epidemic and Tom had got the yard and contents cheap from his widow. He joked that the names had been similar and that it must have been intended by fate, because he would only need half a new sign painting. The place was a mess, though, and he couldn't wait to get things sorted out and the business made profitable again.

As a result, Tom was less interested than the others in what Annie was doing to Netherleigh Cottage and all his energy was devoted to the new yard, though he did agree to find someone to put in a kitchen range and a modern bathroom for her.

When he asked if the boys could keep working with him, Annie smiled and raised one eyebrow teasingly. "I thought you said they'd be in the way."

He shrugged. "I need all the help I can get. Ask me how much use they are in a few weeks' time."

Luke was as nervous going into the junk yard for the first time as he was about everything else. Only when he flinched aside as Tom pointed something out to him did his older half-brother realise how he was feeling.

"Look, lad, I wasn't going to hit you. I don't work like that, let alone you're family. I really need your help here."

Mark put his arm protectively around Luke. "He can't help it. Mam used to hit him all the time."

"Aye, she used to hit me too, till I got too big." He refrained from adding "stupid bitch", as was his wont when talking about his late stepmother. "Come on, we haven't got all day to waste here. We need to move the rest of the junk from Salem Street to the yard first. I thought you two could do that for me. Can I trust you to look after Blackie and the cart, and not to overload it?"

Luke's face lit up. He loved anything to do with animals. Mark's expression was serious as he nodded. If he did well working with Tom, maybe he wouldn't have to go into the mill. Maybe there'd be a place for him in the junk yard. Until he grew up and got his own business, that was. If their Annie could do it, so could he.

As they walked away, leading the donkey and cart, Tom watched them go. "Bloody Emily!" he muttered, remembering the way Luke had flinched, then he turned to start sorting through the piles of rubbish and soon forgot everything else.

"What a way to run things!" he said when the boys came back with their first load, gesturing to the piles of stuff. "Did you ever see such a mess?"

"It's not sorted into piles of the same sort like your stuff at Salem Street was," said Mark. "Where do you want these things putting? And shall we keep the piles separate?"

"Yes, keep 'em separate." Tom ran a hand through his hair. "Lord, I don't know what I want where! I'm still trying to find out what I've got here. Just find somewhere for 'em, eh?"

Mark stared at him for a minute, as if amazed at being given the responsibility, then the two boys walked round the yard, discussing where to put things. Tom watched them, but didn't interfere. This was a small test of their capabilities and he was pleased to see how well they managed. He grinned. Damn Annie! She was always right. But he was not yet ready to admit that to her.

All three of them came home from the yard filthy every

night, but Luke was never too tired to look after Blackie, and often, after he had eaten, he would go outside and look at the plants, and maybe turn over a spadeful or two of earth before it got too dark. He was still the quietest of the four children, but his face had gained some colour and he was losing that cowed bearing.

On the first Wednesday, Tom went off on his round of the small distant farms and left the boys in charge of the yard, and again, they not only coped, but continued sorting out the junk. "All right," Tom admitted to Annie that night, "you win."

"What do you mean?"

"I mean the lads shaping up to be useful to me. I suppose I'd better give them a wage." He saw her expression and added sharply, "Just a small one at first."

She smiled, but said nothing.

The two boys, informed that they were to be paid two shillings each every week, if they worked hard, were ecstatic. After much discussion, they gave Kathy a shilling a week each to save for them and kept the rest for spending. And if most of the first few weeks' money went on sweets for themselves and the other children, neither their father nor Annie said anything.

A few days after the big decision to employ his two half-brothers formally, Tom came home looking jubilant.

"What's the matter with you?" Annie teased. "Have you found a fortune in that junk yard?"

"No, but a man turned up today with a barrow load of stuff, good stuff, too. It was my first time as a buyer. And," he grinned back at Annie, "I've not only bought the stuff off him, but I've hired him to work for me and take over some of my rounds. I'll rent Neil Binns's cart for him – you can't do much with a handcart – and if things work out, we'll buy a second cart."

"You've hired someone already!"

"Aye. He's goin' to work for me an'—"

"Us! Work for us! I still own half that business, and don't

you forget it!" Her voice was sharp and her face was tight with annoyance.

He stared at her for a minute, then conceded, "Work for us, then. He'll take over some of my old rounds. I can't stay in the yard *and* go out looking for stuff. An' the boys are too young for sending out collecting yet – though I might send our Mark out with Fred sometimes to learn the trade. He's called Fred Turner, by the way, this fellow. But I'll keep on fetching the farm stuff myself. I don't want to be shut in the yard all the time. An' I think we can do more with the food, as well. The stuff always sells well at the market. Might see if I can buy from a few more people while I'm at it."

Annie was still frowning. "Can we really afford to hire someone, Tom?"

"We can afford to try it for a week or two, can't we? That's all I offered him."

"I suppose so."

He put his arm round her shoulders and hugged her. "I'll make some real money for us now. You'll see."

"As long as it's honest."

He jerked away from her. "You didn't need to say that. I won't do owt wrong again. I'm planning for years ahead now, like you said, an' I can see that you were right." His anger faded and his grin crept back. "They'll be calling me Honest Tom before we're through."

"I'll be proud of you if they do that," she said softly.

Tom looked round and saw everyone staring at them. He flushed a little, then took a deep breath. "I hope you all heard that. We're goin' to be the most honest business in town, we are. We want folk to trust us Gibsons an' to come back to us, whether it's with the junk or with the food we sell at the market. You lads make sure you understand that right from the start."

Mark nodded. "We will, Tom. Won't we, Luke?"

Luke just nodded.

John Gibson sat quietly in his corner, but when he thought no one was looking, he flicked a tear away from the corner of his eye. Eh, his Lucy would have been that proud of her children! And he was proud of his second lot, too. He was a lucky chap, he was, and no mistake.

After he had eaten, Tom got out some crumpled papers and spread them across the kitchen table. "Er – Annie, will you help me with these accounts?"

"Of course." She moved a chair beside him and soon their two heads were close together, working through the figures.

A shadow fell across the page and Tom looked over his shoulder.

Mark was standing behind him. "Can I watch what you're doing?"

"I suppose so. Do you understand sums?"

"Pretty well. I like figuring."

Across the table, Luke cleared his throat. "Granny Marker allus said she couldn't teach our Mark any more about figuring an' ciphering."

Annie raised her eyebrows at Tom and he shook his head at her mockingly. "All right, lady. I've already admitted you were right. You were probably more right than you realised. Pull up a chair, our Mark, but don't say anything. I don't much like doin' the accounts, but you can't run a business without 'em." Laboriously, he began to add up the columns of figures.

John pulled on his pipe and winked at Kathy. "Long as they don't ask my opinion," he remarked. "Never was any good with figures. Come here, Joanie, and sit on your old dad's knee for a few minutes before you go to bed."

"Shh!" said Tom, frowning round vaguely. "You've made me lose track."

Annie looked round the room thoughtfully. She and Tom would have to find somewhere else for their business discussions. She could see Rebecca bursting to speak and Joanie was whispering in her dad's ear, while Kathy was trying to finish the clearing up quietly. Perhaps they could get a table for the dining room and do their accounts in there. Goodness, there was so *much* to organise! How would she ever get it all sorted out?

Six

FRIENDS, OLD AND NEW

In order to run her salon, Annie had a few special preparations to make. During the second week of living in Netherleigh Cottage, she made a call to further one of them. She had heard that the unmarried daughter of Parson Kenderby of St Mark's gave drawing and painting lessons. Annie knew that she was quite good at drawing. Miss Richards, Marianne Lewis's governess, had taught her the basic rules of perspective and the use of the pencil. She could turn out neat sketches of her ideas for dresses, but she wanted to be able to do better than that, much better. She could not afford to make up half-finished gowns, just on the chance that some lady might take a fancy to them, except for mourning wear, of course, which always sold, but she could do drawings of her design ideas – and if they were coloured in and mounted neatly on card, she would be able to show customers her ideas. Only she had never used watercolours, so she needed help with them as quickly as possible.

She took a deep breath and knocked on the front door of St Mark's vicarage.

An elderly maid answered her knock. "Yes?"

"I'd like to see Miss Kenderby, please."

"Do you have your card, ma'am?"

"No. It's – er – not a social call. I've come about drawing lessons. I'm Mrs Ashworth." She would have to get some cards printed. All ladies carried cards and business people did too. She ought to have thought of that. The maid was looking at her suspiciously.

"Will you please step into the hall for a moment, ma'am? I'll see if Miss Helen is free."

The parson came into the hall as she was speaking. She had not realised that he would be at home. He looked down his long thin nose at her and she gave him back stare for stare.

"Not one of my parishioners, I think?"

"No."

He raised his eyebrows at the lack of a "sir". "New to Bilsden?"

"No, I've lived here all my life." Annie was beginning to feel annoyed. What had this to do with him? She had come to see his daughter, not him. Still, she'd better not offend him, in case he showed her the door. He was notorious for flying into rages.

"Mary Benworth suggested that I consult Miss Kenderby about some drawing lessons." She tried to sound as haughty as her old employer. Strange how she modelled a lot of her behaviour on Annabelle Lewis!

His hostility lessened. "Oh. You're a friend of Mary's, are you? That's all right, then. She teaches in our Sunday school. Very good with the little ones and knows her Bible, too." He bowed slightly and vanished through a door at the side of the hallway.

Well, you're easily satisfied, thought Annie, watching the door close behind him. How do you know I'm telling the truth? I could be here to steal your silver, for all you know!

"Will you please to come this way, Mrs Ashworth." The elderly maid's nasal tones interrupted Annie's thoughts. "Miss Helen will see you in her studio." She led the way along a passage to a room at the back of the house and opened the door. "Mrs Ashworth, Miss."

"Won't you come in? I'm Helen Kenderby. I'm afraid I can't shake hands with you." She waved her paint-streaked hands.

Annie blinked in surprise. She had expected Miss Kenderby to be tall and aristocratic, like her father. Instead, she found herself facing a small woman with untidy hair and a rosy face, whose clothes were covered by a paint-stained smock. This room was at the rear corner of the house, and it was large, bright and airy, with windows on two sides. It was uncarpeted, except for a rug in front of the hearth, and was cluttered with canvases, piles of papers, books, jars and other paraphernalia that Annie did not even recognise. It seemed a strange sort of a room to find a lady in, especially a parson's daughter. Annie tore her eyes away from a statuette of a naked woman and tried to concentrate on the matter in hand. Fancy having that thing on your mantelpiece, though!

"I believe you wish to see me about some drawing lessons – for one of your children, is it?"

"No. I have only the one son and he's not at all interested in drawing. He couldn't keep still for long enough." Annie smiled at the thought, then took a deep breath and said, "It's for myself."

"Oh?" There was no mistaking the surprise in Miss Kenderby's voice. "I don't usually . . ."

Annie rushed into an explanation. "I need to be able to draw better and to colour my drawings – I've never used colours before. It's for my business. But if you only take children . . ."

"No, wait! I didn't mean to imply that I wouldn't take you, Mrs Ashworth. Look, let me wash my hands and order a tea-tray, then we'll start again. You shall tell me about yourself and why you need to learn to draw and paint. I do take pupils sometimes – but only those with some talent. And I've never taught anyone older than fifteen." She smiled at Annie, and added, trying to set her at ease, "My father doesn't approve either of my painting or of my taking pupils. He says there's no need." Her smile faded. "But I want to do something useful with my life. I can't – it's not possible for a lady in my position to travel and paint, as a gentleman might do. It would offend too many people and upset my mother. So I try to foster other people's talent when I find it. I believe that Bilsden needs beauty as much as any other town. Now, just let me wash my hands." She vanished into a curtained alcove.

Her frankness disarmed Annie. She sat and stared round this strange room as she waited. The varnished floorboards glowed a dark ruddy brown in the sunshine that poured in through the windows and everywhere there were splashes of bright colour to cheer you up. Annie decided that she liked it. An honest working room, with its owner's warmth and lack of pretence.

Helen returned. "I hope you don't mind my roomful of chaos, but it's my studio as well as my sitting room."

"I like it very much. It feels welcoming."

The maid returned with a tea-tray and Helen poured out a cup and passed it to Annie. "Tell me about yourself and why you need to learn to paint," she urged.

"Well, I grew up in the Rows." Annie hadn't intended to mention that, but it seemed right to return honesty with honesty. "I worked as a maid until I got married, then I helped my husband in his business – he dealt in, er, second-hand goods – and I started my own business, refashioning the second-hand clothes he brought back. After my husband died – he was a lot older than I am – my brother joined me and we expanded the business. Then I began to make new clothes for people. Gowns.

For ladies. I love designing clothes. I made a dress for Mrs Hinchcliffe recently."

"That blue one? Then you're good. I noticed it last week. It's very pretty. I've never seen Pauline look so well. How did you persuade her into such a pretty colour?"

Annie grimaced. "It wasn't easy. I'm glad you liked it. Pauline wanted me to make her another fawn dress. I refused. Fawn doesn't suit her."

"You overruled Pauline! My dear, you must be very brave, as well as talented. And you were right. How did you guess that that colour would suit Pauline so well? It's an unusual shade of blue. Very subtle."

Annie shrugged. "I just – well, I just knew."

Miss Kenderby went over to the desk and produced a piece of paper and a stick of charcoal. "Draw me something – anything!"

Feeling embarrassed, Annie drew a dress she had been thinking of making for herself. Before she had half finished, her hostess had interrupted her.

"All right. I'll give you lessons."

"Just like that?"

"Why not? You have some talent. I see your needs and I think I can help you. Besides, I admire your initiative. Not many women have the courage to make their own way in life. When can you come to me for lessons?"

"As soon as you like. I need to learn quickly. Most days at the moment I can spare an hour for something as important as this."

"Very well. Come on Mondays, Wednesdays and Fridays from ten o'clock in the morning until eleven. The charge will be two shillings an hour." She used the money for her pet charities, but even so, her father hated her taking any payment.

Annie walked home in a daze. What was she getting herself into? She had moved from Salem Street, taken a lease on a shop in the High Street – well, it was almost ready to be signed – and now she had arranged to have drawing lessons. And she had another expense in mind, even though she was not earning a proper income at the moment! She hadn't told Tom about that. It was a good thing she still had a share in the junk business and that Tom and Alice were bringing some money in. In fact, Alice was managing very well with the second-hand clothes, while Annie was doing nothing but spend, and she'd hardly started. Unconsciously she raised her chin and looked challengingly at the world. Well, you had to spend money to make it sometimes. And she didn't intend to fail. Too many people depended on her.

On the way back, Annie could not resist calling in at High Street, for Jonas Pennybody had let her keep the key to the vacant premises. Number Twenty-Four was at the end of a row of tall narrow houses. All of them had shops on the ground floor, cellars underneath, and the owners lived above them on the second and third storeys. What could be more convenient? But Annie had no intention of living above her salon – and anyway, there would not have been enough room for them all. She had had more than enough of cramped accommodation.

Next door to the vacant shop was Hardy's, the town's only linendraper's. Mr Pennybody had told her that Hardy had wanted to take over the empty premises himself, but that he had haggled for too long over the rent, while Annie had agreed to the amount asked instantly. She went into the shop the back way and, seeing Mr Hardy at the rear of his premises, she said good day to him over the hedge that divided the back gardens, ignoring the sour expression on his thin face.

He was a man of medium height, with sparse grey hair plastered firmly to his skull and steel-rimmed spectacles dominating his narrow features. Even when he smiled, his expression was not warm, and he was certainly not smiling now. Annie wondered whether he was still upset about the lease. Surely by now he had grown accustomed to the idea of having her as a neighbour?

The sight of that Ashworth woman walking round the garden of Twenty-Four as if she owned it made Cyril Hardy furious all over again, and he forgot his usual unctuous politeness. After all, he had only tried to be friendly the last time she had made a purchase in his shop and she had put him in his place in no uncertain manner. Who did she think she was? Everyone knew what women from the Rows were like, especially the ones who found themselves the money to dress as this one did. Well, if she thought she could just walk into a High Street shop in a respectable area, she could think again. It was about time someone told her where she stood, and he was just the man to do it.

"I think you'll find yourself a bit out of your depth at this end of the town, Mrs Ashworth," he said loftily. "We deal with the carriage trade here, you know."

"Oh, I think you'll find that I can cope, Mr Hardy," Annie replied, managing to speak calmly though she was furious inside.

"And I think you overestimate your own capacities, madam! You and your sort should stay where you belong, not try to ape your betters!"

"I think, Mr Hardy, that you are in no position to judge the sort of person I am, or my business capacities."

"Oh, aren't I? Well, we all know what business capacities your sort uses to set themselves up with clothes like that. Not to mention the money to pay for the lease of premises like these."

Shock made Annie speechless for a moment, and by the time she had pulled herself together, he had gone into his shop and closed the door on her. She went inside Number Twenty-Four, slammed the door shut and leaned against it, oblivious to her surroundings and seething with rage. After a moment, she forced herself to calm down and unclench her hands from the tight fists that were straining the seams of her gloves. She took a few deep breaths and straightened her bonnet. "I *won't* let that man see how he's upset me," she said aloud, but she continued to feel sick inside at what he had said. Was that really what people thought of her?

She was still furious when she got back home. "How dared he speak to me like that?" she raged to Tom. "*Mrs* Ashworth, he said, as if he doubted that I had ever been married! Who does he think he is? That shop of his is run so sloppily that he never has half the things you want. You'd think he'd move with the times! Have you *seen* the inside of it? Dark! It's so dark that it's a wonder the customers can see what they're buying! He's too mean even to install gas lights like all the other shopkeepers have. Well, we'll see who finds himself out of his depth! I wasn't going to sell materials, or bits and pieces like embroidery thread, because he sells those, but I've changed my mind now! I'll take business away from him and make him sorry he ever spoke to me like that! You just see if I don't! There's plenty of storage space in the cellars. *I* won't run out of stock!"

Two days later she went to see Jonas Pennybody to sign the lease. What he had to tell her turned her face white with shock. "But I thought it was settled! You said there would be no problem, that the lease was as good as signed!"

Jonas sighed. "I didn't expect . . . My dear Mrs Ashworth, I'm so very sorry! I would never have expected . . ." His voice trailed away. What could he say? For her, this was a catastrophe and there was nothing he could do to change matters.

"Didn't expect what?" she persisted.

"Didn't expect the other shop owners to – to protest."

"What do you mean, protest? What exactly have the other shopkeepers done?"

He hated to put it into words. "I'm afraid they've sent a

petition to Mr Hallam, begging him not to rent the shop to you. All of them in that part of the High Street have signed it, except for the bank. Mr Hallam is now reconsidering the matter of your tenancy."

"But why? What have they got against me? Why should they do such a thing?"

"I think – I can't be certain, but I think it's Mr Hardy who's behind this. He must feel threatened by your business. A draper's shop and a dressmaker's, you know. If you should start selling similar goods . . ."

Her shoulders sagged. "Don't try to spare me, Mr Pennybody. It's not just that, is it? He tried to flirt with me in his shop one day, and I gave him a set-down. He's been surly with me ever since. Then he spoke to me a couple of days ago and he said I wasn't," she had to take a deep breath before she could even say the words, "he said I wasn't respectable enough to run a business in that end of town. He accused me of – of —" She could not finish, for the thought of Hardy's insults still made her choke with rage.

"Oh, dear."

She looked him straight in the eyes. "Mr Pennybody, I have done nothing to merit such an accusation!"

"Mrs Ashworth, I don't doubt that for a moment."

She relaxed a little. "Thank you. I can understand why he's hostile, but," she swallowed hard, "I don't understand why the other shopkeepers should have signed the petition? They don't even know me. I do very little shopping at that end of town!"

"Er – apparently Mrs Hardy is also upset." Mrs Hardy had come along to help her husband to deliver the petition and had made no secret of her feelings about Mrs Ashworth. "She doesn't approve of a woman going into business on her own, besides which, you're a Nonconformist and she's a staunch supporter of St Mark's, as are most of the shopkeepers. And finally, there's your background. The – er – the Rows, you know. And the second-hand trade. They think you'll lower the tone. I tried to reason with them, but they wouldn't listen." He looked at her compassionately. He knew how hard she had worked, and how carefully she had saved her money.

"And Mr Hallam listened to them." Annie sagged in her chair. She could outface the hostility of the other shopkeepers, but Frederick Hallam was a powerful man. If he decided against her, there wasn't much she could do to fight back because he owned most of the suitable property in the rapidly growing town centre. She might just as well pack up and move to another town if she couldn't get a lease on one of his premises.

"Could you – could you not perhaps run the dressmaking business from your home?"

Annie shook her head. "No. I'm not setting up as a dressmaker, Mr Pennybody, but as a modiste, running a salon. There's every difference in the world. I need premises, and very smart premises too, in the best part of town."

"Well, Mr Hallam hasn't definitely said no. He said he would think it over. I'll speak to him again. Maybe your friend Mrs Hinchcliffe could also . . ." Delicately Jonas left the sentence unfinished.

"Maybe." But Pauline had no hold over Frederick Hallam and anyway, Annie did not want to involve her. The fewer people who knew about the petition the better. Numbly, she took her leave of Jonas Pennybody and began walking slowly home.

Half-way up North Street, she changed her mind and walked back down towards the Rows, intending to go to see Tom at the yard and tell him the dreadful news. As she walked along, her thoughts were in turmoil. Wasn't it always like this? You thought you were doing well, you made plans, you started to feel happy, then something happened to spoil it all. It had been like that when she had been planning to marry Matt. Now, just when she thought she had escaped from Salem Street, fate had struck her another blow. A bitter smile curved her lips. And she had been planning to install piped water, worrying about which model of kitchen range to choose!

Before she got half-way to the yard, she changed her mind again. "No," she said aloud, "I won't just accept it! I'll go and see Mr Hallam myself."

When she arrived at Hallam's Mill, she was stopped at the gate. "I'd like to see Mr Hallam," she said crisply. She felt like pushing the gateman aside, so angry was she.

"He's out. I'll send to ask if someone else can see you," said the gateman, a new man whom she did not recognise. "If you'd care to wait here, missus?"

As she was waiting in the sheltered corner of the mill yard, a shadow fell across her and she looked up to find Jim Catterall standing next to her. "Got a problem, missus?"

"Nothing that need concern you." Her heart started thudding, because this man, feared in the Rows, had once attacked her in her own home, and the sight of him reminded her of that awful day, with Charlie lying dead upstairs and Tom fighting with Catterall in her kitchen.

"Are you waiting for something, Catterall?" A tall, good-looking younger man materialised from a doorway behind him. "Shouldn't you be off on your rounds by now?"

"What's it to do with you, Peters?"

"Everything. Mr Hallam made me assistant manager today. You'll be reporting to me in future. So it's *Mr* Peters to you!"

Catterall spat on the floor, made an obscene gesture at Annie and turned on his heel. As he stamped off down the street, Annie took a deep breath and looked at Matt Peters. "Thank you." She would almost rather face Catterall than Matt, who had not spoken to her willingly since he broke their engagement.

"Won't you come through into the office, Ann – er, Mrs Ashworth? Mr Hallam is out, but perhaps I can help you."

His tone was courteous and he was looking at her with that warm but serious expression that was peculiarly his own. She bit her lip, feeling flustered. Somehow she had not expected to meet Matt today, though she should have. She knew he worked in the mill and was doing well there. "I don't think . . ."

"He's leaving a lot of the minor business to me. Is it about the lease on the High Street shop?"

"Yes."

"We can talk more privately in my office."

He had gained a great deal of assurance since she last spoke to him. Like her, he had lost the accent of the Rows and learned to dress properly. Indeed, she had never seen him so well turned out. She assessed him with a dressmaker's eye: double-breasted frock coat, with short skirts and close-fitting sleeves, worn with straight trousers with instep straps in the same speckled dark blue merino. Very smart. The dark blue suited him. But she did not like the single-breasted waistcoat in buff marcella. She would have chosen something in a lighter blue or grey. The outfit was finished with a dark blue silk stock, carefully knotted, and the neat starched points to his shirt collar were immaculate.

As she followed him across the mill yard she noticed that his hair was worn longer than before, with the top cut short and brushed forward. It suited him, as did the full side whiskers. In all, he had the appearance of a man making his way up in the world, not attempting to ape high fashion, but nonetheless turned out very smartly. He even walked with a new confidence, she thought, as they entered a new construction at the far side of the yard.

"Mr Hallam decided that we needed better offices." Matt deliberately kept the conversation impersonal. "This one is mine. It's rather nice, isn't it? Won't you take a seat?" He beckoned to a young man who was standing writing industriously at a high desk in the outer office. "Would you make us some tea, please, Smeales?"

"Do take a seat, Mrs Ashworth," Matt repeated. He waited until she had sat down, before sitting behind the desk, brushing his fingertip along it with an unconscious gesture of pride.

That revealing gesture made Annie feel more at ease. Whatever the anger there had once been between them, Matt Peters had worked hard and deserved his new triumph. "Congratulations, Matt," she said softly. "You've done well. I always knew you would."

He swallowed. This was a chance to end the enmity between them. And it was more than time. She had tried to do it before and he had spurned her gesture, so it was up to him now. And somehow, this time, he wanted very much to mend things. "How are you, Annie?" he asked gently.

Without that scornful look, he reminded her of the old Matt, the one she had loved. She forgot her worries and her nervousness, and smiled across at him, glad to heal the breach between them. "I'm very well, thank you."

"You look well. I hear you've moved out of Salem Street."

"Yes. At last."

"You've worked hard for that. You deserve your success."

"Thank you, Matt."

"And your son – he looks just like you. He seems to be growing into a fine lad."

"Yes, he is. William is all anyone could want in a son." She said this a trifle defiantly, for it was the child who had come between them, after that dreadful day. She remembered it every time there was a snowstorm, and she still avoided walking anywhere on her own after dusk. But she had loved William from the minute Widow Clegg placed him in her arms. Her son had more than made up for her broken dreams.

"I'm glad you're happy, Annie, and I'm just as glad that your son has turned out so well." But Matt could not bear too much of this frank talk. Life was easier if you avoided strong feelings, he had found. "Now," he went on, becoming brisk and businesslike, "won't you tell me why you've come here? I'm sure Mr Hallam will want to hear about it."

His voice had become impersonal again, his features calm and self-contained. Oh, Matt, she thought, why did you grow so cool? You used to be warm and friendly. Then she pulled herself together. She was glad they had managed to speak about the past, glad the enmity had been laid to rest at last, but no more than he did she wish to dwell too much on those days long gone. She had had nightmare after nightmare about the rape, and even now, she woke sometimes in a sweating panic. Her voice matched his in coolness. "You're right. I did come about the lease. There seems to be some trouble."

"The petition."

"Yes. You know about it?" She could feel embarrassment colouring her cheeks and clenched her hands in her lap.

"Mr Pennybody brought it to me."

"Is it – what does Mr Hallam think? Has he made a decision about it yet?"

"No. I managed to persuade him to think it over."

"That was very kind of you."

"I knew that Mr Hardy had wanted the premises for himself, so his motives are suspect. And I also knew that you were perfectly respectable, and so I told Mr Hallam."

"Oh, Matt. Thank you so much." Somehow the words "perfectly respectable" on his lips meant more than if anyone else had said it. After his family's earlier poverty, his desire for respectability and security had been just as strong as hers. She had sometimes wondered if he would have been so cruel to her if it had not been for his mother. Elizabeth Peters equated cleanliness with respectability, and to her, the rape had soiled Annie beyond redemption. Perhaps Matt was out of his mother's shadow now. "If I don't get those premises," she said, trying not to let her voice wobble, "then I might as well move out of Bilsden. There is nowhere else suitable. I need to be where the gentry do their shopping. I need somewhere with style. I want to open a modiste's salon, not a workshop. I've saved my money for years, got it all planned out." She forced herself to stop. She had stated her case; she must retain some dignity, not plead with him like this.

"Yes. I realise all that." He cleared his throat. "Look, Annie, I'll speak to Mr Hallam again, try to explain your dilemma to him. I'll let you know what he says as soon as I can. I can't do any more than that, I'm afraid. He's a man who likes to make his own decisions."

"I do understand that." She rose to go.

He rose, too. "I'll do my very best for you, Annie."

"Thank you, Matt." She was relieved that he had not offered to shake her hand. Somehow, she did not want to touch him. The warmth of his hand might bring back more of those painful memories long buried, memories of the happy girl she had been.

You could never go back, she thought, as she walked away from the mill; you could only go forward. And Matt Peters would not suit her as a husband now. She stopped dead in sheer surprise at that thought, then shook her head and continued walking slowly along. Matt was too conventional, too set in his ways. She enjoyed making her own decisions, being a businesswoman, working on her designs. She didn't think anything or anyone would make her want to give up her hard-won independence now.

Seven

EARLY JUNE 1845

It was two days before Annie heard from Matt Peters, days in which she made everyone's life uncomfortable as she alternated between optimism and misery, frenzied activity and absent-minded staring into space. The four Gibson children were careful not to upset her and even William trod carefully when he was with her. Tom, braver than the rest, had his head bitten off when he made a direct enquiry about how things were going.

Then, at last, a boy brought round a brief note on headed notepaper from Hallam's Mill. She frowned as she studied the handwriting. She would have recognised Matt's firm rounded copperplate anywhere. How could she not? He had taught her her letters when she was a child of ten. He had not written this. Her hand trembled as she opened it, then she let out her breath in a sigh of relief. The note simply requested Mrs Ashworth to come to the premises at Number Twenty-Four High Street that same afternoon at two o'clock, and to come alone, with the object of discussing the lease. Was this Matt's doing? What did it mean? She thought it over very carefully, but there was no question of not going. It was absolutely crucial that she get that lease.

At two o'clock, she arrived at Number Twenty-Four, dressed in her best brown silk and clutching a matching fringed parasol so tightly that her knuckles showed white against its carved bone handle. To her surprise, there was no sign of anyone and the front door was closed.

She knocked on the door. No one answered. She knocked again, with the same result. She could see Hardy's face peering through the window of his shop. Becoming annoyed, she tried the door and found it unlocked, so she pushed it open and went inside, calling, "Is anyone there?" There was no answer, but she thought she heard a sound upstairs, so she went up to investigate.

As she passed one of the bedroom doors, an arm, a man's arm, seized her from behind and swung her round. She would have screamed, but a mouth fastened itself upon hers and prevented her from crying out. She froze for a moment and then began to struggle wildly, kicking out and pulling her assailant's hair in panic. With a curse, the man pushed her away and, to her astonishment, she found herself looking up at Mr Frederick Hallam himself.

He grinned at her and rubbed his shins. "Little wildcat!"

He was standing between her and the stairs, so she retreated as far along the landing as she could, gasping in fright as he started to come towards her.

"Stay away or I'll scream! They'll hear me next door!"

He stopped, looking puzzled.

She waved the parasol threateningly. She should not have come here on her own! If she called for help, would anyone really come to her aid against the landlord? Not Hardy, that was for certain. And if she laid a complaint, who would believe her? Having grown up in the shadow of the Hallams and their mill, she had the utmost faith in Frederick Hallam's ability to bend the law. Her word would not be believed against that of a man who owned half the town. She whimpered in her throat in dismay.

"Oh, come now," he said impatiently, "I'm sorry I startled you, but don't pretend to be timid or coy."

Anger took over from the fear and shock. "Coy? Coy! You grab hold of me, as if I were a – a . . ."

"An attractive woman."

"As if I were a whore," she spat at him. "Did you really expect me to fall into your arms, Mr Hallam?"

"Let us say that I would not have been surprised. Oh, come now, Mrs Ashworth – Annie, isn't it? Don't play the innocent with me! Half the town knows that Charlie Ashworth didn't father that child of yours. You've been very discreet, and I like that, but you're not going to pretend to be outraged if a man kisses you."

She lost her temper completely. "How dare you speak to me like that!"

"Look, I've said I'm sorry. I went about it the wrong way, I'll admit, but you're a damned attractive woman. And a woman like you must be used to such attentions by now."

"Because I come from the Rows?"

"Well – the Rows don't exactly breed fine ladies, do they?"

"What precisely do you mean by 'a woman like me'?"

"An attractive woman." He was growing impatient. Women from her background were usually flattered by his attentions. He'd had his eye on Annie Ashworth for a while and had been looking forward to their encounter today. He looked at her and his annoyance subsided. She was even lovelier when she was flushed with anger. "I just meant that you're a very attractive woman, one a man like me could really – er – appreciate."

"Well, I might have grown up in the Rows, Mr Hallam, but it just so happens that I'm not interested in that sort of thing."

This was playing too hard to catch. "From what Annabelle Lewis told me, you were friendly enough with her husband before she dismissed you. Before you had your baby. And you've been seeing Lewis regularly since then. Don't play the innocent with me, Mrs Ashworth!"

Annie felt sick. And angry. And helpless. "I'm surprised that Mrs Lewis wasted her time spreading such lies," she said coldly. "My child was not fathered by Jeremy Lewis."

"Then why does he still visit you?" Frederick asked with heavy sarcasm. "And take the boy for rides in his gig?"

"As a friend. And only as a friend! A friend of the whole family!" She gestured to the stairs, but did not dare try to push past him in case he construed that as encouragement to grab hold of her again. "I would like to leave now, Mr Hallam."

He cocked his head on one side. "What about the lease? Why don't you persuade me to lease this shop to you?" he invited. "I could even give you a bargain price."

She shook her head and took an involuntary step backwards. "No! No, I won't! I'm not like that."

"You don't mean it," he said easily. Heavens, how lovely she was! He stretched out a hand towards her and she brandished the parasol again. He caught the end of it and twisted the whole thing sideways to pin her in the corner, for he was a strong man. He was smiling again, his eyes running over her face and upper body. He had always been very successful with women. Some of them just needed more persuading than others. Some of them liked to play these little games.

Annie tried to stay in control of herself, but fear was churning along her veins. She found it difficult to breathe as she gazed up at him.

"Am I so repulsive, Annie?"

"Do you intend to rape me?" she asked harshly. "That's how I got my son – whether you believe me or not."

He ran a fingertip down her cheek and she panicked totally,

struggling like a wild thing and sobbing in terror. There was no mistaking that her fear was genuine. Frederick had never seen anyone so terrified. He wanted suddenly to take her in his arms, simply to comfort her, but one movement of his hand sent her cowering against the wall. He stepped backwards, appalled that he should have frightened anyone so much.

She sank to the ground, still sobbing. Not again, she prayed! Oh God, please not again! Why would men not leave her alone? It took her a while to realise that Hallam had moved away and was no longer attempting to touch her. He took another step backwards and she swallowed, trying to calm herself enough to speak.

"You mean it, don't you? You're not putting on an act?" he asked.

She shuddered and it took her a moment to control her voice. "Of c-course, I mean it! And I was telling the t-truth about my son, whether you believe that or not."

"But you'd be a fool not to take advantage of my interest. Why work so hard, when you could live a life of ease? If you really pleased me, you need never work again."

"I don't want to please you or any other man *ever again*!" The words were hissed through clenched teeth. Sweat was pearling her brow. Her face was as white as chalk.

He moved forward, intending to help her up, and she flinched away from his outstretched hand, unable to stop herself from whimpering in fear. He immediately stepped backwards again and his eyes softened. He was a man who liked women and it hurt him to see the fear in this one's eyes. "You really were raped, weren't you?"

"Yes." Tears began to roll down her cheeks and she buried her face in her hands. "Yes! Yes! *Yes!*"

"I'm sorry. I had no idea. I can see now that I've been completely misled about you, Mrs Ashworth."

She gulped back the sobs. "By Mrs Lewis, I presume."

"Yes, among others. May I offer you a handkerchief." He felt ashamed of himself. He had never seen anyone look quite so panic-stricken and he certainly did not need to force a woman into his arms. Nor had he wanted to insult her.

She shook her head and fumbled in her reticule, her hands shaking so much that it took her a while to find her own handkerchief. When she had mopped her eyes, she pulled herself upright, still pressing away from him against the wall and still looking distraught.

He made no attempt to help her up. "I really am sorry, you know," he said quietly. "I would never have behaved like that if I had realised how it would upset you. Or if I had realised that you were a respectable woman."

She could not stop her hands from shaking as she dried her eyes and blew her nose. The handkerchief was sodden in a minute, for the tears continued to flow. She couldn't seem to stop crying.

"Please take my handkerchief." He held it out, but made no other move towards her.

Hesitantly she stretched out a hand, looking as if she expected him to attack her again. "I – I'll be all right in a minute or two," she managed. "I – it reminded me. I can't – can't bear to think it could – could happen again. I don't like people – men – to touch me like that."

His comprehension was immediate. "That's why you married Barmy Charlie."

"Yes. And to give the boy a name. It's why I – why I prefer to work hard, to earn my own living."

"What a waste! You're a very beautiful woman, you know." He spoke quietly and his words were an echo from the past that made her catch her breath again. Danny O'Connor had once said that, then he had caught hold of her and kissed her. She had not felt quite such blind panic then as she had today, though she had fought against Danny as she had fought against

Frederick Hallam. But that was probably because she had grown up with the O'Connors, had known Danny as a child. She wished for the hundredth time that Charlie were still alive. She missed the protection he had given her simply by existing.

She looked across at Frederick Hallam and drew in a deep, shuddering breath. "I wish I weren't attractive," she said, after a moment. "I don't want that – ever again."

He bowed slightly and stepped right back. Annie let out her breath in an audible sigh of relief.

"I won't touch you, Mrs Ashworth, but I can't leave you here while you're so upset. Could we call a truce? We still have some business to discuss."

"As long as you – don't try to touch me again." She shivered.

"Do you hate men so very much?" The words were surprisingly gentle.

"In that way, yes." Oh, God, was she going to be sick? She pressed a hand to her mouth.

"It must have been bad." It was a statement, not a question.

"Yes." It was a hoarse whisper.

"Then please accept my apologies for upsetting you. I made a stupid assumption and I deeply regret the mistake."

She looked at him suspiciously.

He smiled. "My dear, I am not so short of – er – companionship that I'd ever need to force a woman into my bed. But I must admit that you're the first woman of your station to turn me down."

"I've had to struggle to stay respectable," her voice was flat and lifeless, "and I'm not giving that up – not now, not ever, not even to get the lease."

"No. I can see that." He bowed slightly. "I admire your courage and tenacity, Mrs Ashworth."

She could only stare at him.

"Now, if you will agree, we shall forget that these last few minutes ever happened and discuss the lease instead." With scarcely a break he continued, "As you can see, the repairs have been carried out and everything is ready for you."

"You mean – you'll let me have the place? In spite of the petition? In spite of – today?" With a great effort, she tried to answer normally, but her voice still ended with a breathy gasp that was almost a sob, and he found himself touched by it.

"Yes. Of course."

Her sigh of relief was so loud that it would have made him smile if it were not obvious that she was still deeply upset.

"Have you any idea just why the other shopkeepers were so hostile to the idea of your taking over this place?"

"With Mr Hardy, it's because he wanted the shop and – and because I turned down his attentions," she managed a wavery smile as she gestured to the next house, "which I did nothing to encourage in the first place, believe me."

He smiled in return. "Oh, I do believe you, Mrs Ashworth. I most certainly do."

Her smile became more natural. "And Mrs Hardy is hostile because her husband paid me those attentions."

"Hmm. Not a good reason for me to refuse you a tenancy. And you intend to open a dressmaking establishment, I believe?"

"Oh, no! A salon. A modiste's."

His eyebrows were raised. "And you feel capable of this?"

"Certainly." Her lips twisted wryly. "Thanks to Mrs Lewis, I had a thorough grounding in the rules of good taste. I also visited modistes in London and Manchester with her. And," she took a deep breath, because she had told no one else this as yet, "I intend to visit London again before I open my salon."

"A woman of enterprise."

"I believe, Mr Hallam, that I'm quite capable of running such a business. And of making a success of it."

"Then I shall bring my daughter to patronise your establishment and we shall see whether you can do something to correct her deplorable taste in clothes."

Her face became wary again.

"Mrs Ashworth, either we have called a truce or we haven't!" His voice was sharp. "I shall not trouble you with unwanted attentions again, but I don't intend to have to repeat this every time we speak together."

She believed him. His gaze was direct and his eyes were grey and clear. Beautiful eyes, she realised in surprise. In fact, in spite of his age, he was a very attractive man. "I'm sorry. In that case, let's return to the question of the lease for there are some other points I should like to raise." Her voice was steady now, though her eyes were still wary. "With your permission, Mr Hallam, I would like to make a few alterations to the premises."

"Alterations?"

"Yes."

"What sort of alterations? I can't agree to anything which damages the fabric of the building."

"I don't think it'll damage anything," her voice was uncertain, "but it will certainly affect the fabric of the building. I wish to put some plumbing in, you see, and for that we shall have to knock a few holes in the walls."

"Plumbing?" he asked politely, still humouring her because he was worried by her pallor.

She blushed. "Well, an indoor water closet, actually. For my customers' use."

He blinked. This was changing the subject with a vengeance.

She looked at him defiantly. "Ladies sometimes have problems when they're out shopping. It isn't as easy for them to relieve themselves as it is for gentlemen. I thought it – the water closet – though I shall call it the retiring room – would be an attraction."

He gave a shout of laughter. "An attraction!"

She was recovering fast now. "Yes, an attraction! I've

decided to sell things as well as to design and make gowns.
I'll sell embroidery silks, materials, things that ladies like to
buy for their pastimes. And I'm going to serve tea and coffee
and little cakes. I shall make money from that, too. The ladies
of Bilsden have nowhere to meet in town, you know."

He had stopped laughing now. Her ideas were good. They
made excellent business sense.

"Well?" she demanded.

"Well, what?"

"May I make my alterations?"

"Yes. And as landlord, I shall bear half the costs, which is
only fair, because if you leave, you cannot take the
improvements with you."

She looked at him doubtfully, not certain whether he meant
it, not wanting to be beholden to him.

He smiled, a warm smile, very different from the leering
way he had looked at her before. "You know, Mrs Ashworth,
you're a remarkable young woman."

She brushed aside the compliment, completely uninterested
in it. "Thank you. I shall find a builder as soon as the lease is
signed. I believe there's a good man over in Rochdale. I'll let
you know his estimates."

As he watched her go down the stairs, he murmured to
himself, "But it is a waste, all the same."

Annie did not look for a builder until she had visited Mr
Pennybody's office the next morning. She wanted everything
signed and sealed before she took another step, and besides,
she had another matter to lay before Mr Pennybody.

She was well enough known by now for Smithers, the chief
clerk, to greet her by name, settle her in a comfortable chair
and bustle off to find out whether his employer could spare
the time to see her. He was back almost immediately to usher
her into the inner sanctum.

Jonas Pennybody rose and came forward to greet her. "Do take a seat, my dear Mrs Ashworth. Mr Hallam came to see me yesterday afternoon and said that you were to have the shop lease. And on very reasonable terms, too. I'm pleased for you, very pleased indeed. How on earth did you manage to persuade him?"

"I went to see him. Told him about my plans. He said they made sound business sense."

"Indeed they do. And I have the lease here all ready for you to sign. Would you like to read it through first?" The answer was a foregone conclusion, because, as he knew perfectly well, Annie never signed anything without checking every word in the document.

She sat and read through the lease very carefully, it being the first she had ever negotiated. Once or twice she had to ask the meaning of a word and Jonas explained it to her patiently, a twinkle in his eyes.

A little frown creased her forehead as she finished reading the document. "There's just one thing, Mr Pennybody. Will Jim Catterall be collecting the rents?" As far as she knew, Catterall collected all Hallam's rents.

"Catterall? Oh, dear me, no! He's far too rough a fellow for this end of town. My junior clerk, Fitton, goes round on the last Friday in each month to collect the rent money from the central properties. My goodness, we wouldn't send a fellow like Catterall along the High Street! He'd frighten away the customers and then the shopkeepers wouldn't be able to pay their rents." He laughed softly at his own joke, but Annie had too many unhappy memories of Jim Catterall to join in.

"Now, my dear Mrs Ashworth, we must attend to the signing. Smithers! Will you please come through and witness this for us?" The elderly clerk, who must have been hovering near the door, came at once in answer to the call. He watched the signing through narrowed eyes, as if he was there to prevent

forgeries, then he carefully appended his own signature, a very
flourishing, but illegible collection of copperplate letters.
Afterwards, he bore the lease away to have copies made,
carrying it as if it were the Crown Jewels.

Mr Pennybody beamed at Annie. "Mr Hallam asked me to
give you his best wishes for your little business venture. He
said you'd got your head screwed on the right way, and that he
would not forget his promise to bring his daughter in to have a
dress or two made."

She was startled. "Mr Hallam's daughter?" She hadn't
believed that he meant what he said.

"Yes. Miss Beatrice Hallam. His younger daughter. She
was greatly upset by her mother's death and Mr Hallam has
been doing his best to cheer her up lately. His two sons and his
other daughter are married and live elsewhere, so Beatrice is
the only one left at home in Bilsden. Well, one of the sons is
dead now, actually. Tragic to die so young, and him just
married, too. Beatrice has a lady companion living at Ridge
House now, a distant relative, I believe, but the girl misses her
mother. They were very close."

"Oh." It was difficult to picture the owner of half of Bilsden
as a devoted father and family man, but then, Frederick Hallam
had been kind to her yesterday once the misunderstanding was
cleared up. Annie shrugged her shoulders and changed the
subject. She had other business on her mind, something much
more important than Mr Hallam's family life. "Mr Pennybody,
I wonder if you could help me to borrow some money. I believe
it's possible to take out a mortgage on a piece of property?"

"A mortgage? Well, yes, but I confess to being surprised
that you should need one. Your friend, Mrs Smith, left you
quite a tidy sum of money, did she not?"

"Yes. But it's not enough."

"Not enough for what?"

"Not enough to buy the things I need. I intend to have a

very high-class modiste's salon, Mr Pennybody. I shall need more money than I currently possess to redecorate the premises and to make a few alterations, not to mention buying stock, paying staff and meeting living expenses until we begin to show a profit. I intend to attract the custom of ladies from the whole of this area, not just those from Bilsden itself, ladies who would normally buy in Manchester and London. So I thought I could obtain the extra capital I need by mortgaging the two cottages that Sally left me. I thought," she took a deep breath, "a hundred pounds?" She looked at him anxiously.

"You could, in fact, obtain more on those two cottages if you needed it."

"Oh, no! I shan't need more than that! At least, I don't think so. And I do have some money saved. Another hundred will be quite enough."

He nodded at her across the desk. "There will be no trouble with the cottages as security, no trouble at all. It will, however, be necessary to lodge the deeds with me and . . ."

She opened her reticule and passed some papers to him. He began to laugh. "I can see you came prepared, Mrs Ashworth."

She could find nothing funny in that. "Of course!"

"I shall be able to arrange matters very quickly. It just so happens that I have a client who is interested in putting some money out at loan. You go ahead with your plans. The hundred pounds will be available within two days."

"There's no doubt about that?"

"None whatsoever." He did not tell her that he himself would be providing the money. He had absolute confidence in her ability to pay the loan back and it would be a pleasure to help her. Pauline Hinchcliffe was not the only one with an eye for a good investment.

Annie stood up.

"And Mrs Ashworth . . ."

"Yes, Mr Pennybody?"

"I shall bring my wife to visit your – er – salon." He would have no trouble in persuading Eunice to patronise Mrs Ashworth when she knew who had provided some of the finance.

"Please do that, Mr Pennybody. I'm sure we shall be able to help her."

I doubt it, he thought, as he watched her walk out. Eunice has no dress sense, none at all. But she may as well waste her money with you as in Manchester. He did not, however, tell Annie that.

Annie felt as if she were floating down the street. It was all arranged, it really was! The lease was signed and she could start getting her salon ready. The sunshine seemed twice as golden today and, of course, before she made her way home, she went to have another look around Number Twenty-Four.

Eight

JULY 1845

"You're what!" Tom gaped at Annie. "You can't mean that!"

"I do. I'm going to London for a few days."

"What on earth for?"

"To look at the fashion salons and the fabrics and the trimmings, to see what fashionable people are wearing – oh, everything!"

"Just like that. With everything in chaos here and all the work still to do on Number Twenty-Four."

Her voice was defiant. "Yes."

"Just to look at clothes!"

"No! To look at the businesses that sell clothes, to look at how they attract a better class of clientèle."

"But you can look at all that in Manchester."

"Tom, I can't. I really can't. I want my salon to be something special, so I need to go down to London, where there are a lot of high-class modistes and fashion emporiums. If I had the money and if I spoke any French, I'd go to Paris, but I can't afford that just now. And anyway, it'd take too long. So I'm going down to London."

He ran a hand through his hair. "Look, I may not know much about these things, but I do know that you can't go down to London on your own – not unless you want to be taken for a loose woman."

"I don't intend to go on my own. Of course, I don't!"

"Then who are you going with?"

"I don't know yet."

His eyes lit up. "Why don't I go with you?"

"No! I need another woman to go in and out of shops and dress salons with. And anyway, you'd get bored after half a day of the sort of things I want to do."

His expression turned sulky. "I'd like to see London."

She put her arm on his. "You will, Tom, but this is not the time. And anyway, I need you to look after things here. We can't both go away at once."

He was only half convinced. "So who are you going to go with?"

"I – I haven't decided."

"Mrs Hinchcliffe?"

"Pauline? No, I don't think so. She might be willing, but she'd try to tell me what to think. You know what she's like."

"Who, then?"

"I don't know. I'll take Rebecca if I can't think of anyone else, but I'd rather not. Let me think about it, hmm?"

In the event, she found a travelling companion in a completely unexpected way. She mentioned the matter casually to Helen Kenderby the next day during her watercolour lesson and Helen grew thoughtful.

"You're sure there's no one suitable from your family and friends to go with you, Mrs Ashworth?"

"Very sure. I think it'll have to be my little sister."

"How about me?"

"What?" Annie let the paintbrush drop into the water, sending a shower of greyish drops across the page. "Oh, dear!

Look what I've done!" She mopped up the mess with her painting rag, thinking furiously the whole time, then she put the paintbrush down carefully. "Do you mean that?"

"Oh, definitely. I'm in desperate need of a holiday from Father. And I always enjoy visiting London."

"Er – your father—" Annie didn't know how to say this tactfully.

Helen Kenderby's eyes danced with laughter. "What you're trying to say is, would my father approve of my going with you?"

"Well, yes." Annie still got a disapproving glance from the parson every time she met him at the house.

"He won't exactly approve, but as we'll be staying with my aunt, who is his sister, he'll have nothing definite to complain about. I mean, he can't accuse his own sister of not being respectable, can he?" She patted Annie's hand and said gently, "I do go away from time to time, you know. I have to, to keep myself sane. Aunt Isabel loves to have me stay with her and you'd be very welcome to stay at her house, too."

"I couldn't do that! She doesn't even know me!"

"She won't mind. She keeps open house and loves to have young company. She says it cheers her up and makes her forget how decrepit she's getting." She smiled at Annie. "So?"

Annie beamed back at her. "I'd love to go with you."

"Good. That's settled. And if we're to go to London together, hadn't you better call me Helen from now on – Annie?"

Annie was not looking forward to the journey to London because she remembered only too well how tiring it had been when she travelled by coach with Mrs Lewis. But travelling by train came as a delightful surprise to her. On a dull day in July, the Kenderby carriage picked her up from home and took the two women into Manchester, which in itself seemed the height of luxury to one who most often moved around on foot. The coachman deposited them at the London Road station with much shaking of the head.

"Talby disapproves of anything modern," whispered Helen. "Take no notice of him."

The station was only a few years old and was not yet badly stained by smoke like other buildings in the vicinity. It seemed a huge arching cavern of a place to Annie, and she was relieved that she was with Helen who seemed not even to notice the crowds of people jostling around them or the noises coming from the locomotives.

"Ever been on a train before?" asked Helen.

"No. Last time I went to London we travelled by coach. It was bumpy and exhausting." She stared down the platform at the great clouds of steam hissing from the locomotive. A few other people had also stopped to stare at it. Perhaps, like Annie, they were about to take their first ride on a train.

The coachman supervised the transfer of their luggage to the train, still with a disdainful expression on his face, and then, not trusting in mere railway employees, he left his horses in charge of the gardener's boy, who acted as under-coachman on such hazardous journeys, and undertook a second foray into this dangerous world to find the ladies their seats.

As they watched him go, Helen nudged Annie, eyes dancing. "Talby absolutely loathes the railways. Just look at the expression on his face!"

"Why does he hate them so much?"

"Because they've taken away the livelihood of so many coach drivers, his brother among them. He calls them 'dirty great tea-kettles'."

"You could make a lot of tea with a kettle that size!" Annie turned her attention to the passenger accommodation. "The carriages look – ugly."

"Disappointed?" Helen raised one eyebrow.

"Well – I expected something more – exciting, somehow."
She stared at the train which seemed very long to her. She just
hoped that the passenger carriages would not become detached
while the train was travelling along. There were a lot of other
people making their way towards the train, far too many, it
seemed to Annie, to be travelling in a single conveyance. Could
one steam-engine really pull them all?

Talby came back and indicated that he had found their
accommodation. As they walked along beside the train, Helen
pointed out two family saloons which were completely private
with compartments at the end for the servants. "I prefer to ride
in the public carriages, myself," she said, "and not waste my
money. The first-class compartments are perfectly comfortable.
I just hope we have one to ourselves."

She did not get her wish, but as they found themselves
sharing the seating space with an elderly lady and her equally
elderly maid, neither of whom showed any inclination to
chat, they were not disturbed in any way. Before the train set
off, and in spite of the fact that it was summer, the elderly
lady wrapped herself in a large checked rug and her maid
tenderly placed a small pillow behind her mistress's neck. The
maid followed suit with another rug and pillow for herself,
and then both of them leaned their heads back and closed their
eyes.

Annie and Helen exchanged amused glances, but the
weather today was cool enough for them to be glad of their
own travelling rugs in the draughty carriage and they busied
themselves wrapping up carefully. When a man came along
beside the train selling hot bricks, Helen purchased two from
him to keep their feet warm. Then they sat and waited for the
train to start.

"I love your travelling rug," said Helen. "So practical, to
have one with its own hood. Where did you get it from?"

Annie stroked the soft wool and smiled again. "I made it

myself, since you said the carriages were draughty, even in summer. Tom got me some blankets and I thought this might be more practical than just a rug." She did not say how cheaply Tom had bought the blankets for her at the market.

"Well, I hope you'll make me one before I travel anywhere else. If you sell them at your salon, they'll be a great success, I'm sure. Ah, we're leaving. Good."

Annie stared out of the window as the train slowly chugged out of the station, entranced even by the sight of the mean back streets of Manchester. She felt young and free from responsibility today. She could not remember the last time she had allowed herself a holiday from work. Though this wasn't exactly a holiday, of course. Still, it felt like one.

Soon they were thundering through the countryside, and although at first it seemed downright dangerous to rattle past fields and villages at such a high speed, after a while Annie grew used to that, as she did to the rhythmic clacking noise of the train rolling along the metal rails. And the further south they went, the better the weather became, so that she could abandon her wrappings and gaze entranced at a sunny landscape.

Even the stops to change trains were made easily, with porters pushing forward to help the ladies and their luggage into the next train. Like Manchester, Crewe and Birmingham were busy places, with people everywhere. And yet there was a sense of happy purpose to them all, even to the man assiduously sweeping a corner of the station clear of litter or the dignified woman in charge of the ladies' waiting rooms with which the larger stations were supplied.

How awkward it would be if one needed to relieve oneself while the train was moving, thought Annie, as she queued to use the convenience and then washed her hands in a bowl of water obligingly poured by the attendant. "Why can't we just have one train all the way through?" she asked Helen, as they walked across to the new train. "It seems so inefficient to have to keep changing trains like this."

"It's because each stretch of railway is owned by a different company. Perhaps one day they'll get together and sort things out." Helen yawned. "I hope you don't mind if I snooze. For some reason, train journeys always make me sleepy."

Annie did not have the slightest inclination to snooze. She sat staring out of the window, not wanting to miss a single thing. Some of the countryside they passed through was so beautiful that it made her proud to be English. It was only when she went away that she realised how very ugly Bilsden was.

They had brought a picnic basket with them and were able to purchase hot tea, which was poured into their own cups by an enterprising vendor at Birmingham. Annie sipped the dark brown liquid and grimaced. "Ugh! This must have been standing stewing for ages."

"At least it's warm and soothing," said Helen.

When they arrived in London, it seemed astonishing to Annie that they had been able to get there so easily in one day's travel, all for a modest three guineas each. What a difference to the old stage coaches! No wonder people preferred to travel by train when they could.

At Euston station in London, which was even larger and busier than the Manchester station, they took a hackney-cab to Kensington, which was about five miles away. "My aunt doesn't like living in the city," said Helen. "She has a very pretty house in its own gardens in Kensington. She doesn't need to keep a carriage there because it's like a village and anyway, she doesn't go out a lot. She simply hires a carriage from the local livery stables if she wants to go anywhere. While we're staying with her, we can travel to and from London on one of the new horse omnibuses. My father would have a fit if he knew I did that, but I shan't tell him. He doesn't approve of ladies using any public conveyances, not even trains."

That did not surprise Annie. Parson Kenderby did not seem to approve of many things, especially anything modern. During her days in service, she had had to attend St Mark's Church and she remembered his sermons as loud angry harangues against those the parson felt were not living a Christian life, according to the customs of the Established Church, or those who were disrupting the God-given order of the land. Since she had been having painting lessons, she had become aware that his sour tyrannical nature did not change even in his own home.

The elderly Miss Kenderby proved to be as delightful as her niece. She was a tiny woman with neatly banded silver hair and hands twisted by arthritis. "Helen didn't tell me how beautiful you were!" she exclaimed when Annie was introduced. "I've always loved Titian hair." Then she chuckled as Annie coloured. "You'll have to get used to my frankness, dear girl. I'm far too old to waste time on meaningless exchanges of words for politeness' sake."

When the luggage had been carried up the stairs, Miss Kenderby nodded across the hall to her parlour. "I'll expect you two down for tea whenever you're ready. I always used to like to take time to tidy myself after a journey, and I'm sure you'd both prefer to wash and change. Nothing formal about dinner. Day wear only. I've given up changing into evening wear. Can't abide the fuss and botheration at my age. Just come down when you're ready and we'll chat and drink a glass of wine until it's time to eat. I want to hear all about your plans, Annie – you don't mind me calling you Annie, do you?"

"Of course not." Annie tried not to look as Miss Kenderby began to walk slowly and painfully across the hall. Old age was cruel. By the time she grew old she intended to have a lot of money to buy any help she needed.

The next morning Annie woke early while dawn was still glowing in the sky and lay in bed letting anticipation tingle through her body. She meant to make the most of these few days and planned to visit Bond Street, Regent Street and every other place she could find which sold clothes and accessories to those of discerning tastes.

She dressed in her most fashionable gown for this foray and Helen walked round her nodding when she appeared for breakfast. "Yes, you look lovely."

"Quite lovely." Miss Kenderby smiled mischievously. "I think you should play the eccentric lady today, Helen. It always gets the best attention in shops."

Annie looked at her hostess in puzzlement. What on earth did she mean?

"It's a game we used to play when we were travelling in Europe," Miss Kenderby explained. She exchanged glances of complicity with her niece. "You turn up your nose and become very scornful of whatever is offered, then you talk loudly of the better service to be obtained in Paris or Rome or some other place of importance." She sighed and looked down at her twisted hands. "I still miss the delights of travelling, but I couldn't manage it nowadays, not even when you can do much of your travelling in comfort on the train."

She shot a very sharp glance at Annie and added, "Don't waste your life, girl! It passes all too quickly. Make your salon really special, if that's what you want. And don't live only for that son of yours you keep talking about. It's *your* life, too. The Corsican Monster took my fiancé from me, and I didn't start enjoying my life again until I was past thirty and in control of my own money. When my brother married that mouse of a woman, I decided to live on my own and do as I pleased." She chuckled softly. "Theophilus was absolutely furious, but my money was my own by then, so he could do nothing about it. How he roared at me! But his love of family is very strong, so eventually he relented and now he allows my niece to visit me. He hopes she'll inherit my money, as she will."

Helen went across to kiss her aunt's cheek. "I'll never forget all you've done for me, Aunt Isabel. And I don't care about the money."

Her aunt grinned, a street urchin's grimace of amusement that sat incongruously on a narrow aristocratic face with lined paper-thin skin. "You will care one day. But we did have some fun travelling together, didn't we? Now, off with you, and don't forget. Play the eccentric! It ensures the most obsequious attention."

The first adventure of the day for Annie was taking the George Chancellor omnibus into London. It was drawn by four huge horses and it ran from Kensington High Street to the corner of Bond Street in Piccadilly at the very reasonable cost of twopence per person. When they arrived, they strolled first down Bond Street, then they made their way towards Regent Street. Even at this unfashionably early hour, the streets were full of people and carriages were for ever stopping to set ladies down, causing shouts and complaints from those behind whose way they were blocking.

"It makes you realise how small Bilsden is!" sighed Annie, as they stopped under the Colonnade in Regent Street's Quadrant to take stock.

"Let's not think of Bilsden. We'll pretend we've just arrived here from Rome. Now, let's go and look for some modistes."

The first time Helen played the eccentric, Annie nearly spoiled things by giggling. The quiet parson's daughter suddenly became an arrogant lady and her loud commentaries on the poor quality of the goods displayed or the furnishings of the shops themselves made the shopkeepers and their assistants squirm visibly. In London, Helen Kenderby was another woman, vivacious, daring and full of energy. It seemed so sad that although she had the money to become independent, she did not consider it proper to leave home.

One of the places they visited was the Shawl Warehouse of J & J Holmes at 171–9 Regent Street and Annie had trouble hiding her awe at the spaciousness of the premises, the tasteful displays of shawls and the utter superiority of the gentleman assistant who hovered nearby. Unlike the other shop assistants, this man did not seem in the least impressed by Helen's imperiousness or her casual references to Rome, with which she was obviously familiar. Annie was left with the feeling that he would treat Queen Victoria herself in exactly the same way.

When they had visited four other shawl shops, Helen said thoughtfully, "I think I'd like to go back and buy that blue and white Indian shawl we were looking at in Holmes's. It was rather fine, don't you think?"

"You'd need a very special sort of blue dress to set it off, though. Do you have one?"

"Not yet, but I'm hoping you're going to make me one."

"Oh, Helen, please don't think you have to——"

"I'm not offering you charity, my dear. I've been looking at the other women's clothes here in London and then at that dress you're wearing. It's far more stylish than mine, though I bought this in London last year. In fact, your work can stand comparison with anything we've seen so far. You really do have a flair for cutting and fitting. And it's about time I bought some more clothes for myself. I don't pay enough attention to my appearance." She sighed and added very quietly, "Well, who is there to care what I look like?"

They'd care more, thought Annie, if you were always as lively as you are here.

They bought the shawl, then went from one linendraper's and silk merchant's to another in search of exactly the right dress material to set it off. All the time, Annie was studying the ladies they passed and the goods on display. She even dragged Helen into Jay's General Mourning Warehouse which was fronted by a row of large modern windows with clear door-sized panels of glass each topped by a small round window, giving the shop a vaguely church-like appearance. The windows offered tasteful displays of black draperies of all kinds, shawls and veils and black-edged handkerchiefs as well as black ribbons and great loops and swags of black lace.

Inside the shop, Helen made great play with her handkerchief and talked of her dear aunt's recent decline and the need to be prepared, but they bought nothing. Once outside again, they walked briskly along the street chuckling.

The shop which Annie liked best was Howell & James in Lower Regent Street. It occupied several premises which looked from a distance more like private houses than shops. The spacious showrooms offered lavish displays of silks and other fabrics, among which was exactly the right shade of dark blue to set off Helen's new shawl. Twenty yards were cut and wrapped, then the package was whisked away to be delivered to Kensington that very same day. Even though the shawl had not been purchased there, the obliging staff seemed happy to deliver that, too. Nothing, it seemed, was too much trouble for them. This, thought Annie, was the way she would train her staff to treat customers.

By that stage, both ladies were exhausted. "Lunch at Verey's!" said Helen. "The charges are moderate, the cooking is excellent – or it was last time I was in London – and we won't be thought too daring if we eat there unescorted by a gentleman. I need a rest, even if you don't, and they have a retiring room."

By four o'clock, Helen said that her feet were aching too much to carry on and even Annie was feeling that she had had a surfeit of shopping. The two ladies took another omnibus and went home to tell Miss Kenderby about their day and then rest before dinner. Annie used that time to write down her impressions and to sketch everything of note she could remember about the ladies of fashion they had seen. Those they had encountered during the afternoon had been a superior race to the morning crowd, elegant and languid, their carriages blocking the cobbled streets unashamedly and their servants as superior as themselves.

The following day, Annie and Helen visited the Burlington Arcade with its entrance of three tall archways and an interior more like a cathedral than a shopping arcade. Its tiny boutiques sold the most elegant frivolities that Annie had ever seen at prices which made her gasp in amazement. The boots and shoes were varnished, embroidered and beribboned until they seemed too fine to be put upon the dirty ground, the pocket handkerchiefs had more lace than cambric, and the embroidered garters were works of art too beautiful merely to hold up a lady's silk stockings beneath the secret folds of a gown.

When they came out of the arcade, Annie looked at Helen who had purchased things steadily throughout the previous day. "You didn't buy anything here."

"Inflated prices, my dear. Let's go and look at some warehouses which sell very similar goods at much lower prices. I know just the place to start."

Annie was relieved that Helen had the same attitude as Mrs Lewis towards buying things. That afternoon she made several careful purchases for her new business, buttons the like of which she had never seen before, fashionable tartan ribbons in many shades and patterns and some particularly fine Indian muslins.

The next day, they visited several more fashionable modistes' establishments, and again Helen showed herself a skilled actress as she played the eccentric and had the vendeuses tripping over one another to try to please her and the other customers standing back to give her precedence. She might have been a duchess from the way she spoke. Annie remained quiet beside her, but her eyes missed no details of decor and the different arrangements made for dealing with customers.

On their last day in London, Helen insisted on their taking a little holiday from shops and shopping and took Annie for a steamer ride along the river. The smell from the water was rather strong and made the ladies disinclined to sample the refreshments offered them, but if you ignored that, the panorama of England's capital seen from the water was magnificent, a sight which Annie would never forget.

It was as they were leaving the steamer and looking for a cab to take them back to Kensington that they were accosted by a tall, fashionably dressed gentleman who swept off his top hat with a flourish and said, "Annie!" in tones of delighted surprise.

Annie jerked round in shock and blinked up at him. "Danny! What on earth are *you* doing in London?"

"I might ask the same thing. You're the last person I'd have expected to see here."

Annie belatedly remembered her manners and introduced Helen. "Danny and I knew one another when we were young. His mother is a great friend of mine."

"And am I not your friend, too?" he asked, his voice full of innuendo, the soft Irish lilt suddenly more noticeable.

She could feel herself stiffening and she clutched Helen's arm instinctively.

"Well, then," said Helen lightly, breaking the intensity of the moment, "since we've been introduced, shall we move on a little? We seem to be blocking the pathway here. Do you come to London often, Mr O'Connor?"

He was obliged to reply and had soon got a wry smile at the corner of his mouth as he realised how skilfully Helen was controlling the conversation. "Could I invite you ladies to partake of some refreshments with me?" he asked, when he was at last allowed to put a word in.

"We were just going home!" said Annie, and then grew annoyed with herself for sounding flustered. She knew that she was handling this situation badly. Why did Danny always affect her like this?

"But surely you have time to sit and chat with an old friend first?" he said. "I have an appointment early this afternoon, but there's an establishment nearby which provides excellent luncheons and which has a quiet dining room for mixed company." He looked quizzically at Helen as he spoke, and then, before either lady could say him nay, he had summoned a cab with one lift of his finger and was shepherding them into it.

Annie remained stiff and unbending for the first few minutes, then was gradually drawn by Danny into a game of "Do you remember?"

Helen listened in fascination, for Mr O'Connor made no attempt to hide his origins. She could only wonder at her two companions. How many people raised in the Rows could make such a success of their lives? For a moment, the familiar bitterness shot through her that she had not defied her father, had not given her all to her painting. She was even jealous that she had not been born as beautiful as Annie so that she might at least have found herself a loving husband and escaped from her father that way. Only what would her mother have done then? Her mother often begged for reassurance that Helen was not going to leave them. Theophilus Kenderby was not an easy man to have for a husband.

"And what *are* you doing in London, Mr O'Connor?" Helen asked in a lull in the conversation while he cut into his roast beef with obvious relish. "You never said."

"I'm negotiating my next contract for building a stretch of railway," he said. "I specialise in the brick and stonework, though I can turn my hand to most things. Unfortunately, the contracts I've had lately seem to be keeping me away from Bilsden. I had intended to return before this and set up business there as a builder, but it's hard to turn down a good offer."

Annie concentrated on her beef which suddenly seemed as tasteless as old leather. She had enough to do at the moment with her new business and the last thing she wanted was Danny to come back to Bilsden and come courting her as he had threatened to do more than once. She did not want anything else to change in her life.

Helen could not miss the tension that suddenly radiated from her young friend. Not a favoured suitor, then, this one. Which was surprising, because Danny and Annie seemed to get on so well. And he was a very handsome man. He even made Helen's own heart flutter a little, she admitted to herself.

As they parted company after the meal, Annie said quietly, "I'll tell Bridie that I saw you."

"Yes. And tell her I'll be coming home for a visit before long. This contract is near a main railway line and the local squire and parson are determined to prevent Sunday work, so I should be able to snatch a few hours of freedom from time to time."

"Oh."

He looked at her quizzically. "I shall certainly call upon you in your new house, Annie."

"Your mother should come first."

"No. You come first," he said, raising her hand to his lips, then he tipped his hat to them and strode away down the street.

Annie could not hide her expression of dismay.

"You don't favour his suit?" asked Helen.

"No!" The denial was so vehement that Helen looked surprised and Annie felt the need to add quietly, "I want no suitors, Helen. Not Danny, not anyone." But she was beginning to wonder if she really meant that, beginning to wonder if she really did want to live the rest of her life alone. William would not be with her for ever, and then what would she do with herself? Would she grow old like Isabel Kenderby, alone with her servants and lavishing her love on William's children?

Nine

JULY TO AUGUST 1845

"Put that small mirror over on the side wall," ordered Annie. "Yes. That's better! There's a good light over there."

"Yes, your ladyship," mocked Tom. "And where would your ladyship like me to put this sofa?"

"Chaise longue, not sofa. Over here by the fireplace. We want our clients to be able to sit in comfort. Yes, that's it." She ignored his teasing. What they were doing was too important to joke about.

Tom winked at Mark and stood back to look at the chaise longue. Uncomfortable-looking thing! Still, it had an air of class to it. You could see that at a glance. Their Annie certainly had a knack for making things look elegant. She'd better, the money she was pouring into this place! First the trip to London, then a series of visits to warehouses in Manchester. Where would it all end?

He looked round the room while he waited for her next orders. You would hardly recognise Number Twenty-Four. All the downstairs rooms had been repainted in pale colours, not at all practical. Still, the cream walls did look nice and the gilding on the plaster mouldings in the corners looked just right too. How *did* Annie know to do things like that? This carpet square would soon show the dirt, though. He'd thought it a pale, washed-out thing when she bought it second-hand at an auction in Manchester, but now that it was cleaned up, its soft pastel flowers looked – well, he had to admit it, they looked extremely elegant.

He sighed. Annie had nearly driven him mad in the past few weeks, dragging him off to sales and auctions and furniture warehouses. He had lost so much time that the profits from his yard and rounds had dropped considerably, but was she sympathetic? Not at all! She just said it couldn't be helped and they were going to do things properly or not at all. Her idea of properly was to open a shop that didn't even look like a shop! It looked more like a queen's parlour. He wondered what the ladies of Bilsden would think of it. What went down well in London might not please the local carriage folk who were a hard-headed bunch on the whole.

"I think we'll have the plant stand over there by the window. Mark, just run and get that big fern in a pot from outside the back door, will you?" Annie stood tapping her foot impatiently till Mark brought in the plant, staggering under its weight.

Plants, thought Tom, standing back and shaking his head. Bleedin' plants on fancy stands! What was this? A dressmaker's or a glasshouse? He watched scornfully as Mark and Annie lifted the plant and set it carefully on the stand. A tall, thin, table-thing just to put a fern on! And a piece of cloth under the pot with lace round the edges! "My, we are fancy, aren't we?" he said aloud, but Annie did not rise to the bait.

"Now," she said briskly, "we want those little gilt chairs that Alice and Beth have been re-covering. They're up in the workroom."

"Come on, my lad. Her ladyship has spoken."

Annie's lips tightened in irritation as she watched them leave the room and listened to Tom joking with Mark as they went up the stairs. She knew that Tom thought she was fussing too much, but she didn't care. She also knew, because her friend Ellie Peters had heard it from Dr Lewis himself, that everyone in Bilsden, not just the ladies she was trying to attract, was agog to see inside her salon, and that pleased her greatly. Most of them would just have to wait, though. Only a very few people had been allowed to see inside Number Twenty-Four lately.

Pauline Hinchcliffe was one of them, of course. And Helen Kenderby had come along to give her opinion on the colour schemes, but she had not changed anything. All she had said was that Annie didn't need her advice and that everything looked splendid. Annie valued that opinion as she valued Helen's friendship, whatever the difference in their stations. Helen had travelled all over Europe with her aunt before Miss Kenderby grew too old. She had been to Italy and Greece and France, places that Annie had scarcely heard of before she left Salem Street, but which came to life as Helen described them. Helen really knew about art and design and architecture. One day, Annie had decided, she too would go travelling. It was not hard to do now, with the new railways spreading everywhere. Why should she not go one day?

What Annie could not understand was why Helen had come back to live with her parents again when her aunt grew too old to travel. Helen had been left some money by a godmother, a generous amount, she said frankly. Why didn't she just go away again and paint as she so obviously longed to do? She wasn't happy in the parsonage. Anyone with half an eye could see that. Once Annie had ventured to ask her why, and Helen had just shrugged her shoulders and said that her mother, who was a semi-invalid now, needed her, and that she couldn't upset her family. Which was just plain silly. That father of hers didn't care what anyone else thought or wanted; he just had to have his own way. No wonder Mrs Kenderby looked so sad and crushed! No wonder Helen had lost a lot of her vivacity once they returned to Bilsden.

Every morning now Annie walked along the High Street to her salon. She made sure that when she appeared in public she was as fashionably dressed as any lady in the town; indeed, she was more fashionably dressed than most of them. Once at the salon she changed into some older clothes and threw herself into her work, sewing upstairs while the workmen toiled downstairs, or coming down to stand over the men and supervise every tiny detail of the renovations.

The water closet had been installed within weeks. Tom had arranged all that through one of his many acquaintances, a certain Herbert Hutchings. Mr Hutchings said that indoor plumbing was going to become more and more important, and he grew enthusiastic every time he talked about it. He was a self-opinionated young man, but much of what he said made sense. He was delighted to do Annie a special deal on condition that she would recommend him to her wealthy friends and customers, and he was even more delighted when he found out that Mr Hallam was a partner in these renovations.

Mr Hutchings went over to Sheffield himself to select the water closets and other sanitary ware. He said he would find Mrs Ashworth something really top of the tree for the salon, and he did. The closet he chose was made by a firm called Bramah. It had a highly polished mahogany seat and a pattern of flowers under the glaze on the toilet pan. Annie stared at it in amazement when Mr Hutchings reverently unwrapped the sacking in which it had travelled from Sheffield. Fancy having flowers on a thing like that!

Mr Hutchings had brought back on his own initiative a matching flowered handbasin, which Annie was unable to resist purchasing, and she had had it installed next to the water closet, with running water from a shiny brass tap as well, because it stood to reason that the ladies would want to wash their hands and tidy their hair in the mirror of the small dressing table that she also had fitted into the retiring room. Yes, the ladies of the town would soon find out how convenient it was to shop at Annie's salon. The latest ladies' magazines, light refreshments at very reasonable prices and the comfort of a modern water closet.

Tom said she had run mad, but one day he'd realise that she was right. Mr Hutchings had not laughed at her ideas. Nor had Mr Hallam. In fact, Mr Hallam had urged her on. Strange how well he understood what she was doing. She would never have dreamed that he could be so approachable, though he had been nothing but polite and respectful ever since their unfortunate encounter at Number Twenty-Four. There had been no further advances, not the slightest hint of anything like that. She had grown to feel quite comfortable with him, almost as if he were an old friend. Which was strange indeed for a woman from the Rows and the master of the largest mill in town.

While she was making all these changes, Annie arranged for water to be piped to Netherleigh Cottage by the new Bilsden Purified Water Company, and for Mr Hutchings to install one of the new kitchen ranges there as well as a bath and a much plainer and less expensive water closet and handbasin. The range was made by a man called Thomas Robinson. It had two ovens and a big hotplate, and what they called a warming oven too, as well as a built-in boiler which heated the water for you. Mr Hutchings persuaded Annie to have the water that was heated so easily piped into the new bathroom that had been fitted at the rear of the dairy, as well as to the kitchen sink and she could not resist that either. No lugging cans around at Netherleigh Cottage, as she had had to do at Collett Hall. And everything connected to the new sewers and drainage system that Dr Lewis had insisted the town install if they were to avoid further disastrous epidemics.

These were the real miracles of modern science, Mr

Hutchings had said when he fitted the range, patting it with a lover's hand, and Annie absolutely agreed with him. They were the things that made a huge difference to everyone's life, not airy-fairy inventions that meant nothing to real people. Only a few closed stoves had been installed in the whole town so far. The mill owners and manufacturers might pounce on new machinery, but their wives were much slower to introduce such inventions into their own homes and kitchens. Why should they worry, after all, when they did not have the cooking to do and when they had maidservants to empty the dirty water from their baths?

The kitchen range was now Kathy's pride and joy, and she black-leaded it lovingly to keep it gleaming like new. On one of her trips into Manchester, Annie had also bought Kathy a present, a book called *Modern Cookery* by a lady named Eliza Acton. It was full of recipes. Kathy was a slow reader, but she was working her way through it, laboriously spelling out the recipes one by one. The family never knew nowadays what they'd be having for tea, but it was invariably delicious. All four young Gibsons had put on weight, and Rebecca had quite lost that haunted look.

Annie derived a good deal of quiet satisfaction from her improvements. She remembered queuing for water at the tap in Boston Street as a child, and lugging the heavy buckets home to Salem Street. How she had hated it in the winter when the water you spilled felt like icy daggers stabbing your legs! Pauline Hinchcliffe scoffed even at her own household innovations and said she still preferred to take her bath in front of a fire where it was nice and warm. But the owner of Collett Hall didn't have to carry up the big copper cans of water or to empty the dirty bathwater back into the copper cans, jugful by jugful, and then lug it downstairs again. Only those who had had to do such things knew how tiring that job was.

Annie was jerked out of her reverie by Tom. "What?"

"I said, there you are. What do you want done next?"

"I think that's all I need your help for. I can do the rest myself, thank you. Oh, no, what am I thinking about – will you hang the pictures up for me? I've bought some chains and hooks, but the picture rail is too high for me, even when I stand on a chair. You're a few inches taller, so you might just manage it."

"Or I might go and fetch my step-ladders and use them. How many times must I tell you that standing on chairs is dangerous, especially such flimsy chairs as these?"

Pictures in a shop, he thought, as he positioned the wooden steps. What next? Funny pictures they were, too! Some weren't bad, the ones of the moors and the Lake District. But others were of foreign places. You could tell that at a glance. The colours in them were too bright, as if the sun was too hot to go out in. Surely it couldn't really be that hot? Funny thing, that was, Miss Kenderby letting Annie have her pictures to sell. Annie said the parson had kicked up a real fuss about it, saying it was a vulgar thing to do, but for once his daughter had stood up to him. Funny about that visit to London, too. You never knew what their Annie would think of next. And she'd been as thick as thieves with the parson's daughter ever since they got back, in spite of their religious differences.

"There. How's that?" he said aloud, adjusting the first picture to hang straight.

It was Mark who answered. "It's beautiful!" he said, in tones of surprise. "It looks messy when you get close, but it looks beautiful from here."

Tom walked across to stand next to them. "Well, it looks better from further away, I'll grant you, but I still wouldn't call it beautiful. An' the colours are funny. They don't look real." He kept up a running commentary on the pictures all the time he was hanging them, most of it uncomplimentary.

Annie was glad when Tom and Mark left and she could

have the place to herself to gloat over. She adjusted the chairs into groups around the two low tables that had come from Pauline's attic, and which her dad had reglued and polished. Yes, this room was just about ready. Ladies could sit in here and discuss their needs with her, or look at her sketches and materials, or read the latest fashion magazines from London while they drank their tea.

She went across and adjusted the folds of the pale blue velvet curtains which now graced the long narrow windows and which added, she felt, an air of distinction to the room. She had cut them down carefully from some much larger ones Pauline had given her, which had been faded quite badly along the closing edges. They were now as elaborately draped, braided and tasselled as any in a lady's drawing room. She had copied the idea for that from one of Pauline's magazines and had added a touch or two of her own.

There were hours of hard sewing in those curtains alone, but it was worth it. She could have done with some extra help, really, but the women who sewed for her in the Rows were not skilled enough, so she had had to do the fine sewing herself with Kathy's help sometimes on the long straight seams. As if Kathy hadn't enough to do with all of them to look after! It might, Annie decided, be worth getting a woman in for the rough scrubbing and mopping so that Kathy would be free to help her when she needed it. And they would definitely get in a washing woman. But she would still have to find another seamstress, though how she would do that in Bilsden, she did not know.

Walking out into the hallway, Annie peeped into the retiring room and lifted and lowered the water closet seat with a grin. From there she went into the showroom, where a few caps, shawls and mantles were already displayed on stands and bolts of fine muslins and cottons were stacked on the shelves. Ladies could choose material to make their own caps and aprons or they could purchase these articles ready made up. She rather thought when they saw Alice's delightful confections, they would succumb to the temptation of buying them. Maybe Hilda James could take over more of the alterations and leave Alice free to work for the salon.

Another set of shelves held cards of braid, ribbons and lace and packets of embroidery silks, and in front of it was a gleaming mahogany counter. She had stopped worrying about taking Mr Hardy's business away from him since that petition. As far as she was concerned, the more she could do to reduce that man's profits, the better. She had bought most of her bits and pieces in Manchester. No need to pay London prices when a very obliging gentleman, who had a warehouse just off Market Street, was prepared to supply all her needs and deliver them, too.

Annie frowned. She wished Alice could be persuaded to change her mind and live upstairs over the shop, but Alice still insisted that she would hate to live up there and that the quietness would give her the creeps at nights. She'd rather have Salem Street any time and Hilda wasn't a bad old stick once you got used to her finicky ways. Alice was also worried about dealing with the nobs, as she called them, in the salon. She could outhaggle anyone on the market, but she wasn't good at that "fancy talk". She would only let Annie down if she tried. And Annie had to agree with that, however reluctantly.

Annie went upstairs to the big workroom on the first floor. They had not done anything with the other rooms up here yet, or with the commodious attics. That would have to wait. And only one of the cellars had been needed for a storage area. Mr Hallam had certainly provided generous amounts of space when he had these premises constructed. Annie looked round the workroom with pride. "How are things coming on, Alice?"

"Not bad. Look! How d'you like this one?" Alice held out

a froth of white lawn and lace intended to adorn a lady's head indoors. She had a special talent for making caps and other small items and "trimming them up nice".

"That's lovely! Where do you get your ideas from?"

"I dunno. I just fiddle around with 'em till they look nice. An' sometimes the pictures in them magazines give me ideas." Alice couldn't read, and couldn't be bothered to learn, but she would pore over the pictures in the magazines for hours and was almost as well up on the latest fashions as Annie herself.

There was a knock on the front door and Annie, who'd been about to sit down and work on a mantle, sighed in exasperation. "Who can that be? I'm not expecting any more workmen, and anyway, they'd have gone round to the back door. No, I'll go, Alice. I haven't really started yet. You carry on with your sewing."

To Annie's surprise, Mary Benworth was standing on the front steps. She looked so anxious that Annie wondered if anything was wrong at home, but she looked as trim as ever. Mary had excellent taste in clothes.

"I – I'm sorry to disturb you. I know you're not open yet, but – but I wanted to speak to you. I have a – a business proposition that I'd like to discuss with you."

"Well, come in, then. But I must ask you not to tell anyone what it's like inside."

"I won't. I know you want to surprise everyone in the town."

Annie led the way down the hallway to the fitting room at the back where there was the least to see and talk about.

Mary was twisting her hands together. "I – I don't know how to start. It's – Annie, are you intending to take on any apprentices here?"

"Apprentices? Well, yes. Eventually, anyway. But I must see how things go first." Comprehension dawned. "Oh, you have a niece – or a young relative, perhaps?"

"No."

"Then what . . ."

"Annie, you know how we're situated, Father and I. I don't suppose I shall ever marry – I don't seem to – well, I shan't, that's all. But if anything happens to Father, I don't know what I shall do, how I shall support myself. My sister or my brothers would give me a home, but they've all got young families – and anyway, I'd hate being the poor relation. But what else is there? I wouldn't like to go into service – and besides, I have no experience, no references. And I'm not well enough educated to become a governess or genteel enough to be a lady's companion."

She paused, and admitted with difficulty, "I've been worrying about it for a while. Father says I'm foolish and he's nowhere near his grave yet, but, well, he's always been an optimistic sort of person. I'm not. But what can I do? The money he earns – it's his to spend, after all. Why should he save it if he doesn't want to? But I still worry. I worry more as each year passes. Does that sound foolish to you?"

"Not at all. I'd be worrying, too, in your place."

Mary sighed in relief. "So I've decided that I must prepare myself now, perhaps learn a trade." She leaned forward, desperation in her face. "Annie, would you consider taking me on as an apprentice? I know I'm far too old, but I am good with my needle – my aunt was a seamstress and she taught me a lot – and I wouldn't care how hard I worked, what I had to do. I'll sweep your workroom floor happily, believe me, if only you'll give me employment and train me properly!"

Annie sat there stunned. Mary Benworth wanting to work for her! How things were changing. But what the other woman had said made very good sense. Life was hard on unmarried females. Who should know that better than Annie herself?

"I – I'm sorry," Mary faltered, tears brimming in her eyes. "I hope I haven't offended you. I thought – here was my chance, so I thought I'd just speak to you. But if it's not . . ." She jerked to her feet.

"No, don't go! You haven't offended me," Annie said hurriedly. "It's just – you've taken me by surprise. I was trying to think it through. Please sit down again."

Hope flared in Mary's eyes and she sniffed away the tears. "If it's the premium, I have a little money put by. I can pay for my training."

It hurt Annie to see how desperate Mary was. "Never mind that for the moment," she said gently. "Tell me about your sewing. You must like it, to want to make it your life."

"Well, I do like sewing and – I think I'm quite good at it. My aunt always said so, anyway. I make all my own clothes, of course, and Father's shirts. And I'm quite good at embroidery. I've brought some things to show you." She reached for her basket.

"Let me see." Annie examined the garments carefully. They were exquisite. She'd never realised that Mary Benworth had such an eye for beauty or such skill with her needle. And the embroidery was a delight, delicate flower traceries in softly blending hues.

"You couldn't be classed as a beginner, could you? Apprentices usually do the straight seams and the oversewing. You're way beyond that stage. How would you feel about doing such boring work, dusting the furniture, and so on?"

"I'd do anything!"

"Well, I couldn't take you on as a beginning apprentice . . ." Mary's face fell.

" . . . but I could offer you a job." Annie had another of her inspirations. "I haven't much money to spare, but I could pay you a little – and give you free accommodation for yourself and your father up on the top floor here. He doesn't seem to like the house you're in from what he says when he comes round to look after the garden."

Mary gulped and more tears came into her eyes. "Annie, do you really mean that?"

"Of course – and though this house doesn't have a large garden, it does have some land behind it, though it's all in a terrible mess. Your father might be happier here than in your present house."

Mary could not speak, only brush the tears from her cheeks and gulp back the sobs.

"Mind you," Annie warned her, smoothing her skirt unnecessarily to give Mary time to pull herself together, "I shall expect you to do anything that's needed, including dusting the furniture or – or cleaning out the retiring room. I've no time for finicky ways. We're here to make money and to do that we must all work hard."

"I'll do anything you ask gladly. When do I start?"

"You haven't asked about wages yet. That's not very businesslike."

Mary took a deep breath, fumbled for her handkerchief and blew her nose hard. "I'm overwhelmed. I hadn't expected to be successful." She managed a watery smile. "How much are the wages, Annie?"

"Five shillings a week, with the rooms in the attic rent-free. It's all I can afford. I'm stretching myself to the limit setting this place up." Annie smiled. "But if things go well and your skills develop, I shall pay you more later. Only – will your father agree? Did you tell him what you were going to do?"

Mary shook her head. "No. I said nothing. And he'll probably be furious with me at first. But," a twinkle came into her eyes, "I can get angry too. I have my moments. He'll come round in a day or two. He always does. And the garden will help persuade him." She frowned. "I shan't tell him that the accommodation is rent-free, if you don't mind. He'll only spend the extra money he has left from his wages. I'll put it in the new savings bank instead. We might need it one day."

When Annie heard her say this, she realised that Mary was a woman after her own heart and she could not resist giving her a hug. "I think Providence sent you to me. I need another hand." So, she thought, there it is. I'm all set up and ready to go.

Ten

AUGUST TO SEPTEMBER 1845

Annie had intended to open her salon some time in August, but it took longer than she had anticipated to create a selection of items and design sketches to tempt the first customers, as well as to create the stock of smaller articles, such as lacy caps for indoor wear. She, Alice and Mary settled down to a veritable orgy of sewing.

Rebecca, who loved Annie's fancy clothes, found many excuses to visit the salon and help out and within a short time, the child had managed to make herself indispensable to them. After a week or two of observing how her sister shaped, Annie took Rebecca aside and asked if she would like to be apprenticed properly.

"I don't rightly understand what that means, our Annie."

"It means you'll work for me for a number of years and I'll undertake to train you in the dressmaking trade. After that, you can always earn your own living, whatever happens to you."

"I'd like that. I like sewing and fancy things," the child said simply.

Annie approached her father with the offer. "She's a good little worker, Dad, and it'll give her a trade."

"Don't the parents usually pay for their children to become apprentices?" he asked.

"It's likely I'd charge my own sister, isn't it?"

"I don't like to take advantage," he insisted.

"Who's taking advantage of whom?" she retorted. "Look at all the things you've done for me, and you've refused to take a penny for that. How much would I have had to spend if you hadn't been there to repair the furniture?"

His face cleared. "Aye. Well, we'll call it quits then." Almost hesitantly he put an arm round her and gave her a gentle hug. "Eh, lass, what you've done for us!"

"Eh, Dad," she teased, "it's my pleasure."

So Rebecca joined her sister in the salon, proud of her new status as apprentice, not to mention the neat dark dresses and frilly white aprons her sister made up for her. She worked willingly at anything and everything and the only one to regret her new status was Joan, who snivelled miserably when Rebecca left for work the first few days, until she, too, made herself a place in the family, this time as Kathy's helper.

After all that had been settled, the hard work started. Mourning gowns were half made up and tacked together ready for fitting, as Annie had seen done in the mourning warehouses in London. You could always count on sales of mourning. It was late August before she felt ready to open her salon, nearly two months of buying stock and sewing, and three months of not earning any money, except the trifling amounts brought in by the second-hand trade. That was less now that she was not taking a personal interest and Alice was spending so much time in the salon, but Hilda had not done too badly as Alice's deputy, all things considered.

Annie woke up sometimes in the night worrying about the

risks she was taking, but she was now so far along the track that there was no turning back.

When everything was nearly ready, a discreet notice appeared in the recently established *Bilsden Gazette*.

GRAND OPENING

BILSDEN LADIES' SALON

Mrs Ashworth wishes to announce the opening of her Ladies' Salon on the second Monday in September. She will be happy to welcome customers, both old and new, to her spacious premises at Number Twenty-Four High Street. Day and evening dresses, mantlets and other garments will be designed to suit the individual and are guaranteed to enhance feminine charms as well as accord with the very latest London and Paris fashions. A selection of tempting new designs has been sketched for perusal and the most recent ladies' fashion journals can be studied in the salon.

Mrs Ashworth is also able to supply at short notice mourning wear of all descriptions, as well as lingerie, outerwear and a wide range of fashionable accessories, including caps for indoor wear. Ladies are invited to visit the salon and examine her wares at their convenience and leisure, with no obligation to purchase.

Light refreshments will be served free of charge this week to celebrate the opening of the salon, and a retiring room is available for the convenience of lady clients. From then onwards, a small charge will be made to cover the cost of refreshments.

The notice gave the ladies of the district cause for endless speculation over their tea cups. Should they patronise the Ladies' Salon or not? Would a Bilsden dressmaker really understand the latest fashions? What did Mrs Ashworth mean by a retiring room?

Annie would have been astonished if she had known how

hard her friends were working to prepare the way, because they knew how dubious the ladies of Bilsden were about a home-produced modiste. Some people were only too ready to remember that Mrs Ashworth had once lived in the Rows and Mr Hardy was not slow to remind anyone he could of this.

On the other hand, Pauline Hinchcliffe was a tireless advocate for the Ladies' Salon, and she made no bones about her admiration for Annie's skill and her friendship with Mrs Ashworth. She wore another new dress, this time in lavender and white, to a dinner party and astonished both her husband and the other guests by her elegance. When asked where she had purchased such a fashionable creation, she looked surprised and said, "From Mrs Ashworth, of course! Where else can one get a stylish gown made up in Bilsden?" This gave several ladies cause for thought, because for years Mrs Hinchcliffe had dressed dowdily, and she was now setting the style with a vengeance. Could Mrs Ashworth really make that much difference to someone?

Helen Kenderby created an equal sensation when she appeared in church wearing a gown of dark blue shot silk, worn over one of the new horsehair petticoats called crinolines which gave it a fashionable bell shape. With it, she wore the shawl she had purchased in London and a fetching bonnet trimmed with silk flowers, lace and ribbons.

Even her father noticed the dress and was in two minds as to whether he should forbid its wearing. He could not quite formulate a reason for his aversion to the gown, for there was nothing he could point a finger at. The neckline was high enough to satisfy the greatest stickler, the trimmings were moderate, and yet somehow, his daughter looked – well, desirable. Dammit, what was there about the dress?

"Do you like it, Papa?" asked Helen.

"No!"

"Why not?"

"It's not suited to a parson's daughter, that's why not! Draws attention to your – ahem – to your figure. Immodest! Better go and change it."

She smiled. "No, I don't think so. I like it."

He breathed deeply for a moment or two, outraged at her recent displays of independence, then bethought himself of the way she looked after her mother and managed his household. If she left home now to live with his sister Isabel, as she had threatened a time or two, he would have to hire a housekeeper. Even he had admitted now that his wife was not feigning her ill-health. She had lost a lot of weight recently and grown very yellow in complexion. "Well, it's you who has to wear it, Helen, but I tell you again, it don't suit a parson's daughter, don't suit at all!"

She just kept on smiling. She knew beyond all doubt that it suited her more than anything she had ever worn before. Her friend Annie had a magic touch. Just to wear the outfit made her feel good.

After those two appearances, several women determined to try Mrs Ashworth at least once. If she could make such a difference to Helen Kenderby whom they had previously considered faded and dowdy, not to mention a trifle odd and arty, well, what might she not do for them?

Frederick Hallam was less vocal in Annie's support, knowing that any interest he showed in her would be misconstrued, but he managed to drop a few remarks as to her impeccable respectability, whether she came from the Rows or not. He had checked on that before granting her a tenancy in the High Street, he insisted, when people hinted at their doubts. He also made known his intention of asking her to make for his daughter. In addition, he sent a message to those of his tenants who had signed the petition against Annie, and who were still trying to blacken her name, to the effect that anyone spreading calumny about Mrs Ashworth would be in danger of losing his own tenancy. This made even Cyril Hardy caution his shrewish wife to hold her tongue.

The night before the opening, Annie hardly slept. Her confidence was at its lowest ebb. What if she failed? What if no one liked her gowns? Think of all the stock she'd bought! She'd even taken on extra help and the Benworths would be moving into the attics as soon as their tenancy of the house in Church Lane expired. She must be mad! She should have started in a more modest way, not taken such huge risks.

She forced herself to lie in bed till half past five, then she could bear it no longer. She got up and began to dress in her rustling petticoats and one of the bulky crinolines that she had purchased in Manchester. Then she laid out on the bed her new dark green taffeta gown which no one except Alice, Mary and her family had yet seen. She knew she looked both stylish and elegant in it, and it brought out the golden highlights in her auburn hair.

There was a tap on her bedroom door and Kathy tiptoed in. "I've just got your dad off to work an' I've brought you up a cup of tea. Do you want me to do your hair before or after breakfast?"

"I don't want any breakfast, thank you. I couldn't eat a thing!"

"Well, you'll have to try. I'm not lettin' you face today on an empty stomach, and that's flat, Annie Ashworth!"

"Oh, Kathy, I can't eat anything! What if . . ." Annie buried her face in her hands. "I'm terrified!" she whispered. "What have I done? All that money! Kathy, what *have* I done?"

Kathy hugged her. "What you've done is start a successful new business, that's what you've done! Put your wrapper on an' come down for some breakfast, then I'll do your hair afterwards. The dress is beautiful an' so are you."

As they were sitting together in the kitchen, William tiptoed in. "I heard you getting up, Mother." He came and put his arms round her, smacking a hearty kiss on her cheek. "I thought I'd walk across to the shop with you and stay there till it's time for school, if that's all right. I might be able to help a bit." He had boundless faith in his own ability to help people, and it was sometimes difficult to find him enough jobs within a seven-year-old's scope. He hugged her roughly, loosening the knot of hair at the nape of her neck so that the shining newly washed mass tumbled down her back. "Would you like me to come with you?" he asked. "You would, wouldn't you?"

"Good job we didn't do your hair, Annie," said Kathy. "Leave your mam alone, William, do! She's got a lot on her mind."

William looked so hurt that Annie said hastily, "I'd like it very much if you came with me, William, if you're sure you don't mind setting off earlier than usual."

He beamed at her. How tall he was growing! He would soon be eight years old. How could that be possible? She was so proud of her son! There seemed to be no trace of his father in him, unless it was in his height and sturdiness. And that she did not mind. It would not do for a man to be as short as she was.

"I'll bring some more scones and shortbread across to the shop later," said Kathy. "I've got everything ready to bake. Rebecca knows how to set the tea-trays up for you." She had insisted on providing the food for the first week, though if the refreshment service seemed popular, Annie had decided to come to some arrangement with the baker a few doors away.

When Annie went upstairs after breakfast to finish dressing, the other children were stirring and Tom was just emerging from his bedroom. He grinned at her. "Nervous?"

She could only nod.

"You ought to go out like that," he teased. "Set a new fashion in hairstyles." If some of the men he knew could see her now, they'd be queuing up at the door to pester her. Usually, she was turned out in a refined standoffish sort of way, but with her hair like that and her face flushed with nervous excitement, she looked luscious.

In her room, Annie put her new gown on with fingers that had a tendency to tremble, then she twisted to and fro in front of the mirror, to check for the umpteenth time that the dress sat well. Kathy came in and helped to put her hair up, fussing to get the centre parting just so, then massing Annie's long, wavy hair in a low chignon looped with two thin plaits on each side. She insisted on softening the severity of the high white forehead with just a few wisps of fringe before standing back to admire her own work. Finally, she helped set in place one of Alice's small bonnets, a confection in pale fine straw, with a lace-lined underbrim, bunches of artificial flowers and green ribbon bows over each cheek.

"If ladies of fashion have to wear any more petticoats, we shall need help in moving around!" commented Annie when she stood up. "Just feel the weight of this crinoline! It might be the height of fashion, but it's heavy, and these stays are digging into my waist!"

"It's worth it," said Kathy simply, "because you look beautiful, Annie, really beautiful. That full skirt shows off your waist. Tiny waist, you've got. You don't eat nearly enough, though!"

"Your waist is small, too."

"Aye, but I haven't got a figure like yours to go with it. I'm just plain scraggy – scraggy all over." Kathy looked down at her angular figure disparagingly, then shrugged away her envy. "Come on, love!" She opened the bedroom door. "Good thing it's a fine day for the opening, isn't it?"

William came clattering out of the boys' bedroom, then stopped dead. "Mother! You look – you look – you don't look like a mother!" The other boys and Joan crowded out of their rooms in their nightclothes to look at their sister and echo his compliments.

Rebecca, dressed in her own new clothes, had to come and touch the lustrous material of Annie's skirt and stroke the ribbons on the bonnet. "I want one just like it when I grow up!" she breathed.

The wholehearted admiration of her family helped a little, but Annie could still feel her stomach churning with nervousness as she began to walk down the hill towards the High Street with William bounding along on one side and Rebecca walking more sedately on the other. The few people she met hurrying to their own work stared at her, for such wide skirts were not very common in Bilsden, nor were ladies of fashion usually out so early in the day.

Once at the salon, Annie was able to don an apron and submerge herself in last-minute dusting and unnecessary rearranging. Alice came downstairs to say that they had plenty to do in the workshop and Annie was not to worry about them. Mary, dressed very smartly in navy and white in a style which lent dignity to her tall mature figure, reported that the kitchen was ready to provide refreshments. Rebecca scurried to and fro on little errands, while William followed his mother round, pushing and pulling chairs into fractionally different arrangements at her behest.

When her son left for school, Annie stood for a moment at the front door watching him march down the street. She spent a few moments alone in the retiring room, trying to calm herself down, then she went up quite unnecessarily to see that all was well in the workroom. Afterwards she took off her pinafore and wandered round the empty rooms, too tense to settle to any work, too nervous now to do anything but pray that her venture might be a success.

At nine o'clock Annie ceremonially opened and closed the outer door, setting the new brass bell above it jangling. She then placed the new white card saying OPEN in its brass slot behind the glass of the door where it would be seen from outside, before settling down in the main room with some sewing to wait for her first customer. By nine thirty, she was sure that no one would ever patronise her salon, and was too miserable even to rethread her needle. Mary came down to fuss around her once or twice, but mostly the others left her alone. They had done all they could to help. Now, the only thing they could do was wait.

Just before ten, a carriage drew up in the street outside. Annie jumped up and peered through the window, expecting to see Pauline Hinchcliffe who had promised to visit her on the first day, but it was a different carriage and it was Frederick Hallam who got out. He turned to assist a young lady, presumably his daughter, and an older lady who must be her companion. As the doorbell clanged, Annie drew a deep breath and moved out into the hallway to greet them.

"Good morning, Mr Hallam."

"Good morning, Mrs Ashworth. May I present my daughter, Beatrice, and my cousin, Eleanor."

The young woman nodded briefly with a patronising air as if doing Annie an enormous favour by even visiting her salon, and the other woman was just as curt. Beatrice Hallam was rather heavily built for a young woman of only twenty and had a pale complexion and dark hair peeping from underneath a fussy and unflattering bonnet. Her dress emphasised both her pallor and her plumpness, though it was made of the finest materials and its skirts were full enough to be in the very latest fashion.

"Do you require something specific today, Miss Hallam, or would you just like to look round?"

"It's as Papa wishes. He *would* come here this morning!" was the petulant response.

Annie raised an eyebrow at Mr Hallam.

"I'd like to look round now that you've got everything finished," he said. "As landlord, I can't help taking an interest."

Annie saw that he was looking at her, not his daughter. She could see the admiration in his eyes, though in no sense was he trying to flirt with her. Why was she always so conscious of him as a man?

He smiled. "Never mind Beatrice here. She's convinced that she can't get anything fashionable outside London. But I told her it wouldn't hurt to have a look at what you can offer, so here we are."

His daughter glared at him and flushed an unbecoming shade of red.

"I think you will find that I'm abreast of the latest fashions, Miss Hallam," said Annie, every bit as haughtily as the girl.

"I bought this dress in London." Beatrice smoothed it with loving fingertips.

"Did you?"

"Yes. It's the latest fashion, even if it is black."

"You must miss your mother. Do you intend to keep on wearing full mourning?" She looked over Beatrice's head to Frederick Hallam.

"I don't like to see her dressed like a crow, and what's more, black doesn't suit her."

"I could not possibly consider coming out of mourning so soon!" said Beatrice, her voice sounding tearful. The cousin had not said a word and seemed, from the glances she threw sideways at him, to be in considerable awe of Frederick.

"Naturally, you will wish to show respect for your mother's memory. But have you thought of a soft grey or even a lilac, with black ribbons or braid? For a young girl like yourself, that might be considered quite permissible now. After all, it's several months since Mrs Hallam died, is it not?"

"Do you have some materials you could show us?" Frederick Hallam asked at once. "That sounds much more the thing."

"Of course. But none of the designs I have sketched would suit your daughter, I'm afraid. I would prefer to design something specially for her. Something that draws attention to her pretty hands, possibly."

Miss Hallam's mouth dropped open in shock and she stared down at her hands as if she had never seen them before.

Annie led the way into the main room at the front. "This is the salon itself, Miss Hallam. Here, ladies may peruse the latest fashion journals, consult me about their needs and inspect my sketches. Refreshments are also available at a small charge. In the room across the corridor, we have some smaller articles for sale." She watched the amazement on their faces as all three of them stared round the main room.

"I like the curtains," said Frederick after a moment, seeing that his daughter and cousin were not going to speak. "Where did you get 'em from?"

"I made them myself, Mr Hallam. Such draperies are very popular nowadays among people of taste." She did not say that she had fashioned them from some old curtains given to her by Pauline, or that they were not wide enough to close.

"And the paintings? Nice touch, those." He strode over to stare at a particularly bright canvas, retreated a few steps and remained there, eyeing it. "I like 'em."

"They're Miss Kenderby's work."

"The parson's daughter?" He could not hide his surprise.

"Yes. That one's of France. The one over there is of Italy."

"Are they for sale?"

"Of course. That's why they're here. I'm acting as her, um, agent."

He nodded. "And, of course, you get free use of them in the meantime as well as a commission for selling, no doubt?"

She inclined her head in agreement.

"You're a damned good businesswoman, Mrs Ashworth. I'm pleased to have you as a tenant. How much for that Italian one?"

"Ten guineas," said Annie without hesitation, though Helen had suggested, with great diffidence, only three.

"Ten guineas! For a small painting like that, and painted by an unknown woman!"

"It's the skill you're paying for, not the size, and whether the artist is female or not is quite irrelevant," Annie said in her best Pauline Hinchcliffe tone of voice.

"That sort of painting is not fashionable," pronounced Beatrice. "And I think these are crudely done! Really, Papa, what can you be thinking of?"

Her father bristled. "Fashionable, be damned! I like 'em. And I don't like the things your mother chose. It puts me off my tea staring at dead birds and fish. I'll take the Italian one, Mrs Ashworth."

"Certainly. Shall I send it over, or will you take it with you now?" Annie felt breathless. Who'd have believed that her first sale would be one of Helen Kenderby's paintings. Ten per cent commission, they had agreed upon, though Helen had obviously not thought a sale likely. So that made a guinea earned, just like that! It was a good omen.

"I'll take it with me. Shall I reach it down for you?"

"Yes, please. Rebecca!"

Rebecca appeared promptly in the doorway. "Yes, ma'am?" It had taken several days of giggling for her to learn to address their Annie as "ma'am".

"Please fetch down the painting that's on the rear wall in the workroom. Mr Hallam has just purchased this one."

"Yes, ma'am." Rebecca raced upstairs to announce the sale to Alice and Mary in a breathless voice and then carry the painting carefully down the stairs.

Hallam was over by the window now, fingering the blue velvet curtains and the matching braid edging. "And I'd like some of those fancy curtains made, too. Our sitting room's a miserable place and it's got so many patterns in it that your eyes get tired looking at it. I think I'll have the walls painted in a pale colour like yours."

Annie couldn't help showing her surprise. "Curtains?"

"Yes. It'll cheer the place up a bit. You are prepared to make curtains for people as well as dresses, aren't you?"

Why not? Money was money, and it was about time she started earning some. "Certainly, Mr Hallam, but I shall have to come and see the room first. I shall not only need to measure for the curtains, but I shall need to design the top draping to match the proportions of the rest of the room." Helen's lessons had not only given her a knowledge of art, but an understanding of perspective and shape, and a new vocabulary, too.

"I'll send my carriage to fetch you when convenient."

"Next week, if you don't mind, Mr Hallam. As you can appreciate, I'd prefer to supervise the salon myself for the first few days, but any time next week will be fine."

"I'll check when Beatrice is free, then let you know."

She looked at him gratefully, her eyes softening imperceptibly at this sign of his care for her reputation.

He smiled back warmly, but still with that hint of mischief.

Beatrice was staring at her father, open-mouthed. "But, Father, you . . ."

His expression lost its warmth. "You've been pestering me to smarten up the house, haven't you? Well, I've bought a new painting and I've ordered some curtains. You're surely not going to grumble at that, are you?"

The companion tugged at Beatrice's arm, but was shaken off.

"But, Father, I wanted to do it like Mildred's!"

He scowled at her. "And I said I wasn't having that! Mildred's taste is as bad as your mother's was. The one who pays the piper calls the tune, and don't you forget that, my girl!"

Tactfully, Annie moved away to allow them to argue in a semblance of privacy.

Beatrice had flushed scarlet and tears of humiliation stood

out in her eyes. Annie's initial resentment at the girl's air of would-be superiority ebbed away. She was only a silly young thing, after all, trying to seem sophisticated, and her father shouldn't berate her in public. After watching them for a minute or two, Annie could not keep quiet any longer.

"Excuse me interrupting, Mr Hallam, but if you give your daughter no chance to practise, how is she to develop her taste? I should prefer to discuss my ideas for your room with Miss Hallam as well as yourself because she will also have to live with the results. As well as discussing my ideas for her gowns, that is."

He grinned at her unrepentantly. "Very tactful!"

She frowned at him. What on earth had put him in such a mood?

He patted his daughter's shoulder. "All right, then, Beatrice. You can help me to choose. But I'm not having dark wallpaper like Mildred's got – Mildred's my eldest, Mrs Ashworth. Stripes, it is, her wallpaper. Makes your eyes go funny. And lozenges all over the walls in the hallway. I can't abide patterns like that!"

Annie felt a wild desire to laugh. Suddenly, Frederick Hallam seemed as human as her brother Tom, as exasperated by his daughter as any other man, and as stubbornly tactless as her own father could be at times. She felt it wise to change the subject. "Please sit down, Miss Hallam and – er—?"

"My cousin's name is Ramsby."

"Miss Ramsby. As you're my very first customers, please let me offer you some refreshments, and afterwards, perhaps you ladies would do me the honour of visiting the retiring room and giving me your opinion of the facilities offered." She saw the two women relax and continued smoothly, "I have here some sketches of my latest designs which you may find of interest, though I still feel I would rather design something different for Miss Hallam. I also have some dresses partly made up and ready for fitting, plus a full range of mourning apparel."

"I don't believe in staying in mourning for ever!" announced Frederick. "At least, not for two years, like my daughter is talking about. I won't have Beatrice drooping around the house in black. She's too young. And as I said, it doesn't suit her. And, what's more, that thing she's wearing has got too many frills on it. That's what comes of letting her visit her sister and buy a few things in London. None of the women in my family has any taste."

After this masterful discourse, Beatrice was once again scarlet with both embarrassment and resentment, and Annie couldn't help stepping in again. "And yet," she said thoughtfully, "this dress could be very pretty. It's just that – as you so rightly pointed out, Mr Hallam – it has too many frills. And it needs, well, turning into a style more suitable for a young lady."

"It was from one of the best modistes," said Beatrice resentfully, by no means convinced. She stroked the skirt again. The dress clearly meant a lot to her.

"I can tell that," agreed Annie. "But haven't you noticed, Miss Hallam, that strangers will not always know what's best for a client they've never seen before. And I daresay you wanted your dresses made up quickly and couldn't spare the time for too many fittings?"

"How did you know?"

"Oh, because dressmaking is my trade, and because this one is very nearly right, which proves that your taste is developing quite well, whatever your father says."

Hallam's eyes were dancing with laughter as he watched her tactics and Annie had to look away or she'd have burst out laughing.

"Can you alter that dress as well, then?" he asked. "It'd be a pity to throw it away after all the money I paid for the thing. The more I see of those London dresses, the less I like them."

He looked approvingly at Annie's own dress. "Now the one you're wearing is perfect, to my mind."

Beatrice and Miss Ramsby turned to stare at Annie's dress and although their expressions of approval were reluctant, they both nodded in agreement.

Alterations, thought Annie. Am I never to get away from alterations? Aloud she said smoothly, "Of course I can refashion the dress. Miss Hallam and I will discuss the matter when I come over to measure for the curtains, and if she wishes me to look at any other dresses for her, she can tell me then. Now, let me show you our stock, Miss Hallam, Miss Ramsby, and then Rebecca shall bring us a tea-tray."

After they had all taken tea together, Annie suggested that the two ladies inspect the retiring room.

"I'd like to see it, too," said Frederick Hallam promptly.

"Just a peep, then, and only because you're my landlord. It's not meant for gentlemen."

But being Frederick Hallam, he had more than a peep, flushing the toilet, sniffing the scented soap and running the tap. "You're a dangerously clever woman," he said, as he came out again. "I'm just beginning to realise how clever!"

His cousin, who had not opened her mouth, looked puzzled and slightly alarmed at this twist in the conversation and stared at Annie as if she had two heads.

"Let's hope I succeed, then," said Annie, feeling her confidence rising, "or I'll not be able to pay my rent."

"I've got no worries about that. None at all."

Just as the Hallams were leaving, Pauline Hinchcliffe swept through the front door. "Frederick! Trust you to get here before me! How do you do, Beatrice, Miss Ramsby."

Beatrice, clearly in awe of Pauline, bobbed a schoolgirl's curtsey, and Miss Ramsby nodded and smiled, then retreated to the background.

Pauline turned to Annie. "Well, Mrs Ashworth, you must

show me round. I'm longing to see the finished product. But what's that picture standing there for? It spoils the look of the hallway!"

"Mr Hallam has just bought it."

"Good heavens! I didn't know you went in for art, Frederick."

"I don't. As you well know. Can't stand those sentimental things they're all buying. Who wants women weeping out farewells to their lovers all over the wall? *A Mothers' Tears*! *Lost in the Forest*! That's the sort of thing my wife used to buy. Or pictures of dead birds. Pshaw! Load of rubbish! A man doesn't want to feel sad in his own parlour. But this painting is cheerful. You can almost feel the warmth of that sun. It's done by Kenderby's daughter, too. Didn't think she had it in her!"

"Nor did I. Does her father know she's got her paintings up for sale, Mrs Ashworth?" Pauline asked.

"I couldn't say, Mrs Hinchcliffe." Annie had no intention of revealing that the parson did know, and that he disapproved strongly.

When the Hallams had gone, Annie sighed in relief.

Pauline smiled at her. "Difficult, was he?"

"Very! Does he always treat his daughter like that?"

"Yes. He says he's trying to jolly her along. She needs it, too. She's a drooping sort of girl, and when she's not drooping, she's sulking about something. Christine spoiled her. Frederick will never find her a husband unless he furnishes her with a very large dowry."

"He sounded more like he was bullying her than jollying her along. I felt quite sorry for the poor girl."

"Sorry for Beatrice? Don't waste your pity, Annie. She's a spiteful young madam once she's out of her father's sight."

Pauline wandered round the salon, but it was clear that she was not really interested in the things she saw, except to comment on the displays. "I didn't come in to buy anything this time, Annie; I just thought it'd do you good if I was seen to come in. Did Hallam order a dress for that pudding of a girl?"

"No, though he wanted me to alter the one she was wearing. But, Pauline, I was so amazed. He wants me to make him some curtains like the ones in my salon here."

Pauline burst out laughing. "So you've sold a painting and taken an order for some curtains. Fine way to open a modiste's salon, I must say!"

Annie chuckled. "Never mind! It's all money earned. Would you like a cup of tea, Pauline?"

"I should love one. And I'll use your little room, too. That's going to be very convenient when I'm in town."

"Mr Hallam approved of the idea, too. He said I was a dangerously clever woman."

"You are. That's why I like you."

Eleven

PARK HOUSE: AUTUMN 1845

By September Dr Lewis's residence, Park House, had settled down into a new routine. Ellie proved to be a very efficient housekeeper and without offending Mrs Cosden, she introduced a series of minor changes which made life more comfortable for all the servants. Having been a housemaid herself, Ellie saw no reason to make the lives of the girls working at Park House a misery or to fine them, as Mrs Lewis had done, for the sorts of breakages which were inevitable in any household.

The only sour note in all this was supplied by Mabel. Since her former mistress's departure, which had ended her dreams of one day becoming a lady's maid, Mabel had alternated between misery and spitefulness, doing her work sloppily and almost daring Ellie, who was ten years younger, to challenge her about it.

The first crisis came one day early in September when the sun was shining outside and a light breeze was riffling the leaves of the trees in the park and blowing around those which had already fallen to the ground. Ruth, the young general maid, had been helping Mabel to turn out Mrs Lewis's old bedroom, which Marianne had decided to move into. Ellie, who was passing in the corridor, heard a sharp slap and a cry of pain, and stopped to listen.

"Clumsy little bitch! You drop anything else and I'll give you what for."

"It was an accident."

Mabel's voice was low and vicious. "You're not paid to have accidents."

"Ow! Mabel, don't."

Ellie pushed open the door. "Is something wrong?"

Mabel scowled at her. "No. Why should there be?"

Ruth sniffed and wiped away a tear. There were red marks on both her cheeks.

"Why are you crying, Ruth?"

"N-nothing, Miss Peters." Ellie refused to use the customary housekeeper's title of Mrs, which seemed plain silly to her, when everyone knew perfectly well that she wasn't married.

"Go and wash your face, Ruth, and then wait in the kitchen until I ring."

With a scared look at Mabel, Ruth slipped out of the door.

Ellie moved across to the bed, her heart thumping in her chest. She knew that if she backed away from this confrontation, the other woman would continue to take advantage of her. She took a deep breath. "Mabel, we can't go on like this."

"What do you mean 'like this'?" Mabel's tone stopped just short of being a jeer, but it was definitely impertinent.

Anger began to rise in Ellie, and that was a rare thing for her, but she hated to see any creature ill-treated, and the memory of Ruth's tear-stained face and reddened cheeks was still upsetting her. "You know exactly what I mean, Mabel."

Mabel glared at her, then, as Ellie stared steadily back, her eyes shifted away and she huffed one shoulder. "No, I don't know."

"I'll explain it to you, then. I mean that you're making poor Ruth's life a misery."

"Someone has to train her properly. You've been letting her get away with murder since Mrs Lewis left."

"Ruth knows her job and does it to my satisfaction."

"Mrs Lewis wouldn't have thought so."

"Mrs Lewis has gone and she won't be back."

"Oh, yes, she will. She's clever enough to find a way to get round the doctor. *Then* you'll not be able to lord it over everyone like this. In fact, I daresay she'll sack you, just like she sacked your friend Annie. She wouldn't have someone like *you* for housekeeper. She knows better."

Ellie prayed for patience. "You're mistaken, Mabel. Mrs Lewis isn't coming back. Her health is better when she lives near the sea, and that's why she was so sharp-tempered here sometimes. The Bilsden air did not agree with her. She and the doctor have decided that it's better if she stays in Brighton from now on. So Ruth's work is, and will remain, my concern. I'm well satisfied with her. She's a nice, willing girl and I won't have her slapped like that. It's your work I'm not satisfied with lately, Mabel, not satisfied at all." She took another deep breath, "If you value your place here, you'll stop being so spiteful to Ruth and pull yourself together."

"Or what?"

"Or I shall recommend that Dr Lewis dismiss you."

Mabel stared scornfully at her. "You wouldn't dare! And he wouldn't do it, anyway."

"As housekeeper, I'll do whatever's necessary." Ellie's voice became softer and took on a coaxing tone. "Look, Mabel, we all have to live here and I intend to make our lives as pleasant as possible – which includes poor Ruth." Her heart sank when she saw that this plea had made no impression and that Mabel was still looking at her in a scornful sneering way, so she added sharply, "And Dr Lewis would certainly dismiss you if I recommended it. So think over what I've said to you and leave that poor young girl in peace."

Two days later, Mrs Cosden found Ruth crying bitterly in the broom cupboard with a red mark on one cheek. She shook her head over Mabel's stupidity and summoned Ellie. "I thought you should see this, love."

Ruth sobbed and tried to bury her face in her hands. Ellie lifted those hands gently away and sucked in her breath at the sight of the bruise already forming. It looked more like the results of a punch than of a slap. "Stay here with Mrs Cosden, Ruth. I shan't let Mabel hit you again." She straightened her shoulders and marched across to the doctor's rooms, relieved that it was not a time when he saw patients. "Could I please speak to you for a moment, sir?"

Jeremy looked up from the medicine he was mixing, then put down the brown glass bottle of liquid. "Trouble, Ellie?"

"Yes, sir."

"Will you finish this for me, Sam? It just needs five ounces of honey syrup adding." Jeremy ushered Ellie into his office, and offered her a chair. "What is it?"

The memory of poor Ruth's face gave Ellie the courage to continue. "Sir, am I giving satisfaction as housekeeper?"

"You know you are, Ellie. The whole house feels happier, except for Mabel. I don't think that poor woman knows how to be happy."

Ellie took a deep breath. "It's about Mabel that I've come, sir. I'm afraid I'll have to recommend that you dismiss her."

"Is she not doing her work properly?"

"Not very well. But it's not only that, sir. It's the way she's taking out her own misery on Ruth. She's been hitting her, slapping the poor girl's face hard enough to leave bruises. This time I think Ruth will have a black eye from it. I've warned Mabel, but well – she's older than me and she remembers me coming to this house as a general maid – in short, sir, she won't accept my authority as housekeeper, and I don't think anything I do is likely to change her."

"Oh, dear." He stood up and turned to look out of the window across the park.

Ellie watched him, thinking, poor man! All Jeremy Lewis asked of the world was to lead a quiet life, enjoy the company of his beloved daughter and get on with his work as a doctor. She knew he was weak – well, you couldn't help but know it, the way Mrs Lewis had got the better of him over the years – but he was also kindly and caring to those around him. "We could give Mabel a reference, sir," she said, trying to make things easier for him, "and let her stay here until she finds a place. There's no need to put her out on the street."

He turned back, a relieved expression on his face. "Yes, we could do it that way, couldn't we? I just – I would hate to put anyone out on the street, Ellie, the way Mrs Lewis used to do. I'd worry about what had happened to them." He ran a hand through his hair, leaving it in a boyish tangle then came back round the desk to pat her arm. "You sort things out as you wish, then."

"Thank you, sir. And – I thought you ought to know. Mabel keeps insisting that Mrs Lewis will come back."

"You and I both know differently. As I've told you already, I shall not allow Mrs Lewis to return to Park House." For once his voice was firm and determined.

"Yes, sir. But I thought it better to tell Mabel that Mrs Lewis is staying on in Brighton for her health's sake. I thought – well, it looks better for Miss Marianne that way, doesn't it?"

"You did exactly the right thing, Ellie." His eyes were warmly approving. "And you'd better see to hiring another maid to replace Mabel, I suppose. Can I leave all that in your hands?"

"Yes, of course, sir." As she stood up, he came round the desk with that quick nervous stride of his and she bumped into him. She felt a tingle run through her body, gasped and tried to take a step backwards, but the desk was in the way and when he tried to move aside, he collided with her again.

For a moment, they stood there staring at each other, then he took her arms, guiding her firmly to one side of him. As he let go of her, the smile faded from his face, to be replaced by a look of puzzlement.

Ellie could not move for a moment. Her breath seemed to pile up in her throat and all she could do was stare at him. He seemed – he seemed younger today. When you worked for someone you grew out of the habit of looking at him as a man, but today, Jeremy Lewis seemed very much a man, and an attractive one, too. She could still feel his touch on her arm, still see the dawning of desire in his eyes. She knew she had not been mistaken about that, any more than she was mistaken about her own feelings for him. She had always thought him a wonderful man, though she had never told anyone how she felt, not even Annie. Well, what was the use?

There was a knock on the door and they both jerked back into their normal roles.

"There's someone here to see you, sir!" called Sam. "There's been an accident and he's bleeding all over the floor. I've put him in the treatment room."

"I'm coming."

It took a huge effort for Ellie to face Mabel. She went to look for the chambermaid herself. She could not, after all, send Ruth or Mrs Cosden to summon her. She found her in Mrs Lewis's old room, just staring out of the window and making no pretence of working.

"You've been hitting Jane again," Ellie began. "After I warned you not to."

Mabel shrugged. "She deserved it. She spilled water all over this carpet. Just feel it for yourself. It's sopping wet."

Ellie sighed. "It's not that, is it, Mabel. You're just not

happy here now. I think it would be better for everyone if you found yourself another place."

Mabel's mouth dropped open in surprise, then she recovered enough to say in a low vicious voice, "*You* can't sack me! I'll go and see Dr Lewis! He won't let you sack me!"

Ellie held the door open. "Go and see him. He'll only say the same thing. I spoke to him about it first and he agreed with me."

Mabel froze in her place, anger slowly giving way to fear. "But – what am I going to do? Where am I going to go?"

"You should have thought of that before."

Anger returned. "You little cow! You've been in his bed, haven't you, like that Annie Gibson? That's why he's doing what you want."

Ellie flushed scarlet and drew herself up to her full five feet six inches. "I certainly haven't! How dare you even suggest such a thing?"

"You must have been! He wouldn't sack me otherwise. I've been here for years, I have, far longer than you. I was a proper chambermaid when you was just a snotty-nosed little mill girl who didn't know a broom from a cobweb brush! I'm going down to see him." She shoved Ellie out of the way and stormed off down the stairs.

Within minutes, Sam had dragged her out of the doctor's rooms and back into the house. As Ellie ran down to investigate the noise, Mabel succumbed to hysterics in the hallway.

Sam rolled his eyes at his daughter and stood back from Mabel's writhing body. "You should've kept her out of the doctor's way, love."

"I couldn't stop her, Dad. She's a big woman and she's stronger than me."

He shook his head. "Just look at her. I think she's gone half out of her mind. Terrible things she's been saying about you."

The blood drained from Ellie's face. "*What?*"

"About you and Dr Lewis. Nay, there's no need to deny it to me. I don't need telling that you wouldn't behave like that, love." As Mabel's hysterics showed no signs of abating, he pulled the shrieking woman to her feet and nodded to Ellie. "We'd better get her to her room. We can't have the patients hearing this. The doctor says he'll come and give her something to make her sleep in a few minutes. She's run down, he says, and depressed."

But Mabel was not too lost in hysterics to flinch from Ellie's hand. "Don't touch me, you sneaky bitch!" She shoved Sam away and staggered up the stairs without anyone's help, still sobbing, but more quietly now.

Ellie followed her up the stairs and watched to see that she went into her own bedroom, then, when the door had slammed shut, she sagged against the wall. "Dear heavens, what next?" she murmured, but it was the doctor's touch she kept remembering and the strange way it had affected her, not Mabel's behaviour. After a minute or two, she straightened her shoulders and went back down to her father.

Sam shook his head. "It's a bad business, this is. There was a woman in with the doctor when that one ran in, and she heard all that Mabel said. I doubt she'll keep it to herself either."

Ellie put her hands up to her flaming cheeks. "Oh, what shall I do? Whatever will people think?"

"The Lord will know the truth, Ellie. You don't need to fear what people say if your conscience is clear." He patted her arm. "Call me if Mabel gives you any more trouble. The doctor shouldn't be very long before he comes to see her."

But Ellie could not help being afraid of what people would say, and the worry of it all disturbed her sleep for several nights. Like Annie before her, she knew the value of a good name.

Mabel found herself a job working for the Hallams two days later, simply by applying to several of the larger houses in town. When Mrs Jarred, the housekeeper there, applied to

Dr Lewis for references, he explained the scope of Mabel's duties, including her years as part-time lady's maid.

Mrs Jarred looked at him, her expression shrewd. "If she is such a good worker, why is she leaving?"

Jeremy sighed. "Well, to speak frankly, she was bitterly disappointed that my wife did not employ her as a lady's maid and has been unhappy in my household for a while. And now that I've appointed Ellie as my housekeeper, that is a further disappointment. I think she'd be much happier for a change."

"I see." Mrs Jarred frowned into space. "Well, as it happens, we need a lady's maid. Miss Beatrice likes to have someone help her with her toilette." She didn't say that the other maids disliked working for the young mistress for whom nothing was ever quite right. "It will depend on Miss Beatrice, naturally, whether she takes to Mabel. But it might be just the thing." She nodded. "I'll take her on. Well-trained maids aren't all that plentiful in Bilsden. Please tell Mabel to be ready with her things this evening."

When he had seen her out, with his usual innate courtesy, Jeremy heaved a sigh of relief.

Mabel left Park House that evening, with a reference and half a year's wages in her pocket, and with hatred burning fiercely in her heart. As she was leaving, she turned to Ellie who was standing silently on the doorstep and said in a low voice, "I'll get my own back, Ellie Peters. You'll see. I always do. Ask your friend Annie about that."

After this, rumours inevitably started to circulate about Jeremy Lewis and his housekeeper. In the end, he decided that the best way to scotch them was to do as he had planned and get a chaperone for Marianne. He also took the opportunity to move his own things to the spare bedroom above his medical rooms. He wanted to put as much distance as possible between himself and Ellie, for propriety's sake.

He knew he was behaving very stiffly with his young housekeeper nowadays, but he couldn't help it. How could people possibly think that he would behave immorally in his own home?

Jeremy's added reserve upset Ellie. He was such a nice man and she had always enjoyed the way he talked to her and teased her. She hoped he did not think she had been trying to throw herself at him. He was a gentleman and would never even look at a woman from the Rows in that way. She knew that. She had always known that. And besides, he was still married, and she was not the sort to become a man's mistress even if that man had haunted her dreams for years, even if his reaction to her in his surgery had shown that he had now become conscious of her as a woman.

It was Marianne, who was now seventeen, though very young for her age, who was most upset at the idea of having a chaperone come to live with them. "We're happy as we are, Father! Can't we just stay like this?"

"Marianne, at your age you need to get used to being a lady, to calling on other ladies, to attending parties with other young people. I can't help you with that sort of thing."

"But I don't want that sort of thing, Father. I'm not like my mother. I'm not interested in fussing for hours over my clothes and hair. What I enjoy most is helping you in your free clinic, especially with the children. A chaperone wouldn't approve of that."

"And she'd be right. Ladies don't – they don't get involved in the actual caring for the sick, you know they don't. They raise funds and visit the poor and – and things like that."

"You're not going to stop me coming to the clinic!" Marianne clung to his arm, her face raised to his in agonised appeal. "It's the best part of my week."

"Marianne—"

She burst into tears. "Don't stop me coming! Please, Father!

174

It's the only time I feel at all useful. If I were a boy, I could become a doctor like you. It's not fair! Men can do anything and women just have to get married and have children."

"Having children is a wonderful thing," he said softly.

"They why didn't Mother have more? And why does it hurt women so much? You can die from having a child. Even I know that. Or from trying to get rid of one." She flung away from him. "Besides, I want more in life than serving a man, Father, much more!"

"Marianne, just think about it a little, will you, darling? You'll see that I'm right about the chaperone."

She shook her head. "You're not right. I've got Ellie and I've got you, and that's all I need. We don't need anyone else living with us. It'll spoil things."

Jeremy tried to explain about the chaperone to Ellie, though it sounded to her more as if he were trying to convince himself that it was the right thing to do. "How else will Marianne be able to meet someone, get married, have a family?" he wound up.

Ellie nodded. "I think it's a good idea, sir. She needs some company, the company of young people of her own class."

His tense expression relaxed a little. "She's had you, and I hope she always will. Don't think I don't appreciate what you've done for her over the past few years, Ellie. You've been more a mother to her than my wife has."

She coloured. "It was my pleasure, sir. I love her, too. I'll have a word with her about it, shall I?"

But Marianne continued to fight hard against having a chaperone. "I've been thinking about it carefully," she said to her father a few evenings later, "and I really don't want anyone else coming to live with us. I don't want to go calling on people and I don't like silly parties where nobody says what they mean."

"Darling, you've never tried them."

"I've sat on the stairs and watched yours, and they never seemed much fun, with everyone so stiff and formal."

"Parties for young people will be different."

"I don't think so. Not for me anyway. So I don't *need* a chaperone, Father." Her voice softened and became persuasive, "I'm old enough to manage things here with Ellie's help. Why should we need anyone else? I'm as sure as I can be that it'll spoil things."

"I keep telling you. A girl of your age needs an older lady to take her round, to show her how to behave in society. I meant to do it when your mother left. You need to meet people, young people. You need friends, and one day, I hope that'll help you to find a husband."

Marianne went across to sit on the rug at his feet and stare into the flames. "I can't even imagine wanting to get married." She could still remember the way her parents had quarrelled, the coldness between them. "Please, Father, can't we just go on living as we are? Now that Mabel's gone, it's such a happy house."

"I'm afraid not, darling. I've already written to my cousin Dorothy to ask if she knows anyone suitable." He laid a hand on his daughter's head. "That's how things are done with our sort of people, Daughter mine."

"But—"

He had to steel himself to say it. "To put it bluntly, Marianne, it's bad enough that your mother is no longer living with us. We can't make matters worse by letting you grow up without an older woman's care or you'll never be able to live a normal life. In some things, one just has to conform to society's rules." He stroked her hair and she leaned her head against his legs, sighing. "Your mother and I were ill-suited, love. Don't judge marriage by us, will you? Give yourself a chance to find someone you can love. And – and even with a chaperone, it'll be better if you pretend to other people that you write to your mother – as I shall pretend that I go down to see her sometimes."

Her voice was almost inaudible. "Do we have to?"

"Yes, we do. And not just for your sake, either."

She stared at him in surprise. "I don't understand. What other reason could there be? *You* surely don't want to write to her!"

"A doctor must be very respectable, you know, or people won't come to see him, not the gentry, anyway. It's not a good thing that my wife is known to be living elsewhere. To some people the idea of a complete separation between husband and wife is unthinkable, immoral even. It would prevent them from coming to me for help."

"Oh." And that was the last time she protested against the idea of a chaperone. She knew how deeply he cared about the practice of medicine. For him, she would do anything.

Cousin Dorothy wrote back to say that she herself would be prepared to come and chaperone dear Marianne. Dorothy's own father, Jeremy's uncle by marriage, was lately dead and had not left her as comfortably off as she had hoped. Indeed, she had not known where to turn for a home because the family house would have to be sold to pay her father's debts.

Jeremy wrote back immediately to tell Dorothy to come to Bilsden, then went to ask Ellie to prepare a room. "I want you to understand that Miss Hymes will be coming here purely as Marianne's chaperone and companion. She will not be in charge of you or the other servants. *You* will remain the housekeeper and you will be answerable only to me, though of course you will do your best to ensure that Miss Hymes's wishes are all attended to."

"Yes, sir. And I'm glad she's coming, for Miss Marianne's sake."

"Yes." He stared at her, closed his lips firmly and then left the room.

She watched him go, her eyes soft with love. Since that

time in his room the day she had sacked Mabel, she had not been able to feel as comfortable with him as before, and she suspected that he was having the same trouble with her. She was still seeing him as a man, not a master, and that was very wrong. She didn't need anyone to tell her that. She tried her hardest to behave normally with him, but she was finding it more and more difficult. Jeremy Lewis might be a bit weak, but he was kind and caring – and she liked a man who kept himself so clean, whose breath was sweet and whose voice was gentle and low. He was the only man she could ever like in that way.

Miss Hymes arrived a week later and Jeremy, who had seen the cab draw up, came to the door himself to welcome her. In his usual easy way, he introduced Ellie to her and asked her to show the visitor to her room.

"Certainly, sir. Would you come this way, please, Miss Hymes?"

Ellie picked up a suitcase and led the way up the stairs. Miss Hymes made no attempt to pick up any of her luggage, but followed with a stiff-backed gait, her eyes assessing everything as she went. She moved so slowly that Ellie had to wait for her outside the bedroom.

"I presume you have been dealing with housekeeping matters since Mrs Lewis left?" Dorothy Hymes always spoke to servants in a louder voice than normal and never, ever smiled at them or praised them in case they tried to take advantage.

"Of course. Actually, I'm the permanent housekeeper, Miss Hymes."

"You? You can't be! You're far too young. How old are you?"

"I've been in service here for over ten years," said Ellie obliquely.

"That's not what I asked you and you know it!" Miss Hymes stared at her.

Ellie stared right back and said nothing.

"What's your name again, girl?"

Ellie was bristling by this time. "Miss Peters."

"Proper housekeepers are *always* called Mrs."

"I'm not and never have been married. I prefer to use the name to which I'm entitled." She had difficulty summoning up a smile, so she just spoke as calmly as she could. "Now, the bathroom is at the end of the corridor. We have modern indoor facilities here." She spoke proudly, for the doctor had been one of the first people in the town to install a bathroom with running water.

"I would prefer hot water to be brought to my room."

Awkward old bitch, thought Ellie. "If you insist, Miss Hymes. I'll send Ruth up to draw the water from the bathroom for you every morning. Tea will be served downstairs in about half an hour, if that's convenient. I'll have the rest of your luggage brought up."

There was a knock on the door and Jeremy Lewis's voice called, "May I come in, Cousin Dorothy? I've brought up some of your luggage."

"Yes. Yes, of course, Jeremy. But surely there are servants who can do that?" She looked pointedly at Ellie who merely sighed and left the room.

"We have a small household here and no male servants. I think I'm stronger than Miss Peters." He wondered at the time what had made him call Ellie by her full name and decided afterwards, when Miss Hymes's hostility to the young housekeeper became evident, that it must have been sheer good luck. "It's no trouble to me, Cousin Dorothy. I'll just call my man Sam in from the surgery and we'll carry up your trunks together. I'm sorry Marianne wasn't here to greet you, but we didn't realise you would get here so early and she's gone into town to buy some flowers for your room."

"The dear child! But there was no need. Flowers are an

unnecessary extravagance in a bedchamber and anyway, they make me sneeze."

"What a pity! She'll have to put them in her own room, then. Just come down when you're ready. The small sitting room we use when we don't have company is on the left at the back of the hall."

On the stairs he passed Ruth carrying a washbasin and ewer and raised his eyebrows. "Whatever are those for?"

"For Miss Hymes, sir."

"But we have a bathroom."

"She prefers to wash in her room, sir."

He frowned as he ran lightly down the stairs. This beginning did not augur well.

Marianne sneaked into the house the back way with the flowers and caught Ellie downstairs in the tiny staff sitting room off the kitchen. "What's she like?"

Ellie shrugged. "I've only met her briefly. It's too soon to say."

Marianne flopped down in one of the worn armchairs. "You don't like her."

"I didn't say that."

"You don't have to. I know you too well." She sighed. "I told Father we didn't need anyone."

"You *do* need someone, love."

Marianne bounced up out of the chair and hugged her ruthlessly. "No, I don't. Not when I've got you."

Ellie hugged her back, then held her at arm's length, looking down into the eyes that were so like Jeremy's. "Look, Marianne, we've been through all this before. You *do* need someone, love, someone who's a lady born, who can show you how to go on in society. And," she took a deep breath, "if you behave badly or shock her, she'll only blame it on me."

Marianne grimaced. "I realise that. Don't worry. I won't disgrace you or Father."

Within a few days, the consensus of opinion in the kitchen was that Miss Hymes was a sour old maid and a real pain to serve.

Mrs Cosden went still further. "She'll cause trouble, that one will, you mark my words."

Ellie looked surprised. "I don't see why she should."

No, thought Mrs Cosden as Ellie left the kitchen, you wouldn't, because there's nothing mean or underhanded about you. But that woman obviously doesn't like someone as young and pretty as you being housekeeper. She'll try to get rid of you. I've seen the way she looks at you. And I've seen her sort before. Can't leave well alone, they can't. Have to meddle.

A few days later, after the evening meal was over, Dorothy wiped her lips with her table napkin and cleared her throat. "Excuse me, Jeremy, but there is a household matter we need to discuss. Ellie Peters is refusing to let me direct household matters. Surely, it's better if someone with my experience manages things and gives her her orders each day?"

Jeremy and Marianne both stared at her, but he shook his head warningly as Marianne opened her mouth to defend the woman she regarded as a friend. "Miss Peters is and will remain our housekeeper. I didn't bring you here to use you as a servant, Cousin Dorothy."

"But that girl is far too young for such a role!"

"Miss Peters is very efficient and she knows my ways. I don't think her age is all that important though I'd hardly call her a girl."

Again, that scrawny throat was cleared. "Marianne, my dear, would you leave your father and myself alone for a while?"

Marianne's expression became stubborn and again Jeremy intervened. "Yes, go and practise your music, Marianne. You can leave this in my hands."

She stared at him. "You won't—"

"There's nothing for you to worry about," he said hastily.

When the door had closed behind Marianne, he turned to Dorothy with a sigh, but she spoke first.

"Jeremy, dear, surely you can see that it won't do."

"What won't do?"

"Having someone so young and pretty as your housekeeper."

He stiffened. "What do you mean by that?"

She fiddled with the cake crumbs on her dessert plate. "I mean that there's already gossip in this town about you and Ellie Peters. I'm sorry to be the one to tell you this, but for Marianne's sake, I feel we should—"

"There is nothing between Ellie Peters and myself, and there never has been!" he snapped, appalled that anyone could think him so crass as to take a mistress into the home he shared with his daughter.

"Well, I can see that, but it's hardly the point, is it?" that thin inexorable voice continued. "It's what people think is happening that damages a person's reputation. And with poor Annabelle living so far away . . ."

"My wife has nothing to do with this. Her health is such that she is unable to—"

A vinegary smile flickered over Miss Hymes's face. "Really, Jeremy, the whole household is aware of what happened between you and Annabelle, and probably half the town, too. I knew about it before I'd been here two days. In the circumstances, we have to be particularly careful of how we live. I really think you should consider dismissing Miss Peters – for Marianne's sake."

"*Never!*" The vehemence of his refusal came as a surprise to Jeremy himself and caused a knowing look to come into Dorothy's eyes. "Ellie Peters has done nothing wrong," he added more temperately, "and I have no intention of dismissing her. She's devoted a decade of her life to my daughter, has been more of a mother to her than my wife ever was. Ellie's been with us ever since she was a child herself. Her loyalty to myself and to my daughter is beyond question and we owe her the same loyalty in return. Under no circumstances will I dismiss her! Let that be understood from the start!"

The mere thought of dismissing Ellie made him feel furious. It was a simple matter of justice, he told himself, then grimaced. No, that was not all. The house would seem empty without Ellie's cheerful presence. And Marianne would be heart-broken to lose her. No, for his daughter's sake, he would not allow Cousin Dorothy to take over the housekeeping. He would guess that she would prove as miserly as Annabelle had been, not generous and kindly like Ellie Peters. He preferred to keep his staff happy and cheerful. All his staff.

Twelve

LATE SEPTEMBER 1845

On the Monday of the second week that the salon was open, Jeremy Lewis brought his daughter and his cousin to order some dresses. Very fortunately there were no other customers just then, so Annie was free to give them her full attention.

"I hardly recognised you, Annie, in that magnificent dress!" Jeremy said, shaking her hand. "Though I suppose I should really call you Mrs Ashworth in public. You know Marianne, of course, but you haven't met my cousin, Miss Hymes."

The elderly lady looked at Annie as sourly as if she had just swallowed a mouthful of vinegar. Annie could not help but notice that her dress, of a muddy brown hue and made in an outmoded style, did nothing whatsoever for her angular body and sallow complexion. She did not offer her hand to Annie, just nodded once and pressed her lips tightly together.

Marianne, however, stepped forward to shake Annie's hand with the same open friendliness as her father had displayed. "How nice to see you again, Mrs Ashworth. Ellie has been keeping us up to date on your progress here. You salon is quite the talk of the town." She chuckled as she added, "Especially the retiring room."

Miss Hymes sucked in her breath and tut-tutted, and Marianne gave her an impatient glance.

The girl's resemblance to her mother was at first unnerving to Annie, but there was a sincerity and warmth to her that was totally lacking in Annabelle Lewis, and she had her father's bright intelligent eyes as well as her mother's blonde hair.

Annie returned her smile. "I'm glad to hear that. I hoped it would prove a talking point and bring in custom."

Everyone except Miss Hymes laughed, then Marianne asked, "And how is William? Did he get his new puppy? He was so excited about it when I saw him at the farm." She drew the companion into the group by adding, "Father and I visited the farm of a friend of Mrs Ashworth when I was recovering from the influenza, Cousin Dorothy. There was a litter of new-born puppies there, which her son showed me."

"Yes, he got the puppy, but it spends more time with Luke than it does with William. It seems a clever little thing, but it has very sharp teeth, as we've found to our cost."

"I'd love to have a dog of my own," said Marianne.

"We'll look out for one, then," said Jeremy at once.

"Oh, surely not!" Miss Hymes's expression turned even more sour. "Dogs have very dirty habits and they bring fleas into the house. It would not be at all proper, Jeremy. I must protest against it, indeed I must."

With an effort, Jeremy kept his smile calm and polite. He shook his head at Marianne when she would have protested at this edict, but Annie noticed how hard his hand had clenched on the chair back against which he was leaning.

Marianne abandoned the subject of a dog and turned back to Annie. "Beatrice Hallam has already been to visit you, Mrs Ashworth, I believe, and has even admitted that 'for a provincial dressmaker' you show a surprising amount of style. That's very high praise from her, believe me! Since she went to visit her sister in London, nothing in Bilsden is quite good enough for Beatrice any more." Her eyes were again dancing with laughter at the memory of Beatrice's pretentious complaints about the narrowness of provincial life and the delights of London.

At the sight of his daughter's glowing smile, Jeremy's expression relaxed, too. His pride in her showed in his fond looks.

None of them saw Tom tiptoeing along the hallway to carry some supplies up to the workroom. For a moment he stopped dead, staring through the doorway at Marianne as if he had been struck by lightning, then he pulled himself together and ran quickly up the stairs with the boxes. He knew who the smiling girl was, but he had not seen her for a while. He gave a soundless whistle as he reached the workroom door. The doctor's daughter was turning, no, she had already turned, into a very beautiful young woman. She was, Tom drew in a slow deep breath and paused, nodding to himself, oh, yes, she was exactly the sort of person he meant to marry one day. He looked down at himself. But he most definitely did not want her to see him like this, in his working clothes, with his hair blown into a curly bush by the wind and with his hands all grubby and stained.

He was very thoughtful all evening, so quiet that Rosie teased him about it. He stared at his companion as if he had never seen her before and shrugged off her teasing. Rosie was a nice lass, and had stayed faithful to him for some years, but when he took a wife, it would be someone like Marianne Lewis, someone with shiny hair that looked like spun gold, someone whose fresh, unspoiled face had not been marked by hardship and whose body had belonged to no one else but him.

"We'd like to order several dresses from you, Mrs Ashworth," said Jeremy. "My daughter is a little young for high fashion, but she's grown so much since last year that Miss Hymes tells me she has almost nothing respectable to wear." He did not say that one of the things Annabelle had always scrimped on had been her daughter's clothes and that even frugal Dorothy Hymes had been horrified at how little clothing Marianne possessed, though it did not bother Marianne half as much. He glanced at his companions and his eyes glazed over as he looked at Miss Hymes. The woman was a narrow-minded nonentity whose conversation was utterly predictable and whose mind was so totally focused on doing what she considered to be the right thing socially that she had no room in her head for any other ideas.

No longer could he and Marianne sit over dinner and discuss his day's work, and there had been trouble that week when Marianne got ready to come and help him in his clinic. He was already regretting his impulsive invitation to Dorothy to live with them. However, if she was prepared to devote herself to his daughter, he would put up with her for Marianne's sake. He must put up with her. How could he turn her out when she had no home to go to?

"It'll be a pleasure to dress someone as pretty as you, Miss Lewis," said Annie enthusiastically.

"Go away now, Father!" ordered Marianne, taking his arm and turning him towards the door. "Cousin Dorothy has been properly introduced to Mrs Ashworth and as we are to devote ourselves to frills and frivolities, a serious gentleman like yourself would only be in the way."

"Marianne!" hissed Miss Hymes. "You should not tease your father like that in public." She pursed her lips together as if Marianne had committed some social solecism, and Annie again saw a look of irritation pass across the girl's face.

"I should miss it dreadfully if the child stopped teasing me." Jeremy gave Marianne a quick hug, earning another disapproving look from Miss Hymes. "A little liveliness is attractive in a young lady, don't you think, Cousin Dorothy?"

His efforts to make her relax were quite fruitless. Dorothy Hymes worshipped at the shrine of rigid propriety and was quite ruthless with those who transgressed her narrow rules. She was determined to improve the tone of her cousin's household; for she had been genuinely shocked at the lax behaviour of Marianne and horrified at the freedom given to the servants. Like Mabel, she had learned to bide her time. She would get what she wanted in the end, though. She usually did – as her father had found to his cost after he had his stroke. It was a pity that Jeremy was already married or she might have hoped to wed her cousin. A married lady had so much higher a status than an unmarried lady. But there was always hope.

Jeremy bowed to the group of ladies, reminded his cousin to order a couple of dresses for herself, and then left them to their deliberations. If only, he thought, as he strolled back along High Street, there were someone else to look after Marianne! But there was no one else. He had very few relatives. And Dorothy had been so flutteringly grateful to him for giving her a home that he could not ask her to leave, especially now he realised how little money she had. He sighed. Sometimes he wished he were as ruthless as other men, wished he had the gift for taking what he wanted from life. Like Frederick Hallam, for instance. He could not imagine that gentleman landing himself in a dilemma like this. Or if he did, he'd soon find a way out of it.

The next hour was very trying for Annie, because Miss Hymes seemed as determined to order sensible but unflattering clothes as Marianne was to order lavish creations entirely unsuited to a young lady. This was Annie's first real test of the boast she had made to Pauline that she would refuse to make clothes that did not suit her customers. And unfortunately, when the time came to make her stand, two other ladies whom she did not recognise were sitting waiting for her attention.

She took a deep breath. "I'm sorry, Miss Hymes, but I couldn't agree to make you a dress in that material." It was a dull sage green grosgrain that accorded ill with Miss Hymes's sallow complexion and further deadened her already faded mouse-brown hair.

Marianne's mouth fell open in surprise, and the two ladies stopped talking to listen openly.

Miss Hymes stiffened visibly. "I – beg – your – pardon?"

"I said that I could not agree to make you a dress in that material. It would not suit you."

"I never heard such impudence in my life! A dressmaker telling a customer what she can or cannot wear! How dare you, madam!"

"I'm not a dressmaker, Miss Hymes, I'm a modiste, and I have my own reputation to think about. And for the same reason, I cannot recommend pink tarlatan for you, Miss Lewis, not that shade of pink, anyway, which is right for a brunette but would look garish with your beautiful blonde hair."

"Then I must advise my cousin to have his daughter's dresses made elsewhere!" Quivering with indignation and outrage, Miss Hymes led the way to the door and Marianne had perforce to follow, casting a longing glance backwards at the piles of material swatches and the sketches she had been inspecting. Annie escorted them to the doorway, her face calm and wished them a good day, but Miss Hymes did not deign to acknowledge her presence. Marianne threw a quick glance over her shoulder, mouthed "Goodbye!" and followed her cousin outside.

Annie took a deep breath and turned to her other customers.

Before she could speak, one of them addressed her. "You are either very foolhardy or very astute, Mrs Ashworth. Do you always dictate what your customers shall wear?" Her voice was a rich deep contralto and her warm smile showed that the remark was not meant to be offensive.

"I'm not sure which I am," Annie said ruefully, "but I do have my reputation to make and I won't do that by making people unflattering gowns. I don't dictate what ladies should wear so much as help them to avoid the things they definitely shouldn't wear."

"And yet that green is one of your materials, so you must have thought it had some merit."

"Yes, indeed! For a lady with more vivid colouring – one like yourself – or even for me. But it's not suitable for an ageing lady with fading hair and a sa – er – a pale complexion." She hastily avoided the word sallow, fearing to give further offence.

But this lady just threw back her head and laughed, a gurgling laugh that was very infectious. "Sallow," she said. "Your first choice of word was correct."

"But not very tactful. How may I be of service to you?"

"I've just been visiting my friend Pauline Hinchcliffe and she suggested I come to see you. I have a problem which she thought you might be able to help me with. I've recently arrived in the north on a visit and the carriage containing my luggage overturned on the way here. One trunk was crushed and everything in it damaged – and it was the one containing my ball gowns. Unfortunately I now find myself without a suitable new gown to wear for the Lord Lieutenant's ball on Monday next, and I'm reluctant to wear a gown I've already been seen in. I can get something sent here in time from London, of course, but it would be noticed that I'd worn it before, I'm afraid, and taken as an insult. I wondered if you could possibly make me something in such a short time. Oh, I should have introduced myself. I'm Lavinia Darrington, and this is my maid, Sarah."

Annie hoped she had not betrayed her surprise at such an august client visiting her salon. The Darrington family had owned land around Bilsden for as long as people could remember, but the present generation rarely visited the north nowadays and only an elderly aunt was in permanent residence at the Hall. People like them would never normally contemplate buying a gown from a provincial modiste. How on earth had Pauline persuaded Lady Darrington to try Annie's services?

She realised that she was keeping her visitor waiting and took a hold of herself. "I'll certainly do my best to help you, Your Ladyship. Whether I can make a suitable gown in time depends on the material and style you choose. I carry a very small stock of materials and the draper's next door carries nothing of the quality you will require. You'll need to go into Manchester to choose materials, and that will delay us another day. We couldn't do any elaborate embroidery on the gown in any case. It takes too much time and I don't employ a specialist embroiderer." She smiled, wondering if she was being too pessimistic. "I'd love to make you a gown, of course I would, but I'm not going to pretend that I'm able to do the impossible." For the second time that day she felt she had risked offending a customer.

"That's honest, at least. I prefer that. I shall be honest with you in return, Mrs Ashworth. I've come to see you because Pauline assures me that you're very talented, and I've seen for myself that the gowns you made for her are attractive and well cut. But I can't guarantee to wear what you produce until I've seen it. Like you, I have my reputation to think of. However, you seem to know your business, so I shall give you the chance to make me a ball gown. I shall, of course, pay you for your efforts, whatever the outcome."

"If my efforts don't prove satisfactory, Your Ladyship, I shall not ask for payment."

There was a gasp of surprise from the maid and even Lady Darrington paused to stare at Annie. "Are you that confident of success?"

"No, Your Ladyship. I'm not confident about anything, since

I don't know your tastes well enough. You're used to the very best that London and Paris have to offer, and I'm not sure whether I can match their standards – but I am willing to try."

"Then let us discuss the practicalities. There's no problem about material and no need for a visit to the silk warehouses in Manchester. My grandmother was a hoarder all her life and there are bales of silks and brocades stored in the attic. Some of them are spoiled after all this time and others are faded or far too old-fashioned, but among them are some which seem to have possibilities. I brought a few of them with me. Sarah, would you ask the footman to carry them in? Thank you." Lady Darrington looked challengingly at Annie. "Well, how do you feel about making me a dress in time now?"

"Much happier. What about the style, Your Ladyship?"

"I've brought the ruined gown with me to show you. Something similar would be quite acceptable." The maid returned, carrying a parcel and followed by a footman staggering under several linen-wrapped bundles.

The maid undid the parcel to display a torn and stained gown in cream silk. Annie forgot her awe and stepped forward. "How lovely it must have been!" she exclaimed involuntarily. "Surely made by a French modiste?"

"Yes. How did you know that?"

"I was in London a few weeks ago and I saw nothing quite like this in the small details of styling."

"Oh, you were in London?"

"Yes. I shall be going there twice a year from now on. One needs to keep abreast of the fashions, after all, not just what is shown in the ladies' magazine, but what fashionable people are actually wearing." Her voice tailed away as she studied the design and the cut of the dress. "Yes, I could make you a simpler version of this, with less embroidery, I'm afraid, but most of that lace can be washed and used again. I think enough of it has survived intact."

"Oh, I can afford new lace. There's no need to practise such economy." Lady Darrington shrugged her shoulders carelessly.

"But Mr Hardy next door sells nothing half so fine and we haven't the time to go into Manchester to choose more. Besides, this lace has a particularly beautiful design. I'm sure it will wash up again like new, Your Ladyship."

Her Ladyship pulled a face. "Patched-up lace?"

"No, indeed. Lace used in shorter lengths. I should, of course, cut out the damaged parts."

"In that case, do as you please. Now, let's have a look at the materials, Sarah."

The maid had by this time opened the parcels to display their contents. Annie stepped forward to cast a professional eye over them. The materials were indeed old-fashioned, but of excellent quality. "This one would be beautiful," she said at last, touching a deep cream satin.

"I had thought the patterned green," said Lady Darrington. "Patterned fabrics are very popular at the moment."

"No." Annie shook her head decisively. "The cream one would look much better on someone with your colouring and complexion."

The maid looked in shock at this provincial seamstress who was daring to contradict one who was famous for her style.

"Is one allowed to ask why?" Her Ladyship frowned.

"Because of the sheen on it." Annie stroked the material with loving fingertips. "It'll gleam in the candlelight and send a flattering light back on to your skin, and it will look perfect with the lace." She held a piece next to the satin. "See."

"Hmm. You may be right."

"Could I ask what jewellery you plan to wear, Your Ladyship?"

"I had thought of wearing my diamonds."

Again, Annie had the temerity to frown and contradict her.

"No, not diamonds. Not with this. Do you have pearls, Your Ladyship?"

For a moment, Lady Darrington hovered between annoyance and amusement, then amusement won. "I do indeed."

"Then if you decide to wear them, we'll sew just a few pearl drops around the hem, caught up in the lace and ribbon that I shall use to decorate the flounce." The design for the dress was altering in her mind as she spoke.

"Do you have some pearl drops, Mrs Ashworth?"

"Yes."

"Are they real pearls?"

"No, of course not."

"Then Sarah shall remove the pearl drops from another of my gowns and bring them to you. I really could not wear imitation pearls. When shall you have the dress ready for a fitting?"

"By late tomorrow afternoon, Your Ladyship. If you'll just allow me to take a few measurements and leave the ruined gown for me to use as a guide?"

When that was completed, Her Ladyship nodded to Annie. "I'll send a carriage to fetch you tomorrow, then, shall I? Now I really must be going, but first, Mrs Ashworth, I believe you have a retiring room?"

"Yes, Your Ladyship. It's this way." Annie hid a smile. Even the nobility had the same needs as everyone else, it seemed.

When Her Ladyship had left, Annie immediately sent Rebecca off to the mill with a note to Mr Hallam, asking if he would mind waiting until the following week for her to come and measure for his curtains and explaining that she had a very urgent commission to undertake for Lady Darrington. He would not need to be told how important that was to her. After that, she and her staff prepared to abandon everything else to work on Her Ladyship's gown.

Just as Annie was locking the front door of the salon that evening, and wishing that Mary Benworth and her father had moved in so that the building would be occupied at night, Jeremy Lewis appeared. "I hardly dared expect to find anyone still here. Do you have a moment to spare, Annie, or must you hurry away?"

"Yes, Jeremy, of course I've a moment to spare." She led the way back into the salon, wishing for propriety's sake, that she had not sent Rebecca and Mary home. She gestured to a chair. "I was just locking up."

He waited for her to sit down, then followed suit. "You've mortally offended my cousin, I'm afraid."

"I'm sorry about that, but it would have mortally offended me to make her up a dress that was so unbecoming." Her eyes were twinkling as she spoke.

His eyes were crinkled with laughter, too. "Yes, Marianne explained it all to me. Sage green, of all colours! But, Annie, could you not overcome your principles for once?"

Annie shook her head. "No, Jeremy, definitely not. I have a reputation to build and it would do me no good to be known as the maker of such a garment. I'm sorry about Marianne's clothes, though. I would have enjoyed making for her. She's such a pretty girl. You must be very proud of her."

"I am. And who said that you were not making for her?"

"Well, your cousin did."

"My cousin described in graphic detail the clothes she considered suitable for a girl of Marianne's age, and my daughter just as graphically described the fates she would gladly suffer before being seen in such garments. She then went into details about the sort of garments *she* wished to wear, but I gather that you had refused to make them for her as well?"

He raised one eyebrow at her and pulled such a quizzical face that Annie had to laugh. "I sound as if I don't want your custom, don't I? But, Jeremy, I must start as I mean to continue and Marianne wanted things quite unsuitable for a girl of her age."

"Well, I will entrust you with the clothing of my daughter," he saw her surprise and added firmly, "yes, I still want you to make Marianne some clothes – but only if you'll promise to continue to restrain her love of bright colours which are definitely not suitable for a girl of her age and complexion. She hasn't inherited her mother's good taste, I'm afraid, and is more like Ellie in her love of colour. They both have a secret penchant for vivid shades of pink."

"And always red ribbons on her bonnets, for Ellie," Annie said, laughing with him. "She does love them so, and I've never had the heart to quibble at her for wearing them. But won't your cousin be annoyed if I make the clothes for Marianne?"

"She's already annoyed, very annoyed indeed, but I can't have her dressing Marianne as drably as she does herself. With you making the clothes, at least I felt safe in bowing out of the arguments. At the moment I find myself at the centre of the storm and have had to put my foot down. Hardly a judgment of Solomon, I'm afraid. I've insisted that Marianne return to you, but I've given Dorothy permission to use Miss Pinkley's services for herself. Ellie will bring Marianne to see you tomorrow as my cousin refuses to enter your premises again."

"Not tomorrow, please! I've just had a sudden rush order for Lady Darrington." She quickly explained the emergency.

He raised his eyebrows. "Goodness, you *are* doing well, making for the nobility!"

"We'll have to wait and see how the dress turns out. Her Ladyship has not guaranteed to wear what I make for her. Now, I really must go home. They'll be wondering what's happened to me."

"I'll walk across town with you."

"Oh, Jeremy!" She hesitated, not wanting to offend him,

then decided on frankness. "I wish I could accept your offer, but it would cause talk, and you must be as eager to avoid that as I am."

He sighed. "Yes, I suppose you're right." At one time he had wondered if he had fallen in love with her, but he now realised that it was simply loneliness and the friendship he felt for her whole family.

She took refuge in a cool farewell, then waited a few minutes before following him out and locking the front door carefully behind her.

By the following afternoon, the evening gown had been cut out, the seams whipped to prevent fraying and the pieces tacked carefully together. When the Darringtons' crested carriage arrived, Annie wrapped the precious gown in a linen sheet and carried it outside. She hid a smile as she saw Cecil Hardy standing on his doorstep, scowling at her but watching what was happening with great interest.

Annie enjoyed the drive. It was a relief to rest for a while after the early start they had made on the precious gown. Darrington Hall was situated on the very top of the Ridge. Its walls were high enough to discourage the inquisitive from staring inside, so although Annie had lived in Bilsden all her life, she had no idea what the house was like. The gatekeeper was famous for his ferocity towards idle lads with nothing better to do than trespass upon the Darrington demesne, but at the sight of the carriage, he rushed out to open the huge wrought-iron gates and he bowed the carriage through as if it contained royalty.

Annie, riding in solitary state inside, looked out at all this fuss with amusement. What must it feel like to have your own carriage always ready to take you where you wanted? To have servants bowing and scraping at the mere sight of you? She chuckled. That was one thing she would never know. As the house came into view, she looked at it and drew in her breath, so huge was it. Goodness! she thought, whatever do they need all those rooms for? There are only three adult Darringtons and two children, after all, and four of them live in London.

The carriage took Annie along a neatly raked gravel driveway to the rear entrance where a footman condescended to open the door for her and show her up to Her Ladyship's suite.

There Sarah disrobed her mistress, assisted Annie to pin the new gown into place, then stood in silence and studied its fit as they waited for Lady Darrington's verdict.

Her Ladyship walked over to a long gilt-framed mirror on one wall and twisted to and fro in front of it. "Yes," she said eventually, "the fit isn't bad at all. You definitely know how to cut out a bodice, Mrs Ashworth. I'm happy to proceed to the next stage."

Annie let out her breath slowly and stepped forward to unpin the dress. "I'll work on the dress over the weekend, Your Ladyship, but I'll need to have another fitting on Sunday afternoon, I'm afraid, if I'm to be sure it's all right." She would not be able to attend chapel, and her father would be upset about her working on the Lord's Day, but so be it. This dress, of all the ones she ever made, must be quite perfect. This dress could make her reputation.

"Fortunately we have no engagements on Sunday and," Her Ladyship made a wry moue, "we're not sticklers about breaking the Sabbath. And anyway, this is an emergency. I'm sure the Lord will understand my need."

When Sarah had helped Annie to unpin the gown, she followed her mistress into the bedroom to help her dress for dinner, pausing at the door to whisper, "I'll be back in a few minutes to show you out."

Annie wrapped the precious creation in the linen sheet and stood waiting, walking slowly round to study the room, which had a rather forlorn air, as if it was not used to being occupied.

There was a cheerful fire burning in the grate, but there were none of the touches that a lady would normally have put in a room she occupied regularly. Then Sarah returned and Annie hurried downstairs with her to where the under-coachman was waiting to take her back to town.

The next morning, Annie woke early and walked across town to her salon when it was barely light, accompanied by a sleepy Rebecca. She was anxious to make another early start on the gown. When they walked into the workroom, however, they both stopped dead.

"Eeh, our Annie, what's happened?"

Annie could not speak, so sick did she feel at the sight before her. Last night everything had been left immaculately tidy, as always. Now, the room was in chaos. Thread had been unravelled from the spools and lay in tangles of colour across the table and floor. The scraps basket had been upended into the hearth and the bits and pieces were covered in soot and ash. Worst of all, Her Ladyship's gown, left draped across a padded form that Annie used for fitting her garments together, was hanging in shreds, the cotton dust cover discarded intact on the floor, as if ripped off and cast impatiently aside in someone's frenzy to destroy what lay beneath.

Annie found her voice at last. "No!" she cried and rushed across the room, only to stop dead again in front of the ruins of the gown, hands outstretched. She drew back. She was unable to touch it. Her hands trembled upwards to clench into white-knuckled balls at her breast. Tears welled in her eyes, but she felt too numb and shocked to weep. She could only stand and stare around her in horror.

Whenever things were going well, something always managed to spoil them. It had happened again. Was she always to be dogged by bad luck like this? Were things never to go smoothly for her?

Thirteen

MASCULINE INTERVENTIONS

"Oh, our Annie, that beautiful dress!" Rebecca whispered, clutching Annie's arm. "Who could've done it?"

The warmth of Rebecca's hand seemed to penetrate Annie's initial shock even more than the words. She gave a long shuddering sigh and put her arm round her little sister, hugging Rebecca's body to her for comfort. "I don't know, love. I can't – I can't even begin to imagine."

"Shall I run and fetch our Tom? He won't have left for the yard yet, 'cos we set off early."

"Yes. I – I suppose so." Though Annie could not imagine what good Tom could do, what good anyone could do. No one could put those shreds of material back together.

Rebecca rushed out of the house, still brushing tears away from her eyes. Just outside the door she collided with a gentleman, "Oh! Oh, I'm that sorry, sir!"

Frederick Hallam was taking an early morning stroll around the town centre to think out some plans he had in mind for civic improvements while there were few people around to get in his way or to speculate about what he was doing. "That's all right. Hey! Wait!" He grabbed hold of Rebecca's shoulders, having just noticed the tear stains on her cheeks and knowing she was Annie Ashworth's half-sister. "Is something wrong?"

Rebecca choked back her sobs. "Someone's broke into our Annie's salon an' tore up Her Ladyship's ball gown. I've got to fetch our Tom." She pulled away from his hand and raced off down the street before he could stop her. He hesitated by the door, then shook his head and gave in to the impulse to help. There was something about Annie Ashworth that always brought out the best in him, he knew. He had pondered on it several times without coming to any understanding of the phenomenon. As he walked inside, he called out, "Is anyone there?"

He had to call again before a voice answered, "Here!"

He went up the stairs and saw the open workroom door, but stopped on the threshold in shock. "Good heavens! Mrs Ashworth, whatever's happened here?"

Annie turned brimming eyes upon him. "Someone's broken in." She tried to sniff away the tears, but they would keep rolling down her face. "Someone's done this deliberately, someone who knew that I had the best chance I'm ever likely to get to make a name for myself as a modiste." The sobs kept welling up in harsh gulping sounds that hurt her throat. "Who would hate me so much?"

Without thinking he put an arm round her to offer comfort and she was so distraught that she just laid her head on his shoulder and gave way to a flood of tears. But after a few minutes, she slowed down and realised who was holding her. She forced herself to stop weeping and pulled away from him in embarrassment. "I'm sorry, Mr Hallam." Another tear rolled down her cheek.

"My dear Mrs Ashworth, whatever are you sorry for? Anyone would be upset at this. I'm amazed you're not having full-scale hysterics. Who was the gown for?" But he had guessed the answer before she spoke from what the child had said.

"It was for Lady Darrington. There was an accident to one of her carriages on the way north and her ball gowns were destroyed. I was making her a new gown."

"Who would have known about your commission?"

"I thought – I thought only the family and my employees knew. None of them would have d-done this." The tears welled out again, and she smeared them angrily away with the back of her hand. "But – people, the other shopkeepers, would have seen her ladyship's carriage waiting outside."

"Is there anyone who hates you?"

They both stood motionless and then, by common accord, their eyes turned to the wall which adjoined Hardy's shop.

"He wouldn't have done that, surely," Annie said.

"Hmm." Frederick's eyes narrowed as he stared at the adjoining wall.

Sounds from downstairs indicated the arrival of someone else and feet pounded up the stairs. Tom stood framed in the doorway, panting harshly, with William and the other two boys behind him. "Hell, what's happened here, Annie, love?"

William rushed across to put his arms round his mother and Frederick Hallam moved tactfully backwards.

"What does it look like? Someone broke in." Annie hugged her son, and had to swallow hard not to start sobbing again. "Whoever it was has torn Her Ladyship's gown to shreds as well as – as well as—" she could not continue.

Tom strode over to put his arms round her as well, and Mark and Luke hovered nearby. He patted Annie on the shoulder. "Look, you lads, go downstairs and see if there are any windows broken. Try to find how they got in, but don't touch anything."

Only when the three boys had pounded off down the stairs, eager to find some clue as to the culprit, did Tom turn to

Frederick Hallam and give him a questioning look.

Frederick moved forward, tall and elegant against Tom's rough vitality. "I was passing by and saw a little girl run out of here in some distress, so I came inside to see what was wrong. As the landlord, I feel some responsibility for what happens on my premises."

Tom nodded, acknowledging that right, but there was still a slight frown wrinkling his forehead. Landlord or not, it was not like Hallam to get involved in something like this. He usually had bigger fish to fry. So what had got into him this time? When Tom saw Hallam's eyes rest briefly on Annie, he took a deep breath. Oh, no! Their Annie had fought hard to stay respectable. She didn't need Hallam to get interested in her in that way.

Both men turned back to Annie who was still staring at the ruins of the dress.

"What can we do to help?" Frederick's voice was gentle.

"I don't think there's anything you can do," said Annie, stroking the shreds of material, and catching her breath on an echo of a sob. "It's ruined."

"Can't you make her another one?" asked Tom.

"There isn't enough material left."

"Can't you get more?"

"Only in Manchester. It'd take all day to get there and back. And then there wouldn't be time to finish a dress."

Frederick took another sudden decision. He found that he was deeply offended at what had been done here. And if he uncovered evidence that the culprit was Hardy, then the man would find his lease terminated. "Perhaps I could help you there, Mrs Ashworth. My carriage is waiting for me just round the corner. I'd be happy to put it at your service. We could set off for Manchester within minutes."

Annie looked at him, startled, and Tom stared with narrowed eyes, suspicion deepening still further. His ex-employer was not noted for his philanthropy. But he was noted for his womanising.

It was Annie who voiced their doubts. "Why should you do that, Mr Hallam? It's not your problem."

"Because I dislike seeing a hard-working woman like yourself attacked so viciously. Besides, you're my tenant. As I said before, I feel some responsibility for what happened on these premises. We must certainly have stouter locks fitted and perhaps bars on the lower windows at the rear." When they just stood staring at him, he spoke impatiently, "Well, Mrs Ashworth, what do you say? If we spring the horses, we could get to Manchester and back by early afternoon. If you worked all night, you and all your staff, could you not put another dress together?"

Annie stared at him, hope creeping across her face. "Well – well, we could try, I suppose. I'd have to go back home and get some money first."

"I can lend you that. There isn't a minute to be lost from the sounds of it."

"I'll see to things here," said Tom. "You go – but take Rebecca with you." His eyes were challenging on Frederick's face.

Frederick smiled very slightly. No fool, young Gibson. "By all means bring your little sister, but Mrs Ashworth will be perfectly safe with me, I assure you, Gibson. However, I suppose we must observe the proprieties if the salon is to be a success. I'd take my daughter Beatrice with us, but she won't even be out of bed yet. Well, Mrs Ashworth? What do you say?"

Annie took a deep breath and squared her shoulders. "I accept your offer, Mr Hallam."

"Good. Gibson, will you let Peters at the mill know that I shall not be in until later?"

"Aye. I'll do that, Mr Hallam. An' me an' the lads'll find

out how the intruders got in, too, before I call in the parish constables. Not that *they* will be able to do much, but they might as well work for their money, don't you think?"

"They might indeed. Though there's a new sergeant just started who has a bit more gumption than the others." He pulled out a card and scribbled on it. "Give this to Sergeant Miller and say I'd appreciate his personal attention in this matter."

The boys clattered upstairs again, bursting with information, but Hallam quelled them with one raised hand. "Tell your brothers what's happening, Tom. Your sisters and I have to leave at once."

Within minutes, Hallam, Annie and Rebecca were in the carriage, rocking along the main road into Manchester. Rebecca, sitting on the seat next to her sister, stared wide-eyed out of the window. She had never travelled in a carriage in her life and the pace of this drive threw her to and fro like a little rag doll, so that she had to clutch Annie on one side and the hand strap on the other.

"I don't know how to thank you for this, Mr Hallam," said Annie after a while. "I was so shocked when I saw what had happened that I couldn't think straight."

"I've seen my daughter have hysterics over a cup of tea spilled on her gown. I think your self-control was amazing, given the circumstances, Mrs Ashworth."

"What self-control? I wept all over you." Annie was feeling rather embarrassed about that.

"Not for long. And I did not object." He shot a wry glance in her direction but did not elaborate. He would have been happy to hold her for longer, to hold her in a more intimate way, but with the memory of their earlier encounter in the shop before she had leased it imprinted on his mind, he had not attempted to do more than give her a brotherly pat on the shoulders and then release her the minute she started to pull away. To his surprise, he found himself thinking of the brute who had hurt her so badly all those years ago. He would like to smash the rogue's face to a pulp. And that feeling came as a complete surprise to him. It was a long time since he had felt protective towards a woman.

Annie blushed at the memory of herself weeping all over a man like him and caught his eyes on her, warm and friendly, not like his usual cynical expression. "I never thought to ask," she said, conscience-stricken, "but you must have had other plans for today."

"Nothing that can't wait. The mill will function well enough without me, and Peters is quite capable of managing things in my absence." He gave a little cough of laughter. "I don't usually indulge in such impulsive behaviour, to be frank, Mrs Ashworth, but I find I'm quite enjoying the idea of giving this villain a run for his money."

The coachman, having been told to make all haste, did not slow down until they were nearly there. When they joined the Oldham Road and met the press of traffic entering the central district of the city, it was impossible to maintain their rapid pace.

"Look at all them people!" whispered Rebecca, tugging Annie's sleeve. "I didn't think Manchester would be so *big*?"

"It seems to grow and change every time I visit it," admitted Annie. "You should see the new railway station, Rebecca. I couldn't believe my eyes at the size of it."

"Manchester is considered by some to be one of the wonders of the modern world," said Frederick, pride gleaming in his eyes, "and is much talked about throughout the country for its rapid development. We at the Exchange mean to keep it that way, too."

"There's been a lot of hunger round here in the past few years, though, as well as development," said Annie.

Frederick nodded. "Worse in Manchester than in Bilsden. We've managed to keep our workforce mainly employed in

Bilsden, one way or another. And bad as Claters End is, it's nowhere near as bad as Little Ireland in Manchester. There are children born on bare flagstones still there, and the death rate is a scandal."

"I didn't know you cared about that sort of thing."

He grinned at her, a boy's grin that took her by surprise. "I didn't used to care, but as I've grown older, I've come to see that we're all bound up together, masters and men, women and children. If I lose my workforce, I lose my income. If the sanitary conditions are bad, the rich die too – as my wife died in the recent epidemic. I think, with the increasing size of towns, that we employers will have to care more for our people, and for our towns, too. That's what I was doing this morning, looking at our town centre, wondering how we could make it something to be proud of."

He dropped that subject as the carriage threaded its way along the busy Mosley Street. When Annie indicated the warehouse she wanted to visit, he pulled the check-string and the coachman drew up.

"I'll just go and stretch my legs while you're looking at their stock," said Frederick. "I'll join you inside in time to pay for it."

Annie nodded, guessing that he wanted to relieve himself. That sort of thing was so much easier for men. She marched inside, an awed Rebecca pressing close beside her, and asked to see some heavy silks. Luck was on her side, because within minutes she had been shown a bale of lustrous creamy silk that was, she thought, even prettier than the ruined material because it had a slight pinkish tinge to it that would cast a very flattering glow upon a lady's complexion.

She turned towards Frederick as he entered the shop, an unshadowed smile on her face that made him catch his breath at her beauty. "We're in luck, Mr Hallam. This one will be perfect for Her Ladyship. In fact, it's even prettier than the original material, which was rather stiff." While the shopman cut her the length required, she went to search through the ribbons and again found exactly what she wanted, a narrow cream satin ribbon to thread through the lace flounces and bertha, and a broader ribbon in the same colour to frill beneath the flounces and make them stand out. While Frederick was paying for the silk, she stood beside him, so that she could be sure of exactly how much she owed him.

"I'll be able to pay you back on Monday as soon as the bank is open," she said as he put his wallet away.

"I suppose it's no use saying that it doesn't matter. To me, it's a very trifling sum."

"No use at all. There's no earthly reason why you should pay for my materials."

"I thought you'd say that. You're a very independent young woman, Mrs Ashworth."

"Yes. And I like it that way. Independent and respectable." But the word young surprised her and stayed with her. It had been a long time since she had thought of herself as young.

He offered her his arm and she could not refuse that, but somehow she was very conscious of the warm muscular body beneath the fine navy broadcloth of his paletot jacket. She had never thought of him quite like this before. He was older than her by about twenty years, she would guess, but was tall and vigorous. Even his thinning hair somehow suited him. He looked what he was, a man of property and position, a leading figure in his own milieu, a fine distinguished gentleman.

Rebecca followed close behind them, staring around wide-eyed and taking in everything she saw, so that she could boast of it later to the boys. "It were like bein' in chapel, that shop were," she said later, "all quiet an' people talkin' in hushed voices. An' them gentlemen what served us looked right down their noses at most folks, but they didn't look down their noses at Mr Hallam. They jumped about like fleas in a bucket to serve *him*. Eh, you never saw anything like it!"

"Shall we make a very quick pause for something to eat and drink?" Frederick said as they got back into the coach. "I know it's not lunch time, but you must want to – er – wash your hands. I know just the place."

"Yes." Annie suddenly became aware of the needs of her body. "Yes. And I hope this eating place of yours has a retiring room?" She grinned across at him cheekily, feeling more herself now that she had found some material for Her Ladyship. "And then, we'll go straight back to Bilsden and I'll sew all night. I'm *not* going to let this stop me!"

"No. You have a great deal of courage, Mrs Ashworth. I admire that very much."

"Oh. Well, thank you. And – I'd like to say how grateful I am for your help today, Mr Hallam, very grateful indeed."

She could not stop another blush creeping up her face and the warmth stayed there for a while, for she was very conscious of his admiring glances, much too conscious of them for her own peace of mind.

On the Sunday afternoon, a very weary Annie was driven to the Hall where she carried the linen-wrapped gown carefully from the carriage, refusing to hand it over to the footman whom she followed upstairs to Her Ladyship's sitting room. There, she sat and waited in an agony of apprehension for Her Ladyship to finish taking tea and come up to her.

The door opened and she jerked round, but it was only Sarah.

"Did it turn out all right? Can I see it?"

Annie shook her head. "Not just yet. I want to explain something to Her Ladyship before I unwrap it." She ignored Sarah's affronted expression and sat grimly on, her eyes gritty with weariness. The precious minutes ticked past and the nearly finished gown lay hidden under its linen shroud. She had decided not to pull it out until she had explained what had happened.

At last, footsteps came up the stairs and Sarah nodded. "That's her. I can tell her step anywhere." The two of them stood up and waited.

Lady Darrington walked in on her husband's arm. "My dear, this is Mrs Ashworth, the modiste whom Pauline recommended." She looked at the still-wrapped bundle and her fine eyebrows rose. "Is something wrong with it? I'd expected you to have it laid out ready."

"There's nothing wrong, Your Ladyship," said Annie, "but I have something to explain before I show you the gown."

Lady Darrington sat down on the sofa, waited until her husband had lounged over to an armchair by the window, and then nodded to Annie to commence.

"On Friday night, someone broke into my salon and destroyed the contents of my workroom, including your gown. In fact, I think destroying your gown was the main reason they broke in, for they touched nothing downstairs and they didn't steal anything."

Sarah gasped aloud and Her Ladyship looked shocked. "My dear, how terrible! After all your work."

Hard work! thought Annie, who had worked through Saturday night and snatched only a couple of hours' sleep when her eyes grew too tired to focus on the sewing, starting again early on Sunday morning. "Yes. I was both furious and upset at first. But a – a friend took my sister and me into Manchester in his carriage and we found some more material there for you. Actually, I think the new material is even nicer than the satin, and it's almost the same colour, Your Ladyship."

"But – you surely can't have finished another dress in that short time. And what about the fittings?"

"I had your old dress and my pattern pieces to go by."

"You must have worked extremely hard."

211

"Yes. My workpeople and I sat up all night because we didn't want to let you down. I can still alter the seams if the gown doesn't fit perfectly. I've left enough allowances." Only then did she move across and take her creation out of its covering, holding it up in front of her and shaking the soft folds into place.

Lady Darrington moved across to examine it carefully. "Yes, the material is a very similar colour, isn't it?" She felt it between her fingertips. "And it's a good piece of silk. You can't mistake that sort of quality. I'll try it on now, if you please." She turned to her husband. "Darling, will you wait here? I must have your approval if I'm to wear the dress in front of all the county tomorrow night."

Annie went into the bedroom and slipped the dress carefully over Her Ladyship's head, then checked the two side seams on the bodice, breathing a sigh of relief when she found that her estimates had been correct. "Yes. A few finishing touches is all it needs, I think, Your Ladyship, and I can do that before I leave."

Sarah came over to peer at the fit, then stood back to study the style and nodded.

Annie stepped back and waited, heart in her mouth, to hear the verdict. She felt stiff with both anxiety and fatigue, and it took all her will-power to stand still as Lady Darrington twirled about in front of the mirror, then twisted round for another look at the fit of the back.

"What do you think, Sarah?"

"It's a good fit, Your Ladyship."

"Yes. It is. An excellent fit." She frowned into the mirror. "A simpler style than I usually wear, but it's a beautiful weight of silk, just right for an evening gown and the ribbon frills beneath the lace give it a pretty touch. You've made some changes to the original style, though, Mrs Ashworth."

Annie held her breath.

"But I like them. I'll show the gown to my husband and see what he thinks." She laughed. "A wife's object in life is always to please her husband, is it not?"

"I'm a widow, Your Ladyship."

"How sad at your age!" But it was a token utterance. Her Ladyship was more concerned with the gown.

Lord Darrington stood up as his wife entered the sitting room and examined her and the gown with a connoisseur's eyes. He was extremely proud of his lovely second wife, the more so as his first wife had been a plain woman and a dowd into the bargain, even if she had brought him a fortune and given him two sons. "Turn round. Yes, simple but beautiful lines. I like it, my dear. I think you need not fear to be seen in company in it." He grinned. "In fact, all the old biddies will be asking you if you bought it in Paris and if simplicity is the latest style."

They turned with common accord to stare at Annie, waiting in the doorway.

"Thank you very much, Mrs Ashworth! You will let me have your account, including the cost of the new material? No, I insist! Now, will you come and help me out of the dress? Then you can put the finishing touches to it."

"Certainly, Your Ladyship. I came prepared. I wanted to be sure everything was perfect."

That night, Annie slept the clock round, waking lazily long after the others had left their beds on the Monday. She ate a leisurely breakfast in the cosy warmth of the kitchen while Kathy went off to the shops with Joanie in tow. That kitchen range certainly kept things warm, as well as being a godsend with all the hot water it supplied.

Thus it was that when Danny O'Connor knocked on the door, she was the one to open it, her face still flushed from the heat of the fire and the last cup of tea. She stood and stared up at him, her heart fluttering and a feeling of apprehension trickling down her spine, for some reason she could not fathom.

"Oh! Danny. What a surprise!"

"Aren't you going to ask me in, Annie?"

"Oh. Well, I was just going off to the salon, actually."

He put his hands on her shoulders and propelled her gently backwards through the door, feeling her stiffening at his touch. "You can surely spare the time to make me one cup of tea." His smile was lazy and his large muscular body seemed to fill the hallway. "For old times' sake," he added softly.

She turned without a word and led the way into the kitchen, praying that Kathy would soon return. Danny was just too big and too masculine for comfort. "We spend most of our time in here. I hope you don't mind sitting at the kitchen table. We don't light a fire in the parlour until the evening." She could hear the hesitation in her voice as she moved the kettle to the centre of the hob.

Danny walked round the kitchen to look out of the window at the garden, and Annie went across to fumble with the cups and saucers. "Would you like a piece of Kathy's fruit cake?"

"Yes, I'd love a piece of Kathy's fruit cake."

His eyes were mocking her. He knew exactly how she was feeling, the wretch! "And how are Bridie and Mick?"

"They're well. Very well."

She sought desperately for some subject of conversation. "I – I thought you could only get up here at weekends."

"I'm between contracts, so I've taken a few days' holiday to visit my family. And to see you."

With relief, she heard the kettle boiling and went across to pour the water into the teapot. Her hands were trembling so much that she splashed water on to her hand and made a soft mew of pain.

Danny was there in a second. He took the teapot from her and then moved the kettle to the side of the hob. He put the teapot down on the table and before she had realised what he was doing, he had taken hold of her hand to examine the scald. He set his lips to it and she gasped at the thrill that shot through her at the touch of their moist warmth on her skin. "Do you have some cold water, Annie, love? I've found it the best thing for scalds."

To her relief, he let her hand go and made no more attempt to touch her.

"I can manage it myself," she said hurriedly. But when she walked out into the new bathroom to the washbasin there and ran the cold tap on her hand, he was beside her.

"Marvellous, aren't they, these modern bathrooms?" he said, examining the new fittings with great interest and then smiling down at her.

"W-what?"

"Modern bathrooms. I hear the retiring room at your salon is the talk of the town. We have to make do with rather primitive facilities on the diggings, I'm afraid. Ah, Annie, love, don't look at me like that!"

She took a step backwards. "Like what?"

"As if I'm about to rape you. Am I not standing several paces away from you? Surely you feel safe enough with me over here, though it's not where I'd choose to be?"

"I never feel safe with you, Danny," she blurted out.

The pained expression on his face made her try to explain. "It's not that I think you're going to attack me. It's," she shook her head for she was puzzled by her own reactions, "it's the way you make me feel."

"Ah!" His voice grew soft, and the anxiety left his face. "Then you do feel something for me?"

"I didn't say that!" The words came out too sharply.

"Then what in heaven's name did you mean?"

She buried her face in her hands. "I don't know! *I don't know*!"

"Annie, I've been in love with you since the first time I

came back home and you made those two dresses for my mam. You know that, surely?"

"I – I knew you were attracted to me."

"You were married then, so I stepped back, but, Annie, you're not married now. Surely, surely, you don't want to stay frozen like this for the rest of your life?"

She drew in a long shuddering breath. "I – I don't know what I want, Danny O'Connor. I've got my life nicely organised. I like running my salon. I've got my family to look after, so I'm not lonely. I don't *need* a – a—" She turned a bright scarlet as she realised that she had been going to say "husband". Why, she didn't even know that his intentions were honourable. She didn't know anything, any more!

He finished the sentence for her, "Husband. You were going to say husband, weren't you? Why did you stop?"

She swung away from him and walked jerkily towards the door into the kitchen, but he was there before her, blocking the way. "Why did you stop?" he repeated.

"Because you haven't – we're not – because – Danny O'Connor, will you just leave me alone!"

"No. No, that's one thing I don't think I can agree to do." Again those gentle hands were on her shoulders, turning her to face him. "You can pull away from me any time, love. I won't force you to do anything. But I'd like to share one kiss with you, just one." His head was bending towards her as he spoke and she stared up at him, her lips slightly parted, unable to move or speak or think. And then the lips had touched hers, with the softest brushing of flesh against flesh, and he was feathering kisses on her mouth and face until his lips came back to hers, until they sealed her to him in a much firmer kiss.

She sagged against him and as his lips left hers and he simply held her against him, she sighed and let herself stand for a moment with her head on that broad chest, let herself breathe

the scent of his cologne, let herself lean on someone else for a change.

They stood there in a close embrace for perhaps a minute, then she panicked and started to pull away. His arms opened instantly and he stepped backwards. "I won't force anything upon you, my little love. But my intentions are strictly honourable and I'm an extremely stubborn man when I want something. Won't you give me a chance, let me show you that love can be a beautiful thing? That it's a sin to shut it out of your life?"

"I don't know. I – I'll think about it." She heard the sound of Kathy and Joanie returning and sighed with relief as she turned to leave the bathroom.

He stood there for a moment. "Damn the fellow who did that to her!" he muttered through gritted teeth. "If anyone ever deserved to be hung, that one does." Then a wry expression crossed his face. The fellow had done one useful thing: he had prevented Annie from marrying anyone else. For that at least, Danny was grateful. And if he, with his wide experience of women, could not coax her into his arms, then no one could. She would make a most suitable wife, in every possible way.

Back in the kitchen, they all shared a cup of tea and Danny talked cheerfully about his parents and the farm. As he left, he asked Annie to escort him to the front door and after a moment's hesitation, she did so, hurrying out of the kitchen to hide the blush that spread over her face at the look in his eyes.

"Will you let me write to you?" he asked softly.

"I – suppose so."

"And will you write back to me?"

"I – I will if I have time."

"I'll say goodbye, then, love. No, there's a French phrase someone taught me that says it better. *Au revoir*. Till we see each other again, it means."

When she had closed the door, she just stood in the hallway, leaning against it. She wished Danny O'Connor had not turned up like that. He was too disturbing, much too disturbing. She did not want the complications of a man in her life, especially a man like Danny. It was a while before she had calmed down enough to return to the kitchen.

Fourteen

1845–46 ANNABELLE

Brighton
3rd December, 1845

My dear Jeremy,

I was glad to hear from my other correspondents that Marianne recovered quickly from her indisposition earlier this year, and that you have brought your Cousin Dorothy to Bilsden to chaperone her. One cannot be too careful of a young lady's reputation.

I am writing to beg you to allow our daughter to visit me occasionally in Brighton. Whatever our differences, you will surely not deny a mother's right to see her child?

I have told my friends here that I'm living in Brighton for health reasons, and indeed, my health has improved considerably in recent months. The damp air of Bilsden never did agree with me. I hope you will keep to the same story, since a scandal about our separation would damage Marianne's future prospects of marriage and social acceptance, as well as my own present life.

I remain your wife in the eyes of the Lord and the Law,

Annabelle

Bilsden
10th December, 1845

Madam,

There is no question of Marianne coming to visit you in Brighton, nor would I wish you to come to Bilsden to see her. My Cousin Dorothy is as careful as any mother would wish of Marianne's welfare, so your recently acquired concern is needless.

I shall, however, though only for Marianne's sake, agree to keep up the fiction that you are living in Brighton for health reasons.

J Lewis

Brighton
5th April, 1846

Dear Jeremy,

I was deeply hurt by your response to my request to see our child, but must abide by your decision, harsh though it is.

*

I intend to go away for a few days in the near future and shall tell people that I'm coming to Bilsden to see Marianne. For our daughter's sake, I hope you will not contradict this?

Are you sure you will not reconsider your harsh decision and at least allow Marianne to meet me half-way in London?

I remain your wife in the eyes of the Lord and the Law, and the mother of your only child,

Annabelle

Bilsden
12 April, 1846

Madam,

I have no desire for any further meetings or correspondence with you, nor shall I permit you to see Marianne at any time.

I intend to take Marianne away every summer, so if you will inform me of the dates you will be away from Brighton, I shall try to arrange our holidays to coincide with them. That is purely for Marianne's sake.

I will remind you that it was your own choice to abandon your child.

J Lewis

When Annabelle received that letter, she screwed it up and

threw it across the room. "Sanctimonious prig!" she fumed. She continued in a bad mood all day.

Cora retrieved and read the letter at the first opportunity. She was amused at the fuss her mistress was making, when the last thing Annabelle really wanted was a visit from a daughter who was near enough to womanhood to emphasise her mother's age. Mrs Lewis wouldn't have sent an invitation at all if it weren't for the other women talking about their children and pitying her. Cora had heard them, for she eavesdropped shamelessly.

Cora was often amused by Mrs Lewis nowadays, especially her mistress's efforts to remain youthful-looking, but she knew better than to let this show. Instead, she fussed solicitously over her, and oohed and aahed over her appearance. Ever since their arrival in Brighton, Annabelle had put on die-away airs and graces, and had cultivated the impression of someone in delicate health, but she was never too ill to attend a dinner party or receive visitors, and never too ill to fuss about her clothes. Nor did she lack the energy to tyrannise the cook and the other maid.

She had tried at one stage to treat Cora in a similarly autocratic way, but a not-so-gentle hint or two from Cora had put an end to that, and mistress and maid had now developed a very good working relationship. A bit of fuss and flattery went a long way with Annabelle and cost Cora nothing. Looking after Mrs Lewis was an easy job, on the whole, and Cora was enjoying living in Brighton, which she found a big improvement on Manchester and Bilsden.

The need to be careful about money was the thing which irked Annabelle the most about her new life. Mr Minton continued to manage her small investments and to get the most out of them that he could, and Jeremy sent her money regularly, but it was never enough for her to indulge her tastes as she would like, and how she was going to afford a decent holiday in the summer, she did not know. She did not want to dip into her investments.

She tried writing again to Jeremy to point out that she would find it a little difficult to afford a holiday on the small allowance he sent her, but all that got her was an extra ten pounds and the recommendation to try a quiet stay in the country where things were always cheaper.

That same afternoon, Henry Minton dropped in on one of his regular visits to Annabelle.

"You seem a little put out about something," he remarked after a while.

"I am! I've just received a letter from that stupid husband of mine. Of all the miserly creatures! My poor dear daughter's life must be a misery with him, an absolute misery."

Henry leaned back in his chair, amused by her tantrums. "Did he refuse to send you any more money, then?"

"Oh!" For a moment, she was angry at his bluntness, then she sighed and smiled at him. "I could never deceive you, my dear Henry, could I? Yes, he did refuse to send me enough money for my holiday. How he expects me to manage on the pittance he allows me, I don't know! And where am I to go, I ask you? I can't afford London prices, I really can't. But I must get away. And of course, I must spend a few days in Bilsden. People will think it very strange if I never go back to see my dear daughter."

"Oh, come on! Admit it, Annabelle. Your daughter is as dear to you as my wife is to me, and you have no intention of going back to Bilsden."

She pouted and looked at him sideways, not certain whether to be annoyed at this blunt speaking or not. He was grinning at her. Henry had a rather roguish grin and his ways were very direct at times, but he had done wonders with her investments. Even so, she found her lack of income restricting her mode of life, especially in comparison to her friend

Barbara, who was lavishly provided for in her widowhood. After a moment, Annabelle allowed a smile to creep over her own face. She enjoyed Henry's company very much and he could always cheer her up. "I'm admitting nothing, even to you."

"And I thought we were friends," he said mockingly. He sat up again and looked her straight in the eyes. "After all, I've looked after you and your investments very well, haven't I, Annabelle? One day those slum houses will bring you in a rich return."

"But not yet, unfortunately." She gave her cooing laugh, the one she used only on gentlemen she wished to attract. "Still, I am grateful for your help, my dear Henry. You have excellent business sense."

"As do you, my dear Annabelle. Try to be patient with those properties. It isn't quite time to sell them, if you want to make a decent profit."

She sighed, but nodded her head. "I do realise that."

"If I'd had a sensible wife like you, my dear lady, I'd have been a rich man by now" He tilted his head on one side, considering. He'd been wanting to push their relationship a step further for a while now, to break through that polished facade to the woman beneath. He enjoyed a challenge, and this woman was a very big challenge to a man of his tastes. Maybe this was the time to do something about that. "I think I can help you with this holiday."

She was instantly alert. "Oh?" If he was going to ask her to go away with him, she would tell him exactly what he could do with his suggestion. She had not got rid of a husband in order to encumber herself with a lover. There was absolutely nothing to be gained from that.

"That is, if you're prepared to put up with a little boredom for the sake of saving money."

She looked puzzled. A man asking her to become his

mistress would not talk of boredom, surely? "I don't understand you, Henry."

"Well, I have a friend who has a place in the country. He'll be away for the whole summer and has asked me to keep an eye on the cottage for him. There's a woman who comes in as needed from the village to clean, otherwise it's quite a remote location. If you went to stay there, you need see no one. And the woman is very discreet. She would do your shopping for you. No one need set eyes on you, especially if you arrived dressed in black with a heavy veil covering your face," he grinned again, "the grieving widow, as it were."

"It sounds promising. But would I be on my own there?"

"Of course!" He wagged a finger at her. "It wouldn't be proper for me to stay there at the same time, would it, much as I'd enjoy your company? And you're not the sort of woman to have an affair, beautiful as you are. I realise that. You're too much of a lady. Unfortunately." He sighed delicately and looked at her with warm admiration.

"Hmm." She sat frowning at him, still not certain whether to accept his offer. She hated the countryside and always had done, for she had grown up in a small village. However, there was no denying that her means were rather slender as yet and that she would prefer to spend her money on clothing rather than hotel bills. And if she went to London there was always the chance of someone from Brighton seeing her and realising that she was not with her husband. She dared not risk that.

"If you were to let that maid of yours take her annual holidays at the same time, no one – absolutely no one – would know where you were." He looked at her guilelessly, with an expression of boyish honesty on his face that he had worked hard in front of the mirror to perfect.

Annabelle looked at him in silence for a moment, with her head tilted on one side. There was no denying that it would be better to do this without Cora. The minx knew far too much about her mistress's affairs already. "Tell me more about this cottage, Henry."

A month later, Cora departed happily to spend her two weeks' annual holiday with her family who lived near Bilsden. She intended to call on Ellie Peters while she was up there, to see what was happening in the dear doctor's household. You never knew when that sort of knowledge might come in useful, especially with a mistress like Annabelle Lewis. Cora knew that Annabelle resented the hold her maid had over her, even though Cora never pressed the point.

The next day, Annabelle took the afternoon train to London, ostensibly going to visit her daughter in Bilsden. She was travelling alone, something she had never done before, and she felt both elated and nervous. Henry had arranged for her to change trains in London and head out from the city again on one of the smaller railway lines. A carriage was to meet her at the station nearest to the cottage. Really, it was most convenient to have such an accommodating man of business and one who was safely married as well. Annabelle enjoyed the flirtations and the sighing and hand-holding, as she always had done, but was prepared to go no further, not even with Henry, though she did, she had to admit, find him rather an attractive man, so vigorous and masterful. She had never enjoyed sharing Jeremy's bed or found his looks more than passable. As for the marital act, it was a disgusting messy business and it led to the bearing of children, which was even more disgusting. But a light elegant flirtation was a very pleasant pastime for a lady like herself.

Everything went very smoothly. She changed her clothes in the Ladies' Room in London and emerged clad in black and heavily veiled. Her own mother would not have recognised her. A little play with her handkerchief and the other passengers on the train left her completely alone.

When she got out of the train at some tiny halt in the middle of nowhere, she stood waiting, a brave lonely figure, while the porter collected her luggage. As if on a cue, a carriage moved forward.

The driver tipped his hat to her. "Mrs Denby?"

"Yes."

"I was sent to pick you up." He opened the door and helped her inside, then dealt with her luggage. Without another word exchanged, they were soon clopping along a country road.

Annabelle sat in a corner of the carriage, keeping her skirts off the rather dusty floor, and smiled to herself. It would be a boring few days, but she had brought several books, some needlework and her sketching materials. She would contrive to pass the time, and it would cost her virtually nothing. Why, dear Henry had even paid her train fare! That had been an unexpected bonus and she had not made more than a token protest.

When they arrived, she peered through the window and frowned. In the fading light she could see that the cottage was somewhat smaller than she had expected. Not the sort of place she usually stayed in.

The driver helped her out and carried her luggage to the door, pushing it open and depositing her valises in the hallway. He touched his hat. "Everything is ready for you, Mrs Denby. If you need anything else, there's a store in the village as sells most things, an' if you want a woman to clean, just ask there an' they'll find you someone."

She inclined her head and entered the cottage. Someone had thoughtfully lit the lamps in the little sitting room.

"Shall I carry your valises upstairs, madam?"

"No, thank you. I can manage on my own." More play with her black-edged handkerchief and he was gone without the need for a tip. She slid the bolt on the front door, picked up the lamp someone had left lit for her and began to explore the rooms leading off the little hallway. *Much* smaller than she had expected! But at least it was clean. She found the back door and bolted that too.

She was about to go upstairs when she heard a sound. For the first time, the isolation of this place made her feel uneasy. She darted across to peer out of the window of the small sitting room but could see no one outside. It was probably just some animal. There were, she remembered from her youth, all sorts of animal noises in the countryside. She turned and gasped in terror at the sight of a figure in the doorway, letting out a little scream before she realised who it was.

"Surely," said Henry, "you didn't really expect me to leave you here on your own, my sweet? And you'd better put that lamp down before you drop it and set the place on fire. Are you nervous? No need to be. We're old friends, you and I."

Her hand was shaking so much that she had difficulty setting the lamp down safely. She retreated immediately to the other side of a small table, and it was a moment before she could control her voice enough to ask sharply, "What are you doing here, Henry?"

He smiled and began to unbutton his jacket. "I've come to keep you company, my dear. I found that I was free for a few days, and I saw no reason to spend them with my stupid wife."

"I think I had better leave, then. It would not be at all proper for us both to stay here." But she did not like to move, for he was blocking the doorway and he was a big man. For a moment, the expression on his face was gloating, then he changed back into the Henry she knew and she let out her breath in a little sigh of relief.

"But, Annabelle, the carriage has gone. How do you intend to leave?" His voice was calm, as was his demeanour. "It's over two miles to the village, and there's no moon tonight."

"Then *you* must leave, Henry. We really cannot—"

"I've no intention of leaving, Annabelle."

A shiver of fear ran down her spine. She could not believe this was happening, could not seem to think straight. Her heart was thudding in her chest and her hands felt clammy with fright.

He allowed the silence to continue for several minutes, then smiled in a more normal way. "Oh, come, Annabelle, do you think I'm going to rape you? I can get a clean girl any time for half a guinea, you know."

"But – what are you doing here, then?"

"Pretending."

"I beg your pardon?"

"Pretending that I'm married to a real lady like yourself. Giving myself the chance of a few days of gracious living. You'll surely allow me that, Annabelle? A man has his dreams too." He sighed and looked at her soulfully.

Relief flooded through her, but her voice still shook with nervousness. "I still cannot like it, Henry."

"Let's try it for tonight, then. If you still feel uneasy in the morning, then I'll leave, I promise you. But it's pitch dark outside and it's a long way to the village. Besides, they'd wonder what I was doing wandering round the countryside when the gig from the Green Man brought me out here only this afternoon."

"People know that you're here! Henry, how *could* you compromise me like this!"

"You're not compromised, my dear Annabelle. The anonymous Mrs Denby is. And no one's even seen her face. Come, my dear, at least give me a chance to show you whether I can be good company or not, to show you whether you can trust me or not?"

And he was good company, Annabelle had to admit that. His tales of sharp practices and ways of earning a little extra money on an investment were most amusing. And he was surprisingly well read. What was more, he knew all the latest gossip from Brighton. They dined on the simple stew prepared by the woman from the village, but Henry produced a bottle of good wine and Annabelle was persuaded to take a small glass. But only one glass. He need not think he was going to inebriate her and persuade her to do something stupid.

At ten o'clock, she yawned and stood up. "I think I'll retire now."

He stood up and escorted her to the door. "You won't mind if I linger over the wine, my dear? I'm not one to seek my bed early."

"Not at all." She took her lit candle from him with a hand that trembled slightly and made her way swiftly up the stairs.

She found that her bedroom door had a bolt and when she had shot it, she jammed a chair under the door handle, just to be sure. Then she sighed with relief and went to stare out of the window, shivering at the darkness of the garden and the sound of the wind which had started to rise. She would definitely ask Henry to leave in the morning. His presence in the house was making her feel uneasy, though she could not understand why, for he had behaved like a perfect gentleman.

She turned round to start her toilette. She always enjoyed this washing and creaming of her body. She removed her bodice and skirt and hung them in the little cupboard under the eaves, then poured a bowl of water. Cold water, unfortunately, but she had not liked to risk lingering downstairs to heat some water. And anyway, it was nearly summer, not really cold.

Suddenly, the bookcase on one wall swung outwards and before she could do more than utter a small scream, Henry had stepped into the room, clad in a silk dressing gown, with bare legs showing beneath it. "You didn't really think I intended to sleep alone, did you, Annabelle?" The gloating expression was back and his eyes were raking her body.

She grabbed her towel and tried to cover herself, but he only laughed and took a step towards her. "Get out!" she yelled, really frightened now. "Get out of here this minute!"

"It doesn't matter how loudly you scream," he said in a conversational tone. "There's no one to hear."

"Henry, I can't believe that you – that you—" She retreated as far as she could, but the room was small and she soon found herself pressed against the wall. "Please, Henry, don't!"

He said nothing, just reached out and calmly took the towel from her trembling hands.

She moaned and flattened herself against the wall. "Henry, *please!*"

He took her by the wrist and pulled her towards the bed. "My friend who owns the cottage has rather strange tastes," he said. "That's why he needs a quiet place like this. He doesn't like to disturb the neighbours with strange – er – noises. Thanks to him, I think we'll be able to spend a very interesting night together here, my dear, my very dear Annabelle. Quite an uninhibited night, in fact."

She threw herself away from him, screaming wildly, but he just laughed and kept hold of her arm. When she could not shake him off, she lunged forward, scratching at his face with the nails of her free hand. He slapped that hand away before she could touch him and swung her round, catching her flailing hands and pinning them behind her.

He sat her down hard on the bed, then cut her hysterics off by slapping her face. When she continued to sob wildly, he shook her. "Are you ready to listen to me now, or must I slap some more sense into you?"

She could only moan and stare at him in terror.

"Yes," he said softly, "that's more like it." He ran one hand over her bare shoulder and she tried to jerk away from him. "Ah, you're trembling now. Poor little Annabelle. You'll be trembling even more by the time I've finished with you."

He pulled her across to lie on the bed and although she struggled, he fastened each of her arms to the bedposts with the ropes that hung ready down the back.

Why had she not noticed them before? How could this be happening to her?

Then he began to remove her clothes, ripping her chemise. When she was quite naked and whimpering, he stood up and removed his dressing gown, revealing the muscular hairy body usually concealed beneath well-tailored suits.

He hardly seemed to notice her weeping and pleading. He was already fully aroused and was much bigger in every way than Jeremy. He yawned and stretched himself like a great lazy cat.

She lay there, sobbing under her breath, but staring at him in fascination. "P-please, Henry—" she begged.

"If you don't keep your mouth shut, my dear Annabelle, I'll have to gag you," he said, stroking one fingertip up her leg and stopping just before he reached the top. "What is it to be?"

She could only whimper with fear and try to writhe away from him.

"Now, madam, we'll give you something to remember, something that husband of yours obviously couldn't provide."

The first time he took her was rough, but not too different from Jeremy's night-time fumblings. When he rolled off, she shuddered, but could not help letting out a sigh of relief.

He threw his head back and laughed. "You surely didn't think that was it, did you, Annabelle?"

She gasped. "But you – you just—"

"That was only a taster, to keep my little friend down there happy. He's a very energetic fellow, my little friend is, and he's all ready now to start the real business of the evening."

She had not known that pain could be so close to pleasure, or that her body could respond like this. After a while, he untied her, because he said it cramped his style for her to remain in the one position. By the time he had finished prodding and tweaking and stroking, she was numbly acquiescent to his every wish, lying there beneath or above him, as ordered, and moving as his rough hands forced her to.

Eventually, he rolled off her and sighed. "All good things must come to an end."

She thought he would leave her then, so that she could at least wash, but he did not. He stayed there in the bed, a heavy stinking male animal, and the terror stayed with him. Before he blew out the lamp, he grabbed her by the chin and shook her face roughly, staring at her. "Hmm. I think we won't risk anything. You're not really tamed yet." Before she had realised what he meant, he had produced a wrist chain and fastened one of her arms to the bedpost. Then he tweaked her sore nipples one last time, rolled over and fell asleep.

She did not dare sob aloud in case she wakened him. She lay there, listening to his even breathing. She would never be able to sleep, never . . . but her bruised and exhausted body soon slipped into unconsciousness.

In the morning, she jerked awake as a hand slapped her bare bottom. She gazed round wildly and would have screamed, but he put his hand over her mouth. "I really don't like screaming women, Annabelle." He unfastened her arm and allowed her to attend to her needs, then he threw a thin pink cotton wrap at her. "You can put that on, if you like!"

"I – I think I'd rather get dressed."

"That wrapper, my dear Annabelle, is what you'll be wearing today, and it's all that you'll be wearing." That knowing grin was back as he eyed her naked body and she blushed for shame as she remembered what they had done in the long dark hours of the night.

"Please allow me to – to dress properly, Henry. Someone might come to the door."

"No one will come, my pet. We've enough food for a day or two, and when we need more, I'll go into the village and get some."

Only then did she truly realise how much in his power she was. She had hoped that the night had been an aberration, that having slaked his lust on her, he would then leave. "But—"

"I couldn't leave a lady like you here all on her own. It wouldn't be safe." He threw the pink wrap at her feet, chuckled and went over to pee loudly into the chamber pot.

With hands that shook and trembled, she pulled the wrapper on, then stood there, not knowing what to do. She watched as he put on trousers and a shirt, and then shrank back as he pushed her out of the way to remove the chair and undo the bolt on the door.

"We don't need that chair any more, do we? Now, come and have some breakfast."

"I c-couldn't—"

"Then you shall get mine and watch me eat it. Come along, Annabelle. You really must learn to do as you're told." He twined his hand through her long blonde hair and pulled her through the door. "Beautiful hair, you've got. I'm looking forward to seeing it spread out over my chest again later." He jerked her to a rough halt and shook her slightly. "You aren't going to start weeping again, are you? That would put me right off my breakfast."

She gulped and tried to control her panic.

"That's better." He led her downstairs.

By nightfall, he had taken her again several times, where and how he pleased. The last time, he had surprised her into an orgasm, which terrified her even more than his rough handling. "That's it, my pretty lady, you're learning." Then he threw back his head and roared with laughter. "That was the first time you've ever felt that, wasn't it?"

She nodded, lying soft and bemused in the aftermath of passion shared.

"Your bloody husband didn't know how to handle a woman. I do."

Within a few days, she was craving the pleasure he could give her, horrified at her own feelings but unable to resist his skilled handling. She had never realised what it could be like. All those years wasted because of Jeremy's ineptitude!

On their last evening at the cottage, they sat together over a bottle of port. "What's going to happen now?" she asked, since he had said nothing about the future.

"What do you want to happen, Annabelle?"

She swallowed hard. "I – I—"

He sat and waited, smiling across at her. "You'll have to tell me what you want, you know. I'm not going to do it for you."

She did not look at him as she said, "I want it to continue, Henry. Please."

Fifteen

BILSDEN: NOVEMBER 1845

Marianne slammed the door and ran down the path, snatching
Ellie's shawl from the peg by the kitchen door and pulling it
around her shoulders. The door opened behind her and a shrill
voice called, "Come back here at once, you wicked girl!" but
Marianne ignored Cousin Dorothy and continued running. She
could not bear to spend another minute in her chaperone's
company, could not endure the continual carping and criticism
that filled the hours whenever her father was not with them.

If her father had been there, she would have gone to him
and begged him yet again to send Dorothy away. She would
have *made* him see that she would go mad if things continued
like this. But he wasn't there. He was spending a few days in
Edinburgh with other medical gentlemen interested in the
problems of childbirth and he would not be back for several
days.

It was all right for him, she fumed, as she slowed down to a
rapid walk and made her way instinctively up towards the
moors she loved. Her father could escape any time he wanted
from the close atmosphere of Park House, leaving his new

assistant, earnest young Dr Spelling, in charge of the practice. It never seemed to occur to Jeremy that his daughter would also have liked to escape from Bilsden, though he had promised her a holiday in the summer, a holiday without Cousin Dorothy's company.

An hour later, Marianne was glowing from her exercise, in spite of the chill November weather. She stopped to look down at the smoky valley below and breathe in the tangy moorland air in great gulps. Things always felt better up here. Below her, the bells of St Mark's started ringing. "Well, she can just go to church without me!" she said aloud.

"Would you rather have some company, or do you enjoy talking to yourself?" asked a voice behind her and she whirled round to see a stocky young man grinning at her from the next hummock of ground.

"Oh! Mr Gibson. You startled me."

Tom strode down the slope and stopped beside her, gesturing around them. "Lovely, isn't it?" He was hatless and had a leather jerkin over his shirt. His tanned face was relaxed and happy. Tom had never lost his joy at being away from the mill and outside in the fresh air, and he, too, loved to walk on the tops.

Her angry expression softened. "Yes, it's beautiful. The air smells so fresh up here." She looked at him, then looked away. She felt suddenly shy and breathless, and did not know what to say.

He felt the same, for all his experience with women. This one was special, so very special. "You look angry." His voice was soft. "Is something wrong, love?" He used the common term of endearment casually, but he would have liked to say it in quite another tone.

Tears came into her eyes. "Everything's wrong!"

He was careful to keep his distance, not wanting to frighten her away. "Why don't you sit down and tell me about it, then?

They say a trouble shared is a trouble halved." She would think him an idiot, trotting out worn old sayings like that. He wished he were tall and witty, that he were a gentleman, not a working man. But he didn't wish anything changed about her. She was exquisite, with the sun shining on her flushed face, her golden hair streaming down her back and Ellie's shawl pulled tight across her firm young breasts.

Marianne hesitated, looked at him searchingly and then, seeming reassured by what she saw, she nodded and looked round for a place to sit.

"Come up to the top of the next hill. There's a nice dry rock up there that we can sit on. It has the best view around here. I often come up and sit here of a Sunday."

She followed him and sat down primly at one edge of the rock. "You're right. It is a wonderful view." She gestured towards the valley which even on a non-working day looked smoky and grubby. "I don't know why people want to live down there."

"We live down there because we have to, because that's where the money is," he said easily. "But when I'm rich, I'm going to live up on the top of Ridge Hill."

"That's where my mother wanted to live, but my father always said he had to be nearer to his patients."

"Aye. Well, he was right, wasn't he? He's a good doctor, your father is, none better." He tapped his forehead. "See this scar? He sewed it up as neat as one of our Annie's seams when I was only eight. He's patched me up a few times, your father has. I was a bit of a rough lad." He would not pretend with her.

"You're not all that old now."

"I'm a man grown, and I've a bit more sense than to get into scraps and scrapes nowadays, Miss Lewis."

It seemed silly to be so formal here on the moors. "Oh, call me Marianne," she said impulsively.

"Your cousin won't like that."

Her face clouded over again. "My cousin doesn't like anything, Mr Gibson."

"Tom."

"Tom, then. My cousin is the narrowest, meanest creature on this earth. And if I have to live with her much longer, I'll – I'll explode!"

"That's why you came up here today?"

"Yes."

"Had you no other relatives who could have come and lived with you?"

She sighed. "None. And when my mother – when she left – Father insisted that I needed a lady companion. But I don't! Ellie and I could manage things perfectly well without *her* poking her nose everywhere. I don't want to be a fine lady and spend my time making calls on other ladies and doing useless things to fill the time."

"Annie says it'd look bad, you not having an older lady to look after you. I heard her and Ellie talking about it the other week." The irrepressible grin was back on his face. "But I don't think Ellie likes your cousin much, either."

She smiled at him reluctantly. "No. She doesn't. Ellie's never uncivil, but she has a way of standing up for herself. But," her lips trembled, "Father backs *her* up more than he backs me up."

He leaned back. "Aye. It must be hard for you, with only him to turn to. Now me, I've got too many in my family." He rolled his eyes expressively. "The house is full up with nine of us. There's always someone making a noise. That's why I come up here sometimes. To get a bit of peace."

Marianne leaned back and breathed deeply and slowly. "My cousin said I wasn't to leave the house, that it wasn't right to go walking on a Sunday. On a lovely day like this! How often do we get a sunny day in November? We could perfectly well have gone to Evensong, but no, she wanted us to go to that

240

gloomy old church twice. She always does."

"I don't go even once."

"How lucky you are!" Marianne scowled down at the valley. "I hate church. Mr Kenderby preaches the most boring sermons and he's always talking about sinners being punished."

"It's not much better at the Todmorden Road Methodist Chapel, either," he admitted, "and if my dad had his way, we'd all spend half of every Sunday there."

"But you don't go?"

"No. I'm afraid I don't." His eyes twinkled at her. "I'm beyond redemption, I daresay. It's all a lot of mumbo-jumbo to me."

She smiled back at him, then sighed again and because he was so easy to talk to, confided some more. "My Cousin Dorothy's impossible. Why, last week she even tried to alter the new dress your sister had made me. Said it was too tight-fitting for a young woman my age and had too many frills. If I hadn't caught her taking it from my room, she'd have ruined it. At least Father backed me in that. He said she wasn't to touch my clothes."

"She dresses like a washerwoman, your cousin does. I've seen her with her tight bonnets and dark clothes."

He pulled a sour face which had such a look of Dorothy that Marianne could not help chuckling. Then her shoulders slumped again. "I hate living with such – such discord in the house. It's just one thing after another. *Nothing* I do ever pleases her. I sometimes think I'll go mad if I have to spend another hour sitting with her waiting for callers and pretending to embroider. She knows I hate sewing, but she says it wouldn't look right if I didn't have something to occupy my hands." A half-smile crept over her face. "She has to pull my stitches out every night, though. I seem to have absolutely no skill for embroidery, however hard I try." Her eyes were dancing again.

They both chuckled then sat for a while in a comfortable silence.

"I wouldn't want to alter a thing about you," he said softly, treading carefully, but determined to start his campaign. "You're the prettiest girl I've ever seen." Before she could take exception to this, he put a finger to his lips. "Listen!"

Somewhere a skylark was singing, pouring out its rich melody like a paean of praise for the beauty of the day. When the sound faded away, Marianne sighed. "That seems to bring you closer to God than any service in church."

Tom nodded, then pointed. "Look! See that bird over there? It's a kestrel. It'll be hunting mice. I like to watch them soar, then pounce. Wouldn't it be marvellous to be able to fly like that?"

She nodded, still feeling rather pleased at the compliment that had slipped out earlier, yet relieved that he had not pursued that avenue. 'Prettiest girl I've ever seen.' How wonderful that someone should think that of her!

A few minutes later, he stood up and held out his hand to pull her up. "Better start moving again or you'll catch a chill. It's not a warm day, for all the sun's shining so brightly."

She put out her hand to him and he grasped it in his strong warm fingers and pulled her to her feet. For a moment they stood there only a few inches apart. For a moment, he allowed his feelings for her to show in his face. Then he turned away and said briskly, "We'd better get back now. There's rain coming."

"I wish I need never go back."

"Well," he paused and eyed her teasingly, "I'm not a knight on a white horse, but maybe I could rescue you from the dragon for a while. Would you like to come and have a cup of tea with us at Netherleigh Cottage on your way home? Surely your cousin couldn't object to that? My sister is as respectable as they come."

"I'm afraid my cousin absolutely hates your sister. But I'd love to come and have a cup of tea, all the same. My father won't object. He thinks a lot of your sister. Says she's a remarkable woman." She shivered. "I hadn't realised how cold I'd got."

"Come on, then. And we'll get Rebecca to walk back to Park House with us afterwards, so that Miss Hymes can't object to my escorting you home."

When Jeremy returned from Scotland, he was met with a barrage of complaints from Dorothy Hymes.

"You really will have to take her to task, Jeremy. She's behaving in a most unladylike manner. And she's been *so* disobedient! Going tramping the moors on a Sunday and then coming back with that common young man. I don't know what people must be thinking."

Had her voice always had this whining tone to it? Jeremy frowned. Perhaps it was the contrast with the few fascinating days in Edinburgh and the softness of the Scottish voices.

Marianne, who had come down to greet her father, turned round and walked back up to her bedroom without giving him her usual welcome-back kiss. She stood by the window, taking deep breaths to try to calm herself down. For a moment then she had wanted to fly at Dorothy, wanted to push the whining creature out of the way, to stop her spoiling the pleasure of her father's return.

After a while, there was a tap on the door. "May I come in?"

"Yes, Father." But Marianne's voice was dull and her face was wary as she turned towards him.

He was shocked by her withdrawal from him, for usually she flew to hug him and to pour out the tale of her doings. "Don't I get a hug today?"

Her voice was bitter. "A lady does not show her emotions.

She must remain calm at all times. Surely you know that, Father?" She did not move. For the first time ever, she was not sure of her welcome in his arms.

"Then I don't want you turning into a lady," he said huskily. "For heaven's sake, Marianne, come and give me a hug!"

She flew across the room to kiss him and then let him lead her across to sit on the edge of the bed.

"Has she been worse than usual?"

"No worse than she usually is when you're not there. But you seemed to be gone such a long time." A tear trickled down her cheek and she tried to wipe it away surreptitiously.

He cleared his throat. "She said – that you'd been meeting a young man on the moors."

"What?"

There was no mistaking the genuineness of the surprise in her voice. Jeremy relaxed. "Suppose you tell me what really happened, love."

"It was a lovely day on Sunday, probably the last we'll get before the winter sets in. It seemed to have been raining all week." She drew in her breath. "I know it wasn't – wasn't a very polite thing to do, running away, but I couldn't stand the thought of another dreary Sunday. I couldn't bear to go to church twice."

"Twice? But we don't—"

"You don't. When you're away, she insists on me going with her twice."

"Why didn't you tell me?"

"I've tried. But if I told you everything she does, it would just sound like – like her carping. Ellie's the only one who understands how it all gets me down. She can usually cheer me up, but it was Ellie's Sunday off and her mother wasn't well, so she had to go home. When you're not here, Dorothy never stops complaining, Father. I can't do a thing right for her!"

He put his arm round her, feeling guilty that he had not noticed how bad things were getting, feeling guilty that he had not dealt more firmly with his cousin. "But why did she think you'd been meeting a young man?"

"Because I went walking on the tops – yes, I know you don't like me going up there by myself, but I couldn't breathe down here! While I was up there, I met Tom Gibson, Annie's brother. We sat and talked for a while. Isn't that view marvellous? And we heard a skylark, then saw a kestrel. It was lovely. Then, when I didn't want to go home, he asked me to go back to their house for a cup of tea." She began to fiddle with the folds of her skirt. "I knew Dorothy wouldn't approve, but I couldn't see the harm in it. *You* go there for tea sometimes. And Mrs Ashworth is a perfectly respectable person. Anyway, he – Tom – he knew I didn't want to go home, so he took me back to Netherleigh Cottage with him."

"And you had tea there. That doesn't seem a great crime to me."

Her face had brightened just at the memory. "I had a lovely time, Father. There are so many of them living there that they must never get lonely. William's grown a couple of inches, and then there's—" She stopped and laughed, "But you know them, don't you?"

"Yes, I know them. I brought most of them into the world, in fact." That thought made him suddenly feel old. "I was there when Mr Gibson's second wife died and two of his children."

Marianne squeezed his hand. She knew how it upset him to see children die. "Mr Gibson was mending a chair. It was so interesting. The boys were helping him, but," she chuckled, "they seemed to be getting in the way more than anything else. But he didn't mind. The way he looked at them reminded me of the way you look at me sometimes."

He patted her hand. "Yes, well, that's what it's like to be a father."

"I used to think I'd never get married," she said dreamily, "but one day I'd like to have a houseful of children, just like the Gibsons have." The memory of Tom's admiring glance warmed her cheeks suddenly, and she hurried on. "Rebecca and Tom walked back with me afterwards. She's so excited about working in the salon with Annie – *you* don't mind if I call Mrs Ashworth Annie, do you? No, I thought you wouldn't, whatever Dorothy said. And I can call Mr Gibson – young Mr Gibson, that is, Tom? Annie said I could go there for tea any Sunday I wanted. May I, Father? It's such fun there with so many people to talk to."

"Of course you may." If only I could remarry, he thought bitterly. She needs a real mother, and brothers and sisters. She's such a warm loving girl. But Annabelle was there in Brighton and he was still tied to her 'till death do us part'. She had stopped him from having the family he had longed for. She had stopped Marianne from having brothers and sisters. She had ruined his whole life. Almost. At least she had given him Marianne.

They sat together quietly for a minute or two, then he sighed and broke the spell. "So what are we going to do about Cousin Dorothy?"

"How about strangling her?"

"Tch! Tch! What an unladylike way to dispose of someone. Poison is so much more elegant, don't you think?"

"True."

"Seriously, though. I'll have to think of something to do. The trouble is, love, that she has nowhere to go and very little money, so I'm reluctant to turn her out."

"Perhaps if you let me help you a bit more in the free clinic that would make me feel better – and – and I could visit Annie and her family, couldn't I? Kathy said if I went round there during the day, she'd teach me to cook. She's a wonderful cook, you know. Only – well, you'll have to tell Cousin Dorothy that it's all right, or she'll make such a fuss."

"Do you think you can stand her for a while longer, then?"

"I suppose I must. We can't turn her out in the streets, after all, can we?"

"No." He had made a mess of that, too, made a mess of everything, it seemed, except his doctoring. And medicine wasn't enough on its own. A man needed some warmth in his life. A picture of Ellie floated into his mind, with her wholesome cheerful face. He had been thinking about her a lot lately for some reason. She had grown into a comely woman, but best of all, she was a loving sort of person. He and Marianne owed her a lot.

Sixteen

BILSDEN: SPRING 1846

Annie kept her working sketches and a swatch of material from Lady Darrington's ball gown, which had been a great success. It had been a pleasure to create such a delicate confection, and she would never forget how it looked. The lustrous silk of the skirt fell in just the right folds to hang a fraction of an inch above the ground. The bodice fitted Her Ladyship's slender figure perfectly, with not a wrinkle, coming to a point at the waist, and the lace bertha hung off her white shoulders in a demure yet tantalising way. The lace and ribbon flounces enhanced the fullness of the skirt without seeming bulky and the pearl drops gleamed subtly in the folds of ribbon which Mary Benworth's clever fingers had fashioned into delicate rosettes.

When the payment was sent from Darrington Hall, a brief note from Her Ladyship was enclosed saying how pleased she had been with the gown, plus a longer note from Sarah giving more information about how the gown had been admired. Sarah ended by saying she hoped to meet Mrs Ashworth again when they visited Bilsden.

The only blot upon the whole business was that the damage to the gown could not be traced to Mr Hardy. His wife and daughter both swore that he had been with them all that night, and all three of them declared that they had heard nothing from the next shop, nothing at all.

Frederick Hallam admitted that he still suspected Hardy. "But there's nothing I can do about it at this stage," he told Annie. "Unfortunately. However, I have let it be known how *very* displeased I am about the incident, and I hope that will prevent a recurrence."

She nodded. "Thank you. You've been very kind." Strange how comfortable she was beginning to feel with him nowadays.

He refrained from saying that he would like to be a lot kinder. Mrs Ashworth was not that sort of woman.

Of course, once it was known that she had made a gown for Her Ladyship, Annie's salon became very popular. All the ladies in the town had to have at least one gown made by her, though some of them were taken aback to find that she would not allow their tastes free rein. Pauline listened to their grumbles with amusement, and let it be known that she, too, had allowed Mrs Ashworth to dictate what she should wear, which helped prevent some of the ladies from taking huffs.

And then of course, when the ladies found out how flattering Mrs Ashworth's clothes were, how truly fashionable and elegant, they came back for more. By spring, Annie had had to take on two seamstresses as well as Alice and Mary Benworth, and another young apprentice to keep her sister Rebecca company. Hilda James had taken over most of the second-hand-clothes business from Alice and was proving more capable than they had expected. Indeed, that lady was positively blooming in her new life. She and Alice got on well together, living in Annie's old home at Number Eight Salem Street. It was strange, Annie often thought, how things turned out.

"Now we're beginning to get on!" Tom said to Annie with

satisfaction one day. His business was doing well, too, and he was gaining a reputation for honesty that made him smile sometimes. There was no moral basis to this, he admitted that to himself at least. If Annie had not made him see that honesty paid better in the long run, he would have had no hesitation in introducing sharper practices – but honesty was paying, it was paying miraculously well. As was selling fresh untainted produce.

Just before Christmas he consulted Annie, then offered John Gibson a job in the junk yard.

John could only stare at him. "Nay, lad, are you sure about that?"

"Aye, I'm sure, Dad. The way you know how to mend things'll be a real help, an' you'll be able to keep an eye on everything when I'm away."

"I thought folk brought the junk to you nowadays."

"They do. But I'm looking at a few other lines as well, and that means I need to be out and about. The food we sell at market brings in a steady few shillings a week" – Tom always minimised profits when speaking about them – "and I think we could do more with that sort of thing. Have you seen how other folk at the market handle their food?"

"What?"

"Just take a look sometime at how folk selling at the market handle the food. Dirty hands all over it. Makes you sick to watch them doing it."

"Nay, I've never thought owt about that. I'm just glad to earn the bread for me an' my family. I leave buyin' food to the womenfolk."

"Aye, an' so do most of the men round here." Tom shook his head. "Well, I've looked at food because Kathy's *made* me think about it. She's that finicky about what she'll buy, and she's right. If she says someone's cheese is no good or that a farmer breeds tasty meat she's usually right. She's turned into a damn good cook, has our Kathy." He was unaware that this was the first time he had used the word "our", the first time he had accepted publicly that Kathy was part of the family.

"She's a nice lass, too," said John, with his gentle smile. "Our Joanie's really taken to her."

"Yes, well, we're talking about business now, Dad. So, do you want to come and work for me, or not?"

"I don't rightly know. I've only worked in t'mill. What if I make mistakes? What if I don't suit?" He said the last in a low voice. He didn't think he could bear the idea of his own son turning him off, but it had to be faced.

Tom shrugged. "We all make mistakes. I made a lot when I started. It didn't stop me earning my keep." He suddenly realised where John was leading. "An' I won't turn you off, don't worry. You're not stupid. You'll learn quickly enough."

"But what should I be doin'?"

"What I need is a grown man to keep an eye on things when I'm away. Our Mark's got his head screwed on right an' he can do most things, but my customers don't like dealing with a lad like him. They want another man to talk to. An' me, I want a man I can trust at the yard, not someone lookin' for ways to cheat me."

"Well, you know you can trust me. I wouldn't cheat my own."

"I don't just mean that, Dad. I don't want someone who'd cheat the customers either."

John stiffened. "I would *never* do that. You should know without asking. The Lord can see what you're doing when you cheat other folk. I couldn't thole the idea of him seein' me cheatin' when he's been so good to me."

"Yes, well. That's between you an' your Maker. This has got nothin' to do with the Lord as far as I'm concerned. I don't want to cheat anyone because it's bad for business in the long run. Me an' Annie decided a long time ago that we want to make a good name for ourselves in the town."

John sighed at this disregarding of the religion which had saved his sanity when his first wife died and which now gave meaning to his whole life, then he smiled at his son, standing staring at him, foot tapping impatiently. "Aye, well, you an' me see things different, but it all comes out the same. I'm glad you're doin' things honestly. Your mother would have been right proud of you an' our Annie, lad." John blew his nose vigorously then nodded. "I will come an' work with you, then. Aye, I will. I'm gettin' a bit old for t'mill, I reckon." It was typical that he didn't even ask how much the wages would be.

The two of them shook hands solemnly.

"Our Annie says you're to take a week off first, to give yourself a rest before you start."

John gaped. "Nay, what'd I do with myself all day? An' I wouldn't be bringin' in any money."

Tom looked at him. His father seemed smaller to him nowadays, and faded-looking. Annie was right to worry about him. "You need a good rest," he said roughly, to hide his concern. "Get some good fresh air into your lungs. We're not short of bread in this house. An' a week either way won't matter to me."

John nodded, unable to speak for the lump in his throat. And so, for the first time in his life, he spent a week, "livin' like a lord" as he phrased it, going for long walks when it was fine or pottering with his tools or just sitting by the kitchen fire and smoking his pipe while he chatted to Kathy.

To John's further bewilderment, his family used this time to take his wardrobe and appearance in hand. Tom and Annie bought him some new clothes and a fine turnip watch with his name engraved on it in curly letters. The mere sight of it brought tears to his eyes because he had always hankered after one. Kathy cut his hair for him. His little Rebecca hemmed him some handkerchiefs. Mark collected his new boots from the bootmaker and polished them like mirrors, brand new boots, specially made for him. By the time they'd all finished, John didn't recognise himself and he had to keep glancing in the mirror in the hall to make sure it was really him. Eh, if Lucy could see him now!

Only Kathy knew how nervous John was of this big change in his life, but she seemed so confident that he could cope with it all that he took heart. She was nobody's fool, wasn't their Kathy.

And when he did start at the yard, what with Mark helping him with the figuring and Luke smiling at him shyly as they sorted stuff out, he soon found himself settling down happily and taking a real interest. Eh, it were amazing what money there were in junk, and the most interestin' thing of all were figurin' out how to put stuff to use. To his own surprise as much as to Tom's, he came up with a few ideas that brought in more pence. John could never think of money as guineas or even shillings. He had been poor too long.

In the evenings, it was with Kathy and the children that John talked over the little events of the day, while Annie often as not sat and drew pictures up in her bedroom and Tom did his accounts in the dining room that still had only an old table in it covered with Tom's papers and calculations. John liked the kitchen. To him it was the best room at Netherleigh Cottage, the only place where he felt really at home. Even his bedroom felt strange, because he was the only person in it, something that had never happened to him before in all his life. He did not like being alone in the soft bed, however warm and thick the blankets. For him, bed was a warm body and someone to whisper to and joke with. But how could you complain when your children thought they'd done the best they could for you?

So he spent most of his time in the kitchen. And it was a while before he realised that this was partly because Kathy was there, always ready to greet him with a smile and pour him a cup of tea, always ready to pour a cup for herself and to linger with him as they sipped the warm brown liquid and chatted with the ease of old friends.

Like his son before him, once he left the mill, John got some colour back in his face and began to feel more energetic, as well as to put on a bit of weight. He had never expected to feel so well again in this life. In his experience, growing old meant getting poorer and weaker. And it was all thanks to his Annie – and Tom, of course – but mainly Annie. She had started it all off when she married Charlie. John only wished there were some way he could pay her back, but Annie didn't seem to need help from anyone. She was always pleasant, but so busy that she rarely had time just to sit and chat – except when one of her fine friends called to see her. Indeed, she seemed like a fine lady herself nowadays with her beautiful clothes and soft white hands. He would look at her sometimes and marvel that she could have sprung from his loins.

Annie was now so used to dressing and behaving like a lady that she did not realise how much she had changed, and was still changing, except when Ellie teased her about it. As a housekeeper, Ellie had more freedom to come and go than when she had been a maid, so she would occasionally pop into the salon while she was out shopping and if there were no customers, she would stay for a cup of tea and a chat with Annie.

In April, however, Ellie's visits almost ceased because her mother fell ill again and any time she could spare from her duties had to be spent helping her father and giving her youngest sister, Lily, a much-needed break.

"Your mother seems to have been ill a lot lately," Annie said one day when Ellie stole ten minutes to pop into the salon. "Is it – something serious?"

Ellie grimaced. "I'm afraid so. She's been funny for years, but lately, since our Addy got wed, she's – well, she's seemed really strange. And she won't see a doctor."

"Strange?"

"Mmm." Ellie stirred the cup of tea needlessly, swirling the delicate brown liquid round and round the cup and fiddling with the spoon. "She's always been fussy about the house, but now she washes the floor at least twice a day and you can hardly finish a cup of tea before she's taken your cup and started to wash it. She's for ever fiddling with a dishcloth an' washin' things down. Dad's life's a misery, it really is, and I don't know how he puts up with it."

"He's a lovely man, your father is."

Ellie managed a brief smile. "Yes, he is. But she doesn't seem to care about him or think of his comfort. She says all her children have let her down and none of us love her and she might just as well be dead. So when she's not cleaning things, she's sitting weeping, on and on. Her eyes are always red. It makes me shiver to watch her."

"But Lily still lives at home and Matt visits regularly, doesn't he? How can your mother say he doesn't care about her? He's always been her favourite."

"Yes, but she wants him to come back and live at home, too, and he won't. I don't blame him either. An' she wants me to find a husband and get married. You'd think I was committing a crime, not being married, you really would. Apart from me an' Matt, the others are all married, except Lily, who's stayed at home to help Dad. An' even that's wrong, because Mother says Lily only stays because no one wants to wed her, and that she doesn't really care about her parents."

They both sat there in silence for a moment or two, then Annie asked, "Why won't your mother see a doctor?"

"Because she hates Dr Lewis and anyone associated with him." Ellie was fiddling with the saucer, avoiding Annie's eyes. "It's because of you and the way he used to visit you in Salem Street after you'd married Charlie." Ellie looked up at Annie, tears in her eyes. "I think she's gone mad, Annie, I really do. And," the tears were rolling down her face now, "I won't give up my place to look after her, no matter what happens. Dad was asking me if I would, if the worst happened, because Lily can't control her, and I had to tell him no. Am I being selfish?"

"No. Why should you give up your whole life?"

"Well, I can't and I won't. There's Marianne as well, you see. She needs me, too – especially now. But Dad was hurt. He said – he said that children should honour their father and mother an' look after them in their old age. But I can't! I go back home as often as I can, though all she does is complain and nag at me, but I won't do more. And my mother has got Lily. It's not as if she's on her own."

Annie laid her hand on her friend's. "I'm so sorry, love. I hadn't realised it had got so bad."

"No. We try to keep our troubles to ourselves."

"What does Dr Lewis say?"

"He says that even if my mother came to see him, he doubts he could do much to help her. He says doctors don't understand these things very well. He calls it a disease of the brain, but," she took a deep breath and paused for a moment, because it was the first time she had admitted it to anyone, "it's madness, Annie. My mother's going mad."

A few weeks later, Annie decided to celebrate her twenty-sixth birthday with a party for her family and for a few friends. Mary Benworth and her father were to be there, as was Helen Kenderby. And of course, Ellie Peters would be coming, or she would if her mother did not have a bad day.

"Why don't you invite Marianne Lewis as well?" suggested Tom.

"Do you think I should?"

"Of course. You know how she likes coming here an' – an' anyway, I'd like her to come."

She swung round and frowned at him. "What do you mean by that, Tom Gibson?"

"It means she's a nice lass an' I enjoy her company." He said it casually, but he had that look on his face that meant he was concealing something.

"Tom—" She broke off, not knowing how to approach the subject.

"Leave it, our Annie! There's nothing to worry about. I wouldn't hurt her for the world, an' I know she's only young yet, for all she's eighteen. Let's just see how things go on, eh?"

"But you're still seeing Rosie! How can you pretend to be interested in Marianne as well?"

"Aye. Well, Marianne's one thing and Rosie's another. A man has his needs, doesn't he?"

"You sound like Dad when you talk like that."

He hated that prim look she got on her face whenever sex was mentioned. "Well, it's more normal to sound like that than to sound like you. Your face wrinkles up like a prune if anyone mentions men an' women doin' what's natural. The only sort of man you like is one at a safe distance like Danny O'Connor. Letters. What way is that to go on? What'll you do when he comes home an' wants more than just letters?"

She gulped. "I don't know." She had lain awake at night wondering that herself. She did not know why she even answered Danny's letters. It was only encouraging him. But she enjoyed hearing from him. He wrote a lively letter and you could just see the things he described, clear as day, they were. The railway diggings and the mud and the men toiling up and down the slopes with wheelbarrows full of muck.

"Well, you'd better start thinking about it, love, because he won't be staying away from Bilsden for ever, not if I know Danny O'Connor. He told me last time that he was going to start up as a builder. Here. In Bilsden." Tom paused for a minute, then added, "So, will you invite Marianne for me or shall I do it myself?"

"I'll do it." But she was very quiet the rest of the evening. And Danny haunted her dreams that night, which made her angry. Why would men not leave her alone? She didn't want to get married again, didn't want a man to use her body like that. Did she? She had dreamed that Danny was kissing her – and she had not pulled away from him in the dream either. She had cuddled right up to him.

The next day, when Pauline called in at the salon for a chat, Annie told her about the tea party, but not about Tom's interest in Marianne Lewis.

"Why haven't I been invited?" asked Pauline.

Annie gaped at her. "But – but surely you wouldn't—" She broke off, not sure how to put it.

Pauline smiled, that sleek cat's grin she had when she was plotting something. "I was wondering how to start introducing you to a better class of people, Annie. This party would be a good start. If Saul and I came, it would signal to our worthy townsfolk that I regarded you as socially acceptable."

"But I'm not socially acceptable!"

"Why not? I presume you would not eat your peas with your knife?"

"You know why not, Pauline! Because I come from the Rows. Only last year I was living in Salem Street."

Pauline raised her eyebrows. "And while you were there, I would not have considered inviting you to my social functions, but now that you're living somewhere respectable, this birthday party is an ideal opportunity to start. Tell me again who's coming." She listened to the list. "Hmm. Better invite Dr Lewis as well as his daughter. It would look better. And you ought really to invite that cousin of theirs."

"I'd rather not hold a tea party at all than invite her, thank you very much."

"Yes, she is very – er – wearing, isn't she? And I don't suppose she'd come anyway." Pauline shared a grimace with Annie. "Very well, then, an afternoon tea party. Your Kathy is an excellent cook and should be able to cope with that." She raised one thin eyebrow. "Don't you want to invite me, Annie?"

"Of course I do! I just – I didn't think you'd want to come."

"Well, I do want to come." Someone walked off the street into the salon and she raised her voice. "Yes, I quite agree with you, Mrs Ashworth. You have such exquisite taste. And I shall be delighted to come to your birthday party. How kind of you to invite me!"

The two women who had just entered goggled at her.

After that, Annie was fairly trapped.

The thought of the posh company they would be entertaining threw Kathy into a panic.

John found her in the kitchen one day sitting staring blankly into the fire and twisting her apron to and fro. Her expression was so unhappy that he went over and instinctively put his arm round her. "Nay, what's up, lass? Are you not feelin' well?"

She swallowed hard. "It's the party."

"Ah. Yes. All them posh folk?"

"Yes. I'm not – I can't do it, John."

He put his arms round her. "You're like me, you've not been brought up posh an' you've not taken to it, like our Annie has, neither."

She buried her face in his shoulder and burst into tears. "And I can't do it, John! I can't! But if I don't, I'll be letting our Annie down!"

He patted her and shushed her until the tears had stopped, then kissed them away, like he did with Joanie. Only the kiss made her draw in her breath and made him look at her differently. Not pretty, Kathy, but a nice face, to his mind, with gentle grey eyes and a warm smile. The sort of face it was a pleasure to see each night when you came home from work. Suddenly, he found he was kissing her again, kissing her properly as a man kisses a woman, and liking it very much.

They broke apart. "Nay, I shouldn't have done that," he muttered, flushing.

"Why not, John? I enjoyed it," she said pulling him back towards her. "I've been wanting you to kiss me for months."

"But I'm thirty years older than you!"

"Nay, you're not. You're only forty-seven."

"That's nearly thirty years, love."

"Well, I don't like young men. I never have," she said softly. "They aren't kind enough for me. You're a kind man, John Gibson, and," she took a deep breath, "and I love that in you."

He held her close, then put her gently away from him. "Best you think things over, lass. I've not got that many years left to me. You've a long life ahead of you yet, God willing."

"Best we both think it over, then, eh? You might not want to be saddled with a child bride." She chuckled. "Nor you haven't proposed to me yet."

"I'd propose this minute if I thought it was right. But I'm a bit beflummoxed about it all. Kathy, love, you do need to think. it over, an' think carefully, too, before we do owt else."

"All right, John." She knew it would make him feel better if she pretended to think things over, but she didn't need to. She knew her own feelings well enough and had done for a while. It was he who had been slow to realise what was happening between them.

"Right then," he said briskly. "And in the meantime, let's think about this party. You shouldn't be fretting about it. I reckon you can more than cope with the cooking. You're a real good cook, lass."

"But what if things – well, what if they go wrong?"

"With that nice new range and you to do the cooking? They wouldn't dare." He saw a smile curve her lips and chuckled. "That's better. It's allus good to laugh at things. But it wouldn't hurt to have a practice, now would it? You can try out some fancy things on us lot an' we'll see how they go. It'll be good practice for the childer, too. Annie knows what the nobs offer folk at tea parties an' the like. She'll soon tell us what'll suit. She's a great one for plannin' things, is our Annie. Besides, we owe it to her to try, don't you think? I mean, if she wants a posh birthday party, then it's up to us to give her one after all she's done for us."

Never was a tea party so carefully prepared for. Kathy produced a variety of cakes over the next week or two and the family sat in judgment on them. It became the highlight of the day for the evening meal to end with the latest offering from the pages of Kathy's cookery books. The children threw themselves into the tastings and discussions with gusto and gradually the menu was planned.

On the Sunday a week before the party, they held a rehearsal, with everyone dressing up in their fancy clothes and practising eating politely. Even Joanie caught the prevailing mood and sat in smiling silence through the mock tea party, nibbling carefully at her cake and trying not to make crumbs.

"What'll we say to them, our Annie?" demanded Rebecca, who had gained a lot of confidence from working in the salon, but who still liked to rehearse for events which frightened her. And having Mrs Hinchcliffe to tea, not just to tea with Annie, but with all of them, was certainly a daunting prospect. "Whatever will we talk about to *her*?"

Annie smiled. Impossible to tell a chatterbox like Rebecca that children were not expected to talk to visitors. A thoughtful look crossed her face. "Why don't we invite Mrs Hinchcliffe's sons as well? Then you children can play with them and you won't have to talk to her much, apart from saying how do you do. I know that Stephen would enjoy having someone to play with, though perhaps Wesley is too young to come. Tom, can you get a note out to Collett House for me?"

"Yes."

Annie turned back to her little sister and noticed that her two young brothers were listening carefully, too. "Mrs Lewis always used to say that what folk like best is to talk about themselves. So if you're wondering what to say to someone, ask about something – not something personal, but something they do. Like Marianne Lewis. She goes to help out at the clinic down Claters End. Ask her about that, about what she does there."

Mark nodded. "That's a good idea, our Annie. An' we can ask the doctor about his last trip to London. What it's like there." He was going to go to London one day, and to other places, too. He wasn't going to spend all his life in Bilsden like his father had, like Luke seemed happy to. Mark wanted more out of life than that. If he were Annie, he wouldn't have stayed in Bilsden.

Seventeen

MAY 1846

Just before noon on the day of the tea party there was a knock on the door. Annie, who had popped along to the salon for a couple of hours, but was now having the rest of the day off as a birthday treat, went to open it. She gasped, unable to speak for a moment, unable to do anything but stare.

"Aren't you going to ask us in?" asked Lizzie, leaning against the doorpost.

Annie's knuckles were white as she clutched the edge of the doorframe for support. Her sister had hardly changed and Annie was sure that the sly expression in those pale blue eyes still presaged trouble. Behind Lizzie stood May, hand on one hip, the same sneering look as always marring her thin face and making you feel as if she knew all your darkest secrets, knew and was amused by them.

Both young women were dressed in gaudy finery that looked as if it needed a good wash. There could not have been a greater contrast than the two of them. Lizzie was short and stockily built with crinkly hair, like her father and Tom, and May was tall and thin, with straight mousy locks. She had grown so like

Emily, her mother, that it was like seeing the dead come to life again. Or it would have been, if May's cheeks had not been covered in rouge and her lips reddened to an improbable shade of scarlet. Emily might have liked her nips of gin, but she would have died rather than paint her face.

"She doesn't want to ask us in," said May, shaking her head and making tutting noises. "And us coming all the way from Manchester specially to see her, too. Sad, that is, really sad. And her your very own sister, Lizzie."

Annie gathered her wits together. "You'd better come in."

"Better come in!" spat May. "That's a fine welcome, that is!" She seemed to be overflowing with anger today.

Lizzie laid a hand on her shoulder and whispered, "Shh, love!" then she turned back to Annie. "Thanks. Don't mind if we do." Both of them tittered as they stepped forward and collided on the doorstep, then May shoved Lizzie into the hall first.

They had always had this air of sharing secret jokes about the rest of the world, Annie thought, closing the front door and wondering whether to take them into the kitchen or the parlour. One sniff at their perfume in an enclosed space sent her towards the kitchen, even though she knew they would be in Kathy's way there. But she didn't want the parlour reeking of that sickly stink when her guests arrived.

What had brought those two here, today of all days? Annie could not believe that this was just a sisterly visit. She and Lizzie had never got on, never. Even when they were children, Lizzie had been a millstone around her neck, always trailing behind and whining, or else getting her and Tom into scrapes with the other children of the Rows. Why had the two of them come today? The question kept echoing in Annie's mind. Lizzie and May had not been in touch with any of their family since they left Bilsden to work in Manchester several years previously. No one had known how to find them when Emily died, which had grieved John sorely. But no one had missed them except him, for John Gibson loved all his children without reservation.

Kathy turned round from the oven, face flushed and smiling. She saw who had followed Annie in, opened her mouth in a big O of surprise and just stood there clutching a cloth to her bosom.

"I see *she's* still with you," said Lizzie. "Wormed her way right into the family, hasn't she?"

"She always was a little crawler, that Kathy was," said May.

"If you want to stay in this house for more than a minute or two, you'd better be polite to those who live here!" snapped Annie, beginning to pull herself together.

Kathy put the cloth down on the table, ignored the two women who had tormented her as children and made a valiant effort to speak normally. "The sponge cakes have come out well, Annie."

"That's good."

Lizzie walked across to examine the display of food on a side table. "Going to celebrate your birthday, eh, our Annie? I thought you would be. That's why we come 'ere today. We could do with a bit of jollification after the rotten times we've 'ad lately." She moved unasked to sit in a chair at the table. "And I wouldn't say no to a cup of tea, neither, if you're offering."

"I'll make you one in a minute." Annie turned to Kathy. "I know you'll be wanting to get off down to the yard, so I'll take over here. Tom wants his lunch early today."

To Annie's relief, Kathy took her hint, though all the menfolk took their lunch with them when they left in the morning. Kathy nodded and went into the pantry, returning with a cloth-wrapped bundle. She removed her apron. "I'll take it to him now, love."

Annie moved across to the kitchen range and pushed the

kettle into the centre of the hob. She was still having difficulty functioning properly, but she felt she ought to say something. "Well, this is a big surprise," she managed, but the words sounded false, even in her own ears. Dreadful shock would have been a better way of describing the visit. "Do you still like your tea sweet and strong?"

"Fancy you remembering." Lizzie pushed out another chair with her foot and gestured to it. "Sit down, May. It seems her ladyship is going to offer us something, after all."

Face expressionless, Annie set out the teapot and some cups. "Would you like a piece of cake with it?"

"I'd like a bit more than that, actually," said Lizzie. "So would May. We haven't been eating very well lately and I daresay you've got enough extra here to feed us. Crumbs from the tables of the rich, eh?"

It was money they were after, Annie realised suddenly. It must be. Lizzie would never have bothered to come back to Bilsden if she hadn't seen some advantage in it for herself. Lizzie cared nothing for her family; she cared only for herself and May. "Bread and cheese all right?"

"Bread an' cheese will be fine," said May, trying to sound mocking, but the hunger gleamed in her eyes and she licked her lips when she saw Annie bring the cheese out of the pantry.

As she buttered the bread, Annie saw out of the corner of her eye that Lizzie was staring round the kitchen, her eyes narrowed, as if assessing its worth. May was just sitting there next to her, eyes closed, looking totally exhausted. "Did you know your mother died, May?"

Those pale eyes flickered open and May nodded. "Yes. Someone told me. Shame, eh? It were all them kids as wore her out, I daresay. Catch me havin' any! Has *he* got wed again yet?"

"Of course not!"

May rolled her eyes towards the ceiling. "Well, he will.

Can't do without it, he can't. I used to hear 'em at nights. He wouldn't take no for an answer, that sod wouldn't."

Annie slammed the platter of sandwiches down. "If you want to stay here, you'll be careful how you talk about my dad."

"Sorry, I'm sure," said May, but shut up as Lizzie gave her a nudge.

The two of them stopped talking to devour the sandwiches with an urgency that showed Lizzie had been speaking the truth about them not eating well. As they gobbled the food down, Annie clasped her hands together tightly in her lap and sat staring down at her fingers. How upset her mother would have been to know that one of her children was going hungry while the others were doing so well for themselves.

When her unwanted guests had finished the bread and cheese, she buttered some of Kathy's scones and pushed the plate across the table, then had to turn her eyes away again, away from the glistening greedy eyes, the pink snapping mouths and the snatching hands. The silence was punctuated only by gulping noises as the scones vanished, and then by sighs of pleasure and the slurping of tea. Annie held her tongue and waited for Tom to come back, as he no doubt would once Kathy told him who had turned up. This was the sort of trouble which he would deal with better than she could. Especially today. Seeing Lizzie so hungry had upset her, weakened her.

After a while, she decided that she might as well have a cup of tea with them, so she refilled the teapot and gestured to the two visitors to help themselves to more. The cup gave her something to occupy her hands with, but she hardly tasted the hot liquid in it.

"Where are you working now?" she asked, when the silence grew too uncomfortable.

"Oh, here and there," said Lizzie. She exchanged a sly smile with May as she said it.

Annie eyed them both, the pale unhealthy skin tone and the thinness of May's arms. "It mustn't pay very well if you haven't been eating properly."

"No. Not lately it hasn't. We've had better times." Lizzie picked up the last few scone crumbs with a dampened fingertip, licked them off and heaved a sigh of satisfaction. "Nice that was. You allus was a good cook, our Annie." She looked around the kitchen. "In fact, it's all very nice 'ere. Aren't you goin' to show us round the rest of your posh 'ouse? I bet this place has a lot of bedrooms. How the hell much rent do you 'ave to pay for it?"

Thank heavens they didn't know that she owned the house! Annie tried to speak casually. "I don't pay all the rent. Dad and the kids live here as well. And Tom. We split things three ways."

"Yeah. I suppose it's not much more expensive than renting two houses in Salem Street, when you think about it. An' much nicer, too." She pushed her chair backwards. "Show us round, then."

"No, not just now." Annie started clearing the cups and plates up to drown out their murmurs of annoyance about this. She closed her eyes in sheer relief as she heard the front door open.

Tom burst into the kitchen, crashing the door back on its hinges and just standing there staring. "It really is you two! I couldn't believe my own ears when Kathy told me who'd turned up."

"So you just had to come rushing back t'say hello to your dear little sister," sneered Lizzie. "Or did you come back to save Miss Fancy-drawers here from us?"

"What do you think?" He sat on the edge of the table, one leg swinging, looking down at them. They made him shudder, these two. There was something unhealthy about them and always had been. Man haters, he called them to himself, though

270

in truth they seemed to hate the whole world, men and women alike. "Let's not bother with the chat. Just tell us what you came for."

There was a moment's silence, then, "We come for a bit of help," Lizzie said. "We've had a run of bad luck lately an' you lot seem to be doin' all right for yourselves. You are our family, after all."

"And what do you call a bit of help?" he asked, the quietness of his voice in great contrast to the anger in his eyes.

"Twenty pound would be a big help to me an' May. We're broke an' we need some money to set ourselves up again, buy some working clothes an' pay the rent on a decent room. We had all our stuff stolen while we was – away from home."

Tom's eyes flickered once to Annie, as if to warn her to keep quiet, then he stared at Lizzie and May, his face absolutely expressionless. "If you weren't my sister, I'd guess from those clothes that you'd turned whore," he said slowly.

Annie swallowed hard. Tom's words seemed to throb inside her head. It couldn't, dear heavens, surely it couldn't be true! Not that! Surely there must be some other explanation? Hope died as she looked at her sister's face.

Lizzie gave her one of those slow deadly smiles that Annie had always hated. "Nowt wrong with a little whoring," she said. "It brings in more money than workin' yourself to death in t'mill does." She paused for a moment, then added bitterly, "Unless you happen to get caught by them damned new constables, that is. We've just been in the House of Correction, we have, an' we've no mind to go back there. So we need enough money to get ourselves off the streets when we start workin' again. You meet a better class of feller off the streets."

Annie's hands flew up to cover her mouth, to prevent her pain from bursting out. Even Tom's expression registered shock at this blunt admission and the lack of shame with which it was made.

Lizzie's smile broadened and she exchanged grins with May. "Turned right finicky in their ways, haven't they, our dear family. You'd think they'd never heard of Salem Street or Claters End."

"Your Annie allus was a finicky piece," May replied. "She'd fetch a good price laid out on pink satin in a whorehouse, though, that one would."

Tom took a step towards them, fists clenched. "You can stop that sort of talk in this house! In fact, you can stop talking to us at all from now on. Just get out of here and stay out! We don't want anything to do with your sort."

"I thought you'd say that." Lizzie's expression showed no sign that she had taken offence. "I told you that's what they'd say, my precious *respectable* family, now didn't I, May?"

"Aye, you did that."

"So we come prepared to push things a bit," said Lizzie, her voice flat and emotionless, her lips curving into their permanent sneer. "We're not takin' no for an answer, you see, Tom. We need that money bad."

Annie grabbed at Tom, whose face was red with fury, and whose fists were bunched up as if he were about to thump Lizzie. "Violence won't solve it, Tom!"

May nodded at her. "You're still a smart one, Annie Ashworth. Too smart for your own good, sometimes, I allus thought."

"I'm *not* givin' 'em any money," Tom shouted, shaking Annie's hand off his arm, but making no further move towards Lizzie. "So you can just go back to where you've come from, you – you bloody sluts!"

"I'm not goin' back to beggin' for custom on a street corner." Lizzie's voice was flat and quiet. She stared Tom in the face defiantly. "I want enough money to get my own room, an' don't tell me you can't spare it, because anyone can tell that you can."

His fists were clenched tightly on the edge of the table.

"Well, maybe I don't *want* to spare it!"

"Maybe you should think about that again, then. 'Cos if we don't get some money, we'll go an' tell a few people in the town where we've been lately. There's allus someone as'll listen to you in an ale house. Someone's bound to remember us down Claters End. Why, we might even pick up some custom there while we're at it."

Tom lunged towards them again, but Lizzie was out of her chair in a flash and holding it protectively in front of her.

She had always been quick to look after herself, Annie thought, grabbing Tom from behind. "Don't let them make you lose your temper, Tom. It won't get us anywhere."

"I'm not letting those sluts blackmail us out of our hard-earned money."

Annie let go of him and went over to the dresser, where Kathy kept the housekeeping money in a pot. She spilled the coins on to the table. "You're wrong if you think we're rich, Lizzie. But there's the housekeeping money. You can have that."

Lizzie jerked her head at her stepsister. "Count it, May. It doesn't look much to me, but it'll do for a start." She strolled round the kitchen and stood staring out at the back garden while the coins were being counted.

"Two pound nine and fourpence," announced May. "Mean devils." She scowled at Tom. "That'll not be enough. Fancy clothes cost money an' so does the right sort of room."

Lizzie came back to stand behind May, her hands on her stepsister's shoulders, her fingertips rubbing May's neck in a way that was more usual for a man than a woman. "Unless you want us back on your doorstep next week, you'd better give us some more. You'd be stupid not to. If you set us up now to earn good money ourselves, we shan't need to come back here, shall we? You don't think we *want* to come back to Bilsden, do you?"

Annie took a deep breath and looked across at her brother. "Give them what you've got, Tom."

Tom growled under his breath and pulled some coins out of his pocket. "Here." He flung them on the table. "And that's all you're going to get, because that's all I have."

May pulled the coins towards her and counted them. "Six pound ten and threepence. That's not even nine pound altogether."

"Just a minute." Annie went up to her room and came back with ten guineas in a little pouch, as well as two of her old shawls. "Here. I was saving up to buy something, but," her voice wobbled for a minute, "Mam would have wanted me to give it to you. And – and you looked cold when you came in, so you can have these shawls, too, if you like. They're old, but they're good and warm."

Silently, Lizzie walked across the room, took the money and, after a moment's hesitation, took the shawls as well. She started to open her mouth, then shook her head and closed it again. She held one shawl to her cheek for a moment, as if testing the softness. Still in silence, she passed it to May, who huddled it round her shoulders and sighed. Only then did Lizzie say, "Thanks, Annie!" in a quiet voice devoid of her usual mocking tone.

"Couldn't you – earn your living some other way?" Annie's voice came out wobbly and she was very close to tears.

Lizzie looked across at her. "No. We made a few mistakes before, but we'll know better this time. Don't worry. Them constables won't catch us again. An' we've got a fellow to look out for us now, as well." A wry smile twisted her face for a moment. "I never was much good at hard work, love."

Tom decided it was time to intervene. "Right then. Now you've got what you came for, you can get back to where you come from, or I'll not be answerable for my behaviour. An' I'm not as soft as our Annie is, believe me, so I'll do what I have to, to get rid of you. Whatever our mam might have wanted, it's Dad who's alive an' I don't want him seein' you like that."

Lizzie gave him a sideways look, the calculating expression back in her eyes.

"An' just to make sure you don't come back, let me tell you that I've got a few friends who don't like folk upsetting me. They're real good friends. An' they live in Claters End. Not far away. I could be over to fetch 'em in ten minutes."

"Tom, don't!"

"Shut up, Annie! I'm not having 'em coming back to pester us."

"Aye, but would you really do it?" asked Lizzie, hand on one hip, voice sharp. "Set them friends on to your own sister? Whatever would people say if they knew?"

His voice was low and just as vicious as hers. "As far as I'm concerned, you're no sister of mine, Lizzie Gibson, an' May's not related to me in any way. If either of you ever show your face in Bilsden again, I'll make sure that you regret it, really regret it. An' I won't ask our Annie's permission about that either."

Lizzie stared at his determined face for a moment, then flounced her shoulders and nudged May to get up. "Who wants to come back here!"

Tom moved over to hold the door open. "How did you get over to Bilsden?"

"A friend brought us over from Manchester in his cart. A good friend. He'll be waiting for us down at The Shepherd's Rest."

"I'll walk back there with you, then," said Tom.

May moved out into the hallway, still huddling the shawl around her. "We can find our own way."

"Aye, but I'd rather make sure you arrive there safely. An' I also want to make sure you get out of Bilsden straightaway."

He gave Lizzie a push towards the door and she turned on him like a she-wolf, snatching a hatpin from her battered straw hat and brandishing it in his face. "*Don't!*" she yelled. "*Don't ever shove me about again, Tom Gibson.*" Her face was a mask of fury, and her hand was quivering in the air as if she would enjoy stabbing the hatpin into his face.

May poked her head back inside the room. "She's had enough of people shovin' her around in that place. Leave her be, you rotten bully. We're goin', aren't we?"

Tom took a step backwards away from the hat pin and flourished a bow. "My apologies, your ladyship. Just remember that if you don't come back to Bilsden, I'll have no reason to shove you around – or to talk to my friends about you, either."

Annie moved forward again. "Just a minute."

They all turned to look at her.

"You'll need some food for the journey." She could not forget how they had fallen upon the meal she had given them. She did not want her own sister going away hungry, whatever that sister had become.

Lizzie looked surprised for a moment, then shrugged her shoulders. "Aye. Why not?"

"You've gone daft, Annie," Tom snapped.

Annie shrugged, and quickly wrapped some more bread and cheese, and some pieces of cake in a cloth.

As she held it out to them, Lizzie frowned at her. "Why'd you do that? You'd given us the money, an' the shawls. We could've bought summat to eat."

"Save your money. Use it to keep off the streets. Mam would have wanted me to help you." Annie's voice was low and nearly choked with tears.

Lizzie's flat face showed no emotion and her dull pebble eyes were not brimming with tears like Annie's. "The only mam I remember is Emily. But thanks anyway. An' for the shawls. You didn't need to do that."

The two of them moved slowly out of the house, followed by Tom. To Annie, they both appeared very tired under the bluff and bravado. As the front door closed behind them the back door opened and Kathy peered in. "Have they gone, then?"

Annie burst into tears, and Kathy came over to enfold her in a warm embrace. "Nay, love, don't cry." As the tears continued, she shushed her and rocked her, and finally said firmly, "If you don't stop, you'll redden your eyes and then what will your guests think?"

With a great effort, Annie sniffed and hiccuped to a halt. "I'd forgotten about the birthday party. That's the last thing I feel like at the moment." She took a deep breath, wiped her eyes on her apron and looked sideways at Kathy. "Did you hear what they said?"

"Aye."

"I still can't believe it. A sister of mine – on the streets."

Kathy could only pat her arm.

"Don't tell Dad, Kathy. It'd break his heart."

"No, love, I won't tell no one. How about I make you a nice cup of tea now?" It was her solution to every problem.

Annie shook her head. If she tried to eat or drink anything, it would choke her. "No. Let's just get on with the rest of the preparations. Like you said, we've got the tea party to think about. And I'll be better doing something than sitting around thinking."

Tom came back half an hour later. "They've gone," he announced, twisting one of the chairs round and sitting astride it facing them. "And I reminded 'em again what I'd do if they tried to come back. No more softness, our Annie. Giving them that much money was just plain stupid."

Annie's eyes filled with tears. "It'd have broken Mam's heart to see them," she said, her voice husky.

"An' it could still break Dad's heart, if he found out. Oh, you silly bitch!" Tom got up and gave her a fierce hug. "They're not worth weepin' over, them two aren't. They're nothing now, as far as I'm concerned. And if they do come back again, I'll not keep my hands off 'em. They'd better watch out if they try to blackmail me again. I've still got friends in Claters End."

"She didn't need to blackmail us," said Annie. "I'd have given her some money if I'd known she was that short."

"You're too soft for your own good, you are, where your family's concerned! I bet they'll spend most of it on gin."

"I don't think so. May looked ill to me, under all that rouge." She paused and added slowly, "They really had been in prison, hadn't they?"

Tom nodded and kept his arm round her. "Forget it now, Annie. And just pray that we never seem them again – and that Dad doesn't find out. Now, how about some food for a hungry man? I left my lunch at the yard. And I'd kill for a cup of tea."

But although Annie kept herself busy, she couldn't forget what had happened. The thought of Lizzie and of how she and May were earning their living was to give her nightmares for months.

Later that day, Annie looked round the parlour and tried to take comfort from it. Handsome and well-used now, it had curtains at the windows, the stained floorboards were polished with best beeswax and a shiny brass gasolier was hanging from the ceiling with gas wall lights on either side of the chimney breast. A big square of carpet covered the centre of the floor and Pauline's worn rug had been relegated to the bay window.

Her father seemed to be reading her mind as he came to stand next to her. "You've got it right smart in here, love. Fine as a gentleman's house, this is."

Kathy nodded. "Aye. It's lovely. Remember when we moved in an' we had no furniture to put in 'ere?"

Annie watched Kathy walk round the room, straightening

an ornament and patting the plump cushions on the sofa. She was dressed in her Sunday dress, the first silk one she had ever had, and the dusky pink seemed to reflect colour into her pale cheeks. She had protested that the material was too expensive and too light-coloured for her, that she'd be afraid to wear it, that it cost too much, but Annie had taken no notice and had just gone ahead and made the dress up.

"You look lovely as well, Kathy," Annie said softly.

"A real picture," John said, smiling at the now scarlet Kathy. "An' you look good, too, Annie, love. It's nice to see you in a brighter colour for a change."

Annie stroked the heavy aquamarine taffeta of her wide flounced skirt. "I have to wear dark colours for the salon, but I couldn't resist this material when I saw it in the warehouse in Manchester."

"It looks well with your hair," he said fondly. "Darker than your mother's, your hair is, but hers was red, too. You often make me think of her. She'd be that proud of you, love."

She gave him a hug, because she was too emotional to speak after the day's events.

Three of the children came in and perched in a row on the window seat. Luke looked uncomfortable in his Sunday best, William already looked untidy and Rebecca looked as trim as she always did in a new blue dress with a rustling taffeta petticoat that had thrilled her to pieces when Annie helped her to make it.

That boy, thought Annie, looking at her son, can't keep still for a minute. Or tidy. But she couldn't help smiling back when William grinned across the room at her and said for the twentieth time that day, "Happy birthday, Mother."

Promptly at half past three, Mary Benworth and her father knocked on the door. Annie rose to open it. She hoped she looked happy. She hoped her sorrow about Lizzie did not show.

"It's Mr Benworth and Miss Benworth," said William

loudly, waving through the window at them.

Rebecca thrust a bony elbow into his side. "Shush! You don't shout out at people like that. It's not good manners." She had become fascinated since working at the salon with what were and were not good manners.

Luke just swallowed and prepared to endure the afternoon. Meeting people was still an ordeal for him, but his dad had said he had to join in, for Annie's sake.

Five minutes later, Dr Lewis and Marianne arrived, followed closely by Helen Kenderby, and the parlour seemed suddenly full of smiling, talking people.

Then there was the sound of a carriage drawing up and Annie went to open the door for Pauline, her husband Saul and her son Stephen, the guests of honour.

"I'm so glad you could come, Pauline."

Pauline leaned forward to plant a kiss in the air above Annie's cheek, and then pushed her son forward to shake hands with his hostess. "Stephen's been excited all day, longing to meet your son and the other children."

"Happy birthday, Annie!" boomed Saul, from behind his wife. Always a big man, he seemed to be getting stouter every year. And more smug, too, well satisfied with his comfortable life.

In the parlour, Pauline graciously accepted a place on the sofa and looked around the room. "A happy family gathering," she said to Annie.

"Yes. I'm lucky, aren't I?" Annie pushed the recurring image of Lizzie firmly to the back of her mind. "Do you children want to go out into the garden for a while? William, why don't you show Stephen the dogs, and Luke, you can show him the plants you're growing at the moment."

The children trooped obediently out and there was a frozen silence as all the adults looked sideways at Pauline.

Jeremy Lewis hid a smile at the stiffness of the group and,

seeing that no one else was rushing to step into the breach, took it upon himself to speak. "It must have been a lovely drive into town on a sunny day like this, Mrs Hinchcliffe."

"Yes." Pauline smiled graciously round the room, well aware that her presence was causing the constraint. "We had the carriage hood down for the first time this year. It'll soon be summer." She proffered a small box. "A small token for your birthday, Annie, my dear."

It was the signal for everyone else to produce presents and by the time Annie had opened the parcels and exclaimed over their contents, the ice was broken. Within minutes, Saul Hinchcliffe and John Gibson were deep in an earnest theological discussion based on Saul's last sermon, with Kathy listening quietly next to John. Tom managed to get Marianne apart to look at a book of sketches of the Fylde Coast, and the two of them sat happily together on the window seat, exchanging occasional self-conscious smiles. Pauline was soon chatting to Michael Benworth about the best sort of flowers to plant in a windswept moorland garden, while Helen, Annie and Mary discussed the coming band concert in Hallam Park, one of Frederick Hallam's civic innovations that was causing a lot of excitement in the town.

Kathy slipped out after a while to get tea ready, relieved that she had not had to say much. Annie followed her into the kitchen and together they bustled to and fro, getting two big teapots ready and setting the final touches to the new table in the dining room. The adults would eat their tea together in state, leaving the kitchen table for the children's tea.

Mark, who had been minding the junk yard all afternoon, came in through the back door just as they were finishing and Annie realised with a shock that he was taller than her now, almost a man. How had she failed to notice that? Like his half-brother Tom, Mark had matured early, but unlike Tom, he was quite tall and bade fair to become good-looking once he had filled out from his present thinness.

"Do you want to join the adults or the children, Mark?" she asked, on a sudden impulse.

He stared at her in surprise. "Am I allowed to join the adults?"

"I think so. I hadn't realised how tall you'd grown lately, how grown-up you seem, or I'd have suggested it earlier."

"The adults, then. It'll be more interesting to listen to them. But I'd better go and change into my Sunday clothes first, hadn't I?"

"Hurry up, then." She turned to Kathy as he went out. "Isn't he growing up? I hadn't realised." She had been too engrossed in her business and her own concerns and had left the children to Kathy and her dad, even William. There just didn't seem to be time for everything nowadays.

"Aye," said Kathy comfortably. "An' he's a right smart lad, too, is our Mark. Your dad says there's nothing he can't do at the yard, an' he understands the figures best of anyone. He's the most like you, your dad says, him and Rebecca." She wiped her hands on the tea towel and looked around her with satisfaction. "Well, that's it. If they don't like it, they'll have to lump it. I'd better go and tell our Luke that he'll be in charge of the children's tea table, hadn't I?"

"No, tell Rebecca. She'll handle things much better than Luke, and she'll enjoy playing the grown-up lady. She'll not be afraid to tell William to calm down, or Stephen Hinchcliffe, either." Annie peered out of the window and smiled. "I don't know what Pauline will say. Her Stephen's acting like a normal boy today, running round, dirtying his clothes and shouting his head off."

Kathy came to stand beside her. "About time, too, from what you've told me." She turned back to the kettle which was just boiling. "Well, I'll brew up now while you're getting 'em all into the dining room. Don't forget to set another place for Mark first."

As Annie was crossing the hall to the parlour, there was a knock on the front door. "Who can that be now?" she muttered in exasperation. She flung open the door and stopped dead, her hand reaching up across her breast in a protective gesture. "Danny! What on earth are you doing here?"

He held out a bunch of flowers. "I remembered it was your birthday, Annie."

She made no move to take them.

His smile was wry. "No need to say anything. I can see how glad you are to see me."

She flushed. "Oh, I'm so sorry. It was just the – the shock of seeing you. I only got a letter from you last week, and you said nothing about a visit. Er – won't you come in."

"You've got company." He remained where he was, but pushed the flowers into her hands.

She held them to her nose. "They're lovely, thank you. But there's no reason you shouldn't join us, Danny. It's just a tea party to celebrate my birthday. One more person won't be a problem. Kathy's prepared a mountain of food." Her heart was beating rapidly, as it always did when she was close to him. Why did Danny have this effect on her, he and no other man since Matt Peters? She stared up at him, wondering how long he was going to be staying in Bilsden this time. Why had he said nothing about coming? "Do join us." It was far better to have him here with a group of people than coming back later on his own.

She showed him into the parlour and performed a quick round of introductions before taking the flowers into the kitchen and then setting two more places at the table. When she came back she led everyone into the dining room. Taking a deep breath, she fixed a smile on her face as she took her place at the head of the table. She wished the day were over. What on earth had made her organise this ridiculous tea party? What she really wanted at the moment was to go and think things through in her bedroom. After the encounter with Lizzie and May, she desperately needed some time to herself.

And the last thing she felt like coping with, the very last thing, was Danny and his teasing remarks. If he tried to kiss her today, she would scream. She was not enjoying her birthday at all this year. She might be only twenty-six, but she felt more like ninety today.

Eighteen

ENCOUNTERS

The next day was fine and Annie said firmly at breakfast that she was not going to chapel, but for a walk on the moors by herself. Kathy looked at her sharply and John shook his head, for to him chapel was the high point of the week. But the rest of the family did not show much interest in Annie's plans. There was nothing unusual about her going off on her own. Sometimes she would go to the salon after chapel on a Sunday to try out new ideas or to cut out a gown or just, Kathy suspected, to be by herself. And all the family enjoyed a good tramp across the moors. It was John's favourite treat to take his children walking up on the tops.

Kathy followed Annie up to her bedroom. "Are you all right, love?"

"Yes, of course I am." Annie heard her voice wobble and said quickly, "I just have a lot to think about. It was a – a shock seeing Lizzie like that. I can't get her out of my mind. I need some time to get used to the idea. On my own."

"And then there was the shock of Danny O'Connor turning

up again, without warning." Kathy's voice was quiet, but understanding.

Annie fiddled with the things on her drawing table. "Mmm."

"He's always nice as pie to me, but I don't really trust him, you know," Kathy said abruptly. "I never know what to expect from him."

Annie could only gape at her. "You never said anything about that before."

"I know. But I'm saying it now." Kathy cocked her head on one side. "Do you trust him?"

"I – I don't know. I think I do. He's Bridie and Mick's son, after all. We've known them all our lives."

"He's courting you, isn't he?"

"Yes." Annie could not stop a blush creeping over her face. "I suppose he is. Trying to, anyway."

"You've had long enough to think about him. Don't you fancy him?"

"I don't fancy any man." Annie's voice was tight and controlled, but the piece of charcoal snapped in her fingers. "You know that, Kathy!"

"Aye. I know that. It's a pity. Lovin' a fellow is – it's wonderful."

The tenderness in Kathy's voice as she said that made Annie turn round quickly. "You speak as if – as if you're in love with someone yourself."

Kathy's smile was blissful. "Aye, I am."

"Kathy! Who is it?"

"Your dad."

Annie took an involuntary step backwards. "*Dad*!"

"Aye." Kathy set her hands on her hips and stared at Annie challengingly. "He's a lovely man, your dad is."

"I know he's lovely, but Kathy, he's – well, he's so much older than you."

"Aye. But I still fancy him. I don't much like young men."

She was fiddling with the pocket of her apron. "I just – I've been wanting to tell you about it for a while, but you won't say anything to anyone else yet, will you? I know your Tom doesn't want your father to get wed again, an' he'd be right upset if he knew about us. They're gettin' on so well at the yard, your dad an' Tom that I don't want to come between them. Anyway, it's early days yet, isn't it? Who knows what'll come of it?"

"I don't know what to say, Kathy."

"Don't say owt. Just think about it while you're off on your walk." She came across to hug Annie. "I wanted you to know about us. I couldn't go behind your back, love, not in anything." She paused, then added in a more normal tone, "So, when will you be back?"

"I don't know. I feel like having a really long tramp and it looks as if it'll stay fine. Let's just say before tea time, sooner if it rains."

"Do you want me to pack you up something to eat?"

"No. No, I'm not hungry. I ate far too much yesterday."

Kathy watched her go, then stood frowning out of the window for a while. Annie had eaten hardly anything yesterday. Was it Lizzie, or was it Danny who was upsetting her like this?

The fine weather seemed set to continue and the moors were at their best that day. Annie strode up the lane with the sound of church bells ringing in her ears and with sunlight dancing around her like a living thing. It'd be nice to live in a house up here near the top of Ridge Hill, she thought, and in a house with even more rooms than Netherleigh Cottage, a house where you could get away from people without having to go out for a walk or take refuge at the salon.

She passed Jonas Dawton's house with its square tower at one end and its wide lawns. Not as big as Frederick Hallam's house, but a pretty place – or it would be if it were better cared for. Dawton had been hard hit in recent years, they said, with the trade fluctuations, but trade was looking up at the moment, in Bilsden at any rate, and his operatives were on full-time work again. She smiled as she saw some small figures playing hide-and-seek among the trees, regardless of it being a Sunday. With so many children, it was no wonder that Dawton's garden was so untidy. If she didn't have Luke to nag the others and keep them off his precious vegetable and flower beds, her own garden wouldn't be looking so trim either.

She stared at the walls of Frederick Hallam's house as she passed it, smiling again to think of her curtains adorning his huge parlour – no, he called it the drawing room. He had two or three parlours as well, but the drawing room was his favourite, apparently. Beautiful cherry-red velvet curtains now glowed against the newly painted cream walls, with a fine turkey carpet on the floor. She had done well with those curtains, even Beatrice had said so. Frederick had just smiled at her and shown her through the house as he discussed his ideas on decorating some of the other living areas.

Beatrice had trailed behind them like a sulky schoolgirl, her expression resentful when she thought her father wasn't watching her. The other rooms were a mish-mash of patterns and colours that made Annie's eyes ache to see them. The late Mrs Hallam had had appalling taste and Frederick Hallam didn't scruple to say so. Mrs Hallam's daughter scowled at that. She clearly did not approve of the way her father was treating Mrs Ashworth. The mill owner's daughter obviously considered Annie nothing more than a glorified shopkeeper, but Beatrice was too frightened of her father's anger to refuse to entertain Mrs Ashworth to tea.

Annie wasn't at all nervous in Frederick Hallam's company. He was such an interesting man, she thought, smiling to herself as she stood there staring at his grand house. And he cared far more about the people around him than he liked to show. Look at what he was doing for the town! Look at how he had helped her when someone destroyed Lady Darrington's gown! She had been walking too fast and had a stitch in her side, so she stayed there for a moment to catch her breath and continued to stare at the Hallam residence. Ridge House, he called it now. What must it be like to have a house so big? She grinned. That was one thing she would never know. She had done well to get out of Salem Street and to buy a house of her own in Moor Close. She had done especially well to open a business in High Street, but people like her never got to live in houses like these.

It was funny, though. After Salem Street, Netherleigh Cottage had seemed huge, like a palace almost. Now it seemed small and crowded. She immediately felt guilty for even thinking that, but she had to admit to herself that her family was getting her down a bit. There always seemed to be someone making a noise or quarrelling. Her dad took possession of the kitchen every night when he came back from the yard, and he and Kathy sat there as if they owned the place. How long had they been courting? She had thought her dad was too old to take another wife, but he seemed to have found one anyway. Kathy was right about one thing, though. Tom would be absolutely furious. No wonder Kathy was keeping quiet about her feelings for the moment.

Annie wasn't furious. Her dad and Kathy deserved some happiness. They were both lovely people. She did not know what would have happened to her without her dad's help that time when she was expecting William. She owed her father a lot and she knew he really cared about her, about all his children. Danny also said he cared about her, wanted to make her happy. Could she ever come to care about him in that way? The way she had once cared about Matt Peters. Sometimes she thought she might, then at others she wanted nothing to do with Danny O'Connor. All she wanted in life was to earn a decent living and to bring up William as best she could.

Her thoughts wandered back to her home again. She couldn't really keep away from people there. If she went to sit in the parlour in the evening, someone was bound to follow her there. The only place they didn't follow her to was her bedroom. Sometimes she went to sit there quietly, but even so, you could always hear noises. What was wrong with her? Noise was normal in a house. Children couldn't be expected to live without making a noise, could they?

As Annie got further out of town, the air seemed to change, to lose its smoky taste and take on a wild moorland tang. She took deep breaths and sighed in relief as the town dropped out of sight behind her and she was on her own at last. The few people she passed said good day, but showed no desire to linger and chat, which suited her just fine. And after a while, there were no more people.

Her thoughts were still whirling round her head and they were not happy ones. She kept remembering Lizzie and how pale and shabby her sister had looked under that tawdry finery. "Please don't let Dad find out about her," she murmured at one stage. "It'd kill him." She was not even aware of having spoken out loud, but as there was no one near, her words were carried away by the breeze that ruffled her hair and flapped her shawl ends against her body.

She looked down at herself and grimaced. No one would recognise her as the owner of Bilsden's Ladies' Salon today. She had dressed for comfort, perversely rejecting all her newer dresses. She was wearing a simple old brown and white checked cotton dress and a pair of stout shoes as well as a dark woollen shawl. She had had to borrow that from Kathy, since she had given her own shawls to Lizzie and May.

She stopped and just sat for a while on top of a small rise on the edge of the moors. As she stared down into the smoky valley of the Bil, her worries seemed to fade away and she lost herself in the beauty of the day. The calls of the birds and the humming of the insects made little impact on her, but the overall peace of the place did. When she started walking again, she moved more slowly and her shoulders had lost that tenseness.

By lunch time she was several miles away from the town and was wishing she had taken up Kathy's offer of sandwiches. She found a little stream and cupped up a few mouthfuls of water in her hands, then turned round slowly to get her bearings. Goodness, she was quite near to Bridie and Mick O'Connor's farm! She had not realised which way her steps had been leading her. She turned immediately in the opposite direction to Knowle Farm. The last thing she wanted at the moment was to see Danny O'Connor again. She had managed to avoid a tête-à-tête with him yesterday at the tea party, had seen the suppressed irritation in his face and been grateful to Helen for distracting his attention.

Helen liked Danny and thought Annie mad even to think of keeping him at a distance. She had said frankly that if she had even half a chance of marrying someone as handsome, she'd snap it up, never mind the difference in their stations, never mind what her father said. Her father had already discouraged several potential suitors. He just wanted her there to look after him in his old age. He didn't care whether she was happy or not. She had come to realise how stupid she had been to let him ruin her life.

Danny should have warned them that he was coming up to Bilsden, Annie thought for the umpteenth time. He shouldn't just have turned up like that. She hadn't known how to deal with him and she hadn't liked the way Kathy and her dad exchanged knowing looks.

She sighed and pulled the shawl more tightly round her shoulders, realising that the wind was turning a bit chilly. She looked up to see clouds scudding across the sun. Goodness!

She ought to have turned back long before this. She was going to get soaked. Well, a bit of water wouldn't kill her, and if she walked briskly she could be well on her way back before the rain started.

As she turned on to the main Bilsden road, she passed a patch of bilberry plants by the roadside, then another. A few more weeks and it would be time to pick them. The children would love that. Kathy had said she wanted to bottle as many as possible this year, with such a large family to feed. When Annie heard a carriage clopping along behind her, she moved automatically to the roadside to allow it to pass. It was the first sign of life she had seen for a couple of hours, apart from the sheep, the birds and an occasional rabbit. Farms were few up here, huddling mostly in the little valleys away from the wind which always seemed to be sighing across the rolling uplands.

The carriage passed her and then stopped abruptly. Annie stopped as well, feeling nervous. She had been too lost in her thoughts to notice whose carriage it was. But as Frederick Hallam got out, she sighed in relief. She need have no fears of him.

He walked back to join her. "All alone, Mrs Ashworth? You're a long way from home."

"Yes. I was thinking about my plans for the future and I walked too far. I just wanted some time on my own. Netherleigh Cottage is always so full of people." Now why had she told him that? What had got into her lately, treating a man like him as a friend?

He smiled. "We all need thinking time, but some people never seem to get it. I'm lucky. I can order the carriage and go anywhere I please, or I have the choice of a dozen rooms where I can be quiet." It was better, though, when he got away from Beatrice, because her petty carping ways, so like her mother's, occasionally drove him to snap at her. Like her mother, she always seemed half afraid of him and that irritated him.

"Yes, it must be nice to have a carriage." Annie turned to look at his glossy equipage and well-fed horses.

He stared at her profile in warm admiration. Even dressed like that, she was lovely. Her hair had come loose and was hanging down her back in a shining auburn mass. The sun and wind had given her face more colour than usual and it suited her. Her eyes were sparkling with life. It was trite to liken them to emeralds and besides, precious stones were cold things and Annie Ashworth's eyes were warm and alive. Even in that simple gingham gown, she looked trim and attractive. Beatrice never looked like that, however much he spent on her clothes, because she moved about like a lump of dough. This woman held herself with unconscious pride and grace. She would be magnificent if she wore the sort of clothes she made for others. He would like to see her in a froth of ball gown, something ivory or cream that allowed her magnificent hair to blaze with life.

He realised he had been staring at her and cleared his throat. "May I offer you a lift back into town, Mrs Ashworth, or do you prefer to get soaked?"

She laughed up at him. "I don't mind a little rain, but I must admit that it's a long way back and my feet are aching now, so I'll be happy to accept your offer, Mr Hallam."

He escorted her to the carriage, settling her on the seat opposite him, much as he'd have liked to sit next to her, because he knew how nervous she was with men. He tapped the roof with his walking stick and the carriage moved off. "How did the birthday party go yesterday, then?"

"How did you know about that?"

"Word gets around in a small town like ours – especially when Mrs Hinchcliffe is to be one of the guests. That caused a lot of comment among the ladies." Beatrice had been particularly scornful about the foolishness of a lady socialising with her dressmaker. But then, Beatrice was very scornful about almost everything to do with Bilsden since her trip to London.

Annie shrugged her shoulders. "Pauline's been my friend for a long time now, but I have to confess that she invited herself yesterday. I wouldn't have dared ask her and her family to my birthday tea." Her eyes were dancing as she spoke, inviting him to share the amusement of it all.

He would, Frederick realised, and not for the first time, like to share more than a joke with Annie Ashworth. He took a firm hold on himself and said lightly, "Mrs Hinchcliffe seems to take a great interest in your welfare."

Annie's eyes softened. "Pauline's been very good to me. I owe her a great deal. And she's excellent company. She makes me think about the world. There's so much more than Bilsden, isn't there? One day, I'll go travelling myself. Helen Kenderby's been all over Europe and she's told me about it. France and Rome and Greece." Her voice died away in a sigh. "There's so much I want to do and see." Maybe that was why she had been feeling so very restless lately. The trips to London were giving her a taste for travel. They were the high spots of her year.

He looked at her thoughtfully. "I think you'd enjoy Paris most of all. The women there have a special smartness I've seen nowhere else. 'Chic', they call it." He gave a soft snort of laughter as he remembered how Christine had hated Paris, hated going anywhere in fact. She had just wanted to stay in her safe nest of a home. And Beatrice was cast in the same mould. The sooner that girl was wed the better, as far as he was concerned. He would provide a substantial dowry and ask his elder daughter to help find Beatrice a husband. He had delayed taking action for too long.

He realised that he had been silent for a while and looked across at Annie, meaning to apologise, but she was staring dreamily out of the window, lost in her own thoughts.

"A penny for them," he said instead.

Annie flushed. "It's nothing, really. I'm having a very lazy day and my thoughts aren't worth sharing." It didn't occur to her until she was in bed that night that she had felt perfectly comfortable alone with him in the carriage and had felt no compulsion to talk for talking's sake.

By the time they pulled up at Netherleigh Cottage, the rain was beating a tattoo on the carriage roof and the street gutters were running with dirty brown water. Frederick swung Annie down from the carriage, able to hold her for a moment on the excuse of lifting her across the puddles, and then he insisted on escorting her up the path under the shelter of his huge black silk umbrella.

When they got to the door she asked hesitantly, "Would you – er – care to come in for a cup of tea?"

He stared down at her lovely face turned so trustingly up towards him and was tempted to steal a kiss. But when he kissed her, as he surely would one day, he did not want it to be a hurried affair at her door with his coachman watching from the road. "I'd love some tea, but I'm afraid that Beatrice has invited people round and she'll be most annoyed if I'm late. Another time, perhaps?"

"Yes. Any time." She turned and walked inside to find that Rebecca had seen them through the parlour window and was already spreading the news that Mr Hallam had brought their Annie back in his carriage.

As William rushed to give her a hug and the others crowded round to ask why she had come back in a carriage, Annie gave them all a beaming smile. She was not worried now about being surrounded by people. She had not really resolved any of her problems, but the big open spaces of the moors had been a balm to her troubled spirit and chatting with Frederick Hallam was always a pleasure. She felt happy and relaxed, able to face anything.

Danny O'Connor was still looming on her horizon, the most puzzling of her problems, because she did not understand her own feelings towards him, but she felt better able to cope with him now. And anyway, his visits home were always short. It would be different if he were living in Bilsden. He talked about settling down sometimes, but the sub-contracts he kept getting on the railways were too lucrative to miss. So she was safe from his attentions for a while yet.

Nineteen

SPRING TO SUMMER 1847

In fact, it was a full year before Danny's next visit, a year of hard work for Annie whose salon and second-hand clothing businesses were both flourishing. She did not know what she would have done at the salon without Mary Benworth, who was proving to be not only a good seamstress and one who picked up new skills quickly, but also a woman with an eye for the right style to suit a client. Annie let Mary try her hand at designing a few garments, then enlisted Helen Kenderby's help to teach Mary to sketch properly and to use watercolours. The only problem they had was in persuading Mary that she really could do all this, as well as persuading her to wear more fashionable clothes herself. Being so tall had made Mary rather shy about attracting attention to herself.

Letters continued to arrive for Annie from Danny every few weeks, but he did not come home again as there was a frantic scramble everywhere in the country to build railway lines and he was earning the best money he ever had. The letters were untidy scrawls upon pieces of paper that often had dirty smears on them. He used the new gummed envelopes, which Pauline Hinchcliffe scoffed at as a waste of time, but which Annie thought very sensible if you wanted your correspondence to be both safe and private without having to fiddle around with sealing wax.

For all her modern approach to business, Pauline seemed suspicious of many of the new inventions which were changing household life so drastically and said openly that she was glad the gas pipes did not reach as far as Collett Hall. Gas was all very well as a form of lighting for businesses, but it was not necessary for things to be so brightly illuminated in one's own home. Annie, however, relished progress of any kind and was always ready to try something new, which sometimes caused lively discussions between the two of them.

In June that year, soon after Annie's twenty-seventh birthday, Bridie sent Mick across to invite the inhabitants of Netherleigh Cottage to a special Sunday tea at the farm. "Our Danny's just come home again," he said proudly. "An' he thought it'd be nice to have a proper tea party. He's the one for doing things in style, is our Danny."

Annie felt a quiver of apprehension run through her belly. Danny had said nothing about coming back in his letters, and although she had come to enjoy his lively epistles, she still had not arrived at any real decision about the relationship between the two of them. And if she knew Danny, he would use this opportunity to get her alone. She shrank from the mere idea of that. She had found his kisses, few as they had been, far too unsettling. However, she could do nothing but accept the invitation with Mick sitting grinning proudly at her across the kitchen table. "Are you sure it won't be too much trouble to have all of us round?"

"Not at all, Annie, love. Danny said he'd wash the big cart out and put some clean hay in the bottom to sit on. He'll bring it over to fetch you all, and then he'll take you back again afterwards. We can put the hood on, if it's raining, but I reckon the weather will be fine by weekend. I can feel it in my bones."

"That's far too much trouble, Mick. We can walk out to the farm. It's only three miles, after all."

He leaned across to pat Annie's hand. "Sure an' it's no trouble at all. What are friends for? An' save your strength to do your walking on the moors when you get out to our place. Them roads can be dirty places an' you dressin' so daintily, you won't want to spoil your nice things." He took a final slurp of tea. "Good cup of tea, that. Oh, an' Bridie said to be sure you bring your da an' young Kathy here. We want everyone to be there to celebrate with us."

"What are we celebrating?"

He tapped the side of his nose as he stood up to take his leave. "Aha! That'd be tellin', wouldn't it? Wait an' see, love, just you wait an' see. It's to be a surprise. Bridie says not to let the children dress too fancy because they'll want to play with the new puppies."

"All right."

At the door he turned round again. "There, if I didn't nearly forget. Bridie told me to ask if the doctor's daughter would like to come with you. The lass seemed to enjoy herself when she visited us before an' we hear she spends a lot of time round at your house. She's a nice lass, that one is."

So on the Sunday they went to the early morning service at chapel, then, after lunch, everyone got ready with much excited toing and froing between bedrooms and kitchen. Seeing the children's excitement at the prospect of this outing, Annie felt even more guilty about her own reluctance to go.

Tom came and sat beside her as she waited in the kitchen for Danny to arrive with the cart. He raised one eyebrow quizzically. "Not best pleased about this, are you?" he asked quietly.

"It's kind of Bridie to invite us," she said obliquely.

"But?"

Annie fiddled with her wedding ring, not knowing how to answer him.

"But maybe Danny's pushing things a bit." Tom said it for her. "I can always tell him to leave you alone if he's troubling you. But I thought, with you an' him writing all those letters, you'd be glad to see him again."

She sighed, "I am – in a way – and I'm old enough to do my own telling, Tom Gibson, and I would too, if I – if . . ." Her voice trailed away.

"If?" he prompted.

"If I knew my own mind."

There was a chorus of voices shrieking in the parlour where the children had been keeping watch for Danny, and then the clatter of feet in the hallway followed by the sound of the front door opening. Annie tensed, but it was only Marianne Lewis. When Tom heard the visitor's voice, he abandoned Annie to go and talk to her, and his sister was left alone with her worries about the day to come.

A few minutes later, the voices started calling out again and this time Annie heard Danny's deep voice laughing and answering the children's questions. She stood up to go and greet him, unconsciously squaring her shoulders as she left the kitchen. "Hello, Danny. It's a fine day for our outing, isn't it?"

"Annie." He made the word a caress, then took the hand she held out and kept it in both of his while he answered, so that she could only have pulled it away by making a fuss. "It is. It's a lovely day. An' you're looking pretty as a picture."

When he let go of her hand, she mumbled something and went with a flushed face to call her father and Kathy in from the back where Luke was proudly showing off the latest developments in his vegetable garden.

In spite of her efforts to ride in the rear of the cart, Annie found herself up on the driving bench on her own next to Danny, for Kathy and her father insisted on sitting in the back, as did Tom and Marianne. As they started off, she glanced covertly at Danny. He was looking very attractive today, clad in clean moleskin trousers, a cream shirt in heavy cotton and a sleeveless leather jerkin. No sign of the Gentleman of the diggings today. She liked him better like this. His public clothes were always just a trifle showy.

She stared up at the sky. She had half hoped the weather would prevent the outing, but although it had rained during the week, as Mick had predicted, today the sun was shining brightly in a near cloudless sky. Behind her Tom and Marianne sat with their heads together in one corner, oblivious to the scenery, and the children sat in a laughing heap near the tail of the cart, sometimes jumping off it to run behind and then scrambling back on again with much shrieking and help from the others. As usual, Mark was keeping the younger ones in order and William was making the most noise.

Kathy was leaning back against the cart's side next to John, and the dreamy smile on her face was echoed by the fond expression on his. How could Tom not have noticed the pair of them? Annie wondered. Even the children were beginning to link their dad and Kathy together, and she was sure that Mark at least understood how the relationship was developing, understood and approved in his quiet way. Mark was nobody's fool.

But Tom was too engrossed in his own affairs lately to notice. He seemed much taken with Marianne Lewis and that, too, was beginning to worry Annie. The girl had a ridiculous amount of freedom nowadays. Her cousin seemed to have stopped trying to play the strict chaperone, and when you did see the two women together in town, they didn't look as if they were enjoying each other's company. Ellie had said once that Marianne hated her Cousin Dorothy, yes hated her. Well, Annie did not like the woman either, but it was not right for a young lady of that age to visit Tom at the yard so often, or to go for walks alone with him on the moors. Someone should keep a better eye on Marianne.

When they got to the farm, a beaming Bridie rushed out to greet them, followed by Mick who swept the boys and Rebecca off to help him take care of the horses. Bridie insisted on feeding everyone a snack, in case the journey had left them ravenous, which the children agreed it had. When Danny got down from the cart, he stood leaning against the wall of the house, his eyes only for Annie. And it was Annie he sat next to when they went inside to Bridie's huge farm kitchen.

Once the snack had been consumed, Bridie sent the children outside with her youngest son, Rory. They had been promised a chance to play with the young animals, for the stock at the farm seemed to be as fecund as Bridie herself had once been.

"You're lookin' grand, Annie, me love," Bridie said, turning back to her adult guests, who were still sitting around the table. "I keep hearing how well your salon is doing, an' sure you always look as fresh and lovely as a spring morning whenever I see you. Hard work must agree with you."

Annie felt Danny's eyes still on her and so filled were they with – with something she did not like to put a name to that she flushed scarlet. "Bridie, stop your blarney. You're embarrassing me. I'm more interested in finding out what we're celebrating today."

"Ah, yes. It's about time we told you." Bridie clasped Mick's hand and beamed at her eldest son. "Danny, love?"

Danny stood up. "Well, ladies and gentlemen, what we're celebrating today is the founding of my new business. I'm back to stay this time, and I shall be opening up as a builder here in Bilsden in a week or two, once I've got my supplies sorted out and some craftsmen hired. Daniel Connor, builder. Now how does that sound to you?" He addressed his question to them all, but his eyes came back to rest on Annie again.

"Why, it's the best news I've heard since our Tom took me on at the yard," said John at once, beaming with delight. "Isn't it, Annie, love? Annie?"

Annie realised that he was waiting for an answer from her and that everyone else was looking at her as well. She dragged her eyes away from Danny's smug expression and said as calmly as she could manage, "You've done well for yourself, Danny. Very well. But did you say Daniel Connor? Are you changing your name?"

He nodded, ignoring his mother's suddenly sad expression and his father's scowl. "Yes. Daniel sounds more dignified, don't you think?"

Annie gave a slight shrug. "It doesn't sound like you, somehow."

"Well, it will from now on. And Connor will go down better with people than O'Connor." He looked across at Mick whose lips were a tight line of disapproval. "I'm sorry, Dad, but we have to face facts. The Irish aren't generally liked here in Lancashire and I want to be a successful builder."

Tom stepped into the breach. "Have you found somewhere for your yard, then, Danny, or should I say Daniel?"

The grin came back to Danny's face. "That's the best news of all. You know that waste land at the far end of the High Street? Well, Hallam has agreed to let me rent that from him and we're to come to some agreement about me building an office there, with living quarters as well."

Annie sat there frozen, letting the happy voices flow to and fro across her head as everyone discussed the news. Danny had not only come back to Bilsden, but he was opening up a business on High Street only five minutes' walk away from her salon! She felt as trapped as any rat in a cage. Fear trickled down her spine. She was not ready for this, not ready at all. She was not sure she would ever be ready for someone like Danny.

When they had finished exclaiming and talking about Danny's news, Bridie shooed them all outside for a nice little walk "to blow the soot away from yer lungs" while she got the meal proper ready.

Annie lingered in the house, trying to persuade Bridie to let her help, but her hostess was having none of that. In the end, hoping that Danny would have gone off with the others by now, Annie went slowly outside. But he was there waiting for her, leaning against the wall, chewing a stem of tender young grass.

"Annie." Again, the way he said her name was too warm and his eyes were too knowing on her face. "The others have gone on ahead but I thought I'd wait for you. We wouldn't want one of our guests to feel neglected, would we?"

She could see Tom and Marianne in the distance striding out across the fields, deep in conversation, and her father sitting next to Kathy on a sheltered patch of sunny ground, their backs against the dry-stone wall and their faces relaxed. "Let's join Kathy and—" she gasped as a large warm hand grasped her arm and pulled her back.

"No!" Danny's voice was soft but determined.

After one nervous glance upwards, she did not dare meet his eyes. "But—"

He pulled her round the corner of the farmhouse and before she could protest, she was trapped against the wall between his hands. Panic started to rise in her and he must have noticed because he took a half-step backwards and held his hands wide. "You're all right with me, Annie. Ah, love, don't get that look on your face. I only wanted to kiss you. There's no harm in a little kiss, surely."

"I – I don't—" But he was bending towards her and this time, his hands were more gentle upon her shoulders and she could not seem to pull away. With one fingertip, he raised her chin. "Just one kiss, Annie, love. Haven't I been patient all

304

this time? Don't I deserve a small reward for that?"

Before she could reply, he had taken the kiss, his lips so soft and warm on hers that the panic died in her throat and something else took its place. He moved his head back for a minute, studied her face and smiled. "That wasn't so bad now, was it, darlin'?"

She took a deep breath, but his head was bending towards her again and this time the kiss was more urgent. She moaned in her throat, but his hands were cradling her face and stroking her hair and again, something within her responded to his caress in spite of her anxiety. When he pulled his lips away, he just held her close and continued to stroke her hair and murmur endearments in her ear.

She leaned against him and sighed. It had happened now, the thing she had been trying to prevent for a while. And her own body had betrayed her as she had suspected it might. For some reason, she suddenly remembered Matt's kisses and how, at seventeen, she had lived for their moments alone and the touch of his lips on hers. The lingering memories of the slobbering animal-like figure who had raped her began to fade in the face of this pleasant reality.

After a while Danny took her hands in his and tilted her chin up so that she had to look him in the eyes. "That wasn't so bad now, was it, Annie, love?" he repeated.

Her voice was a mere thread of sound. "No. No, it wasn't, Danny."

"Daniel."

"Daniel." Her legs felt so shaky that she stumbled as she started to move and had to lean on him.

His face had a triumphant expression on it as he offered her his arm and reached across with his other hand to clasp the hand she laid upon it. "Let's go for a little walk around the fields, then, Annie, me love, and I'll tell you all about my new business."

By the time she and Daniel got back to the farm, Annie had grown used to using his full name and had also pulled herself together, on the surface at least. She felt that Daniel had gained some sort of a victory over her. She was not sure whether she liked that or not, but she did admit to herself that the kisses had not been – had not been at all frightening this time. And Daniel was a very attractive man. Though she let go of his arm well before they reached the farmhouse, the adults still gave the pair of them knowing glances and only Tom and Kathy's expressions were ambiguous. The rest were openly approving.

The other couples had been too busy with their own affairs to watch what Annie was doing. Tom and Marianne Lewis had got out of sight of the house as fast as they could. Only then did he take hold of her hands and draw her towards him for a kiss. "I've been longing to do that all day," he said in a throaty voice.

She looked at him with all her youthful love shining in her eyes. "Well, I don't mind if you do it again then, Mr Gibson, sir." He had kissed her several times now and she relived those kisses again and again in her dreams and during her waking hours. She dreamed of him often and, being Jeremy Lewis's daughter, she never tried to pretend otherwise, but let Tom see how much she enjoyed his kisses, how much she loved him.

He took her at her word, but was careful not to allow the kiss to become too passionate. For him, this girl was something very special, a golden princess like you read about in story books, so different from dark-haired Rosie with her broad speech and crooked cheeky smile. He pushed Marianne gently away after a while. "Come on, then. That's enough of that. Start walking again, love! Someone'll see us if we're not careful."

"I don't care if someone does see us, Tom."

"Well, I do. I've told you before. We're not doing anything about our future until I'm in a better position financially." He sighed and drew her closer for a moment. "It'll be another year or two yet before I'm properly established as a food supplier, love, so you'll have to be patient."

Her expression had grown unhappy. "It's hard to be patient. I'm not sure I can stand it at home much longer, Tom. Cousin Dorothy is getting – well, she's getting very strange. And vicious. I don't know how Ellie stands her nastiness. Or how Father doesn't notice it."

"Your father's always been a bit lost in his medicine, hasn't he?"

"Yes, but he's got much worse now Mother's not here to keep him in order. He'd forget to come to table sometimes if I didn't go and fetch him. I – I'm beginning to understand a little how she must have felt. What I don't understand is why they ever got married in the first place. I know she still writes to him occasionally, because I've seen the letters, but he says it's only about business matters, usually her wanting a higher allowance. She's never written to me, not once, nor asked me to go and visit her. There's only you with the time to care about me now, T-Tom." Her voice broke on the last word.

He had to kiss her again at that and wipe away the tears brimming in her eyes with his rough fingertip. "Eh, my little love."

"Ellie says we must just endure Cousin Dorothy, because she's got nowhere else to live. Ellie says it's Father who needs our support most, so that he can go on helping people in the town, and that we must just put up with Dorothy. I sometimes think Ellie cares more about my father than about me nowadays." She bent her head and said in a low voice, "Dorothy's been so bad this week that I've felt like running away, only I have nowhere to go." She gulped in an effort to stem the tears.

Tom's arms were around her immediately.

She blinked up at him. "The only thing that keeps me going is the thought that I'll be able to see you and talk to you. You're the only one who really understands how I feel." Surely now he would ask her properly to marry him? But he didn't. He just held her close, then said they must continue walking.

In the field near the house, John and Kathy continued to sit in perfect amity next to the dry-stone wall, hands clasped under the cover of her skirt.

"Eh, it's a lovely day, isn't it?" he said, closing his eyes. After a while, he opened them again and nudged her. "Have you thought any more about what I asked you, love?"

Kathy looked sideways at him. In spite of the white which now threaded his curly brown hair, she never thought of him as old. Since he'd left the mill, he seemed much younger and more vigorous, and often said that he felt like a new man. "Yes, love," she said softly, "I've thought about it."

"And?"

Her face clouded. "You know full well I'd like to wed you, John Gibson, but I don't want to come between you an' your son. You know how dead set he is against you ever marrying again. Can't we just go on as we are?"

He frowned at her. "It's not what I like, treating you like that, and it's against the Lord's word, given to guide us. I want us to be wed proper, Kathy. Man and wife, according to God's holy ordinance."

"Me, too," she admitted. "But Tom would – Oh, let's give it a bit longer, John."

"How much longer? I'm not getting any younger, you know."

She lifted one hand to stroke his cheek. "The end of the summer. We'll do something after the summer, whatever. You know how busy your Tom is with his new food-supply business, how much money he's got tied up in it. It'd be a bad time to upset him at the moment."

"All right, then. But only till after the summer. I'm not waiting any longer than that."

A little while later he asked hesitantly, "I don't think the children will mind, do you? Or our Annie. You said she didn't seem angry when you told her. It's just our Tom, isn't it? I mean, there's nothin' else to prevent us?"

Kathy could not bear the uncertainty in his voice. She squeezed his hand. "Nay, there's nothing else, love. I don't think your Annie will mind at all if we get wed. But John, have you ever thought that she might marry again herself one day? Danny O'Connor's been looking at her today like a dog with a juicy bone."

"She could do worse than marry him."

"I think she could do better for herself."

His eyes widened in surprise. "Eh, what do you mean by that, lass? He's a right pleasant fellow, is Danny – though we must get used to calling him Daniel now, mustn't we? – an' he comes from a family we know and like. He's not short of a coin or two, neither, which is a good thing. Our Annie wouldn't marry a poor man, like you'll have to."

Her eyes were thoughtful and unfocused. "Aye, he's pleasant enough, Mr Daniel Connor is. Too pleasant, sometimes, I think, when he treats me like a queen. But if Annie really cared for him, she'd have done something about it by now. It's her that's holding him back, you can tell that. An' he's getting impatient, too. Charlie's been dead for a few years now. There's nothing to stop them getting wed, except her. So why haven't they done anything about it?"

"Do you think it's still that old – that old business?" He could not say the word "rape", not when talking about his own daughter.

"Perhaps. Any road, she'll have to make her mind up one day." Kathy unfolded his fingers which were tight upon her hand and carried them to her lips. "When she meets the right person. When she's ready. An' about us – we'll leave it for a while before we get wed, eh, John, love?"

"All right, lass. If you insist. But don't let's wait too long."

It was a quiet group of adults who met again for Bridie's hearty farmhouse tea. It was left to the children to do most of the talking, and they had no hesitation in seizing the moment and filling it with talk and laughter. Only Mark noticed how thoughtful their Annie was, how she avoided Danny's eyes, but he said nothing about that to anyone.

Twenty

JULY 1847

A few weeks after the outing to the farm, Frederick Hallam popped into the salon early in the morning, as he sometimes did nowadays. Annie greeted him with real pleasure and when he showed a tendency to linger, she offered him a cup of tea.

"I'll be delighted to accept." He sat down and smiled across at her, pleased at the prospect of a few quiet minutes with someone who was both sensible and beautiful. His daughter had been so sulky this morning that he had cut breakfast short in order to escape from her twitterings and the banging of crockery. He would be glad when Beatrice left the following week to stay with her sister again.

Annie sat down and indicated the sofa opposite her. "Aren't you going to the mill today?"

"Perhaps later."

"You seem to be spending a lot less time there nowadays."

"Indeed I am. Matt Peters is a very capable young man, and honest as well. I'm leaving him to change things to fit in with Fielden's new Factory Act."

"It'll make a difference to people, only having to work eight hours on a Saturday. They'll not be so tired."

"As long as we don't let it make too much difference to the profits."

"You don't sound very worried about that," she dared to say.

"I've decided that it's about time I started enjoying my money, before I get too old, not just making more and more. It's piling up in the bank and asking to be spent."

She wondered how old exactly he was. Middle forties, she supposed, a little younger than her father. Only he seemed much younger than John Gibson, in spite of his silvered hair. "And how do you intend to enjoy the money, Mr Hallam?"

He pulled a wry face, "Well, Mrs Ashworth, to tell the truth, I don't seem able to waste money, however hard I try, and I'm not interested in frivolous pursuits, so I've decided to use it to do something about our town. It's time Bilsden grew up, time it became a more civilised place, a really modern town. Don't you think? Especially with a railway branch line being planned. That'll make a lot of difference to us all."

"I suppose it will."

"Don't you want to see some improvements made to grimy old Bilsden?"

"I've never thought much about it. I've been too busy establishing my salon and looking after my family, I suppose."

"And you don't need to tell me that things are going well here." His voice had become warm and teasing, and his daughter would have been amazed to see how relaxed and genial he looked. "You always seem to pay your rent on time. And even my daughter asks for her clothes to be made here now. By the way, that blue dress with the flowers on is a miracle. Beatrice looks almost pretty in it. Let's hope it catches her a husband in London."

She chuckled, then her face grew serious. "I sometimes think that things are going too well. I have as much work as I can handle without taking on extra staff. And I'm not sure that I want to do that."

He made a sympathetic noise in his throat and she was encouraged to continue. He was such a good listener. "Opening a salon was once my main aim in life, but now that I've got it, I'm finding other things I'd like to do as well. I expect it's these trips down to London, giving me ideas." They were the high spots of her year, and Helen felt the same. But at the moment, with the spring trip just a memory and the autumn trip months away, Annie was conscious of a feeling of flatness. There was nothing exciting to look forward to for a long time.

There was a pause while Rebecca, very smart in a new dress because she was growing so fast lately, brought in a tea-tray. Frederick watched through half-closed eyes as Annie dealt gracefully with the teapot. She had no need to ask him how he liked his tea. She knew his tastes by now.

"May one ask what other things you want to do with your life, then?" He sipped the fragrant brown liquid with pleasure. "Excellent tea, this."

She shook her head and stared down at the steam coming from her cup. "I don't know exactly. I think I enjoyed planning for the salon more than I enjoy actually running it. Isn't that ridiculous?"

He leaned back and took another sip of tea. It tasted far better than that served in his own home, though his cook always bought the very best quality tea available. But by the time Beatrice had banged the teacups around and spilled the milk or sugar over the table, the result never seemed worth all the fuss. "It's not really strange. I think, Mrs Ashworth, if you don't mind my saying so, that you have a man's mind in a woman's body." He grinned, a boyish expression that few people ever saw on the face of the town's most important mill owner. "Not that anyone would want you to look like a man, but it's harder for intelligent women to use their brains in this world, isn't it?"

Such ideas had never occurred to him until he got to know Annie Ashworth, and he still considered her as an exception to womankind. His wife had been so very stupid, and both his daughters took after her. Even his sons were a disappointment to him, for James, the younger, had opted for a profession and was now a lawyer in Leeds. James was now ashamed of the mill from which his family's money came and had made it clear that he intended to put up for sale anything which he inherited in Bilsden. In that he was encouraged by his wife, Judith, who had brought her husband both the prospects of her father's fortune and a rigidly conformist way of life.

The elder son, Oliver, had condescended to dabble in the family business, but had made a mess of everything he touched. He had also been stupid enough to marry a woman with no fortune, however well bred she claimed to be, and then had crowned everything by dying a year later of congestion of the lungs, leaving no child, only a whining complaining widow who never seemed to think the allowance her father-in-law made her high enough and who confidently expected to inherit her husband's share of Frederick's fortune one day. Having seen the way Adelaide wasted her allowance subsidising her gambler of a brother, he had no intention of raising that allowance, and all she would receive under the will was an annuity and a lifelong tenancy of the house she lived in. The house belonged, and would continue to belong, to him and those of his blood.

Frederick remembered one bitter day, soon after Oliver's marriage, when Christine had yet again started pleading with him to give Oliver and Adelaide a higher allowance. He had roared at Christine that he was beset by drooping weeping women and by languid men with pretensions to gentility and no business sense to support it with. He had added that he sometimes wondered if he really had fathered two sons like those. Of course Christine had had hysterics at that. As she grew older it was her only answer to his tirades, or to any other of life's stresses. When he looked back at it all nowadays, he realised that it was no wonder that he had had to seek his fun elsewhere. He had married money and money was the only good thing his wife had brought him.

Things did not seem to have changed much with the rest of the family since Christine's death, but they had changed for him, by Gad! And he intended to make the most of them. It was about time he started enjoying himself.

Annie's voice brought him out of his reverie and back to the present. "You're right, I suppose. It is harder for intelligent women to use their brains, but at least as a widow I can manage my business as I see fit. If I were to remarry, I'd be expected to give up this salon, give up all my business interests and just stay at home." That was a thought that had occurred to her quite a lot recently. Daniel seemed to take it for granted that if – no, to him it was *when* – they married, she would be content to manage his house and bear him the sons for whom he was beginning to long. "I don't think I could bear that," she sighed, and although it was not the first time she had acknowledged that to herself, it was the first time she had said it to anyone else. "I wouldn't know what to do with myself all day."

Was she seriously thinking of marrying that Irish scallywag? Frederick hoped not. Connor might or might not be a good builder, but the fellow would not make a good enough husband for a woman like this. However, he let nothing of his thoughts show in his face as he replied. There was time enough to deal with that later, when he had decided what he wanted to do about his own life. If Annie Ashworth had been going to rush into marriage with Connor, she would have done it by now.

"And yet," he mused aloud, "staying at home was all my wife ever wanted. I had to drag her away from her home and children if I wanted to take a trip, even to London. As for travelling abroad, after her one attempt she became ill at the mere suggestion. In the end I just went on my own." He shrugged. "I don't think it's any secret in the town that the two of us were ill-suited."

She stole a sideways glance at him, amazed that he was being so frank with her today. He looked at her very steadily as he spoke. He had finely chiselled features that were wearing well and his eyes were grey and widely spaced against a complexion many women would have envied. His hair was thinning and was streaked with silver at the temples now, but that only made him look distinguished. Other mill owners seemed to get fatter as their mills grew larger, but Frederick Hallam remained lean and elegant. Annie knew that his grandfather had been a farmer, but this man looked a thoroughbred.

"I probably shouldn't have said that," he added quietly when she did not comment, "but I know you won't repeat it. I've come to regard you as a friend, Mrs Ashworth, and sometimes it's good to share one's thoughts with a friend. As you've shared yours with me."

She stared back at him, then inclined her head. "I'm very honoured by your trust, Mr Hallam."

"Then couldn't it be Frederick and Annie in private? I feel that we've become real friends now, good friends. Have we not?"

"Well, yes, but . . ."

"But what?"

"I – it seems – it seems, well, disrespectful, somehow. The Hallams have been my family's employers for most of my life. It's hard even to think of calling you by your first name." She spread out her hands in a gesture of bewilderment, but her eyes had begun to twinkle at him. "And whatever would your daughter think of such *lèse-majesté*?"

He threw back his head and laughed. "She'd probably have hysterics like her mother used to. If she even understood the word *lèse-majesté*, and if I bothered to ask her opinion. But I shan't do that. You're a successful businesswoman, Annie Ashworth. You call Pauline Hinchcliffe by her first name, why not me?"

She felt breathless, exhilarated and so at ease with him that she dared to ask something that had puzzled her for a while. "But why should someone in your position want a friend like me?"

He captured her hand in his. "Because you're a damn sight more intelligent and entertaining than most folk I meet." He saw the wariness creep into her eyes and let go of her hand. "I don't have any ulterior motives, I promise you, Annie. I'm well aware that you're a highly *respectable* woman, and I shan't do anything to cast doubt on that respectability, believe me. But just in private, couldn't we be real friends? Please?"

He had recaptured her hand, but his expression was so wryly teasing that she did not feel the need to pull her hand away from his. Unlike Daniel's, his touch did not make her feel threatened; it made her feel – she searched for a word and decided that befriended came as near to it as anything. Frederick Hallam was a gentleman, at least he was with her now that he knew her. And she enjoyed his intelligence and his sense of humour very much indeed. It suddenly occurred to her how much she would miss him if he stopped calling to see her in the salon, how much she would miss him if she married. "Very well, then. Frederick it is. But only in private."

He let go of her hand and gave an exaggerated sigh of relief, which made her chuckle. "It would give people quite the wrong impression if I called you Annie in public, would it not?" It would make them think that she was his mistress. But this woman was too good to be anyone's mistress. He stared at her, breath caught in his throat at the anger he felt at the mere idea of anyone taking advantage of Annie in that way. Then he saw that she was staring at him warily again and managed to smile. "Now, pour me another cup of tea, will you, my dear friend – yes, I know it's my third, but your tea always tastes better than other people's – and tell me about your other friend, Mr Daniel Connor. I believe you've known him since you were both children?" Best to find something out about her feelings for the fellow.

"Hardly. He's ten years older than I am and he left home when I was just a child. But his mother has been like a second mother to me. My own died when I was ten and . . ."

Customers rarely arrived at this early hour, so the two of them were able to sit there chatting for quite a while. She told him about Danny's background and how hard he had worked on the railways, how he was another person keen to get on in life, but she did not seem besotted with the fellow. Frederick could not imagine her tossing aside her business to rush into marriage with Connor.

"There are quite a few of you, then, from Salem Street, making a mark upon our town," Frederick said thoughtfully, turning to less personal matters. "There's Matt Peters at the mill and your brother's doing well, too. He's expanded into the regular supply of provisions now, hasn't he? Good idea, if he can keep up the quality. Apparently my housekeeper wouldn't dream of buying her cheese from anyone else but him nowadays."

"I must tell that to Tom. He'll be delighted. He's beginning to consider himself a cheese connoisseur." She chuckled as she added, "And he's also beginning to put on a little weight with all the tasting he does."

"What is there about Salem Street to produce such enterprising people, do you think?"

"Nothing, except perhaps the desire to leave it." Her voice was sharp and bitter for a moment. "I couldn't wait to leave it. I absolutely hated it."

"Why didn't you leave it sooner then, when your husband

died, for instance? You already owned your house in Moor Close, I believe."

"Because times were too uncertain. I needed to save money to finance all this." She waved a hand at the salon around them. "And because I wasn't sure how successfully Tom would manage the junk business."

"You've done well, Annie, built up your business from virtually nothing. I really admire that."

"Thank you, Frederick." She changed the subject. She didn't want to talk about herself or about Salem Street. It wouldn't worry her if she never saw or heard of the place again. "What are you going to do to improve the town, then? Is that a secret, or can you tell me?"

"It's a secret from most people, but I'm sure I can trust you not to repeat what I say." He leaned back and thought about his dreams for the town which his family's wealth and enterprise had helped to create. Without the Great God Cotton, as Frederick sometimes referred to it, Bilsden would still be only an insignificant Pennine village, a mere dot on the map. "I think we must start with the town centre, Annie, and do something to beautify it, so that the town has a heart. You can't call St Mark's the heart of anything, can you? Especially with old Kenderby in office there."

She chuckled. Cantankerous was the best word to describe Parson Kenderby nowadays. He avoided, rather than sought, contact with his parishioners.

Frederick did not try to hide his enthusiasm from her and leaned forward as if to bring her closer to his ideas. "I think we need to build a new town hall for Bilsden. The old one looks more like a barn with windows, and a small barn at that. And some gardens in the town centre would look nice, too, give it a bit of style, don't you think? And of course, when the railway station is built, we'll need a hotel nearby."

"Oh, yes. And perhaps there could be a fountain somewhere

in the gardens? I've always loved fountains. One where children can sit on the edge and dabble their fingers in the water."

"You shall have your fountain, madame." He waved a hand graciously.

"But I didn't mean to—"

"It's a good idea. What else?"

She sat thinking, her head on one side, unaware that he was studying her, admiring the beauty of her hair as a stray shaft of sunlight lit it to a nimbus of flame around her piquant face, and coming back time after time to the sparkling intelligence of her wonderful eyes. "Perhaps we need something to feed people's minds as well as their eyes, Frederick. Our horizons are so narrow here. A proper mechanics' institute? Some men have tried to found one, but they only have the church hall to meet in, and Parson Kenderby insists on supervising all they do there."

"I'm amazed he lets them do anything."

"Well, Helen says he's not as energetic as he used to be. She's a bit worried about him, actually."

"Never mind that old fool. Tell me what else you think Bilsden needs."

"A lending library – as long as it isn't too expensive to borrow books – ordinary working people like to borrow books too, you know, when they have the chance."

"Do you really think such people would use a lending library?"

"Some would. I would have loved it during those years I spent in Salem Street. I could never seem to get enough books, not good books, anyway, though Charlie brought me all he could lay hands on, bless him."

"And do you get enough books now?"

"I don't have much time to read, but no – good books aren't easy to find. We don't have a bookseller in Bilsden, either. I buy books in Manchester occasionally, or when I go to London, but I never seem to have enough to last me between visits."

"You must allow me to lend you some of mine."

"But, Mr—"

"Frederick."

"Frederick, then. I really didn't mean to – to—"

"Annie, I have to confess that books are one of my secret vices and that I have a house full of them. It would be a pleasure to share them with a friend. My daughter uses them only for pressing flowers and the housekeeper complains that they collect dust. I shall send you some across. Poetry?"

"Yes – in moderation."

"And novels?"

She pulled a face. "Most novels seem very silly to me. Do you – do you have any books about other countries?"

"I'm sure I do." And if he didn't, he would make sure he got hold of some. He looked up as the outside doorbell tinkled and was disappointed to see a woman's shadow coming down the hallway towards them. The intensity of his disappointment quite surprised him.

"I'll set those repairs in order, then, Mrs Ashworth," he said, standing up and winking at her. "Thank you for the cup of tea."

"You're very welcome, Mr Hallam." She echoed his formal tones, though her eyes were dancing with amusement. "I'd greatly appreciate you seeing to the matters we mentioned."

Frederick greeted Mrs Dawton and paused in the hallway to listen to Annie's quiet voice discussing the design of a new gown for her customer, then he picked up his silver-headed walking stick and hat from the stand by the door and left. He was very sorry to have been interrupted. He enjoyed his time with Annie more than he enjoyed most things nowadays. She was an exceptional woman. And getting lovelier as she grew older. Perhaps it was the fact that she felt more secure nowadays that had given her that calm dignity. But her graceful movements and the elegant carriage of her head were peculiarly her own.

He waved away his coachman and decided on an impulse to take a walk round the town centre. A library, she had said, and a proper mechanics' institute. Not to mention a fountain. Now where would they best be sited? He was muttering to himself as he walked along, and did not look where he was going until he bumped into someone.

"Jeremy! My dear fellow, I'm so sorry. I had my head in the clouds, I'm afraid."

"More improvements being planned?" Dr Lewis was one of the few people privy to Hallam's intentions.

Frederick tapped his nose. "Thinking about it. I have to live here, after all. I'd like to be proud of my town."

"Have you thought any more about my idea of building a hospital then? We could do with one quite desperately."

"I'm still thinking about it." His eyes were very shrewd as he studied Jeremy Lewis. "If we had a hospital, we'd need someone to run it. How would you feel about that?"

Jeremy's face lit up. "I can think of nothing I'd like better. And I do have an assistant now, so I could afford the time." Then his smile faded. "Unless you're thinking of charging people for their treatment. The people who need a hospital most are the very ones who can't pay for it."

"Don't rich people ever need hospitals?" Frederick teased, scratching at the earth between the paving stones with the end of his walking stick and remembering how beautiful Annie's hair had looked with the sun on it.

"Rich people would rather be treated at home, as you very well know. And I don't blame them, the way most hospitals are run. Filthy places, some of them. I'd bring in the Widow Clegg to run the domestic side of things if I had a hospital."

"Widow Clegg? Is that the old witch from Salem Street? Isn't she a bit old to run anything?"

"No. She's only fifty or so."

"Goodness. She's always seemed quite ancient to me. I remember her caring for our injured operatives when I was quite young."

"She's an excellent nurse. None better. And quite ferocious about cleanliness. I believe she's right, too. There are some theories that a dirty hospital just spreads disease from one person to another. Things like puerperal fever. If that fellow Semmelweiss in Vienna is right, it's no wonder women who use Widow Clegg as their midwife rarely get it. She scrubs everything in sight. Dirty drinking water's a serious danger to health, too. The town owes you a great debt already for starting the water and the gas companies, Frederick. If you were to give us a hospital as well, you'd be a major benefactor, a saint almost." His grin showed how seriously the last phrase was meant.

Frederick chuckled. "Actually, the water and gas companies are making money, which a hospital never would, so I'm not really a philanthropist. Admittedly, they're not making a lot of money, but they are making enough to keep themselves going without my help. I intend to hire managers for them, now. Those companies take more of my time than they're worth. And, my dear fellow, if we're to talk of benefactors, you were as much involved in starting them up as I was. So who's heading for sainthood now?"

"I was only involved with the water company."

"And the gas company."

"Merely to express my medical approval of the gas project when a few fools were spreading rumours about people getting poisoned by it. I didn't have either the money or the influence to get such large projects started. Unlike you. No, only the rich are candidates for sainthood, I'm afraid, in this modern world. Well, I can't stand here chatting all day. I have a sick patient to visit."

Frederick walked on down the street to the very end, where he stopped and frowned. Had he done the right thing in leasing this land to Daniel Connor? The man had some grandiose plans and it would certainly be convenient to have a local builder involved if the new town hall got off the ground but – his frown deepened – was there something just a little reckless about Connor?

Frederick did not like the way Daniel Connor was speaking publicly about marrying Annie Ashworth, as if it were already agreed between them. He doubted that Annie even knew about it, for she'd virtually admitted to him that she didn't know her own mind about Connor, but her brother should warn her. The rumour had spread all over the town already. That was the trouble with small places like Bilsden. Everyone knew each other's business.

If Annie married someone like Daniel Connor, she'd be completely lost to Frederick as a friend. He would miss her. A man in his position had very few friends worth the name, not so many that he could afford to lose one, most especially this one. But he didn't know how far he wanted to go to prevent it. He needed to get away from her to think about that. When he was with her, he had some very foolish ideas. Perhaps distance would help him to get them into perspective.

Twenty-One

OCTOBER 1847 TO SPRING
1848

By October that year, Daniel had his builder's yard set up.
People had grown used to his new name, because he would no
longer answer to Danny, except when it came from his parents
whom he could not persuade to change. A neat brick villa,
with offices on the ground floor and living space above was
taking shape at the front of the yard and was attracting much
attention in the district. Daniel had had no large commissions
so far, but had done some smaller projects around the town,
repairs here and additions there. He now had the possibility of
a commission to build a couple of villas on the outskirts of
town which would be his biggest project so far.

Then Frederick Hallam asked him to build a new brick
storage shed for the bales of raw cotton. Daniel was jubilant
and could talk of little else. He had several consultations with
Mr Hallam himself, wondering why the man bothered to get
involved in such lowly projects. When Daniel was rich, he'd
not bother about the design of sheds, that was sure.

Since it was for the most important man in town, Daniel
gave the shed his best attention. It was built to the highest

specifications and completed in record time though it brought him little profit. That was not important, however. If he could satisfy this man, other customers would follow. And if the powers-that-be did eventually build a new town hall in Bilsden, as rumour suggested they might, it would be Frederick Hallam who had the say about who should build it, Daniel had no doubt about that.

It was strange to see Matt Peters in charge of Hallam's mill nowadays. Daniel remembered him as an earnest lad prone to spout religion when mischief was threatened. And he seemed to have grown into a stuffed shirt, too. Very precise and pernickety, was Matt Peters. Insisted on going through every farthing on every bill for that damned shed. Still, he said that Hallam was pleased with it. And now the villas had been started. It was a reasonable start for a new business, if not as good as Daniel had hoped. When the shares in railways that he had acquired along the way began paying a dividend, there wouldn't be so much need to fuss over details. It was a pity that railway building was slowing down, but it would pick up again. It always did.

Fortunately, Hallam was a prompt payer, or rather, Matt Peters was, because everything, men and materials alike, seemed to be costing more than Daniel had expected. Building in a small town was not quite as easy as it had been on the railways. Nor was it easy to find good tradesmen in sleepy little Bilsden. In the end Daniel brought in Nat Fellows, a man who had worked in his gang on the railways for several years, because the man was not only capable but as strong as a horse.

What he had not bargained for was that Nat would bring his sister with him. Janie and Daniel had known one another intimately in the past. He was surprised now at her thinness, and she admitted that she had been ill. Daniel had to make it very plain to Janie that he considered himself an engaged man nowadays, but even so, she still made eyes at him every time they met and found a chance to brush against him whenever he visited their small terraced house.

It was surprising how quickly Janie filled out once she was eating regularly, and how lovely she looked once she had regained her natural curves. A man would have to be inhuman not to be tempted to dip into the honey pot again, especially a man whose woman was as cool and restrained as Annie was. And after all, Janie was under no misapprehensions about his intentions.

Daniel found it absolutely infuriating that he had not yet got Annie to commit herself to marrying him. She allowed him to kiss her, even kissed him back on occasion, and he knew from the way she trembled in his arms that she was responding to him more each time he held her, but whenever he raised the subject of marriage, she grew very agitated and talked about not rushing things.

He came away from meetings with her feeling frustrated. He had waited for her, borne with her whims, but he was growing impatient. He was no saint. His body had its needs, as Janie well knew, the minx. But he had other needs, too, financial needs which Annie, and only Annie, would be able to help with. That business of hers was thriving and should fetch a good sum, and she had a share in the junk yard. Surely Tom could be persuaded to buy her out? Yes, marrying Annie would give Daniel the ready money he still lacked for the big commissions that would one day come his way, as well as giving him the respectability he craved.

By the following spring, Daniel's own house and offices were finished, in spite of the winter setbacks to the building schedule, and the offices at least were lavishly furnished. The trim appearance of the building made such a positive impression on Jonas Dawton's wife that she sent her husband along one day to discuss adding a new wing to their house, to give their children more space now that they were growing older. Daniel announced the commission to Annie before agreement had been reached, for this was his best project yet, a sign that he was getting established and trusted in Bilsden. It took him a few weeks of negotiations to develop plans which appealed to Mrs Dawton, but in the end the contract was signed as he had known it would be.

He had another, smaller commission from Dr Lewis a short time later. Jeremy needed an extra storeroom for his medicines. He was very impressed by Mr Connor's enthusiasm and quick understanding of a doctor's needs.

Jeremy trusted the young builder without hesitation because he knew he was a friend of Annie's. He even mentioned his dearest dream to Mr Connor, the dream that one day, quite soon, Frederick Hallam would fund the building of a hospital for Bilsden. Mr Connor was most sympathetic about that, understanding the need for a hospital perfectly well, and speaking of modern approaches to hospital design with a surprising depth of understanding. What Jeremy did not realise was that Daniel was adept at getting someone to talk and then agreeing with them.

When Frederick encouraged him to start planning for the hospital, Jeremy was so excited at the prospect of achieving his dream, and so busy planning its design and functioning, that he was hardly aware of his daughter's growing unhappiness or his cousin's increasingly eccentric behaviour.

Ellie was more aware of how things stood, but was torn between her love for Marianne and what she admitted, if only to herself, was an even deeper love for the doctor. She managed to stop the worst of Miss Hymes's spitefulness towards Marianne, but she had other troubles to occupy her mind. She was trying to fit in time each day to help her father with the care of her mother. Mrs Peters now had to be confined to her room and sometimes even tied to her bed to prevent her from injuring herself. As this was in addition to fulfilling her duties at Park House, Ellie was feeling exhausted.

Not even Dr Lewis knew how bad Mrs Peters was, for she became hysterical and viciously destructive if they even mentioned the word doctor to her and Sam, too, had his pride. Sam could not understand why the Lord had seen fit to place this burden upon him, but he shouldered it as best he could and tried to treat his poor wife gently.

He was not the only one with a heavy burden. For Daniel's parents placed another one on their son, just when he could least bear the extra expense. The farm was doing quite well, in that it was providing food and occupation for the O'Connors and their remaining unmarried children, as well as occasional handouts to their son, Peter, who had moved over to Oldham to be near his wife's parents, but who was still struggling to feed his large family. But it was Daniel who still supplied the money needed to purchase what Bridie and Mick couldn't provide for themselves. And always would, probably, given Bridie's generous nature and Mick's propensity to help every beggar who knocked at the back door.

When his mother brought her cousin Finola across from Ireland to live with them, without even consulting him, Daniel was furious. Most of his parents' relatives had died in the various outbreaks of potato famine, or had faded away afterwards, their health weakened by deprivation. Daniel felt sorry for them, of course he did, and from time to time – when he could afford it – he had given his mother money to send to them. Only it was one thing to send small sums across to Ireland, quite another to support an indigent relative who hadn't even got proper clothes to wear and who had to have everything bought for her.

And once Finola was there, he could not refuse to help her. He had to preserve his own reputation as a rising businessman and could not afford to have an indigent relative seen about the town. He could not get it into his parents' heads that things were still a little ticklish. It was taking more time than he had expected to establish himself and his investments had not started paying yet. They would in a year or two, he was sure of that, but he needed all his money for his own concerns and he felt that his parents had done enough for their relatives without bringing any more of them over to England. He told them so very bluntly, to Bridie's great distress.

Daniel was furious when he found out that Finola had already sent for her granddaughter Caitlin, a thin little girl of six, and her grandson Aidan, a scrawny undersized lad of eight, with a cough and a hectic colour that was all too easily recognisable.

Feeling as if he had an army of dependents and no one but him to see the sensible course of action, Daniel tried again to reason with his mother. "Let me find a house for Finola and the children in Manchester. You can't be caring for sick people. You have enough to do already with the farm. There are plenty of Irish folk in Manchester who'll keep an eye on them. Why, they call one part of the city Little Ireland. We don't want the three of them living here, where everyone can see how . . ."

Bridie drew herself up to her full five feet three inches. "Turn my own cousin and the dear children out to live among strangers when they need our help? Let alone Finola doesn't speak English properly. I'll do no such thing!"

"The lad's ill, seriously ill."

" 'Tis only a cough."

"He has the lung sickness."

"He does not! He'll be all right once we've fed him up. He's too thin, that's Aidan's trouble, but he's starting to eat better already. Up at the farm he's able to run about and let the good fresh air clean out his lungs. That's what he needs, not a dark little house in a smoky city."

Daniel turned to his father. "You talk a bit of sense into her, Dad. You know I'm right."

"I wouldn't send a dog out to die on its own," said Mick, puffing on his unlit pipe and scowling at this son whom he hardly recognised nowadays, so like a gentleman did Daniel appear and so grudging had he become about money. "Families should stick together."

"And have you heard the sad tales Finola has to tell?" said Bridie, tears in her eyes. "Sure, they're nearly all gone, the people I grew up with, and their children and grandchildren with them. It's enough to make you weep to think of them all dyin' so young. And no one left but me and Finola to light a candle for their souls."

Finola's tales had made Bridie weep several times that Daniel had seen. And he, too, had heard the tales of the great hunger, heard them so many times by now that he was heartily sick of them. "That's still no reason to risk your own life and mine too with the consumption!"

"I can't believe what I'm hearing!" exclaimed Bridie.

"You're upsetting your mother, boy," said Mick, who was easy-going to a fault, except when it touched his Bridie.

After a few more minutes of fruitless arguing, Daniel slammed out of the house, but he did not leave the matter there. He went to see Dr Lewis and sent him out to the farm to check on the newcomers' health. And when the doctor confirmed his own guess about young Aidan's illness, and said that Finola's health was also very poor, and that she had a touch of a cough, too, possibly the beginning of an infection of the lungs, Daniel tried again to persuade his parents to get the contagion out of the farm. Consumption was dangerous to those who lived with it as well as to those who suffered from it. Everyone knew that, but especially those who'd lived in the Rows, for consumption was endemic in the courts and warrens of Claters End. Daniel had seen several people he knew succumb to it.

Only Janie seemed to understand his worries, because naturally, he wasn't going to burden Annie with his family troubles at this delicate stage in their relationship. He'd told Janie about Annie, but she just laughed. She wasn't after a husband and never had been; just a bit of fun.

But Daniel's efforts to keep his mother's generosity in check were in vain. Bridie was not only obstinate about poor Finola, but was now determined to bring one of Mick's nephews over, a man whose wife had died recently in childbed, and the poor babe with her. Bridie went to visit her son in town to discuss it, because it was a while since he'd been out to the farm to see them. Being Bridie, she was sure that he could not help but be moved by her tale. He would listen to his mother. He was a good son.

Daniel heard her out in silence. How the hell many more relatives was she going to produce? Apart from the cost of helping them all, he'd be the laughing stock of the town if this went on!

"So you could find our Brian a job in your business, Daniel lad, could you not?" Bridie wound up.

"No, Mam, I employ only skilled tradesmen. Brian has no skills." It was not strictly true, but she need not know that.

"He does so have skills. Isn't he the best ploughman in the village!"

"Ploughmen don't have the skills to build houses."

"They can learn."

"Not at my expense they can't."

"You gave that Nat Fellows a job."

"Nat knows the trade."

"Well, Brian could learn it, too."

"Not at my expense, he couldn't. Do you think I'm made of money, Mam?"

"I don't know what I think about you nowadays. Ah, Danny—"

"No, Mam, I can't help you."

"Then Brian will have to try for a place in one of the mills, though they're terrible places and he won't like being cooped up." When Bridie had set her mind on something, she was just as stubborn as her son and she intended to help what was left of her family. "And shame on you, Danny O'Connor, for neglecting your own blood kin!" she ended, storming out of the fine office, her eyes blinded with tears. She was so upset that she went to visit Annie in the salon to try to enlist her help, though the elegance of the place usually daunted her.

The salon was not yet busy, for Bridie was an early riser. The only person there was a gentleman, sitting in earnest conversation with Annie. And when he turned round, it proved to be Mr Hallam himself.

Bridie gasped and stopped dead in the doorway, horrified to think that she was interrupting someone so important. "Oh, you're busy, Annie, love. I'll – I'll leave it till another time."

Annie came forward and hugged Bridie, then frowned at the dried tears on her cheeks. "I'm never too busy for you." She drew Bridie over to the fire. "Mr Hallam, may I introduce Mrs O'Connor who used to be a neighbour of mine in Salem Street. She's our new builder's mother."

It pleased Frederick that Annie showed no embarrassment at introducing him to a woman who was obviously from the lower classes, and Irish too by the sound of her. He had not realised quite how close Connor was to his Irish roots. "Mrs O'Connor," he said thoughtfully. "Not Mick O'Connor's wife?"

Bridie flushed scarlet at meeting her Mick's old employer. "Well, yes."

"He was the best man I ever had looking after my dray horses. There's a job for him back at the mill any time."

Bridie made a woeful attempt to smile at this compliment to her Mick. She also tried again to take her leave, for there was something between these two that still made her feel she was interrupting. "I can easily come back another time, Annie, love."

But Annie would not let go of her. "Bridie, come and sit down, will you. You know I always have time for you and you're obviously upset about something." She was sorry to end her cosy chat with Frederick, but she intended to find out what had upset Bridie so much, to find out and help, if she could.

"My business can easily wait, ma'am," said Frederick, bowing to Bridie. "I'll see you another time about the roof, Mrs Ashworth," he added, with a wicked grin. They kept up a fiction that there was a persistent leak that refused to be cured. It was amazing, said Mr Hardy next door to his wife, how much attention the row of shops in High Street was receiving from their new owner now that they had an attractive woman tenant in one of them. But Cyril Hardy was too afraid of his landlord to try to spread any rumours about this, so he held his tongue and just kept a watch on what "that woman" was doing.

Annie guided her old friend down into a chair. "Just you sit there, Bridie, while I see Mr Hallam out and order some fresh tea. And don't tell me you don't want a cup, for I'm sure you've never refused one in all your life."

Bridie subsided into a chair and nodded. "Well, it would wet the – I mean, it would be very nice, I'm sure, and Mick won't be picking me up for half an hour yet."

In the hall, Annie clasped Frederick's hand briefly in farewell. "Thank you for the books, Frederick. Paris sounds to be such a fascinating place, though there seems to be a lot of trouble in Europe just now."

"I wish I could take you there, trouble or not. You'd love the old buildings and the brightness of the sunlight. The air's so clear it almost dazzles your eyes some days."

She stiffened at this suggestion and he raised his hands in a gesture of mock surrender. "I was only joking. I know better than to offer you such a thing seriously, my dear. I seem fated to travel alone. The one time I did take Christine to Paris, she did nothing but complain about the food."

Annie's lips twitched. She could well imagine that. She had waited on the late Mrs Hallam at table when she was a maid in Dr Lewis's house, and had seen her pick suspiciously at any new dish. "I'll get there one day under my own steam, if I'm meant to see it, Frederick," she said equably and went back to talk to her other visitor.

By the time Bridie left, Annie had convinced her that poor Daniel had his hands so full with a new business that he could not be expected to take a lot of interest in distant relatives. Annie could perfectly well understand his feelings about Finola's grandson, and she had decided immediately she heard the tale not to take William out to the farm again while young Aidan's health was so suspect. Having only the one child made you very protective, she thought ruefully as she went up to the workroom afterwards. She tried to imagine what it might be like to have other children. A daughter or two. Another fine son like William. She tried to imagine Daniel as the father of her children, but she could not, she just could not, and that worried her greatly.

That evening Kathy managed to get a few minutes alone with John, once the children had gone to bed. "John, love," her voice was low and she looked over her shoulder before she spoke, "I've changed my mind. I – I think we should get wed – and soon."

He beamed at her. "Nay, then. What's brought this on? Haven't I been asking you to for months?"

"I – I think now we *need* to." She blushed and looked down.

John stared at her. "Does that mean you're – you're expecting a child?" he asked, his voice breathless with wonderment.

"Aye, I reckon I am."

"Nay, but I'll be happy to wed you tomorrow, if that's the case, lass. It's you as has been holding back, not me."

"I've been worried about Tom. I'm still worried about what he'll say when he hears about the child. Eh, I don't fancy telling him, that I don't."

"He can say what he likes. I'm still capable of supporting a wife and," John's face was one big beam from ear to ear, "and of fathering a child."

"I wasn't sure you'd be pleased about the child," she confessed, fingers pleating the material of her skirt. "I mean, at your age, John . . ."

"I love childer," he said simply. "I allus have. An' you'll make a good mother for this one, none better, Kathy, love. Look at how well you deal with our Joanie. She's getten into a right cheerful little soul since we've been living at Netherleigh Cottage. An' it's all due to you." His face clouded. "All as worries me is – well, I'll likely die afore you do, afore the child is grown, mebbe, an' then how'll you manage?"

"It's a bit late to worry about that, my lad. And I'll manage fine, don't you worry." She raised one hand to stroke his cheek. "I don't think our Annie will turn me out, whatever happens."

Later that evening, Kathy followed Annie up to her bedroom. "Have you a minute to spare, love?"

"Of course. Come in and sit down." Annie's bedroom was now as much a sitting room as a place to sleep in. It had two cosy armchairs near the fire, which in cooler weather was lit every night before Annie came home from the salon.

Kathy closed the door and subsided into one of the chairs. "I need to talk to you about me an' your dad, love."

Annie sat down opposite her, with a sigh of relief, and pulled up her skirt to toast her feet. "Are you still in love with him?"

"Aye. An' we want to get wed." Kathy watched her friend anxiously.

336

"You've decided then."

"Well, it's been decided for us, really." Kathy blushed. "Actually, love, we need to get wed as quickly as we can."

Annie sat bolt upright. "You can't mean that – that—"

Kathy's expression was blissful. "I do mean it. I'm expectin' a babby. Your father's babby." She stared dreamily into the fire. "Eh, I never thought I'd get a family of me own, Annie, love. Never thought a fellow would even fancy someone so thin an' so plain. But your dad really loves me, an' I love him. It's like all me dreams have come true."

Annie went across to hug her. "Then what are you worrying about?"

Kathy sighed and fiddled with her skirt again, then burst out, "It's your Tom. He'll go mad when he hears. I remember after Emily died, you an' he didn't want your dad to marry again. I heard you both sayin' so several times. Especially Tom. I – I'm a bit frightened of tellin' him, if you must know. He can be hard sometimes. He can say things – well, I don't want your dad hurt, nor I don't want—" she broke off and took a deep breath, "nor I don't want to have to move out of here. I never thought you could love a house like I love this one."

Relief flooded through Annie. She did not think she could manage without Kathy either. The house ran so smoothly and the children were well looked after. "You don't have to move out." She knelt down beside Kathy's chair and took hold of her hand. "I'm very selfish, I know, but I need you too. We all need you."

Tears started trickling down Kathy's face. "Eh, that's a load off my mind, love, a real load. I'd hate to leave you all."

The two of them hugged and rocked to and fro for a minute, then Annie returned to her own chair and gazed thoughtfully into the fire while Kathy wiped her eyes. After a moment, Annie began to chuckle. "Kathy, have you realised . . ."

Kathy looked across at her. "Realised what, love?"

"Kathy, if you marry Dad, you'll become my stepmother!"

The two of stared at one another, then both burst out laughing.

"Nay," said Kathy eventually, when they had calmed down, "I never thought of that." Then her mouth wobbled a little as she said, "An' I'll really be part of the family now. I'll really belong to you all."

"Oh, Kathy, you always have been part of the family!"

"Not with your Tom. Not really."

They both fell silent again. "I'll tell him for you," Annie offered. "It'll probably come best from me. When you and Dad go to chapel on Sunday, I'll stay behind and talk to him then. Tell Dad not to fuss about me coming to chapel with him."

"Eh, thanks, love."

Tom stared at Annie. "*What?*"

"I said that Kathy and Dad are going to get married."

"You're joking! You've got to be joking!"

"No. I mean it."

His hands clenched into fists. "Over my dead body! He's not starting another family and then leaving them for us to bring up."

"He's a man grown and can make his own decisions."

"He's thirty years older than her, for heaven's sake! He's an old man. Why can't she marry someone her own age?"

"Because she loves him. And he loves her."

"Love! What that old bugger loves is his—"

"Tom!"

He turned round and went over to stand by the window, breathing deeply. "I'm not having it, Annie. I mean that!"

She took a few deep breaths of her own. "It's a bit late to say that."

338

He turned round slowly. "A bit late?" His voice was quiet and controlled, but it seemed even more dangerous to her than if he were shouting. Tom had changed a lot since they came to Netherleigh Cottage. Grown more serious, more, she stared at him, yes, more powerful, somehow. His new ventures were doing well and he was becoming independent of their shared interest in the junk yard. But he was still counting each farthing, still working all the hours he could, except for his occasional trips down to Claters End where she supposed he was still seeing that Rosie.

She went across to thread her arm through his. "Come and sit down, Tom. Let's discuss this peacefully." His arm was rigid in hers, but when she pulled, he came over to the kitchen table and sat down on a chair next to hers.

"The two of them set you up to tell me, didn't they?" He threw the words at her. "That's why you didn't go to chapel today. They didn't even have the courage to tell me themselves."

"Well, it was me who suggested that I be the one to tell you, actually. We all knew you'd make a fuss. I don't want Kathy upsetting in her condition. And I don't want you hurting Dad and saying things you'll regret."

"Well, you were right about how I'd feel. A fuss you call it! Talking a bit of sense, I call it."

"Tom, please."

He growled under his breath, then looked across at her. "How will we ever get respected in this town if our own father marries the housekeeper and makes a spectacle of himself by fathering one child after another at his age?"

"That's a funny way to look at their marriage."

"Aye, well, it's my way of looking at it." What would Marianne think of him now, with an elderly father having another baby? It was ridiculous, humiliating! More important, what would *her* father think of him? Dr Lewis would surely want better for his only daughter than a man who came from such a prolific family, a man encumbered by a still-increasing crowd of half-brothers and half-sisters. He saw Annie staring at him and threw more angry words at her. "Where are they going to live, then? Have you thought of that?"

"They'll continue to live here, of course."

His voice was flat, but his eyes were still flaring with anger. "Of course. Where else? The one thing we need here is a baby crying in the night, waking us all up."

"Kathy and the baby will be down in Dad's room. We'll not hear it at night." She didn't like the grim expression on Tom's face. She didn't like his quietness. She had expected him to explode into anger. He was keeping something back from her. What was it?

She decided that she might as well get it all over in one go. "I think we'll need to hire a maid as well."

"To wait on Kathy? That's rich!"

"To help Kathy. There are a lot of us. I've thought for a while that she's got too much to do in spite of Mrs Ogley coming in to do the washing. Kathy works from early morning to late at night with never a complaint, but she deserves some time to herself occasionally. She won't accept any money for what she does, either. I've been thinking for a while that we should get her some help."

"If you hire a maid, *you* can pay her."

"I don't mind doing that. And we don't need a fancy maid, just a strong girl to help Kathy. That won't cost much."

Tom pushed his chair back so roughly that it fell over. "Well, that's all settled then, isn't it? And now that you've told me, I'm going out." He strode out through the door without looking back at her, and ran along to his room. A few minutes later he pounded down the stairs again and she heard the front door slam behind him without a word of farewell.

She let out her breath in a long sigh, then went to brew

herself a cup of tea. What she hadn't told him was that her father and Kathy were having the banns called for the first time that day. She wished she had been at the chapel to see John Gibson's proud expression as he looked at Kathy. She felt very alone sometimes when she saw them together, or when she thought how her family relied upon her. It was hard always to be the strong one, the person to whom others turned.

But when she tried to picture herself and Daniel having the banns called, she just could not. And besides, Daniel had been brought up a Catholic. That was yet another impediment to their marriage. Strange, how when she was with him it seemed possible that they might one day marry – not yet, but one day – and then, as soon as she was on her own, she could only think of reasons why they could not, should not marry.

Twenty-Two

BRIGHTON: 1846–48

In Brighton the years had passed swiftly for Annabelle. Once she had discovered the joys of lying with a man, she found she could not get enough of it and she was very bitter about the years of pleasure she had missed because of Jeremy, stupid, soft Jeremy, who did *not*, she said scornfully to Cora, know how to please a lady.

"Yes, ma'am. It must have been awful for you, ma'am. Shall I massage your neck, ma'am?"

Cora was inevitably part of the conspiracy to maintain Annabelle's respectable facade while at the same time allowing her the nights she craved in Henry Minton's arms. The maid's yearly visit to her family in Lancashire always saw her calling round at Dr Lewis's house. Mrs Cosden welcomed her warmly, avid for the latest gossip about Mrs Lewis. Of course Cora didn't tell the cook about Henry Minton – that sort of information might be worth money to her one day, you never knew – but she did tell her about the house and the little holidays and the friends her mistress had made.

Back in Brighton, Cora gradually arranged household

matters to accommodate her mistress, while at the same time managing to line her own pockets. What was sauce for the goose, she told herself, was also sauce for the goose's servant, too. If that servant was smart in how she managed things. The cook was changed to a daily woman – after all, as Mrs Lewis agreed, a household of women did not need hearty cooked meals all the time. The young housemaid was replaced by a daily girl, one with her own secrets to hide, who was very grateful to Cora for finding her the position and who could keep her mouth shut. Cora, and even Annabelle herself sometimes, took care of the dusting and other tidying, and another married woman whom Cora found, who had once been a housemaid was hired occasionally to wait at table when guests were expected. All this meant more work for Cora, but it meant more money, too, and as she did not intend to stay with Annabelle for ever, the money was more important than the work.

Thus there was no one in the house at nights to notice Annabelle's visitor except Cora, and she took care to stay downstairs on a straw mattress in the scullery while they were going at it upstairs. She had to grin sometimes at the noise they made, but she did not betray her amusement to Annabelle. For all this tactful care, Mr Minton was extremely grateful to Cora, and her new savings bank account continued to grow more rapidly than she had ever dared to hope.

And when Henry Minton came up with a new suggestion, one that introduced a series of blindfolded gentlemen into the rear entrance to Annabelle's house during the dark hours of the night, it was Cora, wearing a wig and spectacles to disguise herself, who facilitated that business, too.

Annabelle was at first horrified by what Henry was asking her to do. "How can you? And I thought you loved me, Henry!" She patted her eyes with a handkerchief.

He lay back on the bed, arms folded behind his head. "No,

you didn't. You and I aren't the types to go in for that sort of stupidity."

When she reared up indignantly, he pushed her back and leaned over her, one hand on either side of her head. "Do you realise how much you could earn, my fine lady?"

"I don't care."

He rolled away and lay still, waiting for her to take the bait, as he knew she would.

After a few minutes she asked, "How much do such – such people earn? Just out of curiosity."

"At least five guineas a time, at the upper end of the business." And more, for a guaranteed lady with very liberal tastes in sexual activities and amazing stamina, but milady need not know about that, he thought, hiding a grin by leaning across to nibble her ear lobe.

She pushed him away and sat bolt upright. "I don't believe you! Sin cannot be rewarded in such a – a generous manner. It makes a mockery of all I have ever been taught!"

He raised himself on one elbow. "I'm telling the simple truth. You're a fine woman, Annabelle, and if you'll just learn a few extra little tricks, you can earn yourself twenty or even thirty guineas a week – easily." Until you begin to fade, that is. But she looked as if she had a few good years left in her yet. She should have, all the cream and muck she kept slathering on her face and body. He lay back again, closing his eyes and sighing as if tired.

Annabelle lay beside him, thinking hard. Twenty guineas a week, he had said, or more, and all for doing something she enjoyed very much. The next time he raised the matter, she allowed him to persuade her to try the thing, just once. She would be masked, of course, with the man sworn not to try to see her face. And *of course* the customer would be a gentleman.

It was such fun, such delicious naughty fun, that Annabelle tried it again, and soon she was hooked on both the money and the extra titillation that other men could give her, even when they were not quite gentlemen.

After that, dear Henry brought visitors to the rear entrance of her house regularly, blindfolded and in a closed carriage, so that they had no idea where she lived. Or sometimes he took her to them, and that was rather exciting, too. She always wore a mask and sometimes a wig, and she made a ploy of never speaking to them except for a few husky whispers and moans at crucial moments. The fools always liked to think they had aroused her, even when they were quite inept at the amatory arts.

She also insisted on being paid immediately afterwards each time and Henry found her quite intransigent upon this point. Money was the reason for these "little adventures" and money she must have in her hand to console her for going against her inbred nature as a lady.

None of her special visitors could perform like Henry, of course, and some needed extra stimulus to perform at all, which made her and Henry laugh themselves silly afterwards, for he had begun to watch them through a spy-hole in the bedroom wall. He was not, he said, risking any of the silly devils losing control and damaging her precious body. She found that the thought of him watching only added to the excitement and after one person, definitely no gentleman this one, had been quite rough with her, she was very glad to have had dear Henry within earshot.

The first time she found herself pregnant, Annabelle had hysterics and Cora had to summon Mr Minton as a matter of urgency.

"Now look what you've done to me!" Annabelle sobbed from the bed as he stood in the doorway of her bedroom staring at her. "I'm ruined! Absolutely ruined!"

He walked across to the bed and shook her. "Shut up, you silly bitch! What the hell are you talking about?"

"I'm *enceinte*!"

"*Enceinte*?"

"Pregnant!"

He threw back his head and laughed. "Is that all? You can't possibly be knocked up. It's not so long since you had one of your rest weeks. You've been using that sponge I gave you, haven't you?"

"Of course, I have! And it doesn't work. I *am enceinte*! I can tell. It's just like last time. I'm being sick morning, noon and night. It's disgusting! You've ruined me, Henry Minton!" She was clutching his legs convulsively. "You've got to do something!"

He shook her off and pushed her away from him. "Shut up, you silly bitch, and listen to me. If it's early days, it's quite easy to get rid of your little problem."

She hiccuped to a halt. "What?"

"You heard me. I have an old friend who can attend to such matters for you. She's very good. I've used her services before. I'll bring her to see you tonight."

When he brought his old friend in to see her, Annabelle nearly had hysterics again at the sight of the dirty old woman with matted grey hair and a clay pipe clenched between her toothless gums. "I'm not letting *her* touch me! You can just take her right away again."

He winked at the old woman. "Come on, then, Ma. We'll be off. My friend's decided to keep the baby, after all." He turned as if to leave.

Annabelle's voice was raw with fury. "Don't you *dare* go and leave me like this, Henry Minton!"

He turned round again. "Are you going to shut up then, and let Ma get on with things?"

Annabelle sniffed and pulled at the tangled bedcovers. "Well, I suppose . . ."

"See to it, Ma." He pushed the old woman towards the bed and slammed out of the room.

Annabelle wrinkled her nose at the sour smell that came from her visitor's garments and shrank down into the pillows with a perfumed handkerchief to her nose. Once Henry had left the room, however, she allowed Ma to examine her.

Ma looked dubious as she poked at one of Annabelle's breasts. "It's early days yet. How can you be so sure?"

Annabelle slapped the hand away and glared at her. "Because I keep being sick and because my breasts are sore. It's *exactly* like the first time I was in this condition."

"Ah, one of those, are you? Start spewing up early. It's useful, that, in your trade."

"*My trade! What do you mean, my trade?*" Annabelle's voice was quite audible downstairs, where Henry was sipping a glass of brandy and explaining Ma's presence to Cora.

Annabelle's tantrum had no effect on Ma, who just shrugged and smiled. "I'm talking about the whoring trade, dearie."

"How *dare* you speak to me like that?"

"Well, you don't get a child by praying, do you, and I don't see a husband anywhere around?"

"Mr Minton and I have been – er, have been having a love affair."

"Love! He don't know the meaning of the word, Henry Minton don't." Ma grinned. "An' I heard there was others came to dip their fingers into your honey pot as well." The bony fingers were suddenly painfully tight on Annabelle's arm and Ma shook her as she opened her mouth to protest again. "Don't be stupid, girl. What do I care whether you're a whore or not? It's the women as give it away free that are the fools, to my mind."

Annabelle could only sit and gape at her.

Ma fumbled in her pocket and brought out a screw of paper. "This should fix it, dearie. Don't taste so good, but it usually does the trick. Mix it with honey an' you'll never even notice the taste. An' then afterwards drink a few glasses of gin, an'—"

"*Gin!*" As a pair of knowing old eyes stared at her from a network of dirty wrinkles, Annabelle felt a shiver run down her spine. "I – I don't like gin."

Ma slapped Annabelle's still flat stomach. "Do ye want to lose it or not? Or p'raps you'll enjoy gettin' bigger an' bigger?" Her hands curved suggestively in the air above the soft pink flesh.

Annabelle shuddered and snatched at the screw of paper.

"So do as ye're told, dearie, an' drink a few glasses of gin afterwards. An' that'll be a guinea, if you please."

"A guinea! For a pinch of – of mouldy powder!"

"Aye, lady. But not for the powder. You're payin' for what I know about your little problem. Because if this don't work, there are other things I know how to do, too." She chuckled. "Trust in Ma, dearie. She won't let you down."

"Very well. But not a word to anyone or I'll see you regret it!"

"What do you think I am, dearie – stupid? I don't foul my own nest." She cackled. "You'll be fetching me back to help out again. You've got that look in your eyes. Some of 'em put up with the fellows for money. You do it because you like your trade, as well as the money. An' your feelings show. That's why you're successful. Even when they're payin' for it, men like to think they're irresistible." She ignored Annabelle's sputters of rage, picked up the coin that was thrown at her, then turned on her heels and left, still chuckling to herself.

Downstairs, Henry was waiting for her. "All right, Ma?"

"Aye. If she ain't lost it by tomorrow, give 'er this second lot. An' if that don't do the trick, I'll bring my things over."

But there was no need for Ma to return. The powder worked and Annabelle lost the child. Henry cosseted her better with gifts and soft words, and two weeks later she was at work again.

"After all, life can be so boring if one doesn't have one's little hobby, can it not, Henry?"

"Especially when one is so good at one's hobby."

She preened herself.

He stroked her arm gently. "I've been thinking about things, Annabelle. We don't want word to get out about what you're doing. I think you'd be better working away from home in future, my dear."

She pouted. "Go out into the cold night every time! Really, Henry, is that necessary?"

He tapped his nose. "Trust me, my love. I have your welfare at heart. And – I have another change I'd like you to – er – consider."

"What?"

"I think you'd be better off with a manservant to look after you."

"Whatever for? Menservants cost the earth and they eat like pigs."

"Bodyguard."

"But surely that's not—"

He lost patience with her little games. "Listen to me, you stupid bitch! You've become so successful that others are taking an interest. Do you want to be handled by someone who'll pay you half what I do, and who'll force you to work even during your rest week? Someone who might allow," he trailed a fingertip along her body, "that white flesh to get damaged, if a customer were to pay him enough."

She swallowed hard. "Oh. Well, if you say so. Perhaps you're right. But how shall I explain a manservant to people when I keep such a modest establishment?"

"Say that someone tried to break into your house and that it's made you very nervous." Henry smiled at her. Alf Booling was a cheap form of insurance for this most lucrative of investments. If Annabelle knew how much Henry really got paid for her services, she would die of rage. A real lady was a rarity that some of his customers thoroughly enjoyed, especially a lady with such skilful habits and such soft white skin. Strange how things turned out sometimes. He'd never have guessed that the ladylike Mrs Lewis would be so avid for it, or so good at it, either. He'd only taken her that first time because of the challenge she presented.

Henry even continued to enjoy her services himself when he had no clients lined up, and there were few women who'd managed to hold his interest for so long. It had been a lucky day for them both, he reckoned, when he met Annabelle Lewis.

Twenty-Three

BILSDEN: SUMMER 1848

The troubles across Europe in 1848 seemed to reflect Annie's own moods. When the King of France abdicated and Napoleon III became President, she just nodded agreement as her older customers said that to have anyone with that name in public office could lead only to trouble. When Chartist agitations flared up again around England, she listened quietly to her customers' outrage that working men should consider themselves fit to vote and refrained from expressing her own opinion that working men could vote as stupidly as their betters, and working women too.

When there was a panic about railways investments, she suppressed a sigh as Daniel talked angrily of rich men cheating others out of their life savings. She wished he would find another topic of conversation and she began to wonder why it upset him so much. It was a while before she could get him to admit that he had lost a little money on bad railway investments.

"Just a little," he said, with a wry grimace. "That'll teach me to invest in anything but the sweat of my own brow, will it not, my little love?"

"Don't call me that!"

He just grinned, blew her a kiss and began to talk about his parents.

Things were lightened a little when John married Kathy in a simple ceremony in mid-April, for their joy and love was infectious. Annie insisted that the two of them go away to spend a few days together in a boarding house in Blackpool. The Lancashire gentry had visited that small watering place for many years, but it had recently become popular with the more affluent among the lower classes for summer holidays, especially since the opening of the branch railway line from Preston to Blackpool a couple of years previously.

How things were changing, Annie thought, as she purchased the railway tickets in Manchester and then saw John and Kathy on to the train. What a pity the branch line to Bilsden had been delayed yet again by the Darringtons' opposition to the proposed route! It would have made taking a holiday so easy and helped local businesses. The railways were making a huge difference to people's lives, allowing them to travel and allowing businesses to transport their goods cheaply, but she wondered sometimes where it would all end. Frederick said the changes had hardly begun and Daniel laughed at her fears for the future – why bother when she wouldn't be there to face it? – but she continued to worry about the sort of life William and his children would be facing. And who said she wouldn't be there to face it? She had every intention of living to a ripe old age.

Her depression was not improved by the fact that Frederick had gone away as well, for a month's holiday touring round those parts of Europe which were not in turmoil. She found herself missing him more than she had expected, missing the pleasant half-expectation that he would pop into the salon for a chat. Tom was working long hours and spent any spare time he could with Marianne, John and Kathy were engrossed in each other and although Mark was becoming very grown up lately, he had always held back a little with his stepsister and brother, reserving his deepest love and confidences for Luke and Rebecca. Annie therefore turned to Daniel for the companionship which her own family could not give her.

"Annie, me love," he said, as they walked across the moors one windy afternoon, "isn't it about time you named the day?"

She was so startled by this blunt approach that she stumbled. He laughed and caught hold of her, pulling her into the shelter of his arms, serious for once. "Don't you think you've kept me waitin' for long enough, love?"

Annie looked up at him, leaning backwards against his embracing arms. "Oh, Daniel, why do we have to change things?"

He bent his head to kiss her, not gently this time, but urgently. "Because I love and need you!" he breathed into her ear, nibbling on its lobe, then returning to her lips as she tried to speak. "Hell, woman, haven't I been patient? Do you know what it does to a man, wanting you like this?"

They seemed alone in the sunny wind-swept landscape, alone in the whole world. When his lips eventually left hers, she leaned against his shoulder and stared across the bare curves of moorland, her heart thudding, her body suddenly crying out for the fulfilment it had never known. "I – I don't know." Her voice was hesitant, her words lost in the wind.

"Well, love, that's the first time you've not said no straight off." He pulled her down to sit with him. "Ah, Annie, I can't go on like this much longer. I *need* you, not only for your beautiful body," he caressed it as he spoke, lingering on her breast and tracing out its swell through the soft wool of her pelisse, then his hand went up to cup her cheek, "but also for what's in your equally beautiful head."

"Daniel, I—"

"Don't stop me. Let me tell you how I feel. Shh, be still!"

His hands continued to caress her as he spoke. "I don't just need and love your body; I need your common sense and your company." He kissed her cheek and continued with a touch of bitterness, "And I also need you to help me with my stupid family. That lout Brian's talking about bringing others across now, isn't he? An' Mam's eggin' him on. But most of all," his fingers were tormenting her nipples now, and even through the material, she was responding, moving restlessly beneath him, "most of all, my darling, I need you for a wife, to bear me children and cherish me in my bed at nights. A man isn't built to live alone. Nor a woman, either. What am I working for, if not for our future?"

"Daniel, d-don't—"

"Can you not put me out of my misery, my little love? Haven't I waited for you? Don't you know by now that you can trust me?"

She sighed and lay against him. Yes, he had been patient, inhumanly patient, if Tom's sly teasing and her father's behaviour were anything to go by. And Daniel did love her – more than she loved him, she knew. Was she never to love fully, deeply, as she had loved Matt when she was seventeen? As Daniel's fingers began again to play over her body, the first time she had allowed him such liberties, she could feel her own response and wonder at it. In all those years, only Daniel had done this to her. It must be love. It must. And yes, she did trust him. She could never marry someone she didn't trust, someone who lied to her.

Daniel groaned and pushed himself away from her, breathing deeply, muttering, "Not until we're wed, Annie, not until we're wed!"

Suddenly, she heard herself saying in a voice that trembled, "Then maybe we should get wed, Daniel."

He whirled round, his face alight with triumph. "Do you mean that? Do you really mean it?"

"Of course I do." A stab of doubt shot through her, but she told herself that it was only natural, given her circumstances, given the long years of independence.

He pulled her to her feet, swung her into his arms and twirled the pair of them round and round, laughing and shouting aloud for joy. And when he put her down, she found herself laughing with him, feeling happy and lighthearted, for once.

"When?" he demanded.

"Well, in a few months or so. I need time to – to prepare."

"You won't try to back out of that promise?"

"What do you think I am, Daniel O'Connor?"

"Connor!" he corrected sharply. "And you're going to be Mrs Daniel Connor."

She dipped him a curtsey. "I apologise, Mr Connor." Then she looked at him, head on one side. "Does the name really matter?"

"Oh, yes, my love, it does matter. Us Irish aren't liked. I don't want my sons to suffer the taunts I have had to face."

That reminded her of something else. "But where shall we get married, Daniel? Your – your church doesn't like mixed marriages, I think."

"My mother's church," he said firmly. "I don't have one. It'd be best if we could get married at St Mark's. Couldn't you start worshipping there now?"

"Worship at St Mark's? Whatever for?"

His voice was a little impatient. "So we can get married there. I've been thinking of starting to attend regularly myself, though that old sod of a parson will bore me to tears. It'd be better for business, you see. Most of the leading businessmen in Bilsden attend St Mark's. I've checked it out."

"Oh, Daniel, you turn everything into a joke. Attend St Mark's indeed!" She chuckled and threaded her arm through his, pulling him along again. "Parson Kenderby would die at the sight of a Methodist and a Catholic turning up in his congregation. No, seriously, Daniel, won't there be some difficulties for us?"

He sighed, knowing when to pull back. Once they were married, he'd insist on them attending St Mark's, but for the moment, he didn't want to upset her in any way. "There'll be no difficulties, love, not if your Mr Hinchcliffe will accept me into his congregation. We'll get wed at your chapel, if that's what you really want."

They walked along in silence for a while and he could see the frown on her face, but he said nothing to interrupt her thoughts. Eventually she asked hesitantly, "Won't that upset you at all? I mean, you were brought up a Catholic. Getting married in our chapel will be—"

"Annie, me love, I don't care about that sort of stuff, and I never have."

"Don't you believe in a God?"

"What?" He could see genuine shock on her face. He'd forgotten how that father of hers had rammed religion down her throat, and how she was such good friends with Mrs Hinchcliffe. "Of course I do," he said soothingly. "I just don't think it matters how one worships one's – er – Maker." He suppressed a sigh of relief as her face brightened, then frowned as the smile faded again.

"It'll upset Bridie, though, Daniel. You know it will."

"Look!" He swung her round to face him, almost shouting at her, "Who's getting married, us or them? What the hell do any of them matter at such a time? It's you I'm marrying, not that bloody priest, not my mam, not your family, not one of these churches or chapels, just you!"

The vehemence of his outburst frightened her a little and she drew back.

He forced himself to speak more calmly. "Oh, Annie, you've kept me waiting for so long. What do all these details matter? It's you I love, you I need."

She melted against him, wondering at how good it felt to be held in a man's arms, wondering at the depths of his love for her.

When they got back to Netherleigh Cottage, Annie stopped at the gate. "Daniel, let's not tell anyone yet." The thought of facing all the surprise and questions made her shiver.

"*What*?" He jerked to a halt. "Oh, no. I'm not keeping it a secret."

"I just – I need a little time to get used to it."

"*No!*" The word exploded out of him. "I've waited long enough, Annie. I want the whole world to know about us." He hugged her to him. "And I don't think I could keep quiet about it, if I tried. You've made me the happiest man in Bilsden and I want to shout the news off the roof tops."

She pulled away from him. "Well, I don't want to tell people. Daniel, I need time to think about the salon and the business – it could be very foolish to broadcast this before we've made any real plans." She faltered to a halt. She had never seen such a grim look on his face.

"Do you or do you not intend to marry me?"

"Well, of course I do. Haven't we just—"

"Then why act as if you're ashamed of me?"

"I'm not ashamed. Daniel, you surely can't think that—"

He folded his arms and took a calculated gamble. "I'm not keeping it secret, as if it's something to be ashamed of. Decide now, Annie Ashworth, for I've waited as long as I intend to and I'm not havin' any more put-offs." He held his breath after he'd tossed that ultimatum at her. Had he gone too far, pressured her too much? Hell, she was a difficult catch to land.

She stood for a minute, then let out a deep sigh. "Just the family, then. No one else. I couldn't face telling anyone else yet, and I don't want to harm the business."

"How could it harm the business?"

"If people were to think I was leaving, they might go somewhere else for their clothes."

"Hmm. Well, you've worked hard to build it up. We don't want all that wasted. Just the family, then. But today, Annie. We'll tell them today."

Tom was sitting in the kitchen, reading the newspaper. Annie paused in the doorway, conscious of her tangled hair and rosy cheeks, conscious also of Daniel's hand grasping hers.

She tried to pull it away and failed. "I'd – er – better go and tidy up."

Daniel shook his head. "Not yet, love. Tom, me lad, how'd you like to be the first to congratulate us?"

Tom dropped the newspaper and Rebecca, in the scullery, dropped a cup into the hot soapy water and stared at the open door to the kitchen in shock. Their Annie getting wed! What would this mean for them all? Women who got wed had children. Maybe Annie wouldn't have time for them any more. Maybe she'd turn them out of this lovely house and send them back to live in the Rows. Her dad had hinted they might have to move again one day.

Rebecca stopped washing dishes to listen unashamedly to what they were saying in the kitchen, so that she could tell Mark all about it. Mark was nearly grown up. He'd know what it all meant. She saw Luke bending over some plants outside, but his figure wavered through the blur of her tears. She saw the small figure of Joanie standing by Luke's side. Joanie was laughing. She had come on so much lately, no longer clung to her sister or dad. Rebecca clasped her wet hands at her flat child's chest and swallowed a lump in her throat. Why did things always have to change?

"Daniel! What a way to announce it!" Annie could feel herself flushing and she tried in vain to tug her hand away from his.

Tom looked across the room towards them, eyes narrowed, then quickly changed his incipient frown into a smile. "Well, then, isn't this a surprise! What brought this on? I thought you two were going to be courting for ever."

"She said yes, so I took her up on it before she could change her mind." Daniel patted Annie's arm with a proprietorial air. "It's about time, don't you think?"

Tom walked across and kissed Annie on the cheek. "Congratulations, love. I hope you'll be very happy." He slapped Daniel on the arm and then shook his hand. "Well, I don't need to tell you what a treasure you've got."

Annie listened in amazement as the two men exchanged pleasantries, almost as if she were not there, as if she were a parcel being handed over from one to the other. She was not sure she liked that.

When the other children came inside for tea, and were told the news, they all grew very quiet and stared at the happy couple with apprehension written large on their faces, even Mark.

"Your family don't seem very keen on this," growled Daniel as he took his leave of Annie in the hall.

Her heart was still beating madly from the kiss he had just given her. "It's a big change for all of us. Give them time, love. Stop pressing so hard."

"How can I not press hard when you've made me wait so long?"

When she went back into the kitchen, Tom met her at the door. "Let's go an' talk, love." He led the way into the dining room which was still used more as an office. "Are you sure about this?" he asked bluntly.

She lifted her head indignantly. "Of course I'm sure!"

"Well, you don't look very sure to me. And you don't look all that happy either."

She dropped her eyes, fiddling with the chenille table cover.

"I – I think I'm a bit embarrassed, Tom. It's taken me by surprise."

"Surprise! The fellow's been courting you for years."

"Well, we've only just decided to get married. That feels sudden to me."

"Are you sure that's all it is? Are you sure he hasn't pushed you into it?"

She stiffened and scowled at him. "Don't you think I have a mind of my own?"

"Usually, yes. But Daniel Connor's a soft-spoken devil, with years of experience with women behind him. I just don't – I don't want there to be any problems later."

"Why should there be any problems? Don't you think I'll make Daniel a good wife?"

"Oh, you'll make him a good wife." Better than he deserves, if what gossip said was true. "It's whether he'll make you a good husband that worries me."

She would not allow herself to doubt her decision, especially not to Tom. "I'm sure he will. He's Bridie's son, after all."

"Then if you're sure about the marriage, have you thought what's going to happen about the business?"

"I – we haven't had time to discuss that yet."

"You'll give me first offer to buy you out of the junk business, though?"

"Why should I want to sell it?"

"A married woman doesn't usually keep her business interests, love. Earning money is for the husband to do. Besides, if I know Daniel, you'll probably be too busy having a series of little O'Connors. Look how many children Bridie had. They're a fertile lot, the O'Connors."

Her cheeks were flaming, but it was as much with anger as embarrassment. "I'll do as I please about the business."

"You won't be able to."

"What on earth do you mean?"

"Once you're married, it won't belong to you any more. You know how the law regards married women." He had taken the trouble to find out exactly how things stood from Mr Pennybody himself. "Everything you have, yourself included, will be the property of your husband. Legally, Daniel will be able to do what he wants with it the minute he gets that ring on your finger. Why, legally he'll even own the clothes on your back."

She opened her mouth, then closed it again, frowning. She had not thought deeply about that aspect of marrying. "Daniel won't treat me like that."

"He might. You won't know till you're wed. And what about the salon?"

"I'm not giving that up! Tom Gibson, what's all this about? Don't you want me to get married?"

He shrugged. "Actually, love, I don't know what I want. Strange as it may seem, it's your happiness I care about most of all. You've looked after everyone else so well. Make sure you look after yourself, too."

She had trouble getting those words out of her brain.

When John and Kathy returned, Annie decided to wait until the turmoil of the family's welcome had died down before she told them about her engagement. She listened to their tales of the wonders of Blackpool, its fine sandy beaches and bracing air – the freshly caught fish they had eaten – the other people they had met – the boat ride they had very daringly taken. They were full of it and they both looked so happy, so very happy, that it brought tears to her eyes. She didn't feel like that. Was she even capable of feeling like that?

What was wrong with her that she was already having doubts about whether she had done the right thing in agreeing to marry Daniel? It was just a fit of depression. Soon, she too would have that fulfilled, happy look to her, though she would not, she decided, risk getting pregnant beforehand like Kathy had. That sort of thing would have to wait until she and Daniel were married. She grew annoyed with the stab of longing that shot through her body at the thought. And nervous. She might have borne a son, but she had never known what it was to take pleasure in a man. Her thoughts faltered and she turned with relief to answer a question from her father.

After a little while, Tom grew impatient. "Aren't you going to tell them your news, Annie?"

She glared at him. "I don't need prodding from you! I can speak for myself, thank you."

"Pardon me for breathing!" He grinned across at her.

John's gentle voice prevented any further sharp words. "Tell us what news, love?"

Annie looked down at her hands. "That I've agreed to marry Daniel."

"Nay, then, lass! That's a grand piece of news." John got up and gave her a big hug. "I couldn't want anything better for you than to be as happy as me and my Kathy are."

Kathy came across to hug her as well and Annie tried to keep a smile on her face. "Are you sure about it, love?" Kathy asked softly, for Annie's ears alone. "You don't look very happy."

Annie nodded. "Mmm."

"Nay, lass, you don't look all that happy about it," said John, watching them and unconsciously echoing his wife's words.

"I'm embarrassed, if you must know, Dad. To get married again after all these years. It's such a big change. I – I don't know where I am."

John nodded, appeased. "Aye, it will be a big change, stayin' home will."

"Who says I'll be staying home?" Annie snapped. The way everyone assumed that she would stop taking an interest in her salon was beginning to annoy her.

"Well, you'll have to once the babbies start coming, won't you?" he said peaceably. "It stands to reason. An' besides, you won't *need* to go out to work."

Kathy interrupted hastily. "Well, I hope you'll be very happy, love. If anyone deserves it, you do."

"Thank you. Er – I want to keep it secret for the moment," Annie said, as they all sat down again. "Only the family is to know. I don't want anyone in the town told yet. It might be bad for business."

"All right, love." John squeezed Kathy's hand and beamed at her. He could not refrain from touching her at every opportunity and the smile had hardly left his face since they returned. Even his daughter's news had not dented that aura of bliss.

Would she ever be that happy? Annie wondered suddenly. Did she even have it in her to trust anyone so blindly?

Then John's smile faltered. "Eh, I never thought. He's a Roman, isn't he, Daniel? Eh, love, how shall you be wed to a papist? You'll never turn!"

"We'll be wed in chapel, like you were, Dad. Daniel doesn't have – er – any strong feelings about where he worships his Maker. He says it's the same God."

John's face was still troubled. "That means he's the one who'll have to do the turning. An' what will Bridie an' Mick say about that?"

"I don't know. Daniel hasn't told them yet. We'll cross that bridge when we come to it. I wanted to tell you first."

"Me an' John'll start lookin' for a house of our own, then," Kathy said bravely. "There won't be room for us all here." She tried to smile, but the thought of leaving this house was very hard to bear.

Annie stared at her in surprise. She had not even considered the question of where she and Daniel were going to live. What was wrong with her? Why could she not be like other women, making plans and thinking about her husband's needs? Her first thought had been for her business and when Tom had talked of buying her out of the junk yard, she had been furious, was still furious at the idea. She let the talk eddy around her, smiling and nodding occasionally, but when she wasn't making an effort to smile, her face felt as if it were a piece of wood, stiff from masking the worry in her heart. She needed to see Daniel, to talk to him. There were so many things to discuss. And this time, she wouldn't let him charm her out of discussing their two businesses.

"You've what!" Pauline stared at Annie. "To Daniel Connor? Surely not!"

Annie could feel anger surge up within her and hoped it didn't show on her face. "What's wrong with Daniel Connor, pray?"

"He's not good enough for you, that's what's wrong. Not nearly good enough."

Annie laughed bitterly. "On the contrary, Pauline, it's me who's not good enough for him. So far I've done nothing but cause trouble between us and throw impediments in the way of us getting married."

"What do you mean, trouble?"

"I don't want to sell my business."

"Any why ever should you?"

"Daniel thinks – well, it's not suitable for a married woman to keep her business, is it? Married women s-stay at home – and look after their children." She hoped her smile as she said this looked genuine.

Pauline's eyes narrowed. "That depends. Is Mr Connor's business bringing in enough to keep you in comfort?"

"I – I don't know." Daniel had refused point blank to discuss the details of his business with her, first trying to tease her out of asking, then retreating behind a shield of anger. It was the first time Annie had realised how strong the mould was in which men who were not poor placed their wives. Daniel was determined to be the breadwinner and to support her as a wife should be supported and from that standpoint he would not budge. In the end she had let the matter drop, afraid that their raised voices would disturb the rest of her family. But she did not intend to leave it at that. She could surely help him in some way, perhaps by taking over the accounts and paperwork. She could do that at home. She would go mad if she had nothing to do but look after a house.

"Then I would advise you to find out about how things stand before you commit yourself," declared Pauline, bringing Annie sharply back to the present. "You're an excellent businesswoman. Does he think you wouldn't understand his affairs?"

"Daniel says he wants to – to cherish me. He says I've never had time for myself."

"He wants you to spend all your time fussing over him, you mean." Pauline saw that she had raised Annie's hackles and sighed. "Well, you'll have plenty of time to work things out before you get married, surely. When are you thinking of? Next spring?"

"Daniel says there's no need to wait."

"And what does Annie say?"

Annie looked at her friend and her smile wobbled visibly. "Annie doesn't know what to think. It's all happened so quickly."

"Then don't let him rush you into it."

"He says—" Annie broke off, unable to believe that she was continuing to parrot Daniel's opinions like this. "No, we both think that we're not all that young and – and if we want children, we'd be best not waiting too long."

"Hmm." Pauline let the matter drop and condescended to discuss the new dress she wanted making. But she had not

finished yet, not by a long chalk. She did not like the way Mr
Connor was pushing Annie into marriage. She decided to talk
to Tom Gibson about it and ask how he felt.

In fact, no one displayed unalloyed joy at the prospect of
Annie marrying Daniel Connor, though his parents were at
first delighted to welcome her as a daughter-in-law.

"About time, too," said Bridie. But when the question of
religion cropped up and they found that Annie did not intend
to turn Catholic, Bridie's joy turned to tears and she begged
Annie to reconsider. "You'll not want to damn the souls of
your children, surely?"

"It's not only Catholics who go to heaven, Mam," joked
Daniel, but Bridie turned on him like a fury and then, when
she could not move him from his decision to get wed in the
Methodist Chapel, she wept for days and sent the priest round
to see first him and then Annie.

Even Helen Kenderby's congratulations were stiff. "I envy
you, Annie," she admitted. "He's such a handsome man. You're
very lucky."

"Why am I the lucky one?" demanded Annie. "Why isn't
Daniel lucky to be marrying me? After all, I'm bringing him a
good dowry, aren't I?"

Helen's words continued to echo in her mind, even after
she had gone to bed that night. When she and Daniel were
apart, the doubts kept creeping into her mind. When they were
together, he banished the doubts and his kisses made her long
to be his wife. But he still refused to contemplate her continuing
to be involved in the businesses, even behind the scenes; in
fact, he still refused to discuss his own business matters with
her at all. And last night he had broached the idea of finding a
buyer for the salon.

"Over my dead body!" she had declared in a rage. Only
then had he backed down. But she could not get Tom's teasing
words out of her mind. Once they were married, Daniel

wouldn't need her permission to sell the salon. Everything she had worked so hard for would belong to him. Dared she trust him, dared she trust anyone with that?

Twenty-Four

LATE SUMMER 1848

Marianne Lewis continued to live in a state of open warfare with her Cousin Dorothy, while her father grew ever more absent-minded and immersed himself in his work and the joy of planning his hospital at last.

As the summer passed, he read with concern about the cholera outbreak in London, a bad outbreak, very bad. It was hitting other places, too, but please God, not Bilsden, which at least had a clean water supply. The sanitation situation was not as good as Bilsden's water supply, though. Claters End continued to trouble him and to spawn miniature epidemics. He really would have to get Hallam to do something about this. The trouble was, Hallam did not own Claters End. The land and slum houses were owned by a miscellany of small investors, none of whom seemed concerned about the health of their tenants.

On the home front, at Park House, relations between his womenfolk remained tense, but he still could not see how to tell Dorothy to leave. She seemed so happy with her little charities and her church work.

Marianne, who had by now learned to assert herself in the things which mattered to her, simply retired to her room when things grew too bad. She locked the door against her cousin and refused to answer when Dorothy knocked. After a while, Dorothy stopped provoking fights, realising that she would never tame this headstrong girl and that in the last resort, Jeremy would always come down on Marianne's side. Dorothy wanted very much to stay on in the comfort of Park House, because her only other alternative would be to throw herself on the mercy of some distant relatives of her father or to find some very cheap lodgings. Her father's affairs had proved to be in such a state that she was left after his death with an income too small even to keep her in modest gentility. Everything had had to be sold to pay the debts. Jeremy had managed that for her. Dear Jeremy.

One day, she vowed, one day when Marianne was married, she would have Jeremy to herself, and then she would change a few things at Park House. The first thing she would do would be to get rid of that impudent young woman, Ellie Peters. When his daughter had left home, Jeremy would realise how indispensable his cousin was to his comfort and he would always side with a relative against a servant.

And if Dorothy were very very lucky, his wife would die and then he would be free to marry his cousin, not for the usual disgusting reasons, but simply because a man needed a wife to look after his domestic affairs, especially a man who was a doctor. People preferred their doctors to be married, and there were enough rumours about Jeremy and Annabelle's separation already. In the meantime, if Dorothy let Marianne have enough freedom, the girl would surely *have* to get married, the way she was playing around with that Gibson fellow, and the sooner that happened, the better, as far as Dorothy was concerned.

As he always had, Jeremy shrank from stirring up trouble

His daughter had stopped complaining and seemed happy enough these days, though quieter than before. Dorothy, too, had become quieter and did not fuss as much or intrude into his life. He was glad that Marianne spent a lot of time over with Annie and her family, for he knew that she would be quite safe there. Everything had gone wrong when he had brought Dorothy into their life, almost as badly as it had gone with Annabelle. He was just not fated to be happy and successful, except in his work. And fortunately there were so many developments to study in the field of public health that he was kept busy and was often away learning from whomever he could. Every now and then he persuaded Frederick Hallam to take an interest and together they achieved something really important for the poor of Bilsden. And then there was the hospital. It would be a while before that could be started, but when it was, he intended it to be a marvel of modern science. What more could one man do for his fellow creatures?

Jeremy rarely even thought about Annabelle these days, except when he received her annual requests for a pretence of a meeting during the summer. She still persisted with that pretence, but it caused him little trouble to meet her requests, for he and Marianne now made a habit of taking a summer holiday together, without Dorothy. It was the highlight of his whole year. Such a pity that it had had to be postponed this year.

Ellie, who was more aware of the true state of hostilities between Marianne and Miss Hymes, worried about the girl sometimes, but she, too, consoled herself with the thought that Jeremy's daughter would come to no harm with Annie and her family. She helped her father move into a more isolated house and hire a strong woman to look after his wife. This left her sister Lily with a little more freedom, but her father was not best pleased with this situation and still said occasionally that if Ellie were doing her duty, she would have come home to

look after her mother herself. That was what families were
for. Between them, Ellie and Lily could have managed their
mother without bringing in a stranger.

Marianne was now a firm favourite with John Gibson, for
she visited the junk yard regularly. At weekends, she sometimes
went to tea with Annie and her family, but more often she
went off for long walks on the moors with Tom. It was easy
enough to make everyone think she was somewhere else, and
Annie, normally so sharp to see through any subterfuge, was
rather abstracted nowadays. How Marianne prayed for fine
weekends that summer! How she fretted if it rained!

She made a token effort to join in the social life in the town,
but did not make any close friends. The other young women
could only talk about clothes and prospective husbands, and
she found the young men to whom Dorothy and the town's
matrons introduced her vapid and mindless. They either talked
all the time about their fathers' businesses, or they spouted
bad poetry and made sheep's eyes at her. Neither approach
pleased her, for Tom talked to her about real things, about his
business and the sources he had discovered for the supply of
food to the townsfolk, a surprisingly lucrative field. She was
the only person besides Annie to know about his plans for a
big new grocery emporium in the High Street. Being part of
that, hearing it planned, making suggestions, pleased her
greatly. It made her feel special in Tom's life, and she wanted
to be special to him. He had taken her father's place in many
ways now and had become the centre of her existence.

When Kathy's body thickened and she started making
preparations for her child's layette, it was Marianne who took
the most interest in her condition. At first shy of the doctor's
daughter and her fancy way of talking, Kathy soon came to
regard her as a friend, and the two of them formed an admiration
society for the future Master Philip Gibson, or perhaps the
future Miss Louisa Gibson.

"I'd like a baby of my own," Marianne said dreamily to Tom one day as they sat in their favourite spot on the tops, looking down at the sooty vale of Bilsden.

His breath caught in his throat at the tender expression on her face. She had never seemed so beautiful. "I'd like one too," he said hoarsely. "I can think of nothing more wonderful than for you to be the mother of my child."

"Tom, does that mean that you . . ." Her voice trailed away and she flushed as she looked at him sideways.

"It means I want you to be my wife. Surely you knew that already?"

"Yes, but you've not said anything about – about actually marrying. You've hardly ever even t-touched me." She blushed vividly, not knowing how to put things into words without seeming too forward.

Tom just held his arms out to her and she threw herself into them. "That's because I'm human, love. If I touch you, I'll want more than just a touch, and I know I can't have it yet – not till we're wed. It's not only me and my business that's holding things up. I've been waiting for you to grow up."

"I shall be twenty soon."

"Yes. Very old." He caressed the nape of her neck, then raised her chin so that he could kiss her properly. "But the main reason for waiting is that I want to have enough money behind me so that I'll know you'll never go short." And Rosie, poor Rosie, was still as willing as ever, so he'd not been too frustrated, though to tell the truth, he was sick and tired of Rosie and her silly prattle of folk they had once known in Claters End, sick and tired of reining in his response to Marianne's slender body and glorious silky hair. And Rosie had got a bit fat and crotchety lately. It didn't suit her.

"I don't care about the money," Marianne said, pressing against him. "You know I don't."

"Well, I do. I must." He traced the line of her jaw with one fingertip, then kissed her lips. "Oh, hell, love, I'm trying so hard to do the right thing. Don't make it worse for me." He held her away from him. "I think it's time to get it settled between us, though, properly settled. Marianne Lewis, will you marry me or not?"

Her smile was radiant. "Oh, Tom, I can't wait to marry you! Let's go and ask my father's permission today."

Prudence reasserted itself, in him at least. "Marianne. Look, will you just stop – mm – kissing me and listen for a minute."

It took him a while to stop her kissing him, and to stop giving in to the temptation to caress her just once more. Eventually, however, he insisted they settle down on the coarse grass with their backs to a rocky outcrop. She fitted into the crook of his arm as if she had been made for it and he could only hope his arousal was not too visible. In some ways, she was very innocent still, for all she was nearly twenty. "Let's be sensible for a minute, love."

"I hate being sensible. It's Cousin Dorothy's favourite word."

"Well, sometimes you have to be sensible. I think we should wait to tell people."

"Tom, no! Oh, Tom, why? Are you ashamed of loving me?"

"You know I'm not."

"Then why?"

"I told you, love. I'm not well enough established yet. Your father, any father worth his salt, would want a girl like you to do better for herself than marrying a rough fellow like me. come from Salem Street, love. You've seen it. You live in a comfortable house and you always have done. Your father is a gentleman. I can't change where I was born, but I can change what I have to offer you. You don't know what it's like being poor. You've never wanted for anything. And I don't intend that you ever shall."

"Except love," she said softly. "I've always wanted for love."

"Your father loves you."

"Yes. When he's not too busy looking after his patients or planning his hospital or new sanitary improvements for the town." She sighed and snuggled against him. "I know my father loves me dearly in his own way, but he's not often there to show it. And he doesn't cuddle me like this. No one ever has."

"There's Ellie as well."

"Yes. But she's worried about her mother. And anyway, it's not been the same with Ellie since Cousin Dorothy came to live with us." Even thinking of Dorothy, who made her life unhappy in so many petty ways, made Marianne's fingers clench tightly on Tom's arm, so tightly that he winced and pulled them away. And then he found that Marianne was in tears and he had to comfort her, comfort her and love her better. And when that loving developed into something more than just a kiss, neither of them was able to stop it, for the fires had been pent up for too long.

Afterwards, she leaned against him, oblivious to the chill breeze on their naked limbs, and smiling at him like a white and golden angel. "Now I really do belong to you, Tom."

He buried his head in her breasts. "Oh, my little love, I'm sorry, so sorry!"

"Whatever for?"

"For taking advantage of you." And he knew that he had done that, even if she did not. A man, even a man from Salem Street, did not take a young woman as innocent as this one on the grass of the moors, did not take advantage of her love for him.

"Tom, I wanted you just as much as you wanted me."

"I'm older than you. I'm the man. I should have had more sense than to—"

"Than to what?" she teased, face alight and flushed with love. "Than to love me? Are you sorry about that?"

"No," he groaned into her soft sweet-smelling flesh. "But we both know it was wrong."

When he pulled his head away and stared down at her, she saw that his eyes were full of tears. "Tom, what's the matter? Tom, you do still love me, don't you?"

"Of course I do. But I hadn't meant to take advantage of you. I just – I love you too much. I wanted everything to be proper between us." When she just laughed up at him, he shook her slightly. "What if you're with child? What will people say then?"

She sobered for a minute. "I could be, couldn't I?" Then her face broke into a beaming smile. "Oh, I do hope I am. No one could stop me marrying you then. We'd have to get married straight away."

In Brighton, Annabelle again found herself pregnant and sent a message round to Henry to send for Ma at once. He came himself.

"Hell, you surely can't be pregnant again!"

"Well, I am. What does it matter? Ma'll be able to fix it for us."

"Not this time."

She clutched her wrapper to her bosom. "What do you mean, not this time?"

"Ma died last week. God knows how old she was. She just died in her sleep, poor old sod."

"Oh, no!"

"I'll find someone else, don't worry."

"See that you do!"

He grabbed hold of her hair and pulled her roughly towards him. "I'm getting a bit tired of you taking that tone with me!" He shook her and then slapped her face as he let her go.

She drew away from him, gasping and startled. "There was no need for that."

"I think there was. Maybe it'll remind you to watch your manners with me from now on, my girl!" He smiled to see the way she shrank back and moderated her tone. He'd put up with her "I'm a lady" posturings and protestations for long enough.

"But you will find someone to help me, won't you? You will, Henry."

"I will if you behave yourself." Just to emphasise his power over her, he let her wait for three weeks before he did anything, by which time she was ready to lick the ground he trod upon if only he would help her. The pregnancy was affecting her badly, making her sick and unable to work.

When at last he came to see her again, he was surprised at how unlovely she was looking. The last of his attraction towards her was fading, but as she was unable to work, it was time to act. She would be more docile now, he reckoned. While she was ill, he had found another woman to take over Annabelle's regulars and she was doing very well. He had also found himself a younger piece to satisfy his own needs, a girl of fourteen with very firm flesh and very biddable ways. He found young Nelly a pleasant change after the years of Annabelle Lewis and her airs and graces.

Three days after the new woman visited her, there was a frantic note to Henry from Annabelle. Sal's potion had not worked. Please could he find someone else! As his income was beginning to be affected, Henry went to berate Sal.

She just shrugged. "There's times, Mr Minton, when the babies don't want to be moved. I've seen it afore."

"Keep trying."

Sal tried all her potions, but nothing would dislodge this damned baby.

"You'll have to let her dig it out, then," he told Annabelle crudely, fed up with the whole business, fed up most of all with this stringy-haired, puffy-faced woman with the red eyes and quivering mouth.

"*Dig it out!* What do you mean, dig it out?"

"Bit of wire. Easy enough to do. You just poke the baby out with it. I'll get her to come round tonight to see to it."

Annabelle stared at him in horror and it was a moment or two before she found her voice to ask, "Will it h-hurt?"

"Of course it will, you stupid bitch! But it's better than having the sodding baby, isn't it?"

"I – I suppose so."

When Sal turned up that night and got out her equipment, Annabelle nearly fainted. But the thought of the baby growing within her made her submit. The first attempt was so painful that she screamed loudly and pulled away. She could not stop sobbing for quite a while afterwards. And it did no good, for this baby still refused to be dislodged. Cora, sickened by the brutality of these measures and by Sal's indifference to others' pain, held her mistress's hand and began to wonder if it was time to leave this position and set up for herself in a little shop. She had not bargained for this sort of thing happening and she did not like it.

When Sal picked up her piece of wire again an hour later, bloody still from her first attempt, Annabelle shrank back, then began to scream, "Don't touch me! Don't you dare touch me again!"

Nothing Cora and Sal could say would persuade her to change her mind. Nor did Cora quite dare to hold her mistress down, as Sal suggested. The two women held a hurried conference outside the bedroom door.

"*He* won't be pleased," said Sal. "You'll have to make her lie still. If she hadn't twitched around the last time, I'd have got it first go, like I usually do."

"I can't make her do anything. She's the mistress, not me. Besides, she's stronger than she looks. I don't think I could hold her down, even if I tried."

"Why don't you bring Alf Booling in to hold her down, then?"

"I daren't. She'd sack me."

Sal shrugged, gathered together her things and left, grumbling all the way out about "finicky madams as don't know what's good for them".

Henry was round first thing next morning. "Well? Did it work?"

Annabelle shuddered. "No."

"What do you mean, no? It always works."

"I couldn't stand the pain. Henry, surely you can—"

He threw his head back and laughed. "You stupid bitch, you don't have any choice about this. Either you let Sal do her business or you have the child."

Annabelle glared at him. "She's not touching me again with that – that implement of torture."

"All right. Your choice." He stared down at her. She was looking old, as well as haggard. Well, it had been a good thing while it lasted. He shrugged.

"You're not just going to leave me!"

"What else can I do if you refuse to be helped?" He turned to leave. She had now lost every bit of her attraction for him, and also all usefulness. "I'll take Alf with me. You won't need him for a while. Call me when the baby's born, and I'll see if I can find you some more work. Of course, it won't be such classy work, with stretch marks on your belly and with sagging tits."

Pride made Annabelle draw herself up and point to the door. "*How dare you* speak to me like that! Get out of my house this minute."

For the next two days, she lay in a darkened room, nursing her sickness and brooding on the future. This trouble had made Henry lose all his ability to blind her to what she was doing and she began to wonder, in sick shuddering horror, how she could ever have let herself be used like that. What if people found out? *What was she going to do*? She sent for her Bible and prayed as she had never prayed before.

On the third morning, she rang the bell to summon Cora. "I've decided to have the baby."

Cora could only gape.

"Well, what choice do I have, you stupid girl?"

"Ma'am."

Annabelle realised that she was alienating her only ally. "I'm sorry, Cora, I shouldn't have spoken to you like that."

She wants something, thought Cora. Well, she'll have to pay for it.

"I've decided not to oblige Mr Minton any more. I've also decided that I need a holiday. We shall go away to the country, somewhere where I'm not known, and when I've had this child, I shall leave it on the doorstep of an orphanage. I shall tell people here that I'm going to try to live in Bilsden with my husband again."

"But won't they find out you're not there?"

"It's a risk we must take. But I shall need your help." For the first time, the hard voice faltered. "You won't let me down, will you, Cora? I'll – I'll make it worth your while."

Cora looked at her mistress and found herself agreeing to help. The poor bitch was well and truly lumbered now, wasn't she? And if Mrs Lewis was prepared to raise the wages, Cora was quite prepared to stay with her. For the time being, anyway. A bit more money saved wouldn't hurt before she set herself up in her shop.

"Of course I'll help you, ma'am. Haven't I always?"

Annabelle dissolved in tears and clung to Cora. "You can't rely on men. They always let you down. Don't ever rely on a man, Cora. If they're not weak, they're selfish. I should have known better. From now on, I shall not associate with men at all. I shall live a very quiet retired life. Only the Lord has not abandoned me. In Him I shall place my trust from now on. But first I must be rid of this." She stared down at her still-flat belly and shuddered. "It's my punishment and I will endure it. And afterwards, the Lord will surely forgive me for my sins."

Cora stared at her mistress in surprise. This was the first time she had ever heard Annabelle Lewis sound religious. She could hardly believe her own ears. But as the months passed, Annabelle's fervour did not change; it only grew deeper. All this religion made for a very dull sort of life, but Cora put up with it. The money was too good to be missed. But she wasn't staying long after the baby was born, money or no money. She didn't enjoy a quiet life, or evenings spent reading the Bible.

Twenty-Five

OCTOBER TO NOVEMBER
1848

Kathy's baby was born in October, after an easy labour.

"It's a little lad," said Widow Clegg, dumping the squirming bundle wrapped in an old piece of sheeting into Kathy's eager arms.

"A boy!" Kathy breathed, hugging the bundle to her and dropping tears of joy all over her son's little pink button of a nose.

The Widow finished her tasks, then summoned the father to the birth chamber. "There you are, John Gibson. Another son for you."

John leaned over to kiss Kathy and then beamed down at the infant, squalling now for the comfort of its mother's breast.

"And," said the Widow sharply from the doorway as she prepared to take her leave, "don't give this wife another babby for a couple of years. You're too ready to jump into bed, you are, John Gibson. You wore your poor Emily out. Let this one have a bit of time to recover in between babbies."

John breathed deeply, but said nothing as the door banged shut.

Kathy smiled up at her husband. "She's a terror, isn't she, Widow Clegg? She's been scolding me for the past half-hour about not having any more babies for a while. Still, Dr Lewis says she's the best midwife in town, so she must know what she's talking about."

He smiled down at her and reached for her hand, swallowing hard to shift the lump of emotion from his throat and blinking the moisture from his eyes. "Aye, well, you deserve the best, my bonny lass. Shall we still call him Philip, or have you changed your mind?"

"Philip's a lovely name. An' John for you as well."

"Philip John it is, then."

Her smile faded. "Your Annie an' Daniel will be wanting to set the wedding date, I reckon, now that I've had my baby."

"I've never understood why she's kept putting if off. But then," he squeezed her hand again, "you women allus like to keep us fellows guessing. Look at how you kept me waiting to get wed. If it wasn't for our Phil here, you'd still be sneakin' into my room at night."

"Philip. I don't want his name shortened. An' I kept you waiting because I didn't want to upset your Tom."

"You never want to upset anybody, Kathy Gibson. Proper little peace-maker, you are. Eh, look at him squirm! He'll be a strong little fellow, that one will. Our Tom were just the same."

They both watched their son fondly, then Kathy said wistfully, "I wish Annie would wait till next spring to get married, like she said she was goin' to. It's Daniel as wants them to get wed quickly, not her."

"Nay, lass, why ever should she wait? It's not as if they're goin' to be short of money, is it? They'll be well set up, with a place like this to live in."

"I know that. But I think Annie still needs time to get used to the idea. She's not really been wed before, you know, John, for all she's got a child. Poor Charlie weren't a husband to

386

her, though he were a lovely fellow an' a good father to William. It's like this is her first time. Only she's not a young girl. She's got used to havin' her own way in life, as well as to runnin' her own business. It's a hard thing to give all that up."

He nodded, but he was more interested in the antics of Master Philip John Gibson, so Kathy let the subject of his eldest daughter drop. But she continued to worry about Annie's future. Try as she might, she could not trust Daniel Connor. And there were rumours in town that he was not a quick payer these days. Kathy hadn't liked to tell Annie about that.

The following day, Daniel came round to Netherleigh Cottage to admire the baby, then on his way out he pulled Annie into the parlour and set both his hands on her shoulders so that she had to face him. "Well, are you going to find any more excuses or can we settle on a day now?"

"It wasn't an excuse. You don't want my father and Kathy living here with us, and I couldn't very well ask Kathy to find a new home when she was pregnant."

"It was an excuse and we both know it." His voice was firm and he was not smiling, for once. "I let you persuade me to wait because I thought you still needed time to get used to the idea of getting married, as well as time to decide what to do about your businesses. You've had your time now, Annie. Either you allow me to place an announcement in the *Bilsden Gazette*, or we'll call the whole thing off." He pulled her suddenly towards him and started to kiss her and when he released her, she could only sigh and stand within the circle of his arms.

"You don't seem to have taken a dislike to me," he teased.

She smiled up at him, but the smile soon faded. He always made her feel like this, uncertain of her own wishes.

"At least, let me announce our engagement in the paper," he insisted.

There was a moment's silence, then she nodded. "Yes."

She had kept him waiting long enough. Few men would have put up with that. Surely it augured well for their life together that he had been so patient?

"And we'll name a day right now. Give Kathy a few weeks to recover, say the last Saturday in November. Will that suit you?"

Annie stared at him. She could not speak for a moment or two. Late November. Only seven weeks away. It was still too soon. But it wasn't fair to keep him waiting any more. She knew that she was just being stupid, dithering like this. Any other woman would have been over the moon with a handsome man like Daniel wanting to marry her. Helen had said so openly. Poor Helen. She had seemed even more unhappy at home since her mother had died. Only Daniel seemed to have the power to cheer her up lately.

Daniel held his breath. He could not afford to wait much longer, if truth be told, though he had kept the true state of his business affairs from Annie. His investments had gone sour, there had been a downturn in trade and consequently folk were not wanting much built. He had to get some money from somewhere to tide him through until better times. If folk knew he was to marry Annie Ashworth, that would help for a while.

Annie continued to stare at him, her lovely eyes wide and, though she did not realise it, a trifle fearful. "Oh, Daniel, I don't know."

He'd just have to push her. Dammit, why was this woman, of all those he had known, so hard to manage? "I'm beginning to think you don't want to marry me." With an effort he kept his voice lightly teasing.

"Of course I want to marry you." Of course she did. Whatever Kathy said about waiting. Whatever Tom hinted at. Annie sighed. Besides, word had got around and half the town knew about their engagement already. It was just plain silly to delay things any long. "Yes, Daniel. The last Saturday in November will be fine."

She was not aware of how closely he was watching her, or of the sigh of relief that he suppressed when she agreed. She was just grateful that he did not push his attentions on her and that he left soon afterwards, so that she could have some time alone to get used to the idea of becoming Mrs Daniel Connor at last.

Tom was not as tactful as Daniel. He cocked a knowing eyebrow at his sister and said bluntly, "So he's pushed you into it, then."

"I don't know what you mean!" Annie's voice was sharper than she had intended. She took a deep breath and added, "Most brothers would wish me happy, not – not say things like that."

"I'm not most brothers. And I'm still not sure that you really want to marry him."

"Of course I do! Why else would I have got engaged to him, for heaven's sake?"

"Why indeed? A moment of weakness. A desire for a handsome man. Even you must have some desire for a bit of loving."

"I don't like that sort of talk."

"Why not? Feelings are natural enough for women, as well as for men. You've kept yourself away from men for too long, Annie, but surely you want to—"

"*Don't*!" She pressed her hands to her burning cheeks. "Tom, don't go on at me!" Her voice quavered a little "I've made my mind up and – and nothing you say will make me change it. But I don't like you t-talking like that."

As Mark and Luke came in just then, Tom had to let the matter drop, but he could not forget the fear on her face. He soon realised that Annie was taking care not to be alone with him and that worried him. If anyone, and that included Daniel Connor, ever hurt Annie, he would personally make sure they paid for it in blood. He had heard some rumours lately about Daniel, but when he had tried to find out more about how things stood, people just clammed up. There was nothing you could put your finger on, just tight-lipped expressions and a reluctance to talk about their business dealings with Mr Connor to the brother of the woman he was engaged to.

Tom decided that he had better make more of an effort to check it out. He wasn't having Annie hurt. It was a new thing for Tom to feel protective towards her, when for so long she had been the strong one, the older sister, so he went about it slowly. He had to be sure.

In early November, Annie was called away from sewing her own wedding gown to attend to two new customers in her salon, smart women who said they came from Manchester way.

She was surprised. "May I ask how you heard about me?"

"Oh, we heard about you from a friend, well, an acquaintance, really. We need some really special gowns for our cousin's wedding, so we thought we'd come and see you."

"Might I ask who your acquaintance is?"

"A Mrs Dawton. We met her at a friend's house. When we admired her gown, she told us about you and your salon."

The two women seemed different from Annie's usual customers and neither wore a wedding ring, so they were hard to place socially. But if they knew Mrs Dawton, then they must be all right. Annie was used to such referrals by now.

She answered their questions patiently, if a little absent-mindedly, as she displayed her swatches of material and sketch cards for their perusal. Sharp questions they were, too, she began to realise, even through her abstraction. Nobody's fools, the Misses Brierley. Probably the sort of women who had less money than people thought and who desperately wanted to keep up appearances. In the end, they did not place an order, but said they would think about things and return another day.

"It doesn't do to hurry such things, does it?" the elder Miss Brierley asked, smiling. "We never rush into anything. Oh – I believe you have a retiring room?"

"Certainly. Won't you come this way?"

Annie left them to their ablutions while she served Mrs Corby with some fine muslin for a new best apron. Mrs Corby was in such a hurry that the transaction was soon over. After Annie had put away the bolt of material she noticed some pins on the floor and got down on her knees to pick them up. She was therefore hidden behind the counter when the two strangers walked into the front display room on their way out.

"She's got it well set out here," one of them said.

"Yes, she's a good businesswoman. No wonder Mr Connor wants such a high price for it."

"So you think it'll be worth it, then?"

"Well, we'll probably be able to knock him down a bit, but I should say it's a little gold mine here, even at that price. We'll have to study the accounts, of course. I do insist on that."

"He was very definite that he wouldn't give the accounts to us till he was sure we were serious about buying it," the other remarked, then sighed. "She's a lucky woman to be marrying such a handsome man, isn't she? And one who cares about her business like that."

"Very lucky. I wonder if there are any more unattached gentlemen in Bilsden." They both laughed rather bitterly, then their voices and footsteps faded away and the front-door bell clanged behind them.

Annie straightened up, pins forgotten, and stared blindly through the window, not really seeing the two women as they walked away down the street. After a moment or two, she fumbled across the room and sank down on one of the little gilt chairs kept for those customers who liked to take their time about a purchase. There was no mistaking what the two women had been talking about. Daniel had started trying to sell her salon. Already. Before they were married. Without even asking her.

When the doorbell clanged again, she had difficulty in pulling herself together and was only just rising to her feet as Helen Kenderby walked in. Since Annie's engagement, Helen's visits had declined in both number and length, and Annie had sensed a coolness between them, a distance there had not been before.

"Helen," she said, trying to smile a greeting.

Helen paused in the doorway and then came quickly across to her. "What's happened? You look like you've had a shock."

"Nothing." But a tear winked out of Annie's eye, even as she spoke.

"Are there any other customers here in the salon at the moment?"

Annie stared. "No. What—"

Helen went out again to the front door, removed the OPEN card from its brass holder and turned it to CLOSED, then locked the door. When she came back into the front display room, she took Annie's arm, and walked with her into the rear room. "I think you need a cup of tea, my dear." She rang the little hand bell.

Annie could not seem to summon up the strength to stop her friend taking charge. She felt as if everything were happening very slowly and as if her body no longer belonged to her. Waves of shock were still making her feel faint.

Rebecca came hurrying into the room to answer the summons. "Yes, ma'am?" Then she gaped at Annie, who was just sitting staring in front of her like someone in a trance.

Helen intervened. "Your sister has had a shock, Rebecca. She needs a nice hot drink. Can you bring us some tea?"

Rebecca stared at Annie, then stared again as she saw how white her sister's face was and how distant was the look in her eyes. "Shall I fetch Miss Benworth down?"

"No. I'll deal with this. I've put the CLOSED sign up on the door. No one will come in for a while. Just get us the tea, then go and ask Miss Benworth to keep the others away."

She spoke with the voice of authority and Rebecca obeyed her immediately, pausing again at the door to stare back at her sister. She had never seen their Annie with that look on her face, and it really upset her. "Is she all right?" she whispered.

"Rebecca, get the tea!" Annie's voice was a mere whisper, but it sent her little sister rushing off.

Helen went over to sit next to Annie and take hold of her hand. "Tell me," she said simply. "Whatever it is, tell me."

Annie gulped, but could not seem to find the words.

"Aren't we still friends?"

Annie tried to speak, but suddenly, it was all too much for her. She burst into tears and buried her face in her hands, sobbing incoherently.

Helen sat there and patted her back, making soothing sounds. She didn't press for an explanation, just made sure Annie could feel that she was not alone.

It took a while for the sobbing to lessen. When a wide-eyed Rebecca carried in the tea-tray, Helen nodded approvingly. "Good girl! Pour your sister a cup, will you?" When Rebecca had done this, she nodded towards the door. "I'll look after her, don't worry."

Rebecca stood hesitating beside them.

Annie raised her tear-stained face. "It's j-just the shock," she managed. "I've had a sh-shock. I'll tell you about it later. I'll be all right soon. Thanks for the tea, love."

Rebecca's footsteps tapped quietly up the stairs to the workroom. There, everyone wanted to know what had happened, and when Rebecca confessed to being no wiser than they were, they discussed what might have happened in hushed voices until Mary Benworth at last brought an end to the gossip and told them to get on with their work. But like them, she was worried. Annie never gave in to trouble. Something really dreadful must have happened to upset her like that.

Downstairs, Annie made a huge effort and tried to pull herself together. "I'm s-sorry."

"What for?"

"For losing control of myself like this."

"That's what friends are for." Helen passed her a cup.

The warmth of the tea was soothing, but after a moment the cup began to rattle as Annie's hands started shaking again.

Helen took it from her. "I'm not leaving until I find out what this is all about. You need to talk to someone. Tell me what's wrong, Annie."

"I – I don't—"

"Sometimes it's hard to talk to your own family. Tell me. You can't bottle it up inside you."

Annie opened her mouth to speak, but the tears welled up again. "It's Daniel." She could not for a moment force any more words out, then she said in a rush, "He's put my business up for sale. Without – without even asking me." The sobs were welling up her throat again.

"Daniel has? How did you find that out?"

"I – there were two customers – at least, I thought they were customers – I overheard them discussing it as they were leaving. They were interested in buying the salon, but they said he was asking a h-high price for it."

"Well, he would be. You've done things in style and made a great success of it. Is that all? Is that what's upset you so much?" Helen frowned.

"Isn't it enough?"

"But surely you love Mr Connor? He'll want you to give up working here when you're married. Men usually do."

"I – thought I loved him." Annie stared down at the sodden handkerchief in her hands. "He was going to show them my

394

accounts, you see. That's what's upset me most of all."

"I'm afraid I don't quite follow."

Annie's voice was calmer now, but it had an edge of despair to it. "He lied to me. I offered to help him in his business after we were married, and he – he kept avoiding the issue, saying there was no need, that I'd be too busy in our home."

"He doesn't know you very well, then."

She stared across at Helen. "No, he doesn't, does he?"

"A woman like you would go mad in a month, sitting at home with nothing to do but the housework. Even I know that. I didn't say anything before, but if we're being honest, I must say that it has worried me. Go on, Annie."

"Well, in the end, Daniel teased me into giving him my account books to prove that I c-could do it. Only, I can see now that it was all a trick. To get hold of the accounts. I never – I never thought he'd lie to me like that."

Helen nodded at her to continue.

"I can't bear the thought that he lied to me," Annie said suddenly, savagely. "*I can't bear it!*" She turned to Helen, her expression bleak. "Is that wrong? Shouldn't I love him whatever he does?"

"You might. If you truly loved him. I've sometimes wondered about that. Do you think you do?"

Annie's lips were still trembling and it was a moment before she spoke. "No. No, I don't."

The words were whispered, but very definite. For a moment, something flashed in Helen's eyes, then she dropped her lashes to veil them and contented herself with patting her friend's hand.

"I'm going to look a fool," Annie said after a minute.

"Are you?"

"Yes."

"Why?"

"For jilting him."

"Are you going to do that?"

"Yes." Annie's voice was quite firm as she said, "I can't – I just can't marry someone who would lie to me about important things like that."

"It must be your own decision. I won't try to influence you one way or the other."

Annie picked up the cup and this time managed to take a drink without Helen's help. The warmth was vaguely comforting. "I can't have loved him, can I? Not if I let this stop me marrying him."

"I don't know. We all love in different ways." Helen saw Annie staring at her and added with a short laugh. "I was in love once myself, you know. My father sent him away. And I allowed him to send Frank away. Later, when I realised how stupid I had been, I vowed that if I ever loved anyone again, and if that person wanted to marry me, I would allow no one and nothing to come between us."

They sat in silence for a few minutes, each busy with her own thoughts, then Annie started speaking, not looking at Helen, just thinking aloud, trying to understand her own feelings. "After the rape, I think I was frozen, somehow. I never – never missed having a man. Not in all those years. And then when Charlie died, Daniel started courting me, k-kissing me. I found that I was just like any other woman. I needed to be held, needed to be wanted and I enjoyed the kisses. They were all – people were falling in love around me – even my own father. I thought something was wrong with me. I wanted to be in love. I wanted to be like everyone else."

She fell silent for a moment, then gave a short bitter laugh. "So when Daniel came back to live in Bilsden, when he continued to court me, it seemed – it seemed as if I ought to marry him. How could I not love him when I responded to his kisses like that? I thought I just wasn't capable of strong feelings."

Helen said quietly, "It's possible for your body to respond without you loving someone, Annie. Believe me, it's quite possible."

Annie's reply had an echo of sheer surprise. "Yes, it is, isn't it? Only no one ever told me, no one talked about love, so I didn't think about that."

"So you got engaged to Daniel."

"Yes. But I kept putting off naming a day. There was just something that made me not want to – to go through with it."

"I have wondered about that. Didn't your brother say anything? Or your friend Pauline?"

"They tried. I wouldn't listen."

"And now?"

"Now I know I can't marry him." Annie's voice was firm. "I just can't do it. I shall never be able to trust him again."

"It'll cause a lot of talk. Can you face that?"

"I'll have to."

"It'll affect your business."

Annie shrugged and looked at Helen wryly. "I once talked about that to Frederick Hallam. The business isn't everything to me, you know. It's not even the thought of selling it that's made me change my mind about marrying Daniel. It's his lies – and the way he wanted to imprison me in his home."

Helen stood up. "If you need to talk, you know where to find me, Annie. Whatever happens, please believe that I've always been your friend, always cared about you."

Annie stared at her in puzzlement, but Helen didn't explain these cryptic words, just pulled on her gloves, kissed Annie's cheek and left.

Annie sat down and poured herself another cup of tea, more for the warmth of holding it in her hands than because she wanted to drink it. It was a while before she stirred herself, then she stood up, straightened her shoulders and went to change the notice on the salon's door back to OPEN. "Business must go on," she murmured, standing in the doorway for a moment in the late autumn sunlight. As she held her head up to its comforting caress, she added softly, "And life must go on too."

Then she took a deep breath and walked briskly back upstairs to the workroom. "Rebecca, please go and clear away the tea things." She turned to Mary. "I won't work on the wedding dress any more today. I'm not sure about the design of the flounces." She was not yet ready to tell anyone about herself and Daniel. But she was ready to go on with her life. She had done it before and could do it again. And if she was alone again, well, she could face that, too. She would still have William, still have her family around her.

Twenty-Six

NOVEMBER 1848

"You little slut!" Dorothy's shrill tones echoed round Park House and Marianne, trapped by her cousin in a corner of the morning room, winced away from the flecks of spittle that accompanied the shriek of fury, the torrent of abuse. For once, she felt unable to defend herself against her cousin's rage and guilt made her cringe back against the wall.

The sound of Dorothy's hand slapping Marianne's cheek masked the sound of the parlour door opening. Jeremy crossed the room swiftly to catch hold of his cousin's arm as it was raised for another blow. He pulled it back, then moved to stand protectively in front of his daughter. "Have you gone mad, Dorothy?"

Ellie slipped into the room behind him and closed the door. She had run downstairs as soon as she heard the shrieking start.

Dorothy tried to get past Jeremy to attack Marianne again and he held her away forcibly.

"Someone has to teach your slut of a daughter a lesson!" she panted, struggling to get away from him. "I *told* you the girl had been let run wild, but you would not support me in controlling her. Oh, no. And now see what has come of it. The shame of it all! A gentleman's daughter to behave in such a way! There are no excuses for that sort of filthy behaviour, none at all, and if you don't turn her out of the house this very hour, then you don't know your Christian duty, Jeremy Lewis."

Ellie had by that time crossed the room and taken the weeping Marianne into her arms. "Nay, love, don't take on so. We won't let her attack you again."

Jeremy was hampered by Dorothy, who was clinging to him and weeping against his chest, and this stopped him from getting to his daughter. If he let go of his cousin, she would surely fall over, so hysterical had she become. Across her head, his eyes met Ellie's, a question in them. She shrugged her shoulders and shook her head slightly. She, too, was astonished by this outburst.

"Come and sit down, love." Ellie kept her arm round Marianne's shoulders and guided her across the room, jerking her head to indicate that Jeremy should sit the sobbing Dorothy down opposite them.

"We can't discuss this until you've calmed down, Dorothy," he said, half carrying the thin body across to the sofa.

Dorothy collapsed into a heap at one end of it, making incomprehensible wailing noises into her handkerchief. Once he had let go of her, once she had realised how unkindly he was staring at her, as if it were she who had done something wrong, she made a huge effort to calm down. Now was not the time to alienate him. "I'm sorry, Jeremy. It was the – the shock. The thought that a young lady could betray her family like that. *Your* daughter, of all people. I could not bear it for your sake."

Marianne pulled away from the protective circle of Ellie's arms to face her accuser. One cheek still showed the imprint of Dorothy's bony hand upon it. The other was chalk white.

Jeremy frowned at his cousin. "I think you'd better explain

these accusations, Dorothy, and your behaviour today."

"Ask her!" Dorothy threw a triumphant glance towards the girl opposite. "She won't be able to hide it from you for much longer, anyway. And she's not a child! I've been telling and telling you, but you would not listen to me and just see what has come of it!"

Jeremy abandoned his cousin. "Do you know what she means, Marianne?"

His voice was as gentle as ever and its loving tone brought tears to his daughter's eyes. Marianne knew she was going to hurt him, but it was too late to worry about that. She had no doubt that Tom would stand by her, no doubt whatsoever, and this gave her courage. She raised her eyes and stared across at him pleadingly. "Could we discuss it in private, please, Father? I was going to tell you soon myself."

Dorothy snorted loudly. "She's a liar! As well as a whore."

Ellie jerked to her feet. "There's no need for such language, Miss Hymes. I'm sure it would be better to leave Marianne and her father alone. Let me get you a nice cup of tea. You've been—"

Red spots flared in Dorothy's sallow cheeks. "I'm not leaving. I was brought here to chaperone that – that hussy. And I would have prevented this happening had you not all spoilt her, taken her side against me. It's my duty now to make sure you're aware of what's been going on, Jeremy, and that you do something about it." Her voice rose. "*The day of retribution must come for all sinners*. I did my best for your daughter, but she takes after her mother. Only a truly wicked woman would abandon her husband and child like that. Only a truly wicked young woman would give way to her lust. *But the sinners shall be punished*."

Jeremy tried in vain to stop the voice from shrilling its abuse across the room. "Dorothy, you're overwrought. Let me—"

"Of course I'm overwrought. And so would any decent

woman be when they discovered that someone in their household had been behaving immorally." Dorothy's eyes glittered triumphantly as she pointed a quivering bony finger at Marianne. "But this is one thing she cannot hide, one thing nothing can excuse. *Be sure the Lord's wrath will find you out, for He sees all.*"

Jeremy laid his hand on her arm. "Please, Dorothy."

She wrenched her arm away. "Your precious daughter, who can do no wrong in your eyes, Jeremy, is *with child*!" Her expression was triumphant, not shocked.

Jeremy looked across at Marianne. "My dear, she doesn't know what she's saying. She's too upset to—"

Marianne suddenly ran out of patience with them all. "Oh, she does know, and she's right, Father. I am with child. But I'm proud of it, not ashamed. I *want* the child."

"*You hear*!" Dorothy's voice rose again. "Jezebel! Strumpet! She shall burn in hell, Jeremy. Oh, yes, the sinner shall burn. Especially a sinner who has no shame like her."

Jeremy was staring at his daughter as if he had been struck by lightning, his mouth open in shock, his face drained of all colour.

Marianne sank down on to the sofa and buried her face in her hands, unable to watch the pain etch its way into his face. "Don't look at me like that, Father. I love him. And he loves me. You might be able to live without love, but I can't. And I'd do it all again. I don't regret a thing."

Dorothy shrieked in outrage and burst into loud hysterical sobbing again, building up to a crescendo that had her thrashing around like a fish on a hook.

Jeremy did not seem able to move, let alone speak. He made no attempt to help his cousin, just sat staring across at his daughter.

It was left to Ellie to deal with the situation, because she had to protect the two people she loved most in the world.

'We can't discuss things with Miss Hymes making that noise. If you'll go and get some laudanum, Dr Lewis, we'll give your cousin some and take her up to bed. She's overwrought." She turned and gave the girl she loved like a daughter a quick hug. "Sit down and wait for me, Marianne. We can't talk about it with her shrieking like a banshee."

Marianne gave Ellie a quivering smile. "Are you still going to talk to me, now you know?"

"Of course I am, love. And so is your father, once he's over the shock."

Marianne leaned back against the sofa, closing her eyes to blot out the unlovely sight of a scrawny middle-aged woman having violent hysterics, or a father staring at her as if she had broken his heart. After a minute, she put her hands over her ears and waited for the ululations to stop.

Ellie laid a hand on the doctor's arm and gave it a shake, murmuring the word, "Laudanum!" again.

Jeremy jerked into awareness of what needed to be done. He left the room swiftly and returned holding a cup with a spout. He had to force the liquid between Dorothy's teeth, and then they all waited for it to take effect, and for those dreadful shrieking and moaning noises to die down. He looked across at Marianne and tried but failed to smile encouragement.

When Miss Hymes began to quieten, he turned to Ellie. "Would you fetch Sam? Tell him I'll need help carrying her upstairs."

Ellie hesitated, her eyes going to the hunched-up figure on the sofa. "I want to be with you when you talk to Marianne, Dr Lewis. If there's any blame, I must share it. I should have been more careful – I've been neglecting her lately. So I won't let her take all the blame."

He gave her a bitter smile. "You look as fierce as any mother defending her young."

Ellie looked at Marianne again and her eyes softened. "Sometimes I feel like her mother."

"God knows, you're the only one she's ever really had." Dorothy moaned and scrabbled at him, so he gave Ellie a push. "Go and get Sam. I won't do anything until you come back." He looked across the room and his doctor's instincts took over. "Put your head between your knees, Marianne. It's the shock that's making you feel faint. I'll be back in a minute."

She stared at him as if she didn't understand what he was saying.

"Please, darling. Head between your knees."

At the word "darling", her lips quivered, then she dropped her head towards her lap.

Ellie went with the two men as they carried Miss Hymes up to her room. She threw a quilt over the angular body and then left Sam guarding Miss Hymes's door. "No one is to go in to her!" she ordered. "No one!"

"It should rightly be another woman staying with her," he protested.

"We don't want the other servants to hear what she's saying. Look, I'm needed downstairs. Please, Father, just stay with her. I won't be long."

"Very well."

As Ellie slipped back into the parlour, she breathed, "Thank God!" Jeremy had his arm round his daughter, who was sobbing tiredly into his chest. Ellie went across to sit on the other side of Marianne, took hold of her hand and patted it briskly. "Now love, let's calm down and talk it all over quietly. There's been enough screaming and crying from that fool upstairs."

Marianne stared at her blankly for a moment, then let out her breath in a long sigh. A shadow of a smile crossed her face. "She is a fool, but," she gulped, "she was right in one thing. I – I am with child. At least, I think I am." Her hand was clutching Ellie's so tightly that Ellie's fingers had gone white.

Ellie waited for Jeremy to speak and when he didn't, she asked, "Whose is it, then? Or need I ask?" keeping her tone matter-of-fact.

"It's Tom's, of course. Surely you guessed?"

"I guessed how you felt about him, yes, and how he felt about you, but I trusted him not to – I thought he would look after you."

"He tried to. It's as much my fault as his, you know. I wanted him to love me. And he was the one who was sorry about it afterwards, not me. It was my fault, too, that we did it again, and I'm not sorry about that, either!" She stopped with a gasp. "I'm sorry, Father. I – I've never wanted to hurt you. But I do love him so much."

Tears were trickling down Jeremy's face. "I've failed you, neglected you."

"We can go on all day, blaming ourselves." Ellie's tone was sharp. "It won't do any good. We have to think what to do next. Couldn't you – help her to get rid of it, Doctor?"

Jeremy stared at her. "Kill the child, do you mean?"

Marianne jumped up off the couch and stood there, shivering with horror. "You can't mean that, Ellie!"

"Oh, I do. You're too young to have your life spoiled." She remembered how Annie had suffered.

"Well, I won't let you do it! I *want* Tom's child! And he'll want it, too." She was out of the door before either of them could say anything, running from the house and across town with the swiftness of youth.

Jeremy moved to follow her, but as he got to the front door, Ellie caught hold of his arm, "If you run after her, the whole town will wonder what's wrong."

He stared down at her so blindly that she was more afraid for him than for Marianne. "You're not going to – to cause a fuss, are you?" She felt him sag against her for a moment.

Jeremy took strength from the warmth and steadiness of

405

Ellie's body against his. He would have liked to put his arm round her and hold her close, to draw comfort from her, but that could not be. His shook his head and straightened up. "No. It's too late for fusses. We must just make the best of things. And at least Marianne seems sure that Tom will want to marry her."

Ellie kept hold of his arm. He looked so bereft, her heart ached for him. "I'm sure he will, too. I've seen the way he looks at Marianne, like she's the most precious thing on earth. Oh, he'll want to marry her all right. But it's not a good way to start a marriage and people will talk when the baby's born early."

"Let them talk. It's Marianne who counts. And the baby."

"You'll make a good grandfather," she said softly. "I'm sorry I said that about getting rid of the child. I was only thinking of Marianne."

"I know." He squeezed her hand briefly and straightened up, alone again. "Now, I must follow her and see Tom Gibson."

"Take her cloak with you. She'll need it coming back. It's a cold day. And Doctor—"

"Yes?"

"Don't be too hard on Tom. He really does love her. You can see it in his face."

"If you saw it, then I should have seen it, too." Jeremy caught hold of her hand as she held the cloak out to him. "What would we all do without you, Ellie Peters? You make even this seem so – so normal."

"Well, it is normal, isn't it? Girls have always got themselves into trouble with the men they love. What's not normal is people like your cousin who have no love in them, only spite and bitterness."

He was staring down at her, his eyes showing the love and admiration he dared not express. "Yes. But no one could accuse you of that, Ellie. You're full of love. I only wish—

He bit off what he had been going to say.

She watched him walk down the street. "I wish, too," she said softly, then she straightened her shoulders and went upstairs to check on Miss Hymes, who was now snoring softly in her bed.

"What's happened?" Sam asked.

"Miss Marianne's in trouble." She patted her belly suggestively.

"A child, you mean?"

She nodded.

"Nay, she's nobbut a lass."

"She's nearly twenty, Father. And Tom Gibson will marry her."

Sam's expression was disapproving. "Them Gibsons do nowt but cause trouble."

Ellie's mouth dropped open. "How can you say that, Father? What have the Gibsons ever done to you?"

"Enough." He was remembering a time when seventeen-year-old Annie had demanded money from Matt, who had got drunk for the only time in his life when he found that the girl he loved and was to marry had been raped. While drunk he had told people that Annie was expecting a child. The money she had demanded had been for betraying her condition and making her lose her job, and Sam could understand her desperate need for the wages she would have earned, understand but not forgive easily the way she had gone about getting it.

But his wife had never understood. From then onwards, Elizabeth had hated Annie Gibson, and that hatred had come between her and their daughter Ellie, who had remained stubbornly loyal to her friend. Well, she and Annie had worked together in Dr Lewis's house for years and they were closer than most sisters. But his wife's hatred had also made her refuse to see Dr Lewis when she became ill, and that Sam could not help blaming on the Gibsons. If you never tried to get help, you always wondered whether you had failed someone, as he felt to have failed Elizabeth.

He also remembered a talk he'd had with Matt only the previous year, when he had asked his eldest son why he had never wed. It was one of the things that had preyed on Elizabeth's mind and it seemed sad to Sam that while some of his children had wed and had children in their turn, they had moved away from Bilsden, depriving him of his grandchildren. The children who had stayed in Bilsden had not made any effort to marry, not Matt, not Ellie and not Lily. He sometimes watched little children playing in the street and ached for grandchildren of his own living nearby. So one day he'd just asked Matt straight out what had gone wrong.

"I've never found anyone else that I could love," Matt had said simply, in reply. "Annie spoiled me for other women. I was a fool not to stand by her. I know that now. But it's too late. She'd never have me, now."

And here was another Gibson causing trouble for poor Miss Marianne. Oh, Sam knew they never meant it, but nonetheless, they seemed to leave a trail of troubles behind them, that family did. His wife, in her rare moments of lucidity, still blamed Annie for both Matt's and Ellie's unmarried state. He had listened to her ranting and raving about Annie and the Gibsons for hour after hour. And maybe she was right, in some ways at least. Certainly, Tom Gibson had done wrong in this. Miss Marianne was young for her age and Tom had been wrong to take advantage of her innocence.

Sam shook his head. Well, it was done now. If Tom repented, the Lord would surely forgive him, and he, Sam, must try to do the same. Like his daughter, Sam had no doubt that Tom would want to marry Miss Marianne.

That day Annie did not go to the salon, but sent a message to ask Daniel to come and talk to her at home, urgently. She waited with grim determination for him to arrive and when he would have taken her in his arms, she stepped quickly backwards. "Don't touch me!"

The smile left his face. "What's wrong?"

"Two ladies came to visit me in my salon. The Misses Brierley."

His smile flickered for a moment, then he raised one eyebrow. "What's that supposed to mean?"

"Don't play games with me, Daniel. You know the name. You've been negotiating with them about my salon."

"It's always a good idea to seize the moment. They want to buy. We want to sell."

"*We* don't want to sell."

"Ah, love, we've been through all that. You know you won't be able to run the salon once we're married." He moved across to take her into his arms, but she was as rigid as a wooden doll and when she pulled away from him he let his arms fall.

"The worst thing of all, as far as I'm concerned, is that you lied to me when you took my account books." Her face was pale, but her voice was steady. "I can't bear that, Daniel."

"Ah, I'm sorry, love. I'd never have hurt you willingly. I don't know what got into me." He stretched out a hand towards her. "Say you'll forgive me."

She took another step backwards and stared at him, head on one side, considering. "How easily the apologies roll off your tongue."

The smile faded. "For heaven's sake, Annie, let's sit down and talk this over calmly."

"I am calm. I was upset yesterday when I found out, and I was upset during the night as I lay awake thinking about us, but today I'm quite calm. Sad, but calm." She walked across to stand by the fireplace, staring into the flames, then she pulled the ring off her finger. "Take this back, Daniel. I can't marry you now." She had put it into his hand before he realised what she was doing, then she returned to stand by the fire.

"Annie!" He stepped towards her, but stopped when he saw how chill her expression was. "In God's name, you can't mean that!"

"Oh, I do mean it. If you'd lie to me and deceive me before we got married, you'd do the same afterwards. I won't live with the fear of that. And besides," she paused, then shrugged, "we both know that I don't really love you, not the way a wife should. You pushed me into getting married, and it might have worked, because you're a good-looking man and can be charming when you want, but it can't work now. Not when I've seen how easily you can lie to me."

"Annie, I'll never lie to you again. I swear I won't!"

She just shook her head. "It's no good. I won't be able to trust you, you see. Leave it at that, Daniel. Just take your ring and go."

Anger was beginning to replace the coaxing expression and tone of voice. He glared at her, fists clenched against his sides. "Just like that!"

She nodded. "Yes."

"Do you even have a heart inside that pretty shell?"

She swallowed, but could not defend herself. She knew there was something wrong with her. That realisation had racked her throughout the night. She was lacking as much as he was. But it didn't change things between them. She could only shake her head and then, when he said nothing, she managed to say through lips that felt numb, "Let's at least part with dignity. Please."

He gave an angry snort. "Oh, no! Dignity be damned! If you do this to me, Annie Gibson, I'll make very sure that I'm not the only one who suffers."

"What on earth do you mean by that?"

He made one last try, forcing a tender expression on to his face. He seized her hand and pulled her towards him. He was strong enough to ignore her struggles, so she stopped struggling and just stood quiescent next to him as he said, "Annie, please, just give me the chance to make it up to you."

"No. I can't. It's over."

The smile faded and a bitter expression replaced it, then anger and disappointment exploded out of him. "By Christ, you're a cold fish! I'm well out of things there, at least. A man needs a warm and willing partner in bed. But if you want us to part with *dignity*," he said the word with immense scorn, "then you'll have to make it worth my while."

"What do you mean?" The words came out as a whisper, so shocked was she by his change of tone.

"I mean you'll have to give me some money, to help me stay in business, for if it gets known that you're not going to marry me, the creditors will be buzzing around me within the day."

Her voice was harsh. "Creditors! How can you possibly have creditors? You've only been in business a short time. What happened to all the money you earned on the railways?"

He held up the ring. "Well, this didn't come cheaply, for a start, and there are sundry other unpaid bills. It costs a lot more to set up as a builder than I'd expected, especially when you have a family like mine hanging round your neck, always wanting something. I needed your money quite desperately, Annie. Without it, I'm ruined – and if it comes to that, if I am going to be ruined, I'll make sure that I take your good name with me."

Her lips were white, her whole body rigid with incredulity. She felt as if she had strayed into a nightmare. "What do you mean by that?"

"I mean, my *dear* Annie, that I'll tell the world how you and I were lovers. How you can't get enough of it. They won't like to think of their favourite modiste behaving like that. You've fought all your life to keep your good name, have you not? Well, now you're going to have to pay me to keep it."

She felt as though the room was spinning around her and her voice seemed to come from a great distance. "You can't be serious!" But the expression on his face was so vicious that she knew he was, even before he replied.

"Oh, I am, Annie. I'm very serious."

"Then you – you can never have loved me, either."

He gave a snort of amusement. "What's love? A whimsy for rich people who have nothing better to do than sigh over each other. I fancied you, Annie. You're a beautiful woman with an attractive body. You'd have made me a good wife, a good mother for my children. And best of all, you had money. What more could any man want?"

"Love." Her voice was a mere scrape of a sound. "A man could want love, Daniel. Have you seen the way my dad looks at Kathy? That's not a whimsy; that's real. And love is what every normal woman wants, too. I'm not that different to other women." She fought to stay calm. She would not let him see how he'd hurt her. "How much money do you need?"

He named a figure that made her head reel. It would take all her money, every bit of it. She'd even have to sell the cottages to meet that price. "I don't have that much."

"But you could raise it."

"Perhaps." She had no intention of paying him, but she needed to buy time, to see if there was some way she could stop him from carrying out his threat.

"Well, don't take too long to do your thinking, Annie. And in the meantime, don't say a word to anyone about us not getting married. It's keeping the creditors at bay, you see. I repeat, if you do ruin me, then I won't hesitate to ruin you in return."

She felt desolate, destroyed, but she nodded and remained standing there, willing herself not to break down in front of him.

"It'll be worth it to keep your good name," he mocked. "You care more about that and your little business than you'll ever care for a man."

"I'll let you know."

"Don't keep me waiting too long." He turned and walked out.

Only when the front door had closed behind him did she shudder and sink down into the nearest chair. After a few minutes' reflection, she made her way towards the kitchen.

At the sight of her white, strained face, Kathy rushed across to put an arm round her. "What's wrong now, love?"

Annie stared at her for a moment as if she did not recognise her. "My engagement is over. And Daniel Connor is threatening me."

"Threatening you!"

"Yes. He wants my money. Would you go and fetch Tom for me, Kathy? Please? I need to see him."

Kathy nodded and pulled off her apron. When she saw Annie's blank expression, she picked up Philip John, wrapped him in a shawl and took him with her.

Annie didn't even notice the child. She watched Kathy go, then went back to sit in front of the parlour fire. She felt numb, unable to think clearly. Tom was the only one who might be able to help her to deal with Daniel Connor. She did not think she could bear to face him again on her own. All she knew was that she did not intend to give him her money. A little money, perhaps, in the last resort. But she would not destroy her business and abandon her security for him. She had worked too hard for it.

Then Annie had another thought. Frederick. He was back. She knew that. She had met him once or twice in the street and received a bow and polite greeting, nothing more. She had been disappointed when he did not come to see her, but not surprised. He knew she was engaged to Daniel. And as an

engaged woman she had no right to feel so disappointed at not
seeing Fredrick, no right at all. Just as she had no right to ask
him for help now, much as she longed to.

Twenty-Seven

MARIANNE AND TOM

As Marianne ran through the streets, she became aware that people were staring at her and for a while she slowed down into a rapid walk. But she was so afraid of pursuit that she kept turning to peer over her shoulder and she did not respond to people's greetings because she simply did not notice anyone else. She knew from her work in her father's clinic that poor women sometimes got rid of unwanted babies, though she was not sure exactly how. But this baby wasn't unwanted and no one was going to take it away from her. No one. Not even her father.

When she saw the junk yard at the end of the street, she broke into a run again, terrified that something might stop her at the last minute from reaching Tom. By the time she pounded through the gates, her breath was sobbing in her throat. Tom, who had caught sight of her through a window, came rushing out of the office, leaving a customer standing there open-mouthed. She flung herself into his arms and burst into tears.

Hearing the clatter of footsteps and the sound of a woman's weeping, John came hurrying out of the main shed. He stopped to stare at Tom and Marianne in amazement.

"Can you finish off dealing with Jim Barnes for me, Dad?" Tom's arm was around Marianne's waist and she was clinging to him as if he were her only hope of salvation. He didn't wait for a reply, but led her round the corner to what they called the tea place, a cosy little room with a fire. The family ate their lunches here and kept a kettle near the boil all the time. He could feel Marianne trembling, but he said nothing until he had her sitting down. "Shh, love. Calm down and tell me what's wrong."

She sat down, but the tears were still rolling down her cheeks. "My father's found out." She clutched his hand.

"Found out about what?"

"About you and me. And – oh, Tom, I haven't had a chance to tell you yet, but I'm going to have a baby."

"What!" His hand tightened on her arm. "Are you sure about that, love?"

The smile shone through her tears like a ray of sunlight. "Oh, yes. Well, as sure as anyone can be at this stage. It's early days, but I'm feeling sick in the mornings and I've missed twice."

"Well, I'll be damned!" A grin crept over his face. "A baby, eh?"

"Are you pleased?"

His answer was to crush her in his arms, murmur soft endearments against her cheek and cover her whole face with kisses.

And that was how Jeremy Lewis found them. As he stood in the doorway, the fierceness of his anger abated at the sight of them so closely embraced and most especially at the sight of the joy on Tom Gibson's face. You could not doubt that Tom loved Marianne, or that he was happy about the child. Jeremy stood there for a while, then, when they didn't notice him, he rapped on the door and cleared his throat.

Tom swung round. "Dr Lewis! Won't you come and sit down?" His eyes were wary and he kept his arm protectively round Marianne's waist.

"I'm not getting rid of the baby," Marianne threw at her father.

"I'd never ask you to, darling," said Jeremy. "You didn't wait to hear my answer to Ellie."

She looked at him, hope warring with anxiety in her face.

"I'm rather looking forward to becoming a grandfather." He held his arms out and she hurled herself into them, laughing and weeping at the same time.

Tom watched them for a minute, then went to swing the kettle over the middle of the fire. "You both look as if you need a good hot cup of tea."

"I take it you're going to do the right thing by my daughter?" Jeremy asked, letting go of Marianne and trying not to feel sad as she immediately went back to nestle against Tom. Watching her, Jeremy could not withhold a sigh. Already he had lost his daughter to the other man. The young couple's closeness made him feel not only old, but also cheated. It seemed only yesterday that he, too, had been looking forward to having a child of his own, several children. And then had been denied them.

"I'd have been round to see you about us before now, but I wasn't sure you'd want someone from Salem Street for a son-in-law," Tom said, feeling a sense of relief to have it all out in the open. "I was waiting until I was a bit better established before I asked you. And," his arm tightened around Marianne, "I'm sorry it had to be this way. It wasn't what I'd intended and I'm not proud of myself."

"I don't care about that." Marianne raised one hand to caress his face.

"Well, I do!" said Tom. "I've told you before, love, that I want everything to be perfect for us."

417

John Gibson, having got rid of the customer, came and poked his head in the doorway. "Everything all right here?"

Tom turned round and beamed at him. "Very right, Dad. Me an' Marianne are going to get married."

"Well, now!" said John, astonished. "That's you an' our Annie both in the one year. Eh, I wish your mother could have lived to see this day." He held out his hands to Marianne, who took it upon herself to give him a hug. "I couldn't be happier, lass!" he said kissing her soft cheek.

"And it seems, John, that you and I are about to become joint grandfathers," said Jeremy, trying to suppress a feeling of jealousy at the radiant faces of the young couple. Annabelle had never looked at him like that. In fact, no one had ever looked at him like that in his whole life. For some reason, Ellie's face came into his mind, but he banished it with a sigh. He was not free to think of other women.

When Kathy hurried into the yard, carrying young Philip on one hip, she found everyone except Mark sitting in the tea place chatting over cups of steaming liquid. She stopped in the doorway, reluctant to banish the look of quiet joy from John's face, then she pulled herself together. "I'm sorry to disturb you, but there's trouble. Annie needs you, Tom. And quickly, too. She's waiting at home."

Tom jerked to his feet. "What's wrong?"

"I think you'd best get home an' let her tell you that. Daniel Connor was round an' she says the engagement's off."

Jeremy stepped forward to put his arm round his daughter. "You get off, Tom. I'll take Marianne back to Park House. Will you come round tonight to discuss arrangements, though?"

"Try to keep me away!" Tom's irrepressible grin peeped out again. "You'll soon be sick of the sight of me at Park House." He strode across the yard, his expression becoming thoughtful as soon as he was out of Marianne's sight. Only something very serious would have made Annie send for him like this. Why had she broken her engagement?

Kathy waited until Jeremy and Marianne had left, then turned back to her husband.

"What's up?" John asked as he tickled his son's cheek and admired the child as if he hadn't seen him only a few hours previously.

"Annie's quarrelled with Daniel Connor. They'll definitely not be getting wed now. An' John – he turned real nasty."

"Danny did?"

"Yes."

"Nay, whatever's got into him?" He shook his head. "You allus said you didn't think he was the right one for her, didn't you?"

"Yes, but I'd never have believed he could get that nasty. When she told me about it I felt like smacking him one on the face myself!" She related what had happened, and then had to restrain John from going along to Daniel's yard at the end of High Street that very minute to knock a bit of sense into the fellow. Violence wasn't the solution. It wouldn't seal Daniel Connor's lips.

When Tom burst into Netherleigh Cottage, he found Annie still sitting in the parlour, pale but determined. Like Kathy, he could hardly credit Daniel's behaviour when she told him. "Well, you're not paying him anything," he said at once. "If necessary, I'll find someone to fix him up good and proper."

"Oh, no, you won't! We're not risking all we've achieved. I've told you before that I won't have you breaking the law."

"How the hell else can we stop him?"

She bowed her head. "I'm not sure that we can. If it were less money, I might be inclined to – to help him a bit. But it'd take everything I have to give him what he wants. I'd have to sell the cottages, perhaps even my share in the junk yard."

"Well, I wouldn't let you give him anything. Not one farthing." Tom opened his mouth, hesitated, then said. "There's something else you should know about him, love. He's been visiting Janie Fellows, the sister of his foreman, at night. The person who told me reckons that the two of them have known each other for a long time, since before he came back to Bilsden."

"Are you sure?"

"Yes. Very sure. This Janie's a right flaunting piece of goods. Apparently Danny isn't the only one who visits her."

Annie's fists were clenched in her lap. "Why didn't you tell me about that before?"

"I wasn't sure if it was true. I had to get proof before I said anything or you'd not have listened to me."

She shuddered. "And all the time Daniel was kissing me, telling me I was the only woman for him, he was – was—" Bile rose up her throat.

Tom took a deep breath. Best distract her, if he could. "Er – there's something else you ought to know."

"What more can there be?"

He put his arm round her. "This is a bit of good news, love. Well, I think it is. Marianne an' me are going to get wed."

She managed a faint smile at that. "Dr Lewis has agreed, then?"

"He had to. Marianne's expecting my child. How do you fancy being an auntie?"

That jerked her out of her apathy. "Tom Gibson, you haven't gone and got Marianne Lewis pregnant?"

He shrugged. "I knew you wouldn't like it. I didn't mean to get her into trouble, but you know what it's like sometimes."

Her face tightened and there was such a look of pain in it that Tom could have kicked himself for his clumsiness. "No. I don't know what it's like," she said bitterly. "I think there must be something wrong with me." She bit off the words of reproach. What right had she to reproach anyone? She had made a complete and utter mess of her own life. She had been

taken in by a handsome face and cozening ways. Thinking of
Daniel Connor lying with another woman while he was courting
her made her feel sick with disgust. And every time she thought
of him trying to blackmail her, trying to take her hard-earned
money away, she felt furious.

Tom hugged her again. "Eh, love, we'll work something
out."

"I can't see how."

He could feel the tension in her body. "Neither can I at the
moment, but we've always managed before. Give me some
time to think about it. I'll come up with something. You'll
see."

"Mmm." But as she watched him leave, Annie felt anger
and bitterness still boiling within her and she could find nothing
to give her hope. Nothing. And then the anger abated, leaving
her feeling very tired, more weary than ever before in her life.
She did not attempt to go to the salon, just sat staring into the
fire. What was wrong with her that she could not love someone
or find someone to love her? And what had she done to deserve
all this? Hadn't she had enough trouble in her life?

When Tom was half-way back to the yard, he met Helen
Kenderby coming out of the house of one of her father's
parishioners. He nodded and would have passed by, but she
stopped him.

"You look upset. Is something wrong, Mr Gibson?"

"There is – a problem."

She laid a hand on his arm to detain him. "I saw Mr Connor
earlier, coming from the direction of Netherleigh Cottage. He
didn't see me. He looked upset, too. Is Annie all right?"

Tom snorted. "No. And it's all his fault."

Helen did not let go of his arm. "Would you have a moment
to tell me about it? I care greatly about Annie." And about
Daniel Connor, too, heaven help her. He was, quite simply,
the most attractive man Helen had ever met and she lusted

after him in a way that disgusted her sometimes. A man who was betrothed to her best friend, for heaven's sake!

"I'd rather—"

"Please."

"Let's just say that the marriage will not now be taking place, Miss Kenderby. And that if Connor does what he's threatened, then Annie will be ruined."

"*What*!"

Tom regretted his outburst. "Look, I didn't mean to say anything. I was just so – so furious with that bas— er, with him."

"What has he threatened?" She clutched his arm. "Please. You must tell me!"

"He's threatened to tell folk that Annie was his mistress if she doesn't give him some money. A lot of money. His business is in trouble."

"I see. Would it be any help if I went round to see Annie?"

He shook his head. "Not at the moment. She's too upset. Excuse me, I have to get back to the yard." He raised his hat to her and moved on.

Even after Tom had disappeared round the corner, Helen stood staring after him and it was not until a passer-by murmured, "Good morning, Miss Kenderby!" that she realised where she was and moved on.

Tom returned to the yard, but could not settle to work. A couple of hours later, he stopped in the middle of a sentence and stared at Mark. "That's it!"

"What?"

"There's something I need to do. I have to go out. Keep an eye on the yard for me." Without further explanation Tom strode off down the street, his expression grim and determined. He knew Frederick Hallam had returned to Bilsden, and he had seen how Hallam looked at Annie sometimes. This was a case for desperate measures, and if anyone in town had the power to prevent Daniel from ruining Annie, it was Hallam.

At the gate of Hallam's mill, he demanded to see the owner. The gateman passed him on to Matt Peters.

"It's Mr Hallam himself I need to see," Tom insisted.

Matt shuffled some papers and then pushed them aside. "I usually deal with everyday matters for him."

"Then you won't be the one to deal with this." Tom saw the frown on Matt's face and pulled himself together. You got nowhere by annoying folk. "Sorry! It really is Mr Hallam himself I need to see. It's a personal matter. And urgent." He had no intention of revealing his business to Matt Peters. As far as Tom was concerned, Matt had let Annie down when she needed him and he would never forgive him for that, or trust him with her affairs again. Relations between the two of them had been very stiff for years. His father had forgiven Matt, had said it was water under the bridge, but Tom never forgot an insult or a wrong done to him or his family. Besides, like the other lads of his generation, Tom had been jealous about the way Matt Peters had been helped and trained by Frederick Hallam.

"I'm afraid I don't usually allow—"

Tom spoke through gritted teeth. "It's Annie. She needs his help."

"Annie! What's wrong?"

"I'll tell Mr Hallam that, not you."

"I too have Annie's welfare at heart," Matt said stiffly.

Tom slammed his fist down on the shiny desk top. "Well, if that's true, just go an' tell Mr Hallam that Annie's in trouble and needs his help. See what *he* says to that." He saw that Matt was still hesitating and added savagely, "If you won't do it, I'll go an' find him myself if I have to punch you senseless first to get past."

Matt drew himself up. "Very well, I'll do as your ask, but please wait here. Mr Hallam may have someone with him.

I'm sure your sister wouldn't thank you for bandying her name about in front of other people."

Stiff-necked bastard! thought Tom as he watched him leave. I'm glad she didn't marry him.

Two minutes later, Matt was back. "Mr Hallam will see you." He ushered Tom into Frederick's office. "Mr Gibson, sir."

"Thank you, Peters." Once Matt had left, Frederick didn't waste time on civilities. "What's wrong with Annie?"

"She's in trouble. Bad trouble. There's not much I can do to help her, but you might be able to do something." He looked at Hallam thoughtfully and added, "If you don't she may well be ruined."

"Tell me about it, then."

Tom hesitated, not sure how much to tell him.

"I'll help her if I can, Gibson. Never doubt that. I think very highly of your sister."

Tom nodded, satisfied. He had suspected for a while that Hallam and Annie were on rather closer terms than was generally known. Rebecca had innocently let a few things drop about early morning visits to the salon, but unlike the rest of the family, Tom had not been taken in by excuses about the roof leaking or damp in the cellars. He knew that the row of shops was perfectly sound. And he had never forgotten how Hallam had helped Annie when Lady Darrington's dress had been ruined. He had supposed then that Hallam wanted Annie for his mistress, but he knew that Annie would not agree to that, so he had left her to deal with Hallam as she thought best.

"It's Daniel Connor, Mr Hallam. Annie's decided that she doesn't want to marry him. She found something out about him which upset her. Let her tell you about that herself. But apparently Connor turned nasty and threatened her. And if he carries out his threats, she'll be ruined."

Frederick got up from his desk and pushed the chair back

so violently that it fell over. "I'll go and see her at once." He strode round the desk, yelling, "Boy!"

A lad poked his head round the door. "Sir?"

"Tell them to get my carriage out. As quickly as they can."

Footsteps pounded off across the yard.

Frederick went into the next office, heedless that he had slammed the fine new panelled door right back on its hinges. "Peters! I'm going out. Deal with anything that turns up here as you see fit. I don't think I'll be back today." Only then did Frederick notice that Tom was still standing in the doorway to his own office. "Leave it to me, Gibson!" he said curtly. "You get back to your business."

Matt and Tom both stared after him as he strode across the mill yard.

"Is Annie hurt?" Matt ventured.

"Not physically, no. But *another* fellow has just let her down." Tom spun round on his heel and followed the mill owner across the yard, leaving Matt to sit and chew the wooden handle of his new patent steel-nibbed pen and then ruin the nib as he stabbed it in and out of the inkwell. Bitter thoughts scalded through him. He had forfeited the right to help Annie years ago, but never had he regretted it more. Like Tom, he suspected that Hallam was interested in Annie, and like Tom, he believed that she would never agree to become his employer's mistress. But who knew whether this trouble might change that? It might put her in Hallam's power. And Matt would not be able to help her, even if he wanted to. Not against a man as powerful as Frederick Hallam.

At Netherleigh Cottage, Frederick jumped down from the carriage and yelled at the coachman to stay right there and be ready to move off at a minute's notice. He didn't wait to be asked inside, but knocked and immediately pushed open the front door, calling, "Where are you, Annie?"

"I'm in here."

As he walked into the parlour, Annie jumped to her feet. "Frederick, what are you doing here?"

"Your brother told me you were in trouble, so I came to see if I could help." As he strode across the room, he could see the tears trembling in her eyes. He took her hand and drew her towards him. When she tried to pull away, his grip tightened. "Let's sit down, mmm?" His daughter would have stared to hear the tenderness in his voice and to see the concern on his face. "Tell me what's happened, my dear. Tell me everything. I'm sure I'll be able to think of something to help you."

"Oh, Frederick, I—" Her voice wobbled and she took a deep breath, trying not to break down. She had forgotten how comfortable she felt with him, what a rock of reliability he always seemed. Since his return from his travels, his cosy early-morning visits had stopped and on the few occasions they had met in the street, she had sensed a coolness in him, a distance that had not been there before. She knew why. A married woman could not have male friends. But she had missed their little chats, missed them quite dreadfully. It had seemed to her sometimes that one had to give up everything one enjoyed when one got married.

"You look as if you've had a nasty shock." He did not say that Tom had told him something about her troubles. He just left it to her to tell him in her own way.

She tried to speak, but a tear spilled out and sobs thickened in her throat.

His hand was gentle on hers. "Take your time, Annie. It doesn't matter what's wrong. I'm here to help you."

She could not hold the tears back any longer then. She felt as if everything were happening very slowly as he took her in his arms and held her against his chest. The agony of the betrayal welled out of her and sobs shook her body. And she could not have said whether she was weeping for what Daniel had done to her or for all the other pain that she had lived

426

through. She only knew that in Frederick's arms she felt safe, safe and loved.

He sat there and patted her back, making soothing sounds and rocking her a little, just letting her weep out her pain. As he stared down at the glowing auburn hair and the shaking shoulders, a great wave of tenderness overwhelmed him, followed by another wave of fury that anyone should have hurt her so much.

It took a while for Annie's sobbing to lessen. "I'm s-sorry." She tried to pull away, but Frederick's arm tightened around her.

"What for?"

"For c-crying all over you like this."

"That's what friends are for. Real friends, anyway. Now, tell me what's wrong. Tell me everything. We'll work something out together. See if we don't."

Those involved said afterwards that they had never seen so many troubles pile up at once. When Tom went round to see Jeremy Lewis that evening, he found Marianne sitting waiting for him in the parlour, demurely clad in palest pink. She did not dare throw herself into his arms under the severe gaze of Ellie, who was far less forgiving than her father about this trouble, but the way she looked across at Tom spoke her love as clearly as if the words had been spoken aloud.

"Dr Lewis has been called away," said Ellie, interrupting their unspoken communion. "I'm here in his place to discuss the arrangements."

Marianne patted the seat beside her on the sofa and Tom, after a quick nod from Ellie, went and sat down. Under the cover of her full skirts, Marianne's hand slipped into his as he said, "Father received a telegram late this morning. It came all the way from Brighton in only a few hours, would you believe? Apparently my mother is seriously ill. He's had to leave for the south. If he caught the train in Manchester, he'll be in London by now."

"It doesn't rain but it pours, does it?" said Tom. He would have liked to hug her, but one glance at Ellie's face stopped that impulse before his arm had done more than twitch. Ellie was only a year or two older than he was, but tonight her basilisk stare quelled even his ebullient nature.

"Dr Lewis has asked me to discuss the wedding arrangements with you." Ellie's voice was as chill as her expression. She still felt angry every time she thought of what Tom Gibson had done to her girl, whether they loved each other and whether both had been willing participants or not. He was old enough and experienced enough to know better.

"I can think of nothing in the world I'd like more than to wed Marianne," he said firmly. "How we do it is up to you ladies. Just tell me what you think best and I'll do it."

Ellie's stern expression relaxed just a trifle. "Right, then. The sooner the wedding takes place, the better, for obvious reasons. But don't think you'll fool anybody, Tom Gibson. Folk are bound to talk once the baby is born. They can all add the dates up. The main thing tonight is to decide where you get married, the Methodist Chapel or St Mark's. Dr Lewis has no preferences about that. He says he'll leave it to you two. All he asks is that you'll arrange to have the first banns called next Sunday."

Tom turned to Marianne. "Where do you want to get married, then, love?"

"I think the chapel would be best. I – I don't think Parson Kenderby will be very accommodating. He's been very strange lately. I've hated listening to his sermons. He seems to be preaching only hellfire and damnation. I don't want him to marry us."

"I'll go and see Mr Hinchcliffe first thing tomorrow morning, then. He doesn't preach hellfire and damnation, no since he got married. He comes to town most mornings, in case any of his congregation need to see him, so I'll send a lad round to the chapel to watch out for him. But Mr Hinchcliffe will want to see you as well, I should think, Marianne. And your father."

Tom looked so happy as he exchanged glances with Marianne that Ellie could not help snapping, "And while you're up that end of town, you should go inside the chapel to pray for the Lord's forgiveness for what you've done, Tom Gibson."

Tom had had enough. "You can just stop nagging at me like that, Ellie Peters! It's not the end of the world. We were going to get wed anyway."

She was unmoved. "It'll be a long time before I forgive you, a very long time. Marianne is like a daughter to me, an' I never thought a Gibson would take advantage of her like that. I thought I could trust a Gibson. And whatever you do about it now, folk will always remember that you had to get wed quickly and why. That's the way the world is."

Tom sighed and sagged against the back of the sofa. Marianne's smile faded and she bowed her head. Ellie had not stopped scolding her all day. Not just about what she had done, but about how she had hurt her father.

"Now," Ellie went on, satisfied that she had brought the seriousness of Tom's offence home to him, "I have a piece of paper here, signed by the doctor, giving Marianne permission to get married. You'll need that to show to Mr Hinchcliffe. The doctor might not be able to get back to Bilsden straight away if Mrs Lewis is bad. If Mr Hinchcliffe wishes, I can go to see him with Marianne in Dr Lewis's place."

"Right. I'll find out what he wants."

"And you'll arrange to get wed as soon as the banns have been called."

"Yes, ma'am!" Tom gave a mock salute. Nothing kept him down for long.

Ellie was not to be teased into a smile. "That's all that needs to be sorted out just now, then. You can leave the dress and the reception to us. The guests can come back here for a bite after the wedding. You won't want a big do, in the circumstances." She stood up. "Now, I think Marianne needs her rest. She's had an exhausting day."

"Oh, Ellie," pleaded Marianne. "Can't I just have a few minutes alone with Tom?"

"Certainly not! You'll get more than enough of that once you're married." Ellie went to open the door and stand by it, foot tapping impatiently.

Tom sighed, rolled his eyes at Marianne, planted a defiant kiss on each of her cheeks and took his leave. Once outside, he let out his breath in a long whoosh of relief, then the irrepressible grin stole back over his face. In a month at most Marianne would be his wife. No one could stop that now. And soon he would be the father of Marianne's child. He could think of nothing he wanted more in life.

The grin was replaced by a thoughtful expression. He could never have married a woman like Rosie, fond of her though he was. He deeply regretted that he had not broken completely with her sooner. Still, there was no helping that now. You couldn't turn the clock back. And Rosie would not make trouble for him, not if he made sure she didn't want for anything. He owed her that, at least.

Then he forgot everything else but Marianne. He'd have to find somewhere for them to live. He wasn't going to take Marianne back to Netherleigh Cottage. He intended to make sure they started their life together in privacy. And in comfort. He could afford to dip into his savings a little to set them up properly in furniture and such. And they'd have to hire some help around the house. Kathy would be bound to know a girl who could do the scrubbing and such. And the cooking. His Marianne wasn't going to do any of the rough work, not his lovely girl. He would make sure she did not suffer from this. He would make absolutely certain that she was happy from now on. Nothing would ever come between them.

Twenty-Eight

ANNABELLE AND JEREMY

That same night an exhausted Jeremy Lewis boarded the last train from London to Brighton. It was full of happy city dwellers, of all classes, going to spend the weekend by the seaside, and quite a few were already having sing-songs. Their exuberance grated on his nerves as he stared out of the window of the first-class compartment at the dark landscape rushing past. The thought of Marianne's condition still upset him, even though he had forgiven her and Tom. He had not expected his beloved daughter to go down this track towards marriage. And he was not sure that he would have chosen a man like Tom for her, either.

The thought of seeing his wife again was upsetting him even more than thoughts of his daughter. He had not set eyes on Annabelle since she left Bilsden. He would have preferred never to see her again. Even her letters left a taint in his mouth.

The message from Cora had said that her mistress was desperately ill, however, and he could not ignore that. The trouble must be serious indeed for Annabelle to allow so much money to be spent on a telegram. Only rich people could normally afford to use the new telegraph service across long distances, when it was charged by the mile, and Jeremy knew how parsimonious Annabelle was with everything but her own comfort.

The address on the telegram had puzzled him, too. A small village, he presumed. What was Annabelle doing there when she already had a house of her own in Brighton? He had never even heard of this village before. The telegram had instructed him to leave the train several stops before Brighton and to take a cab to the address given.

He leaned his aching head back against the seat and sighed. He wished this jolting journey would end. He felt absolutely exhausted. It had been a harrowing day. He was getting too old for such alarms and excursions. Far too old. He was about to become a grandfather!

Jeremy almost missed the stop, for he had dozed off, so he had to toss his luggage out of the door and jump on to the platform as the train was starting to pull away. He ignored the stationmaster's reprimand for such careless behaviour and looked round for a cab.

A few minutes later a tired old horse was pulling the only vehicle available for hire slowly along the dark country lanes, splashing through puddles and splattering the verges with mud. Its interior smelt of dust and the seats were hard and uncomfortable. When it stopped at a small cottage which stood on its own at the end of a lane, Jeremy sighed and prepared for an unpleasant experience. "Can you wait for me?" he asked the driver. He had no intention of staying here for the night, whatever Annabelle's condition.

The driver sucked in his breath and shook his head. "I dunno sir. 'Tis gettin' late."

"I'll pay extra."

"Ah. Would that be in advance?"

"If you require it." Jeremy gave him half a guinea and the

man nodded. He got down to put a nosebag on the horse and pulled out a large blanket to wrap round himself. "You take your time, sir. I'll be here waiting. Nice fine night it is, now that the rain's stopped. Pity there isn't a full moon, eh, then I could have read my newspaper?"

Jeremy knocked on the door of the cottage and could not for a moment recognise the woman who opened it. Cora had always been trim and pretty. Now, her clothing was awry, her hair hung lank about her shoulders and her face was greasy white with fatigue. And surely that was dried blood spotting her dirty pinafore? "Cora?"

She burst into tears at the sight of him. "Dr Lewis. Oh! Oh dear, you're too late!"

"What do you mean, too late?" A chill trickled down his spine as he moved into the narrow hallway and followed her bobbing lamp into the kitchen.

"Mrs Lewis died this afternoon."

"Annabelle? Annabelle's dead?"

"Yes, sir. I'm sorry, sir."

"What on earth did she die from?" He had always thought Annabelle would outlast him.

Cora gulped and began to twist the corner of her apron. She had been dreading this moment all evening. "She – she'd had a hard labour, sir. And then she started bleeding." She peeped sideways at him, but he was simply staring at her as if he could not believe what he was hearing. She rushed into an explanation. She had to make him understand that she had done her best, that it was not her fault Mrs Lewis had died. "We tried to stop the bleeding, but it went on and on. I didn't know people had that much blood in them. The midwife said it happens like that sometimes." Her voice trailed away, and more tears flooded from her reddened eyes. "She – she just lay there and died, sir. I don't think she felt any pain by then. Four hours ago, it was."

For the second time that day, it seemed to Jeremy as if the earth trembled beneath his feet. "Annabelle?" he managed, after a few moments. "*Annabelle's had a child*?"

"Yes, sir."

Fury surged through him. "Who the hell's is it?"

"I – I don't know, sir." Cora buried her head in her hands and burst into tears. The last three days had been a nightmare.

Jeremy's fingers were hard and bony on her shoulders, and when she did not quieten down, he shook her roughly. "You must know whose it is, Cora. You're her personal maid, for heaven's sake! You *must* have known she was," the words stuck in his throat for a moment, then he spat them at her, "having an affair."

Cora only sobbed more loudly.

From upstairs came the wail of a new-born infant. Jeremy spun round. "Is the child still alive, then?"

Between sobs, Cora gulped out, "Yes, sir. It's a little girl. But she's very small. The midwife doesn't think she'll live."

"Show me." The doctor took over from the wronged husband and he snatched up the lamp, pushing Cora before him towards the stairs.

In the bedroom, Annabelle's body lay beneath a clean sheet, illuminated by one flickering candle on the bedside table. Jeremy walked slowly over to the bed, bringing a circle of brighter light with him.

"I got Mrs Webster to lay her out before she left," said Cora, making no attempt to lift the sheet.

Jeremy put the lamp down on the bedside table, lifted the sheet and looked at his dead wife. What he saw made a murmur of surprise rise then fade in his throat. Annabelle's face was more at peace than he had ever seen it, and in death her expression gave no clue to the viciousness of her nature. But he was looking at the face of an ageing woman. The hair was more grey than gold and the skin looked sallow and wrinkled.

"She – she hadn't been well," mumbled Cora, edging towards the door.

Jeremy was across the room in a flash. "Where do you think you're going?"

"Well, sir, now that you're here, you won't need my services. I've done all I could for her." She tried to shake his hand off her arm. "I've been paid, sir. You don't owe me no money. An' I don't know nothing about babies, so I won't be any use to you, not now."

"If you attempt to leave before I give you permission, I'll set the police after you."

She began to weep. "But it wasn't my fault. She made me help her. I wouldn't have done it if she hadn't made me!"

"Made you do what?"

"Help her. She made me help her. She an' that Mr Minton."

Jeremy struggled to make sense of this. "Was he the one? The father of the child?"

"No, sir. At least, I don't think so, sir."

"What the hell do you mean, you don't think so?" he roared, taking her by the shoulders and forcing her to look him in the eyes. "Stop hedging around and tell me what's been happening? *Tell me, Cora!*"

Cora was white with terror. He would kill her when he found out.

"Well?"

"Mrs Lewis – she went into business with Mr Minton. They – she – she used to receive gentlemen callers." Cora shrank before the fury in his eyes and cowered against the wall, too frightened even to sob. "They gave her money."

"Are you telling me that my wife had turned whore?"

"Y-yes, sir. But very exclusive, sir. She – it was for the money. She needed the money." No reason to tell him that his wife had thoroughly enjoyed her new trade until this last pregnancy.

He stared at her for a moment, then he said flatly, "She did *not* need the money, not that badly, at least. What you mean is, she wanted the money. She always was greedy for money." Bile rose in his throat. All those years of denying him his marital rights, of denying him more children, and then Annabelle had turned whore and done it with anyone who would pay her. He would have paid her himself, it if had meant that she would bear him another child.

The silence was broken by a faint whimper from the side of the room. "Don't you dare try to leave!" Jeremy growled, then went over to the drawer that was being used as a cradle. The infant's face was screwed up and looked pinched and unhappy, but it had a look of Marianne as a child. As it started to fret and sob, he reached out to pick it up, rocking it against his chest as tenderly as any woman. "Shh, now. Shh, little one," he said softly and the head squirmed against him, seeking a breast to suckle as tears welled from the screwed-up eyes and trickled down the tiny cheeks.

Still cradling the baby, he swung round to Cora. "What preparations did your mistress make for this baby?"

Cora swallowed hard. "None, sir."

"None? What do you mean, none? Even Annabelle must have had some plans for her child."

"She – she was going to leave it at the foundling hospital, sir."

A grimace of a smile pulled his face into ugly lines. "Oh yes, I can quite believe that. She had not an ounce of maternal feeling in her." He continued to rock the baby to and fro, and when he pushed the little thumb aside to examine its face again, the baby grasped his finger and held on tightly. "Poor soul!" he murmured. "Poor little soul!"

Then he became brisk. "Is there another bedroom here?"

Cora gaped at him. "Yes, sir."

"Then let us move everything there. Annabelle has no furthe

need of our attentions. Bring the drawer and that candle. I want to examine the baby."

It did not take him long to establish that the infant was healthy, if rather small. The midwife had been wrong. With proper care, the child had a good chance of surviving. If she could be fed, that was. He stared at her little face in silence. He could not escape from the resemblance to Marianne, and that kept tugging at his heart.

Cora hovered behind him as he wrapped the child up again. "Shall I – shall we take it to the foundling hospital, sir? I know where it is."

He glared at her. "Certainly not!"

"But sir, what shall we do with it?"

"First we shall find *her* a wet nurse. Don't refer to the baby as 'it', if you please. And then," a wry grimace twisted his face, but there was not the fury in it that there had been before, for the baby had done nothing to deserve his wrath, "we shall arrange a funeral for the mother." He looked down at the now slumbering child. Like him, this was an innocent victim of a woman's greed and selfishness. Whoever the father was, this infant was Marianne's half-sister and the poor little creature did not deserve to be left to the untender mercies of a foundling hospital.

Cora looked at the bundle in his arms and then back up at his face. "But the child, sir? You'll have to do something with the child. We can't just leave it – I mean, her – here."

"I shall call her Catherine, after my grandmother. And I shall take her home with me to Bilsden."

Cora forgot her place. "You'll never!"

"Oh, I shall. But I shall require you to promise me faithfully, Cora, that no word of this will ever get out. As far as the world is concerned, the child is mine, the result of a weekend meeting with my wife in London earlier this year."

"Sir!"

"Is that clear, Cora?"

She could only nod and say, "Yessir." He had run mad, but who was she to stop him? All she wanted was to get this over with and find herself a new life, as far away from Brighton and that Henry Minton as possible. The way Minton had abandoned Annabelle Lewis had made Cora realise just how ruthless he could be. She wanted nothing more to do with him. And she would not, she decided, tell him anything about what had happened to the baby. Dr Lewis deserved that from her, at least. "I promise, sir," she added.

Jeremy looked at her face and nodded, as if satisfied by what he saw. "Then go and ask the cab-driver to bring the midwife back for us."

"Mrs Webster, sir?"

"If that's what she's called. She must help us to find a wet nurse. Midwives usually know of someone. And, Cora – if you stay to help me for a while, I'll see you don't lose by it. I'm sorry if I was abrupt with you just now."

"Yes, sir." She had forgotten how kind he was. A real gentleman, Dr Lewis. Then Cora smiled to herself. Mind you, that wouldn't stop her using this knowledge to her own advantage if she were ever again in need. The good doctor wouldn't want anyone to know about who had really fathered the baby – especially if he were bringing her up as his daughter.

She shrugged off a slight feeling of guilt as she walked downstairs to speak to the cab-driver. It was a hard cruel world and you had to look out for yourself in this life, because no one else would. That thought made her decide to move back to the north. She could just as well open her shop near her family and Minton would never find her there. She would be able to keep an eye on what was happening at Park House. It never hurt to have something to fall back on.

In Bilsden, Frederick left Annie with the promise that he would go and talk to Daniel Connor himself. "Don't worry. I'm sure I'll be able to persuade him to moderate his demands."

"The more I think about it, the less inclined I feel to give him anything, Frederick."

He nodded. "We'll work something out, you have my word on that." He kept a cheerful expression on his face until he was outside, then he allowed his face to settle into a frown as he told his coachman to drive slowly along the High Street to Connor's building yard.

Once there, he sat for a moment in the carriage, staring at it, his eyes narrowed in thought, then he got out. "Wait for me here!" he said curtly to the coachman. He rapped sharply on the door and scowled up at the ornate sign saying Daniel Connor, Master Builder. "Master rogue, more like," he muttered under his breath. When there was no answer, he rapped again, more loudly this time. Still no answer.

As he was raising his hand to try the knob, the door opened. Daniel Connor stood staring at him, shirt in disarray, cravat missing and cuffs flapping against his wrists. His face was ruddy, the reek of brandy hung around him and he was swaying on his feet. When he saw who had knocked, he tried to straighten up and smile, but it was a poor shadow of his normal charm and his eyes were not focusing properly.

Frederick rapped his cane on the door frame. "Well! Aren't you going to invite me in, Connor?"

"Er – it's not convenient just now, I'm afraid, Mr Hallam. I'm in the middle of – er – drawing up some plans. Could I maybe call round and see you later, at your convenience?" He blinked at his visitor. His head was thumping both from fury with Annie and from the brandy, and all he wanted was to be left alone.

"I need to see you now. About your ex-fiancée."

Daniel stared at Hallam then he began to smile, a twisted nasty smile. "Aah. Clever Annie. She hasn't wasted any time finding herself a protector, has she, the bitch?"

Frederick surprised himself by knocking the sneering face to the ground. It was a long time since anything had made him feel so angry. "If," he said icily to the groaning figure below him, prodding it with his walking stick, "I ever hear you speak of Mrs Ashworth like that again, I shall be happy to repeat my action."

As Daniel scrambled unsteadily to his feet, Frederick pushed him inside, all too aware of his coachman staring goggle-eyed at him from a few yards away.

Inside, Daniel shook off Frederick's hand and led the way into the office. Papers were strewn across the fine polished desk and a nearly empty bottle bore witness to his attempts to find solace. "Please take a seat," he managed, enunciating the words very carefully. He'd have liked to return the blow, to punch the damned fellow's face in, but Hallam was the richest man in town and that held Daniel back. Or at least, so he told himself. There was also the question of the scorn upon Hallam's face and the ease with which he had knocked Daniel down.

Frederick waited until Connor had sat down, then followed suit. "I believe you've been making threats to Mrs Ashworth."

"What's between Mrs Ashworth and myself is none of your damned business."

"I'm making it my business."

Daniel snorted. "Thank you. That'll lend credence to any rumours I choose to spread around if she doesn't do as I've suggested."

"That, sir, is blackmail."

"That, sir, is sheer desperation!"

"If you carry out the threats you've made, Connor, I'll see you do no more business in this town."

Daniel shrugged. "If Annie doesn't see her way to helping me, then I'll do no more business anyway. In which case, sir, I have nothing to lose." And from that standpoint, he was not to be moved. All he would agree to, and that only upon the loan of five guineas for "immediate expenses", was to wait a day or two longer before taking any further action, and to allow Frederick to examine the building company's accounts to see whether anything could be done to help the ailing business.

It was a grim man who came outside again, carrying Annie's account books, which he had found among the tangles of papers on the desk, as well as Daniel's. "What happened here is not to be discussed, Robert," he said to the coachman.

"No, sir. Wouldn't think of it, sir." Once his master was in the carriage, Robert grinned. It had been a good punch, that one. Bang on the mark. He wouldn't like to be in that Connor's shoes, not with Mr Hallam looking like that. You didn't cross Mr Frederick Hallam, not if you were smart. He was a good friend and employer, but a ruthless enemy.

Back at Netherleigh Cottage, Frederick found Annie much calmer. She must have been watching out of the window, for she opened the front door before he had a chance to knock. "Not good news," she said immediately. "I can see it in your face." She gestured to him to come inside.

As they crossed the hall, she paused for a moment to stare at her reflection in the mirror on the far wall. She had never, she thought, looked worse. There were dark circles under her eyes, her cheeks were pale and strain was pulling down the corners of her mouth. Only her hair blazed back at her, bright even on this dull day. She tried to tidy it, but looked up to find Frederick standing in the parlour doorway watching her.

"Don't worry about how you look, Annie." His voice was gentle and when he held out a hand to her, she did not hesitate to take it and allow him to lead her back into the parlour.

"I'm not paying him anything," she began. "I've been thinking about it. I won't give him my money, whatever he threatens. He'll only waste it as he's wasted his own. What did he say?"

"He was drunk when I found him, and I'm afraid I didn't help matters by knocking him down when he spoke slightingly of you."

That brought a smile to her face. "Why, thank you, Frederick. I hope you blacked his eye for him."

"If I didn't, and if it would make you feel any better, I'd be happy to go back and do so." His smile was warm on her for a moment, but then it faded. "Unfortunately, he's absolutely determined to damage your good name. He seems almost to hold you responsible for the failure of his business. I could make no headway against his pig-headedness."

She realised that Frederick still had hold of her hand and flushed vividly as she looked down at it. But she did not try to pull away. The warmth and strength of it was comforting. It felt so right to hold it.

"Annie." His voice was quiet but insistent.

She raised her eyes, but what she saw in his face made her feel breathless and unable to speak. And when he bent his head to kiss her, she did not pretend that she did not welcome his lips upon hers. She did nothing but put her arms around his neck and kiss him back. It was as if she had come home from a long journey. It felt so very natural to be in his arms that she wished she need never leave them again.

Twenty-Nine

ELLIE PETERS

Jeremy Lewis arrived back in Bilsden a few days later, accompanied by a country girl found for him by the midwife. Hetty, unmarried and in disgrace with her family, had lost her own baby recently and had been happy to act as wet nurse to little Catherine. People on the train stared to see a man with a baby and nursemaid, but then their eyes fell to the black band around his arm and the black weepers trailing from his top hat and they looked away again.

Hetty soon lost her awe of the doctor and she enlivened the journey for him by her frank enjoyment of this new experience and by her tender care of the baby who was starting to get roses in her cheeks and was already crying less. It was as if her nursemaid's placidity had communicated itself to Catherine.

Hetty had accepted without question Jeremy's explanation that his wife had been in delicate health and had not been able to live with him in the smoky atmosphere of Bilsden. "Well, I daresay it won't affect me, sir. I'm allus healthy, I am. It surprised us all when my baby died, poor little fellow, but my mam says it's a good thing, with me not being married like.

He was a bonnie baby, though, an' I fair cried my eyes out when we buried him." Her eyes fell upon Catherine and she smiled again. "Eh, she's a little love, isn't she?"

In Manchester, Jeremy hired a carriage to drive them all to Bilsden in comfort. He would be glad when the railway branch line that was being planned was built. It always annoyed him that he could travel swiftly in the modern way to everywhere except his own town.

By this time, even Hetty was tired, and he was relieved when she and the baby both fell asleep within minutes of climbing into the carriage. Left alone with his own thoughts as they rocked along the road to Bilsden, he pondered yet again on the best way of establishing that little Catherine was his child.

He had sent a letter to Marianne and Ellie to explain that he would be delayed for a few days, but he had not given any explanation of why. He was sure they would agree with what he had done, but he found himself dreading the inevitable confrontation with Cousin Dorothy. She was well aware that he had not had any meetings with his wife and after the trouble she had stirred up for Marianne, he was sure that she would not easily accept Annabelle's child into the house. And even if she did, she would make poor Catherine's life a misery. It was time now for him to take a stand with Dorothy. More than time. And he must not weaken, whatever she said or did.

When the maid opened the door of Park House, he swept the half-awake Hetty and the baby inside and into the morning room and asked Susan to send Miss Peters and Miss Marianne to him at once. "Please sit down in here for a moment, Hetty. I'll just put a bit more coal on the fire. No one is expecting us, so they won't have a bedroom prepared."

Catherine started to wail and Hetty looked down at her fondly. " 'Tis time for her feed, sir."

"Yes. Why don't you feed her in here? By the time you're

finished, we'll have a room arranged for you."

"All right, sir." Calmly she began to unfasten the fine new woollen jacket that he had insisted on buying to keep her warm. Such kindness she had had from him. The best master anyone could ask for, in Hetty's opinion, and just let anyone try to say different.

Jeremy walked out into the hallway to find Dorothy waiting for him.

"My dear cousin," she cooed, her eyes lighting up as she noticed the black armband. "I gather that you were not in time. How sad life is sometimes! And how exhausted you must be after your journey! You must allow me to send for a tea-tray."

Marianne appeared on the stairs. "Father! I was just having a nap. I'm sorry I wasn't downstairs to welcome you." She ignored Dorothy's glare and went to give Jeremy a hug.

"How are you, my dear?"

"I'm well, but so sleepy."

He smiled. Some women were like that. And he could see that she was well by the rosiness of her cheeks and the happiness in her eyes. Please God, she would never have to face a marriage with one who did not know the meaning of the word love. "I'd like to speak to my daughter alone first, if you please, Dorothy."

Dorothy obviously did mind, but he paid no attention to her scowl.

Ellie appeared at the back of the hallway, having just been alerted by Susan to the fact that the doctor had brought with him a baby and its nursemaid, and that he was wearing mourning.

Jeremy looked at her in relief. "Could you help the young woman I brought with me, Ellie, and find her and the baby a room? She's in the morning room. She'll be staying with us until further notice."

"Certainly, sir."

447

He watched Ellie walk along the hallway, a half-smile on his face. Now he knew he was home. There was something so wholesome about his Miss Peters. Being away had made him realise how much he appreciated Ellie's quiet cheerful presence and her sensible attitude to life. It had also made him realise how wrong he had been to do nothing about Dorothy. It was his fault that Marianne, desperate for affection, had turned elsewhere to seek it. Well, that sort of weakness was over now. Catherine should have a better start in life.

He led the way into the parlour, gave Marianne a hug and said simply, "How wonderful it is to be home! Come and sit down, darling. I'm afraid I have some sad news for you."

"Mother's dead."

"Yes."

"I'm sorry, of course, but I can't care deeply. Please let's not pretend about that, Father."

"No. We needn't pretend with each other."

"What did she die of?"

He took a deep breath. "Childbirth."

"*What*? But—" She broke off and stared at him.

"We need not discuss how that happened. It's enough that there's a baby in need of a home and that the baby is your half-sister. So I brought little Catherine back with me."

Marianne looked at him for a moment, tears in her eyes, then came over to hug him again. "You're the kindest of men, Father, the very kindest."

"You don't mind?"

"No. I don't like to think of any child without a home. Especially now." She looked down at her own still-flat stomach.

He nodded and had to wait a moment for the lump of emotion in his throat to dissipate before he could speak again. "We won't let all this stop you from marrying Tom, though it'll have to be a quiet affair, of course, because of the mourning. Have you made all the arrangements for your wedding?"

Her eyes lit up. "Oh, yes. We're to be married in the Methodist Chapel just before Christmas. Tom's even found us a house to live in and Ellie's found us a maid who's living there at the moment. Megan's scrubbing the whole place through from attics to cellars, and Ellie and I go round every day to get things ready. There's so much to buy – crockery and linen and so on. Ellie said you wouldn't mind if we spent the housekeeping money on it."

"Of course I don't. Remind me to give you some trousseau money tomorrow."

"I won't forget."

"Good." He yawned. "Now that I know you're all right, I think I'd like to have a wash and a rest. It's been a long tiring week. Can you and Ellie see to Hetty and the child?"

"Oh, yes."

As they opened the door, they found Dorothy waiting for them in the hall, her expression determined. "A word with you, if you please, Cousin Jeremy."

He sighed, pushed Marianne towards the morning room, then turned to follow the thin figure back into the parlour. "Is something wrong, Cousin Dorothy?"

"Is it true that you've brought that woman's child back with you?" she demanded. "I could not believe my own ears when the nursemaid told me whose the infant was."

"I've brought my new daughter back with me, yes."

She stiffened. "That child is not your daughter, Jeremy, and you have no responsibility for it. I'm well aware that you haven't seen Annabelle since she left this house."

"Oh, but I have. I met her in London a couple of times. I saw no reason to tell you about it. I knew it would only upset you. I'm afraid we – er – allowed ourselves to be carried away." He had no intention of trusting Dorothy with the true tale.

Her breath hissed into her throat like water spilled on a hot griddle. "I don't believe you! You hated her too much. That

449

child can only be your wife's bastard!"

"I intend to raise Catherine as my daughter, and you would be wise to accept her as such. She's Marianne's half-sister, whatever else she is or is not."

Dorothy came closer and all of a sudden her voice was coy and coaxing, though this sat ill with the calculating expression on her sallow face. "Jeremy, it's unfair to do this, unfair to Marianne and unfair to yourself. Surely some provision can be made—"

"A foundling hospital?"

"The very thing! I understand your generosity, but what's bred in the bone will out in the flesh. The offspring of such an illicit and sinful liaison can only—"

He could not bear to listen to her hypocritical platitudes for a minute longer. "You're speaking of an innocent child, Dorothy."

"I'm speaking of your wife's bastard and I will not share the house with her. You have no right to ask that of me."

"I've no intention of asking it of you."

She looked puzzled. "But you said—"

He steeled himself to answer honestly. "I know you haven't been happy here, Cousin Dorothy. I also know that you haven't enough money to maintain an establishment of your own. Never think that I shall abandon you. We are cousins, after all. I shall help you to find somewhere else to live and then I shall make you an annual allowance."

Although he spoke kindly, she could sense the coolness towards her, and anger that he would keep the child and turn her out made her lose control of her temper. "The only decent thing you could do for me, Jeremy Lewis, would be to marry me. I came here at your behest. I've done everything humanly possible to look after your daughter, and it's not my fault if she's gone astray. I warned you how it would be. I warned you!" Her voice was becoming shriller and shriller.

"I could never marry you, Dorothy," he said firmly. "Never. I've had one experience of a loveless marriage and I have no intention of repeating that mistake."

She dragged out her handkerchief and began to sob into it, then, when he remained where he was, she threw herself against him, clutching his jacket. "You owe it to me. You owe it to me to marry me!"

He tried to pull away, but she clung even more tightly, sobbing loudly. "Please keep your voice down, Dorothy."

"No! I shall demand my rights. *You owe it to me!*"

The door opened and Ellie came across to join them. "Dr Lewis, I'm afraid I couldn't help overhearing what Miss Hymes was saying. I thought you might need some help."

"I do."

The look that passed between them made Dorothy's sobs redouble, but when Jeremy would have tried to comfort her, Ellie shook her head and gestured to him to stand away. She stepped in front of him, slapped Dorothy's face and forced the other woman to sit down on the sofa. "We've enough trouble here without you having hysterics again, Miss Hymes. No! This time be quiet and listen!"

Dorothy subsided, but continued to rock to and fro, sobbing incoherently into her handkerchief.

"You wouldn't really like to marry him, you know." Ellie sat down and took Dorothy's quivering hand into hers.

"Yes, I would! Only married women are respected in this world."

"You'd like to share his bed? Bear his children? Raise little Catherine?" Ellie's voice was inexorable.

Dorothy drew away, her back rigid. "We're both beyond the age of that sort of thing, and how dare you speak of it to me, you – you unprincipled hussy! At Jeremy's age, gentlemen require caring for. They require the services of a wife only as a housekeeper."

451

"I wouldn't," said Jeremy, taking his cue from Ellie and stepping forward to stand at the end of the couch. "I'm a man of – of strong passions." For a moment, laughter threatened to overcome him, then he regained control of his face muscles. "Why do you think I go away on so many trips?"

"W-what?" Dorothy had stopped in mid-sob to gape at him.

"I need a woman in my bed," he declared. "If you were my wife, I would demand my conjugal rights from you – every night."

Ellie looked firmly at the ornaments on the mantelpiece and dug her fingers into her palms. It was a moment before she could speak steadily. "I tried to warn you, Miss Hymes," she whispered. "I knew what he was like."

Dorothy's mouth was open and she was frozen with shock.

"Now that I am free," said Jeremy, striding up and down in front of the fire to avoid Ellie's eyes, "I shall of course remarry. I want to enjoy the comfort of having a wife in my bed and I hope to have a lot of children. Are you really offering to warm my bed and bear me several children, Cousin?"

Dorothy gulped and shook her head, looking at Ellie in a panic now.

"Perhaps you should explain to Miss Hymes what you intend to do for her," said Ellie, rising to leave.

"Don't go!" Dorothy grabbed Ellie's arm and pulled her back down on the couch. She looked across at Jeremy as if he had suddenly grown horns and a tail.

"It is my intention," said Jeremy, "to provide you with an adequate allowance, such as would enable you to live in genteel lodgings, to clothe yourself decently and to participate in the social life of the neighbourhood. I thought somewhere like Bath or Tunbridge Wells might suit you."

"H-how much?"

"We shall agree on that when we're both calmer. But rest assured that I shall provide enough to keep you in reasonable

452

comfort." Dorothy need never know that it was Annabelle's money he would be using. He had been astounded at how much Annabelle had left when Cora had showed him where her late mistress kept her account books. He had left instructions with a reputable lawyer to terminate Mr Minton's involvement and to dispose of the estate. All of Annabelle's money would come to him by default, since she had not left a will and he intended to keep most of it for Catherine. "However," he spoke to Dorothy as sternly as he could manage, "this money will be yours only on condition that you say nothing to damage the reputation of my dead wife or my new daughter."

Dorothy struggled to her feet, a dazed expression on her face. "I shall give the matter my – my earnest consideration." Tunbridge Wells, she thought. I shall go to live in Tunbridge Wells. She had friends there already and had long envied them their peaceful life.

Ellie helped her to the door and stood to watch her stumble up the stairs.

"Don't go yet, Ellie."

Jeremy came over to close the door, then took Ellie's hand in his. "As usual, your good sense sets everything to rights. What would I do without you, Ellie?"

She found herself blushing.

"Now is not the time to speak. We must allow a decent period of mourning. But Ellie, afterwards—" His smile and the kiss that followed it left her in no doubt of his intentions. "Afterwards," he said as he moved resolutely back from the temptation of her soft body, "I should like to get to know you better – with your father's permission, of course."

There was no mistaking his meaning. Ellie's eyes were like stars as she looked at him. "Oh, Jeremy!" It was the first time she had ever allowed herself to address him by his Christian name and her voice lingered on the word, making a caress of it, "Jeremy, nothing on this earth would please me more."

She watched his face light up and remained where she was as he left to go and deal with his other problems. For a while she just stood there, remembering his kiss and the promise of his words. "Afterwards," she said softly, as she prepared to set about her duties again, "afterwards, my dearest Jeremy, you shall be loved as you deserve."

Thirty

STORMS OVER BILSDEN

Tom was not the only one to contemplate with longing the idea of paying someone to murder Daniel Connor. During the next few days, Frederick tried several times to bring Annie's ex-fiancé to see reason, but drunk or sober, Daniel clung stubbornly to his threat to drag Annie down with him.

Annie went back to work in the salon, finding the uncertainty easier to bear if she kept herself occupied. Her staff all agreed that she was looking tired and there was a conspiracy among her family and employees to try to spare her from any trouble or upset.

A few days later Helen Kenderby came into the salon and asked if she could speak to Annie privately. "I met Tom last week and I'm afraid I persuaded him to tell me a little about your troubles, Annie."

Annie sat like one carved from marble. "I prefer not to talk about that."

"Yes. I do understand. Only tell me one thing and I'll not trouble you again. Is your engagement with Daniel Connor really at an end? Irrevocably?"

"Oh, yes. Quite irrevocably. And if he's sent you to ask me to reconsider, you can tell him to speak to Tom or to Frederick. I don't want to see him, not ever again." Annie gasped as she realised that she might have revealed more than she had intended.

Helen's expression was inscrutable. "Is Mr Hallam helping you in this, then?"

"Trying to." Annie couldn't keep the bitterness out of her voice. She didn't think anyone would be able to prevent Daniel from carrying out his threat, but she had refused Frederick's offer to pay him off in no uncertain terms.

She looked at Helen who had been a good friend to her and suddenly the words were pouring out, the whole tale of Daniel Connor's villainy and the reasons for it.

Helen listened carefully, not interrupting. "So Mr Connor is nearly bankrupt, you think?" she asked, when the tale was ended.

"I'm sure of it. Mr Hallam and Tom have both had to lend him small amounts of money to keep him quiet. But he's *not* going to take my money away from me, whatever he does!"

"No," Helen's voice was quiet. "No. We mustn't let him do that. You've worked so hard for it." She picked up her gloves and fiddled with them for a moment. "Please believe me, Annie, that only my genuine concern for you prompted me to call here today."

Annie blew her nose. "You've been a good friend to me, Helen. Now, tell me how your father is keeping?"

"I think my father is going mad. I'd have gone to live with my aunt long ago if it hadn't been for my mother. Now that she's dead, I'm seriously considering my options. It was only for her sake that I stayed here." She gave a wry smile. "I think there must be a streak of the gipsy somewhere in my family. I have this longing to travel. I shall probably move away from Bilsden quite soon."

Annie gave her a hug. "I shall miss you."

"No. I don't think you will. Or not much, anyway. You have so many people to care for you. Family and friends – and even Frederick Hallam now." She noted Annie's flush, but did not comment on it, only said, "I envy you, my dear." When she left, she did not look back.

The following morning, Frederick called in at the salon early. When Annie kept her distance, he made no attempt to take her in his arms, though he was longing to kiss her. "May I beg a cup of tea from you, Annie?"

"Of course. I sent Rebecca to make one as soon as I saw you coming along the street."

"You're looking much better today."

"The shock's worn off a little." Annie fiddled with the braid on her skirt, unable to meet his eyes. She didn't know why she felt so shy of him, when she had dreamed every night of the way he had held her.

"No regrets about the broken engagement?"

"I think, if it were not for Daniel's threats, I'd only feel relieved that the engagement is over. Have you – seen him again?"

"Not since yesterday. I tried to get him to see reason, but he was adamant, as your brother probably told you." The discussion had degenerated into a blazing row, and if Tom had not been there, Frederick suspected that he might have tried to pound Daniel Connor's head to a pulp. He couldn't remember getting so furious in all his life.

Without thinking, she laid a hand on his arm. "I value your concern for me, Frederick."

"I fear we may have to pay him off. Annie, won't you let me—"

"No! Frederick, I absolutely forbid you to give Daniel Connor anything. I shan't speak to you again if you do. I mean that!"

"I can easily afford it, my dear."

That word brought more colour to her cheeks. "No! Why should he have my money? Or yours? He's done nothing but waste his own. If he carries out his threat," she had to pause to steady her voice, "I shall sell the salon and move away from Bilsden. Perhaps I shall open a salon somewhere else. Perhaps not. I shall have to think about it."

"Oh, no!" He pulled her round into his arms. "I'm not having you leave the town. You know how I feel about you—"

She had been dreading this moment. "Frederick, I won't become your mistress."

"Ah! Is that what's causing this reserve?" A crooked smile appeared on his face. "I'm not asking you to become my mistress. I wouldn't insult you like that. Annie, my dearest Annie, will you marry me?"

She stood motionless for a moment, then emotion crumpled her face. She would like nothing better than to marry him, but with her background it wouldn't be fair to him. "I couldn't let you make that sacrifice, Frederick."

"It wouldn't be a sacrifice. And who is there to be upset anyway? My family is grown up, and I'm old enough and rich enough to please myself. I can't think of anything I've ever wanted as much as I want to marry you."

She took a deep breath. "Your family would be shocked if you married me, and well you know it. As would everyone in Bilsden. And Beatrice—"

"Beatrice is engaged to a gentleman in London. Her sister has proved to be an excellent matchmaker." And the generous dowry had helped considerably. "After the wedding, I doubt she'll ever come back to Bilsden. She tells me often enough how she loathes the place."

Annie's eyes softened. Poor Frederick! He had had nothing but disappointments from all his children. "That still doesn't change things as far as you and I are concerned. Frederick

I'm honoured by your proposal, deeply honoured, but gentlemen like you don't marry women from the Rows. It would cause a major scandal in the town." She tried again to pull away from him, but he would not let her.

"I thought people from Salem Street were respectable," he teased.

Her voice was suddenly fierce. "Don't mock me, Frederick. You know exactly what I'm saying."

"Does that mean that you're turning me down?"

"Of course I am. It's not – it's just not possible. We're too different." And she loved him too much to marry him. With her background and her sister Lizzie, it could only lead to trouble.

His eyes were hooded and his fingers were like steel bands on her arms. "It's very noble of you, Annie, but I can only think of one reason I'd accept for your rejecting me."

"Oh?" She tried to keep her face expressionless and her voice steady, but she wanted to throw herself against his chest and tell him yes, then nestle against him. She stiffened herself against the urge. "And what reason is that?"

"If you didn't love me."

She drew in a breath that was almost a sob.

Before she could speak, he raised her hand to his lips and said gently, "I love you, Annie, more than I would ever have believed possible. If you say you don't love me, can't ever love me, then I'll stop annoying you, but if there's any chance that you might return my affection, then I shall not stop annoying you until you agree to marry me."

"I *can't* marry you."

"Look me in the eyes and tell me you don't love me, then," he commanded, raising her chin with one fingertip.

She stared at him, her eyes wide with pain. "I – I – Frederick, it doesn't matter how I feel. The difference between us is bad enough, but once Daniel Connor has carried out his threat,

ANNA JACOBS

it'll ruin any chance we might have had of – of making a success
of our marriage."

"Does that mean you do love me?" he insisted, taking her
head in both his hands and placing a gentle kiss on each of her
cheeks.

"Far too much to marry you," she managed.

Someone pushed open the shop door and he allowed her to
draw away from him. "Discussion only postponed," he said
softly.

"I won't change my mind."

"You will! I shall make you."

That evening, Annie sat with a half-smile on her lips and
listened to Tom listing all the things he would like to do to
Daniel Connor. Somehow the thought that Frederick Hallam
loved her enough to want to marry her had lightened the misery
she had felt since she found out about Daniel's duplicity. And
although she knew that marriage to Frederick was not possible,
still she could not help dreaming. She realised that Tom was
waiting for an answer and blushed. "I'm sorry, I was miles
away."

"Thinking of Frederick?" he asked. "Rebecca said he came
to visit you at the salon this morning."

She nodded, unable to deny it. "What a kind man he is!"

"That's not kindness. He's in love with you, isn't he? I
watched him staring at you the other day. If that's not love
I'll go an' jump in the river."

"I – don't want to talk about it." She smoothed her skirt
carefully, avoiding Tom's eyes.

"Why? Don't you love him?"

She clenched her hands together tightly in her lap, staring
down at them. Of course she loved Frederick! That love had
crept up on her little by little, taking her by surprise. What she
had felt for Danny had been only physical attraction, she knew
that now.

460

Tom laid one hand upon hers. "Look, I won't tease you if you don't want to speak about it, but don't lie to me, Annie, love. You do care about Hallam, don't you?"

Unshed tears sparkled in her eyes and as she nodded one rolled down her cheek. "Yes."

"You won't become his mistress, will you, though? Not after all you've done to stay respectable. You wouldn't be happy living like that, love. I know you too well."

"No. I won't become his mistress." She hesitated, then decided that her brother at least deserved to know the truth. "Frederick has – he's asked me to marry him, Tom."

"Hallam has!"

"Shh! Keep your voice down. I don't want anyone else to know."

"But that's all right, then. Surely you're not going to turn him down?"

"I love him too much to marry him." She stared bleakly into the fire. "I – I won't even have a good reputation to bring to him."

"I'll kill that bastard Connor!" He jumped to his feet.

Annie stood up and caught hold of his arm. "No, Tom. It's not just that. I couldn't marry Frederick even if Daniel Connor hadn't threatened to blacken my name."

He allowed her to pull him down beside her on the sofa. "Why ever not?"

"Because of Lizzie and May."

It was the last thing he had expected to hear. "But we got rid of them."

"For the moment."

"Look, if they come back again, if they try anything on, I promise you I'll get rid of them again. I'll even pay them regularly to stay away if I must. Annie, don't ruin your life. Think of your own happiness, for once."

"I am thinking of it. I couldn't bear it if Frederick – if he grew to despise me. And I couldn't bear to bring scandal to his name. He's very proud of how well his family have risen in the world. And although he tries to hide it, you can tell how much he loves Bilsden. Look at all he's done for the town. He's got such plans . . . I can't risk anything that might prevent him from holding his head up in public."

He could hear the tears she was holding back so he just hugged her close. "We'll find some way to work it out, love."

"Perhaps." She blinked her eyes hard and tried to smile at him. "And at least you and Marianne are going to be happy. I'm pleased about that. Really I am."

Later that evening, there was a knock on the door. Luke went to answer it and came back into the kitchen holding a letter. "It's for you, Annie. A little lad brought it, but he said there was no answer."

She took it reluctantly and then gasped aloud as she recognised the handwriting. "It's from Daniel."

Tom could see that her hand was trembling and took it from her. "Let me open it, love."

She shook her head and snatched the letter back. "No. I'll face whatever's inside it myself. Please excuse me, everyone."

Tom exchanged glances with his father and Kathy, then followed her out into the hall. "You're not facing it on your own." Before she had realised what he was doing, he had taken the letter from her again. "Come on. Into the parlour. I'll read it to you and then we'll work out what to do together."

But when he tore open the letter and read the first few lines, his mouth fell open and he stared across at Annie. "He's changed his mind, withdrawn his threats. He's not going to cause you any trouble."

She snatched it out of his hand. "Does he say why?" But the letter was very brief and gave no reasons for Daniel's change of heart. "Frederick must have bought him off," she said slowly. "It's the only explanation."

"That's marvellous!"

"It's *not*. I particularly asked him not to."

"He can easily afford it."

"I won't have it! Tom, will you come with me to see Frederick?"

"Now?"

"Yes, now."

"But I was just going round to see Marianne."

"You've seen Marianne every night this week. You can spare me an hour tonight, surely? Go and find a cab. I'm not walking up to Ridge House in this weather. Just listen to that rain. It's not stopped all day."

Tom pulled on his overcoat, grimaced as he opened the door, then opened his umbrella and walked briskly into town to the livery stables. As he walked, he made an important decision and soon began to whistle cheerfully, in spite of the rain. He paid for the hire of a carriage and stood fidgeting impatiently at the livery stables while the horses were harnessed and a driver sent for.

Annie was waiting for him at the house, dressed again in her smart working clothes. "Go and put your best overcoat on!" she commanded, "and change your shoes. That's your old coat, and it's wet and your shoes are muddy, too. We want to look respectable."

"Yes, ma'am." He grinned as he ran upstairs. That sounded more like their Annie.

As they were rumbling up the hill towards the big house on the Ridge, Annie's hand crept into Tom's. "Thank you for coming with me. I – I need you tonight. He'll expect me to say yes to him, now, and you know why I can't."

Tom held his peace, but in the darkness of the jolting vehicle his lips took a firm determined line that made him look more like Annie than usual. "I'll be there looking after you, love," he said quietly. "You've spent the last eighteen years looking

after everyone else in the family, me included, and it's abou
time someone else looked after you."

"It was all worth it. We've done well, we Gibsons, haven'
we, Tom?"

"Very well." But he hadn't missed the way her voice
wobbled as she spoke.

At Ridge House, Tom dismissed the driver, ignoring Annie'
protests that they would need the cab to return home. Tom
was pretty sure that Frederick would send them home in hi
carriage, but if things went right, maybe not for a while. He
went to hammer on the front door.

When he heard their voices, Frederick himself came to gree
them, his eyes lighting up at the sight of Annie. Within minutes
they were installed in a snug sitting room with Helen
Kenderby's vivid picture glowing down at them.

"What's wrong? What's that fellow done now?" Frederick
asked as soon as the maid had closed the door.

Annie held out the letter from Daniel. "I received this tonight.

He read it through, then whistled and raised his eyebrows
at her. "I'm delighted for you, of course, Annie, but I don'
understand why you've come to see me – and in such a storm
too! It could surely have waited till morning?"

She was very stiff and on her dignity. "Frederick, I asked
you not to pay Daniel Connor off. I thought I could trust you
not to do that. You promised me."

"I didn't pay him off."

She and Tom both exchanged puzzled glances. "But you
must have. Why else would he have changed his mind?"

Frederick got up and walked across to the little writing desk
in the corner. He picked up a letter and brought it back with
him. "I received a note today, asking me to pass the enclosed
letter on to you tomorrow. It's from Helen Kenderby. She didn'
sign the note, but I persuaded the lad who brought it to tell me
who gave it to him."

Annie tore open the envelope, read the letter inside and then exclaimed, "No! I can't believe it!"

"What's happened?"

Tom hid a grin as he saw Frederick sit down and put his arm round her shoulders, and he noted with satisfaction how Annie leaned her head against Hallam for a minute, before jerking it away. "What's happened?" Tom asked impatiently, when she made no attempt to enlighten them.

"Helen's gone off with Daniel. She says – she says she's going to marry him and pay his debts. I can't believe it!"

Frederick took the note out of her hand and scanned it rapidly, before holding it out to Tom.

"Well, talk about the Devil's own luck! That villain's got hold of someone's money, after all," Tom said, once he had finished reading. "But Helen Kenderby's too nice for him, much too nice."

Annie was sitting frowning, unaware that Frederick had taken her hand in his. "Helen's always found Daniel attractive. I couldn't help noticing that. But I'd never have believed she would want to marry him, not after all he's done. She says *she* asked him to marry her!"

"I don't envy her," said Frederick. "Connor will make a rotten husband. And he'll throw her money away as he threw his own."

Annie had a sudden memory of Helen playing the imperious autocrat in the London shops, of Helen lively and unconventional once away from her father's stern shadow, and of her Aunt Isabel who would surely keep an eye on her and leave her another fortune in such a way that Daniel Connor could not touch it. "I wonder if he might not be in for some surprises," she said slowly. "I wish she had told me what she was planning, though."

"I'm glad she didn't. You're that soft, you'd have tried to talk her out of it," Tom scoffed.

Frederick cleared his throat. "Gibson, do you think you could leave your sister and me alone for a few minutes?"

"Don't you dare leave me, Tom!" said Annie, suddenly realising that Frederick had one arm around her shoulders and was holding her hand with the other. She tried in vain to pull away from him.

Tom stood there grinning down at them. "I think you'll both be happier if I stay."

"I most certainly will not!" snapped Frederick. "For Christ's sake, man, we don't need a third person at a time like this."

Suddenly, the world seemed full of joy to Tom and he could not stop beaming at them. "You do if you want Annie to say yes."

Both the figures on the couch went rigid and looked first at him, then at each other. Then Frederick gave a wry smile. "I hope you know what you're doing, Gibson."

"I do, Hallam."

"I'll never speak to you again, Tom Gibson, if you interfere," said Annie. "And you can just let go of my hand, Frederick Hallam."

But he only pulled her closer. "Annie, you're not leaving this house until you promise to marry me. There's nothing to stop us now, nothing at all."

His closeness was making the breath catch in her throat. She forgot about Tom. "Frederick, there's too much between us. I can't – it still wouldn't be fair of me to marry you."

He too had forgotten Tom. "Because you come from Salem Street? My dearest love, my great-grandfather was a farmer, and not a rich farmer, either. It's well known that he made his money from some very dubious deals. The difference between us is not so unbridgeable."

"Oh, Frederick, if that were all, I'd say yes quite happily." She could not resist reaching out to stroke his cheek and he seized the opportunity to press a kiss on the back of her hand.

"Tell me what else there is, then, love, and we'll deal with it. For I'm absolutely determined to marry you, whatever you say."

Tom stepped forward. "I'll tell you why she's refusing, Hallam." He was not smiling now. Like Annie, he realised that Hallam might well turn away from them in disgust, but he was willing to take the chance.

"Tom, no!"

"It's his decision as well as yours, love," Tom said, then looked at Frederick. "We have a sister, our full sister Lizzie, and a stepsister called May. The two of them have turned whores. They mostly keep out of our way – they work in Manchester – but they came back to blackmail us for money once, and the probability is that they'll be back again. Especially if Annie marries you. Not many whores end up rich, do they?" He paused, then added, "That's what Annie's trying to save you from."

Frederick prevented Annie from standing up, but spoke to Tom. "Is that all?"

Tom smiled in relief. It was going to be all right. "That's all."

Annie sat motionless within the circle of Frederick's strong arms, not daring to hope.

Frederick's breath was warm on her cheek. "You don't think I care about that, do you, my little love?"

"Well, I care. I care about you. I won't—" The words were muffled by his kiss, and after a while, her protests faded and she found herself returning his kiss, clinging to him and murmuring his name in her throat as they paused for breath.

Tom grinned down at the pair of them, then left the room and found his way into another sitting room across the hallway. He poked the fire to life. Might as well wait in comfort, he reasoned, then he beamed at himself in the mirror over the fire and yanked the bell-pull hard. When a maid came into the room, he said confidently, "I daresay your master has some good wine stored in his cellar."

"Yes, sir."

"Champagne even?"

"I believe so, sir."

"Then I think it'd be a good time to bring up a couple o bottles. We'll have something to celebrate shortly." He winke at her and tapped the third finger of his left hand, unable to keep the news to himself. "Your master and my sister are jus sorting a few things out."

Her mouth was a big O of astonishment, then she giggled "All right, sir. I'll go and fetch some bottles up right away."

Inside the library, Frederick was kissing away Annie's las protests. "I don't care about your sister," another kiss butterflie down her cheek, "or whether you come from the Rows," hi lips traced a line of fire down her neck. "You don't leave thi house until you've agreed to marry me."

"But my—"

His fingers loosened the pins and sent her hair cascadin across her shoulders and then started to tease their way throug its flaming depths. "If it worries you so much, we'll find you sister and," a smile stretched his face into an echo of th mischievous youth he must once have been, "save her fror sin."

"But, Frederick—"

"We'll set her up in a shop, or buy her a guest house i Blackpool, or whatever seems appropriate, but," he buried hi face in her hair and his voice was muffled by that and by th passion he felt for her, "Annie, my love, my dearest love, can't bear it if you don't marry me."

Suddenly, all the fight went out of her and she sagged agains him. "Are you sure, Frederick? Are you really sure of this?"

"I've never been so sure of anything in my life."

"But your family—"

"To hell with my family!"

A glorious smile curved her lips. She looked at his face, at the love in his eyes. For the first time in days, her eyes began to sparkle with life and happiness welled up within her. "Then I suppose I'd better agree to marry you, hadn't I?"

This time, she returned his kiss with fervour and the last of the barriers between herself and men, barriers that had been in place ever since she was seventeen, dissolved away. She could sense a new lightness inside her and the room seemed filled with the radiance of her joy. "I've never felt like this before," she whispered in wonder. "Oh, Frederick!" She leaned forward to kiss him of her own accord.

When she drew away, Frederick raised the subject he had been dreading. "I'm older than you," he said quietly. "Much older."

"Are you? I hadn't noticed." All she had noticed was that with him she felt no shyness, no reluctance. With him, she felt only a rightness and a burning desire to be held close. She smiled at him. "That doesn't matter, Frederick."

"It will one day. You're very likely to be left a widow."

She shivered. "Don't talk about that!"

"We must."

She shook her head. "It isn't important. One never knows what life will bring, Frederick. I learned that a long time ago. You can plan everything carefully and then something will happen to overset everything. I could just as easily be the one to die first. Your age will only matter if we let it."

"Ah, my darling girl, I'll make you so happy!" He crushed her to him.

An hour later, Annie noticed the time and pushed him away. "We must go and find Tom. Whatever will he think of us?" She adjusted her clothing, blushing at the appreciative expression on Frederick's face, then she scrambled her hair into a loose knot at the nape of her neck. She could not resist reaching out to smooth away a lock of hair that had fallen across Frederick's brow. "Am I tidy?"

"You're beautiful, Annie." He caught hold of her hand, kissed it and led her in search of her brother.

Tom raised a glass as they entered the sitting room. His speech was a little slurred. "I decided not to wait for you. I hope you don't mind my ordering the champagne, Hallam, but I rather thought we might have something to celebrate."

"We have." Annie's face was blissfully happy. "Frederick and I are going to be married, Tom."

"Very soon," said Frederick, pouring two more glasses of champagne and handing one to Annie.

"Not too soon," Annie protested. "People will talk."

"Soon," he repeated. "And let them talk. We won't be here to listen to gossip."

She clinked her glass against his and took a sip. "Oh?" Her eyes were full of light and happiness. And that same happiness was mirrored in Frederick's face.

Watching the two of them, Tom found tears rising in his eyes and made a great play of blowing his nose. "Where will you be, then?" he asked when neither of them spoke.

"We'll be in London," said Frederick firmly. "My wife and I will be honeymooning in London, and when we tire of it, we may or may not travel round Europe for a while. We'll decide that later."

The tears of joy for Annie would not be held back, so Tom took a great gulp of champagne and let himself choke on it. By the time he had mopped his face, he had regained control of himself. Well, control of everything except a huge grin. He had never seen his sister look so happy. He had no doubt whatsoever that Frederick loved her as much as he himself loved Marianne. He raised his glass in a silent toast

470

to his own darling, drained it and then reached out to fill it
again.

"To you Annie, love!" he said loudly.

"To you, Annie, my darling!" echoed Frederick.